THE INEVITABLE FALL OF
CHRISTOPHER CYNSTER

A CYNSTER NEXT GENERATION NOVEL

STEPHANIE LAURENS

ABOUT THE INEVITABLE FALL OF CHRISTOPHER CYNSTER

WITHDRAWN

#1 New York Times *bestselling author Stephanie Laurens returns to the Cynsters' next generation with a rollicking tale of smugglers, counterfeit banknotes, and two people falling in love.*

A gentleman hoping to avoid falling in love and a lady who believes love has passed her by are flung together in a race to unravel a plot that threatens to undermine the realm.

Christopher Cynster has finally accepted that to have the life he wants, he needs a wife, but before he can even think of searching for the right lady, he's drawn into an investigation into the distribution of counterfeit banknotes.

London born and bred, Ellen Martingale is battling to preserve the fiction that her much-loved uncle, Christopher's neighbor, still has his wits about him, but Christopher's questions regarding nearby Goffard Hall trigger her suspicions. As her younger brother attends card parties at the Hall, she feels compelled to investigate.

While Ellen appears to be the sort of frippery female Christopher abhors, he quickly learns that, in her case, appearances are deceiving. And through the twists and turns in an investigation that grows ever more serious and urgent, he discovers how easy it is to fall in love, while Ellen learns that love hasn't, after all, passed her by.

But then the villain steps from the shadows, and love's strengths and vulnerabilities are put to the test—just as Christopher has always feared. Will he pass muster? Can they triumph? Or will they lose all they've so recently found?

A historical romance with a dash of intrigue, set in rural Kent. A Cynster Next Generation novel—a full-length historical romance of 124,000 words.

OTHER TITLES BY STEPHANIE LAURENS

Mastered by Love

Black Cobra Quartet
The Untamed Bride
The Elusive Bride
The Brazen Bride
The Reckless Bride

The Adventurers Quartet
The Lady's Command
A Buccaneer at Heart
The Daredevil Snared
Lord of the Privateers

The Cavanaughs
The Designs of Lord Randolph Cavanaugh
The Pursuits of Lord Kit Cavanaugh
The Beguilement of Lady Eustacia Cavanaugh
The Obsessions of Lord Godfrey Cavanaugh (July 16, 2020)

Other Novels
The Lady Risks All
The Legend of Nimway Hall – 1750: Jacqueline

Medieval (As M.S.Laurens)
Desire's Prize

Novellas
Melting Ice – from the anthologies *Rough Around the Edges* and *Scandalous Brides*
Rose in Bloom – from the anthology *Scottish Brides*
Scandalous Lord Dere – from the anthology *Secrets of a Perfect Night*
Lost and Found – from the anthology *Hero, Come Back*
The Fall of Rogue Gerrard – from the anthology *It Happened One Night*
The Seduction of Sebastian Trantor – from the anthology *It Happened One*

Season

Short Stories

The Wedding Planner – from the anthology *Royal Weddings*

A Return Engagement – from the anthology *Royal Bridesmaids*

UK-Style Regency Romances

Tangled Reins

Four in Hand

Impetuous Innocent

Fair Juno

The Reasons for Marriage

A Lady of Expectations An Unwilling Conquest

A Comfortable Wife

/

THE INEVITABLE FALL OF
CHRISTOPHER CYNSTER

THE INEVITABLE FALL OF CHRISTOPHER CYNSTER

Copyright © 2020 by Savdek Management Proprietary Limited

ISBN: 978-1-925559-33-0

Cover design by Savdek Management Pty. Ltd.

Cover couple photography and photographic composition by Period Images © 2020

Savdek Management Proprietary Limited, Melbourne, Australia.

www.stephanielaurens.com

Email: admin@stephanielaurens.com

The names Stephanie Laurens and Cynster, and the SL Logo, are registered trademarks of Savdek Management Proprietary Ltd.

❀ Created with Vellum

CHAPTER 1

AUGUST 12, 1851. WALKHURST MANOR, KENT.

*S*eated behind the desk in the manor's library-cum-study, Christopher Cynster leaned back, raised his hands, and ran his fingers through his thick locks in frustrated resignation. After a moment of staring unseeing at the desktop, he lowered his hands and muttered, "Apparently, I require a wife."

There was no one else present to hear the admission—a lowering one given how long it had taken him to reach it, to jettison all self-deception and face that sobering reality.

About him, the large house lay quiet, basking in the warmth of the summer afternoon. The windows to either side of the desk stood open; he could hear bees humming and birds twittering in the bushes and borders surrounding the old stone walls. Other than the staff, evidenced by the occasional sound from the rear of the house or outside, there was no one else in residence; Christopher's parents were gadding about the Americas, his younger brother, Gregory, was visiting friends in the Peak District, and his sister, Therese, was busily managing her husband, her children, and her own household in Lincolnshire.

Christopher fixed his gaze on the various reports arrayed before him. He picked up a pencil and tapped the end on the corner of the leather-bound blotter.

If Gregory and Therese could see him now...

If they learned of his reluctant conclusion, they would laugh themselves into stitches, then Therese would set about arranging a wife for him, while Gregory would grin and look on.

He spent a moment tendering heartfelt thanks that both his siblings were far away.

That would allow him to work out a strategy to rectify the issue on his own—without interference.

As Vane and Patience Cynster's eldest son, while his parents were away, he had stepped into the role he'd been trained all his life to fill; he'd sat and stood at his father's right hand for so many years that managing the estate was all but instinctive.

Being the eldest son, he would, eventually, inherit the manor estate; from his earliest years, he'd understood that it would be his responsibility to ensure the continuing prosperity of all his grandfather and father had amassed and brought into being, not only in Kent but also through investments elsewhere. Vane Cynster had a flair for managing crops of all kinds, and Christopher had inherited the knack; he was confident in his ability to continue in his father's footsteps.

Yet being the eldest son and therefore the senior representative of his branch of the family presently in England had also meant he hadn't been able to slide out of attending the family's annual summer gathering at Somersham Place, the principal residence of the Duke of St. Ives. The current duke, known as Devil, was his father's cousin and closest friend, and Devil's duchess, Honoria, was Christopher's mother's bosom-bow. Although this year—for the first time in his life—Christopher would have preferred not to attend, Honoria's invitation-cum-summons had been couched in such a way as to make not appearing impossible.

Aside from all else, his grandmother, Horatia, his grandfather, George, and his great-aunt, Helena, would have been shocked if he hadn't shown his face.

So he'd gone and whiled away the day in the bosom of the wider Cynster clan and, as usual, had spent most of his time consorting with his cousinly peers—with Sebastian, Michael, Marcus, Lucilla, Prudence, and their spouses. This year, that group had also included Louisa and her husband, Drake Varisey.

Other than a few of the recently added spouses, Christopher had known the members of that group literally all of their lives. He'd even known Drake and Antonia, Sebastian's wife, from their earliest years. Yet now...he was very definitely the odd man out.

The only one unwed.

Not that the others had so much as alluded to that, for which he'd been grateful, but their elders hadn't been anywhere near as reticent; virtually every one of them had arched a brow and inquired when he was going to bestir himself and find a wife.

He'd smiled and avoided answering the question. Previously, he would have concocted some faintly jocular reply, gently suggesting they should lay aside any expectation of seeing him front the altar, but this year, all such glib assertiveness had deserted him.

Something had changed. Over the past year, some part of his psyche he hadn't known he possessed had awakened, stirred, and stretched and now actively wanted the sort of future his peers had secured—one with a spouse by his side and a family of his own.

Until now, he'd assumed he wouldn't marry—that, along with Pru, he would be one of the two in their group who would happily face the future unwed. He'd seen himself as the bachelor uncle to his siblings' children— the one overseeing the family finances, to be ultimately succeeded by his brother's son.

To his mind, there had been no reason for him to marry—no need to risk love and the complications it brought, the emotional vulnerabilities it entailed.

With her adamantine refusal to consider marrying, Pru had been, he'd thought, of the same mind, and if she, a female, could hold firm against the inevitable pressures brought to bear by their parents, aunts, and grand-parents, then so could he.

But then Pru had traveled to Ireland and changed her mind. Or Deaglan Fitzgerald, Earl of Glengarah, had changed it for her... No; Christopher knew that not even Glengarah had the power to sway Pru once she'd made up her mind.

Pru had met her fate in Glengarah—she'd accepted that and, with what had appeared to be clear-sighted alacrity, had embraced the future Fate had placed before her.

Christopher had danced at Pru's wedding and had left feeling just a little betrayed.

Not by Pru but by Fate—by Fate's intervention that had led to Pru finding happiness and what was patently her true place and, by contrast, throwing into stark relief the restless, dissatisfied yearning that had, by then, sunk its claws into his soul.

On returning from Ireland, he'd attempted to reclaim the life he'd once found satisfying. He'd thrown himself into socializing with his friends and had attended several early-summer shooting parties in the north.

Nothing he'd done had eased the yawning emptiness inside him; if anything, it had grown.

Grown more distracting. More compelling.

In late July, he'd returned to London to celebrate his birthday with his parents and siblings, then had waved his parents off on their journey to America before coming down to Kent to take up the reins at the manor. After settling into the familiar rhythms of summer in the country, he'd reluctantly headed to Somersham.

He'd returned late last night. Now, brooding over his hours at the Place, on all he'd seen and felt, he had to admit that the spur that had finally punctured his resistance to matrimony had come in the form of very small people.

He'd watched Thomas, Lucilla's husband, chasing their twin daughters, Chloe and Christina, both squealing and shrieking, around the lawns. The laughter in Thomas's eyes and the sheer joy in his face as he'd caught one, then the other, lifting them high to yet more ear-splitting squeals, had clutched at and squeezed Christopher's heart.

Meanwhile, Lucilla had stood proudly rocking her and Thomas's weeks-old son, Manachan. She'd been chatting to Niniver, Marcus's wife, who had been holding their son, Richard—until the proud papa had relieved her of the burden of the sturdy six-month-old boy. Yet given they'd been at the ducal estate, pride of place in the baby stakes had gone to Sylvester Gyles Cynster, born a few weeks before Manachan to Antonia and Sebastian and therefore destined, eventually, to inherit the dukedom.

Antonia had been radiant, while Sebastian had never—ever—looked and acted so besotted over any other being, not even his beautiful wife.

Christopher knew that last for a fact; among their group, he and Sebastian had spent the most time together throughout their lives. They'd seen less of each other in recent years as their involvement in managing their respective fathers' estates had increased, but prior to that, they'd moved in the same exclusive circles and, having similar interests and attitudes, had been largely inseparable.

As for the rest of the group, Michael and his wife, Cleo, were expecting their first child in a month or so, while Louisa, pregnant with her and Drake's first child—very possibly Drake's heir and therefore another future duke—had been trying her best to downplay her condition, difficult given she'd started to swell about the middle and had Drake hovering constantly at her side.

While Pru's state was not as far advanced, the glow in her cheeks had left little doubt of her condition, but Deaglan—a wise man even if he was Irish—was doing his level best not to hover like Drake.

In multiple ways, Christopher's visit to Somersham Place and the Cynster Summer Celebration had proved the last straw. The joy and happiness that had radiated from his peers...

I want that.

Consequently, after dealing with estate business that morning, after lunch, he'd settled in the comfortable surrounds of the library-cum-study to confront his need to acquire a wife and embark on what, therefore, loomed as his most urgent personal task.

Finding the *right* wife.

The concept remained nebulous; he accepted that much of his difficulty in defining what he wished for in a wife stemmed from his refusal, until now, to even think about the future he had, so belatedly, realized he actually wanted. He hadn't made any reasoned decision to remain a bachelor; he'd simply assumed that was what he would prefer and had fallen into that rut, which, until recently, had suited him well enough.

It no longer did, so...

"What sort of wife do I want?" He narrowed his eyes. What manner of wife did he need?

He thought of the ladies with whom he'd dallied over the last decade and more; as with other gentlemen of his ilk—of his wealth, social status, and age—their number was not insignificant. Yet virtually all had been married ladies of the haut ton with whom he'd enjoyed short-lived affairs; he'd never envisioned marrying any of them—he'd never assessed their attributes in that light.

Likewise, his belief that he had no reason to consider the numerous young ladies paraded before him by society's hostesses had led him metaphorically to turn his back on the entire genus of marriageable females; consequently, he had no yardstick—no frame of reference or list of qualities—to guide his choice.

It was easier to list the traits and characteristics he could not abide, such as silly, frivolous females, those ninnyhammers with more hair than wit who, these days, bedecked themselves with ribbons, bows, feathers, frills, and furbelows. The ton was currently littered with such females, and their tittering and vapid conversations never failed to abrade his nerves.

He needed a wife with whom he could share an intelligent conversation. Beyond that...?

I really have no clue.

Where to look for her, his ideal wife?

At present, the ton were dispersed throughout the country. In mid-September, the major families would return to London for the autumn session of Parliament and the concurrent social round; the balls and parties of the haut ton held through those weeks would, he suspected, be the most useful hunting ground...

He shied at the vision that thought evoked. The instant he appeared at more than two events, the hostesses would realize what he was about, the matchmakers would descend, and his life would become well-nigh unbearable.

He locked his jaw and forced himself to consider the prospect; he felt as he imagined a horse might in refusing a fence.

And it wasn't just his dislike of the inevitable brouhaha that was holding him back.

It was galling to admit that cowardice played a large part in fueling his antipathy toward marriage. Family lore stated that for a Cynster, with no exceptions, falling in love was a requirement for a successful marriage. From all he'd seen, that rule held true, no matter the resistance of the male or female involved.

Falling a victim to love wasn't an outcome he had wished to embrace. Being in love meant being close to another, sharing thoughts, hopes, and dreams, and most pertinently, leaving oneself open to hurt. To betrayal and rejection, loss and grief.

He had never been in love, so couldn't speak from experience, yet he could see how it would be. He could imagine the pain. He'd seen it in non-Cynster friends.

Other acquaintances had avoided the snare by marrying, but not for love. Those marriages seemed to rattle along well enough, but Fate had decreed that particular path was not one he would be allowed to take.

The Cynster curse, as he thought of it, was inviolable and unavoidable; as a Cynster, if he wished to marry—as he now accepted he did—he would have to embrace love and risk the consequences.

He tapped the pencil he held on the blotter once, twice, then nodded. He would slip back to London in September and see whether any of the current crop of unmarried ladies would suit. Or more specifically, if Fate deigned to steer him toward one; when it came to it, he had no idea how Fate and love might strike.

With his way forward decided, he refixed his gaze and his attention on the accounts spread before him.

The restlessness inside him swirled and seethed, unappeased; his inner self wanted to forge ahead, find the right lady, marry her, and get on with building his desired future. He'd never been the sort to overthink things; he much preferred action, yet in reality, what else could he do?

"Wait until September," he muttered, then forced his mind to concentrate on the plan for the next round of crop rotations.

The clock on the mantelpiece ticked on. It had just whirred and chimed for the half hour when Christopher heard firm footsteps rapidly nearing.

A sharp rap fell on the door.

He looked up. "Come."

The door opened, and George Radley, the estate manager, looked in.

At the sight of Radley's tight-lipped face, Christopher dropped the pencil and pushed back his chair. "What?"

"Goats. The Bigfield House herd have got into one of our hop fields."

Christopher cursed, rose, and strode for the door. He waved Radley ahead of him. "I take it you mean the field bordering the lane?"

Grimly, Radley nodded. "And the plants there are just coming into flower."

"Naturally!" Equally grim, Christopher strode with Radley for the stable.

Ellen Martingale sat behind the desk in the study of Bigfield House and stared at the sheets of figures spread before her. She felt like tearing out her hair. Hopper, the estate manager, had left her to wrestle with the projected harvests from the estate's grain fields; it had taken her a good half hour to realize she needed to know which grains were grown in which fields to make any use of the information.

"Argh!" She tossed down the pencil she'd been using in an attempt to estimate the crops' total worth. She glared at Hopper's sheets. "Who would imagine that managing a 'straightforward farming estate' would be so complicated?"

A "straightforward farming estate" was how the family solicitor, Mr. Vickers, and Hopper referred to the Bigfield House lands. Ellen absolved Hopper of being deliberately difficult in not noting down which grain grew in each field; the man was trying his best, just as everyone involved was. But sadly, Hopper was an unimaginative sort; a local man, country bred, he consistently failed to allow for Ellen's lack of local knowledge—indeed, her complete lack of knowledge of farming.

She sighed, closed her eyes, and massaged her temples. A faint headache threatened, and she really couldn't afford to have it develop further.

The truth was she harbored zero ambition to manage the many enterprises of the Bigfield House estate; she was sitting there, being slowly driven insane, only because there was no one else willing and able to shoulder the burden—and there were so many people dependent on the estate functioning as it should, she couldn't just allow the farming to bumble along without any oversight.

Of all those under the Bigfield House roof, she was the best qualified to manage the reins her poor uncle could no longer grasp. Her younger brother, Robbie, her aunt Emma, the staff of the large house, all the estate workers, and even Mr. Vickers were counting on her to keep the estate's wheels rolling, however slowly, in the right direction.

That, Mr. Vickers had assured her, was really all she needed to do.

A pity the good solicitor knew nothing about farming himself!

After a further minute of indulgence—of closed eyes and blessed peace—Ellen drew in a calming breath, lowered her hands, opened her eyes, and studied the sheets before her. Then she looked around the small study. "Perhaps there's a map that shows what crops are grown where?"

She was about to push back her chair and go hunting when a tap fell on the door. "Yes?"

Partridge, the butler, a tall man with a rotund belly and spindly legs—in his butler's garb, he forcibly reminded her of his namesake—poked his head around the door, spotted her, and came quickly in and shut the door behind him.

Alerted by his furtive movements, she stared at him, her *"What is it now?"* conveyed without words.

Partridge cleared his throat and announced, "Mr. Christopher Cynster has called, miss, and is asking to see Sir Humphrey."

"Well, he can't."

Partridge inclined his head in a careful way that suggested there was some doubt about that. "Mr. Christopher is the eldest son of the Cynsters of Walkhurst Manor, miss. You've met the elder Mr. Cynster and Mrs. Cynster—Mr. Christopher's parents—several times."

Unease welling, Ellen said, "I thought they'd gone traveling to America."

Partridge dipped his head. "Indeed, miss. And Mr. Christopher—being the eldest son—has come home to manage the estate."

And is doubtless making a much better fist of it than I am here.

She rose. "Be that as it may—"

"Mr. Cynster has called because there's been an incident with the goats, miss."

She'd asked Robbie to move the goats into a field while the ornery animals' pen was being repaired. With growing trepidation, she asked, "What incident?"

"I believe the herd somehow found its way into one of the manor's hop fields. One where the hops are just coming into flower."

She didn't need to be told that was not a good thing; she'd already discovered goats ate just about anything. Quashing the urge to close her eyes and groan, she stepped smartly out from behind the desk. "I'll speak with Mr. Cynster." She'd weathered his parents' visits; one way or another, she'd manage the son's. "Sir Humphrey doesn't need to be disturbed."

Mr. Cynster certainly didn't need to exchange words with her uncle.

She swept past Partridge on her way to the door. "Where did you leave Mr. Cynster?"

Partridge swiveled to follow. "In the front hall, miss."

Thank heaven for small mercies. She opened the door, stepped into the corridor, swung right—and ran into a wall.

One of solid muscle.

"Oh!" She would have staggered, but hard hands grasped her forearms and steadied her.

Her senses fizzed; her nerves leapt. The skin on her arms, under the firm grip, flushed hot.

She stilled and looked up—into a pair of agate-brown eyes. Mid-brown flecked with mossy green and caramel and set beneath almost-straight dark-brown eyebrows, those alluring eyes widened, then captured her gaze and held it...

Time seemed to suspend. She realized she wasn't breathing—that her lungs had seized in a most peculiar way.

And she couldn't stop gawping.

Yet as she studied those fascinating eyes, the expression in them hardened, sharpened; even as she stared, something like suspicion rose and swirled in the moss-and-caramel depths.

No—no suspicions allowed.

She swallowed and forced her lungs to operate at least enough to hold giddiness at bay, then scrambled to locate her wits and harry them into order.

Christopher found it impossible not to stare—and stare—at the vision before him. He'd felt the jolt of pure sensation when they'd collided, and the startling frisson of awareness that had streaked through them both when he'd seized her arms had put the implication beyond doubt.

His every sense had locked on her. When it came to women, he was an experienced wolf, and every instinct he possessed had focused, unrelentingly and unwaveringly, on her.

He saw her eyes widen, her pupils flare. Saw telltale tension afflict her, constricting her breathing, while the seconds ticked past and he held her—because he hadn't yet managed to force his fingers to ease and let her go.

He knew—to his soul knew—what those signs plus those afflicting him portended, but...

Impossible.

She looked like a doll, one some young girl had dressed in her most gaudy finery. Hair the color of ripening wheat formed a corona of large curls about her head. Someone had attempted to scoop the silky mass high, into a knot, but numerous curls had slipped free to bounce about her face and shoulders—competing with the trailing ends of a mass of ribbons wound about the knot.

The face thus framed was a sculpted oval, perfect in every delicate line and sheathed in a milk-and-roses complexion that was so unmarred and pristine it looked painted, as if the lady truly was a doll come to life.

Large green-flecked hazel eyes, presently wide and fringed by long brown lashes, plus lush, full lips tinted a pale rose did nothing to counter the unnerving illusion. The lady's slender neck led down to delicate collarbones and a figure that, courtesy of their collision, he now knew well enough to describe as nicely curvaceous. Yet the doll-like theme rolled on, with her curves clad in a dress that, had he not seen it with his own eyes, he would never have imagined adorning a flesh-and-blood female.

In some lightweight material suitable for summer days, the gown—although in a pretty shade of teal—sported multiple frilled layers about the modest neckline, with more below the waist and about the hem. The skirt was fashionably full, but the combination of narrow white lace and darker-teal ribbon that edged every frill made a mockery of any claim to elegance.

Yet despite what his eyes could see—every evidence that this young lady was the worst sort of frivolous female—his senses continued to insist that she was a pearl beyond price.

He almost shook his head to dispel his confusion. No matter what his obviously scrambled instincts were screaming, there was no way in hell he would ever pursue a lady such as she.

That resolution had him easing his grip and releasing her. Lowering his arms, he ensured his face was devoid of expression and bestowed a curt nod. "Good morning. My apologies. I'm looking for Sir Humphrey."

He went to step past, but she shifted and blocked him.

"Um..." She hauled in a breath and tipped up her chin. "I regret Sir Humphrey is not receiving."

What the devil is going on? Christopher frowned at the irritating female. He hadn't called at Bigfield House for quite some time, and what little he'd seen while returning the goats suggested all was not running as smoothly as it should. He'd wondered if Sir Humphrey had simply over-looked things.

He opened his mouth to insist on seeing his neighbor, but the lady—*who the devil is she?*—insinuated herself more definitely between him and the study door and suggested, "Perhaps I can assist you."

The look he bent on her stated very clearly: *I seriously doubt it.*

Holding fast to her rising temper, Ellen kept her gaze on Christopher Cynster's handsome face and fought to keep her expression mild. Chiseled planes and aristocratic features, broad shoulders, narrow waist, and long legs garbed in typical gentleman's country attire of well-cut hacking jacket, buckskin breeches, and top boots, all cloaked in an aura of rigidly controlled physical power wielded with arrogant confidence, unquestionably constituted a potent distraction, but regardless of her silly reaction to his touch, she, he would discover, was made of sterner stuff.

She should have guessed that the Cynsters' eldest son would be a London rake—a wolf of the first order was her experienced assessment.

She tipped her chin a notch higher and calmly inquired, "Was there some specific issue you wished to address with my uncle?"

The agate-y eyes narrowed. His head tipped as he studied her. "Your uncle?"

She arched an eyebrow. "Indeed. I am Sir Humphrey's niece—Miss Ellen Martingale."

He held her gaze for a second, the set of his features giving nothing away, then he smoothly inclined his head. "Miss Martingale." He seemed to come to some decision and went on, "I'm here because of Sir Humphrey's goats. I'm aware they are his pride and joy, but somehow, the herd got loose, crossed the lane, and pushed their way into one of the manor's hop fields. As you're no doubt aware, the hops in this area are just beginning to flower, a critical stage when, unfortunately, goats are especially attracted to the crop."

His eyes searched hers as if to gauge how much she'd understood.

She returned his stare levelly while her mind raced.

His lips thinned, and he went on, "I've just spent the past hour with my men, rounding up the goats and returning them to Bigfield House."

She blinked. "Ah. The goat pen is being repaired—that's why the wretched animals weren't in it." Looking past his broad shoulder, she frowned. "I thought my brother had shut the goats into the front field—the one on our side of the lane."

"He might well have done so, but you can't hold goats in a field fenced only by hedge—not when they can scent ripening hops on the other side. The animals pushed their way through your hedge into the lane, then broke through the hedge on our side to get to our hops."

Ellen felt her eyes grow round as her lips formed a soundless "Oh."

Cynster seemed to be fighting a glare, but then, somewhat to her surprise, he conceded, "As luck would have it, my estate manager spotted them fairly soon afterward, and we got them out before they'd caused much damage."

Conciliation was surely her best way forward. She clasped her hands before her and earnestly said, "I'm terribly sorry—I assure you it won't happen again."

Christopher nearly snorted; he wasn't all that appeased by her assumption of humility. He still wanted a word with Sir Humphrey. "It *can't* happen again, but while returning the goats to their pen—and yes, I saw that it's now repaired and in good state—I noticed that the barn roof needs attention, and the rear corral fence is shaky and needs to be fixed. I drew Hopper's attention to both issues." He paused, then drew breath and more diffidently said, "I know the staff are, understandably and quite laudably, loyal to Sir Humphrey, and I haven't sought to question them further over what, on the surface, appears to be an uncharacteristic lack of attention to detail."

He met Miss Ellen Martingale's pretty eyes. "I thought I would have a word with Sir Humphrey himself."

He went to step past her, and quick as a flash, she blocked him again.

Her eyes sparked, and she snapped, "As I've already mentioned, my uncle is not receiving."

He arched his brows. "Are we back to that?"

Without further warning, he reached for her waist, clamped his hands over the frills, and lifted her, swung around, and deposited her on the runner behind him. Then he swiftly released her, turned on his heel, and strode into the study.

"Sir Humphrey?" Christopher scanned the room. In this season, at this time of day, he'd expected to find Sir Humphrey behind the large desk.

The desk was strewn with accounts and ledgers, but no Sir Humphrey presided over them.

An agitated rustle of skirts and petticoats heralded the arrival of his would-be denier.

To his surprise, she caught his sleeve and hauled him around—and with fire and fury in her eyes, planted her hands on her hips and all but stamped her foot at him. "How dare you, sir!" Then she flung out a hand toward the desk. "And as you can now see with your own eyes, as I told you, my uncle is not receiving!"

Rather than glance at the uninformative desk, Christopher studied her flushed cheeks and bright eyes. There was something behind her anger, something more along the lines of fear.

Something *was* going on.

"Your uncle has known me for all of my life. Receiving or not, he will see me." With that, he strode rapidly for the door.

Predictably, she rushed after him. She was on his heels as he paced along the corridor. "Where are you going?"

"I don't yet know." He spared her a glance. "Why don't you tell me?"

"You can't just barge in!"

"Watch me."

Ahead in the front hall, Christopher spotted Partridge, the butler. Approaching the mouth of the corridor, Christopher rapped out, "Partridge, where's your master?"

He heard a gasp and dodged to the side to hide the outraged female trying to signal around him.

As he'd hoped, Partridge responded instinctively to the voice of authority. "In the conservatory, sir."

"Thank you." Christopher tried to keep the smugness from his tone and failed.

From behind, he heard a heartfelt "Damn it!"

But he'd already turned and was all but jogging toward the conservatory, which stood at the end of a long corridor, virtually at the rear of the house.

He ignored the muttered imprecations and the patter of feet behind him. He felt a tentative tug on his jacket and ignored that, too.

The conservatory was a large one, constructed of glass panes framed in white-painted wood. He spied the top of Sir Humphrey's gray head rising above the back of a wicker chair set before the wide windows at the end of the room. Gentle sunshine poured in, bathing the chair and its occupant.

Christopher slowed as he neared, instinct prompting him to look before he leapt.

He drew level with the chair and saw Sir Humphrey gazing out at the rolling lawns, bright garden beds, and the green-and-gold patchwork of orchards and fields beyond.

Sir Humphrey's expression appeared tranquil, and his lips were lightly curved.

Christopher walked farther, to where Sir Humphrey could easily see him. "Sir Humphrey?"

"Heh?" Sir Humphrey looked up at Christopher.

The lack of immediate recognition in the old man's faded blue eyes sent unease cascading through Christopher. He held out a hand. "It's Christopher, sir. Christopher Cynster."

He'd last seen Sir Humphrey a year ago, and the physical change in the man, while obvious, wasn't enough to raise alarm. But the vacant expression in the blue eyes staring up at him was deeply disturbing.

Then Sir Humphrey's eyes widened, and recognition flared. Sir Humphrey beamed and clasped his hand. "Excellent! Well met, my boy! Good of you to call."

Sir Humphrey glanced around, then waved at another chair. "Here— sit down."

Christopher glanced briefly at Miss Martingale as he moved to comply; she was standing back, out of Sir Humphrey's sight, and all but wringing her hands.

After tugging the chair closer to Sir Humphrey, Christopher sat and leaned forward.

Sir Humphrey was still smiling. "Good of you to call, Vane."

Christopher paused, then gently corrected, "It's Christopher, sir. The pater and Mama are off traveling in America—they called on you before they left."

And why hadn't his parents seen what he was seeing and warned him?

"Oh?" Sir Humphrey frowned. "America...oh yes, I remember. Went to visit someone, didn't they?"

He has no idea and is trying to conceal it. Obligingly, Christopher said, "The pater is looking into farming equipment and techniques, while Mama is purely sightseeing."

Sir Humphrey nodded. "And you're holding the fort while they're away, heh?"

Christopher knew his parents would have mentioned that. He nodded. "Yes."

"Need some advice, then? Is that what's brought you here?"

Christopher glanced at Miss Martingale. She now stood with her arms folded; both stance and expression radiated irritated resignation. Carefully, he said, "I came because your goats got loose. I brought them back."

"My goats?" Sir Humphrey's gaze brightened. "Why, I'd almost forgotten I had them!" He focused on Christopher. "I say—are they all right?"

The sudden flare of imminent agitation had Christopher saying, "Quite all right, sir...although"—he glanced again at Miss Martingale and was relieved to see she'd lowered her arms and was walking forward—"I thought I should mention that their hooves need trimming."

"Oh." Sir Humphrey's eyes clouded with confused concern.

Miss Martingale placed a firm hand on Sir Humphrey's shoulder. "No need to worry, uncle. I'll speak to Hopper. He'll see that the goats are taken care of."

Sir Humphrey looked up at his niece, and his features relaxed. Smiling, he raised a gnarled hand and patted her fingers. "Thank you, my dear. I know I can rely on you and the others. Very comforting, it is, and that's a fact."

As Sir Humphrey's gaze swung back to him, Christopher rose and held out his hand. "I'll leave you now, sir. It was good to see you again."

"Indeed, indeed." Sir Humphrey grasped his hand with a surprisingly firm grip. "My thanks to you for calling, Vane. Glad we had time to catch up. I expect I'll see you at the meet next week, heh? Give my regards to Patience, won't you?"

Faced with the earnestness in Sir Humphrey's gaze, Christopher managed a reassuring smile. "Yes, of course." He glanced at Miss Martingale. "Until next time, sir."

With that, he walked slowly to the conservatory door. Halting, he turned and saw Miss Martingale bending solicitously over her uncle, settling him again.

Eventually, she straightened and walked toward Christopher. He waited until she neared to quietly demand, "What the devil's going on?"

Her lips compressed to a thin line, and her gaze grew as hard as diamonds. She studied him in silence, assessingly, measuringly, then said, "As you insist on knowing, come to the study, and I'll tell you what you deserve to know."

He nearly humphed at her presumption, but there was a strength in her voice—in her attitude—he hadn't seen before.

She might look like a doll, but there was steel beneath the distracting façade, and every instinct he possessed warned that treating her dismissively would be a serious mistake.

He stood back to allow her to precede him through the door, and with outward meekness, followed her along the corridor.

Ellen slumped into the chair behind the desk and watched as her unexpected and unwished-for visitor pulled an armchair around to face her and sat—every movement executed with elegant grace. If she had to have a nosy neighbor of her own generation, she deemed it grossly unfair that he was so visually—and in so many other ways—distracting. She had enough on her plate without that.

But he'd seen her uncle and was now as sober and focused as a judge. He would have questions galore, and she needed to decide how much to reveal.

Can I trust him?

She wished she could have sought advice from Hopper or Vickers or even Partridge. But Cynster was there now, in front of her, and she had to make up her mind purely on her own observations.

She studied him openly. After a moment, he cocked a dark eyebrow at her, with a certain languid arrogance asking without words if she'd seen enough.

She grimaced faintly; the impression she'd got from the exchange in the conservatory—and even more, his reaction to her uncle's state—was that Christopher Cynster was an honorable gentleman and not the sort to take advantage of another's misfortune.

Who knows? He might even be a help.

Apparently losing patience with her hesitation, he offered, "The last time I saw Sir Humphrey, admittedly over a year ago, he was hale and hearty and striding about his acres, keeping everyone in line. I know my parents visited him before they left, and that would have been not quite two months ago. They spoke with me afterward, yet said nothing about your uncle having...difficulties." His voice hardened. "Yet now I find him with his mind wandering."

Ellen inwardly sighed; she wasn't going to be able to keep much, if anything, from him. "We—my younger brother, Robert, who is Sir Humphrey's heir, our maternal aunt, and I—came to join my uncle's household last October."

Cynster frowned. "Why was that?"

Impertinent, yet... "Primarily because Sir Humphrey wished it. He's been our guardian—my brother's and mine—since our father, Sir Humphrey's older brother, died in '44. We had a house in Belgravia, and our mother was London born and bred and wished to remain there, for the social whirl above all else. But she contracted a fever in the summer of '49 and passed away. After our year of mourning, as Robbie is Sir Humphrey's heir, Sir Humphrey, backed by Vickers, the family's solicitor, pressed us to sell the London house and, together with our widowed aunt, who'd lived with us for many years and who Sir Humphrey knew well, come to live here, at Bigfield House." She shrugged lightly. "Robbie and I were agreeable, as was our aunt Emma—none of us were as fond of London as Mama—so we sold up and came down to Kent and became a part of this household."

She paused, then went on, "It seemed sensible all around. We all thought it would give Robbie time to learn how to manage the estate."

"Including what it takes to safely corral goats," Cynster drily remarked.

"That would be the least of it," she returned acerbically. "Robbie's only twenty and rides well, but that's the limit of his country expertise. Hopper and the farmworkers, orchardmen, and herdsmen know what's needed, or so I've been assured, but they—like me—have been run off their feet trying to keep up with things"—she drew breath, raised her chin, and looked at Cynster challengingly—"since we realized Uncle Humphrey wasn't able to anymore."

He studied her, then prompted, "What happened?"

"Nothing dramatic—that was part of the problem." She thought back to their arrival and the weeks and months after that. "When we first took up residence here, Uncle Humphrey seemed quite normal—to us and everyone else. Emma has known Humphrey for most of her life, and she didn't see or sense anything amiss. None of the staff suspected a thing, and as you probably know, most of the senior staff have been at Bigfield for decades and are very loyal to and protective of my uncle. Not even Vickers, who has known and worked closely with Humphrey for most of Humphrey's adult life, had any idea my uncle's mind was failing. As you saw, physically, he's still quite hale and whole, and at first, it was just minor things—slips of memory that anyone might make—like calling Robbie by my father's name. His condition came on gradually, and we strongly suspect that Uncle Humphrey grew quite adept at hiding his difficulties."

She paused, then continued, "Eventually, we realized that, at times, Humphrey actually thought Robbie *was* our father—that during those times, Humphrey was living in some version of the past. Vickers now believes Humphrey had some sense of his failing faculties, and that was why he was so insistent we left London and came to live with him."

"He foresaw his own decline?"

"So Vickers thinks. He may well be right. There are still days when you might imagine Humphrey is back to his former self, but the next day, he'll have retreated again." She gestured toward the conservatory. "You've seen how he is—he lives more in his memory than in the real world."

Cynster looked genuinely perturbed. "I can't believe my parents didn't sense something was wrong."

She smiled faintly. "Humphrey rallied when they visited—he made a huge effort to stay focused. There are times when he can manage that, but as the days pass, more and more, he simply can't bring his mind to bear."

Cynster held her gaze for a long moment, then stated, "You're trying to hide your uncle's decline from the neighborhood."

She tipped her head. "Not so much from the neighbors as from the agents the estate deals through—the ones who purchase our fleeces, fruits, and crops." She watched Cynster closely as she said, "According to Hopper, if Humphrey's condition becomes widely known, then with no experienced man to step into his shoes, when it comes to selling our produce, there's a good chance the estate will be taken advantage of." She paused, trying to gauge his reaction. "Vickers agrees, so I'm trying to hold the fort here and cope with the day-to-day decisions while Robbie does his best to learn the ropes from the ground up, as it were."

From the awareness and concern Cynster allowed to show, she concluded that Hopper and Vickers hadn't been wrong. She rubbed her forehead, where her earlier headache lingered. "We all, Vickers included, thought Robbie would have five years at least to learn how to manage the estate before, eventually, taking over from Uncle Humphrey. But things didn't fall out that way, and we're all doing our best to manage the situation as well as we can—meaning as Humphrey would have wanted and expected."

When Cynster said nothing but stared frowningly into space, she more waspishly stated, "I assure you we will cope—one way or another. And now, if your curiosity is satisfied, perhaps you'll allow me to get on with these projections."

Quite where her spurt of temper came from, she couldn't have said, but she was certain of its target.

Christopher heard the underlying anger in her words, presumably due to having been forced to reveal such information. She wasn't the sort to relish being forced to do anything, much less acknowledge such a weakness in an uncle she plainly cared for.

But her revelations had left him with a lot to think about; he needed time to sort through all the ramifications. In the circumstances, he decided to accept her dismissal, regardless of how snippily it had been delivered.

He got to his feet. "Thank you for being so frank."

She met his gaze and, he suspected, fought not to narrow her eyes.

He hid a smile, but then sobered. He hesitated, then felt compelled to say, "Our families have known each other for decades, and the manor and Bigfield House have always supported each other through any adversity. If we at the manor can render any assistance in this instance, know you have only to ask."

She searched his eyes and, presumably, confirmed his sincerity. With a graciousness that was singularly remarkable given the ribbons bobbing about her ears, she inclined her head. "Thank you for the offer. If we have need of assistance, I'll remember it."

He noted that she didn't say she would ask for his help, but he'd said what he'd needed to say, and so had she. He nodded in farewell. "I'll see myself out."

She didn't leap to her feet and insist on showing him to the door. She remained where she was and, with a direct and level gaze, watched him leave.

Once in the corridor and out of her sight, Christopher shook his head.

He passed through the hall and walked out through the open front door, into the afternoon sunshine. A groom stood waiting at the bottom of the steps, holding the reins of Christopher's gray hunter, Storm. After taking the reins and thanking the lad, Christopher stepped to Storm's side —and paused.

Despite his initial expectations evoked by her doll-like frippery, Miss Ellen Martingale had displayed not the slightest sign of harboring even the faintest interest in him.

Given her status as an unmarried young lady beyond her first blush, that alone was odd.

Yet compounding that oddity, she'd shown no sign of wishing to investigate the searing attraction that had flared so unexpectedly between them.

Indeed, she'd done her level best to pretend that attraction didn't exist.

After a moment spent reviewing their recent interaction, Christopher softly snorted, stuck his boot in the stirrup, and swung up to the saddle. He settled, lifted the reins, and urged Storm down the drive.

He might have thought he was losing his touch, but he knew it wasn't that. No. It was Miss Ellen Martingale.

She was a strange bird—one quite different from any other lady of her station. From any other lady he'd ever met.

CHAPTER 2

The following afternoon, Christopher was, once again, on Storm's back. The big gray needed frequent exercise, and Christopher found an hour of riding over his fields to be an excellent way of keeping up with developments.

Such as the altercation he heard occurring in the lane running between the Bigfield House estate and the manor's fields.

He steered Storm out of the field across which he'd been cantering and into the lane. As they trotted toward the sounds of escalating argument, Christopher distinguished two male voices, the more mature of which—deep, calm, and controlled—was familiar, although he couldn't immediately place it. The other voice was more youthful—and more strident and aggressive.

On rounding the next bend, Christopher beheld a sight he'd been expecting to see, if not that day, then soon. A long row of gaily painted covered wagons was drawn up in the lane. The lead wagon, decorated in vivid shades of red and gold, had swung to turn in to the grassy meadow bordering the stream that cut across the Bigfield House and manor fields.

Although the meadow belonged to Bigfield House, in this season, being already harvested of its hay, the field had become the traditional halt for the gypsy caravan that supplied labor to the local farms for the hop and apple harvests.

However, today, the wagons' advance into the meadow was being blocked by a young gentleman on a leggy roan.

Pleased to see that there were nine wagons lined up behind the first, Christopher walked Storm forward as the young man declared, "I repeat, you can't set up camp here."

The Romany seated on the bench of the first wagon, the reins held loosely in his hands, sighed and said, "And I repeat, we always use Sir Humphrey's field. Clearly, I need to speak with him—"

"You can't," the young man retorted. "My uncle isn't receiving visitors at present."

The gypsy looked exasperated.

Wholly focused on their exchange, neither man had noticed Christopher's approach, but the ancient personage seated beside the Romany had. Wrapped in colorful shawls, Gracella, matriarch of the clan, caught Christopher's eye, nodded imperiously, and tweaked her grandson's sleeve.

Glancing around, Aaron saw Christopher, and his dark-featured face lit. "Ah—Cynster. Well met!" He held out a hand.

Drawing Storm up beside the wagon, Christopher adopted his most charming smile and half bowed to the stout, elderly woman. "Gracella. You and yours are very welcome here."

As regal as Victoria, Gracella inclined her head. Her face bore traces of faded beauty, her expression was unruffled yet alert, and her dark eyes saw everything and held a wealth of experience.

Still smiling—he was truly glad to see the gypsy troop—Christopher leaned across and clasped Aaron's hand. "Aaron. You and your tribe are a welcome sight."

Aaron snorted and waved toward the young horseman. "Perhaps you can explain that to this gentleman here and that we are permitted to use the meadow."

Christopher had already transferred his gaze to the younger man. Still smiling affably, he guessed, "Robert Martingale?"

The young man blinked, then carefully nodded. "Yes."

"I met your sister yesterday, and she mentioned you. I'm Christopher Cynster, currently in charge at the manor." Christopher nudged Storm forward and extended his hand.

At the news Christopher was a neighbor, Martingale relaxed; a trace of relief showed in his eyes as he gripped Christopher's hand. "A pleasure to meet you, sir. M'sister mentioned you'd called." Recollection of the reason for Christopher's visit sent color into Robert's pale cheeks. "I must apologize for the goats, sir. I had no idea they could be so…well, *determined*. And destructive with it."

Christopher chuckled. "As it happened, no real harm was done. Your sister explained that being town bred, you and she are having to learn how things are done in the country."

He'd said that as much for Aaron and Gracella as Robert; the comment also gave him an opening to address the current impasse.

"Oh." Robert looked from Christopher to the gypsies. "Is this"—he waved at the waiting caravan—"one of those country things?"

Aaron grinned wolfishly—all teeth.

Christopher shot him a warning look, then said to Robert, "As a matter of fact, it is." He waved Robert to accompany him and walked Storm farther into the meadow. "Why don't we let the wagons through? You have my word they have your uncle's permission, as they claimed. They can start setting up while I explain."

Christopher glanced over his shoulder and saw Robert turning his horse to follow—and Gracella nodding in approval and Aaron smiling in relief.

After drawing Storm up to one side of the meadow, Christopher waited until Robert halted his horse beside him and the wagons started to rumble past, heading for a natural dip above the stream, then folded his hands on his pommel and said, "All the landowners hereabouts—indeed, most landowners in Kent—have a special relationship with the various gypsy caravans you'll find in the county during harvesttime. Picking fruits and hops is labor-intensive—we all need extra hands to help bring in our harvests. That's where the gypsies come in. The men, the older children, and even some of the women help with the picking. Gypsy bands are usually extended families and, like this one, return year after year, traveling the same routes and helping out at the same farms."

He tipped his head to where Aaron, with the help of some of the other men, was siting his wagon. "In the case of this band, Aaron's father used to lead it, and according to my father, Aaron's grandfather led it before that."

Robert was frowning. "So this band of gypsies helps with the harvest on our estate?"

"Not just at Bigfield House. Although it was Sir Humphrey—and his father before him—who volunteered this field for the gypsies' camp, this band helps at five estates while they're here. Then they'll move to another area where they'll also have been helping with the harvest for decades.

They tend to move east to west, south to north, as the crops and orchards ripen." Christopher huffed. "Sometimes, I think they know our fields better than we do."

"So," Robbie said, "they've arrived at the right time to help with our..." He glanced at Christopher. "What's the next crop to be harvested?"

Christopher hid a smile. "Hops, but it'll be a week or so before they're ready. In the meantime, I expect Aaron and his crew will help the Entwhistles at Grove Farm and the Huntlys at Moreton Manor to prune their cherry trees. If that doesn't get done now, next year's crop will suffer."

"Will these gypsies also help with our apples?"

He nodded. "This group usually remains until the harvests around here are done, and that's usually in early October, depending on the weather." He paused, then added, "We feel lucky to have them—they're a reliable and trustworthy crew."

"I see." Robert straightened in his saddle. "So having the help of this band of gypsies—being able to hire them as day laborers—is essential to getting our harvests in, and without them, we'd be in trouble."

"That's it in a nutshell." Christopher watched as Robert, jaw now set, nodded, more to himself than anyone else.

"In that case"—Robert swung down from his saddle—"I'd better go over and apologize."

Christopher said nothing, but he, too, dismounted and followed Robert as he strode determinedly across the grass to where Aaron now stood, hands on his hips, directing the placement of the other wagons about the shallow dip.

Two yards behind Aaron, Gracella was sitting on a stool before the caravan she and Aaron shared.

Robert strode up and had sufficient nous to nod politely to Gracella before addressing Aaron. "I say," Robert said, drawing and meeting Aaron's gaze. "I apologize about that." Robert waved toward the entrance to the meadow. "I didn't understand, but now I do." He held out his hand. "Welcome to Bigfield House."

Aaron's gaze flicked to Christopher, who had halted some yards behind Robert, then a grin split Aaron's weathered face, and he gripped Robert's hand. "Ah, well—we all have to learn. Best we put it behind us, eh?"

The readiness of Robert's smile confirmed his relative youth. "Thank you." He bobbed again to Gracella, then said, "I'll leave you to get settled."

With that, he turned and made for his horse, passing Christopher on the way.

Obviously approving and, Christopher suspected, mildly impressed, Aaron tipped a salute to Christopher.

He returned it with a nod. "I'll call back later."

He followed Robert and caught up as Robert mounted his horse. Christopher grabbed Storm's reins and did the same. As he settled in the saddle, he met Robert's eyes—a paler, less dramatic hazel than his sister's. "Given this"—Christopher waved at the gypsy encampment —"was news to you, perhaps I should accompany you to Bigfield House, in case your sister has any questions about the arrangements with the gypsies."

Robert's expression lit. "Would you? I have to admit I wasn't looking forward to explaining this to her—she's a trifle tense at the moment, what with all the other things she's having to deal with."

Christopher waved Robert on; as he followed the younger man out of the meadow, he realized he was smiling in anticipation.

Ellen was seated behind the desk in the study, her elbows planted to either side of a lengthy report on the anticipated production from the estate's orchards. She was struggling to make sense of the figures and had sunk both hands into the curls at her temples, ready to clutch. Her expression was one of sheer frustration when Robbie strolled in—followed by Christopher Cynster.

Abruptly lowering her hands and rearranging her features, she stared, then hurriedly rose. "Mr. Cynster. I wasn't expecting you."

He smiled and inclined his head in greeting. "I met your brother while out riding."

She managed a vague nod in response, exceedingly glad that the desk sat squarely between them. That smile had set her senses skittering and her nerves flickering in an even worse fashion than the day before.

Damn. She'd hoped the effect he had on her would fade. Apparently not.

How irritating.

Mentally gritting her teeth, she waved her nemesis to a chair and, resuming her seat, glanced questioningly at Robbie.

Entirely at ease, her brother informed her, "I encountered a band of gypsies turning in to the lower meadow. I tried to stop them, but luckily, Mr. Cynster happened along and saved me from making a complete fool of myself."

She blinked. "Oh?" She'd always understood gypsies to be troublemakers.

When Robbie simply slumped in a chair and said nothing further, she looked at their neighbor. "What do I need to know about these gypsies?"

The smile hadn't left his lips, flirting about the ends in a distracting fashion. "What you need to appreciate is that the Bigfield House estate needs the services of this particular band of Romany in the same way we at Walkhurst Manor do, as well as the Huntlys at Moreton Manor, the Entwhistles at Grove Farm, and the Cummingses."

She frowned. "Why do we need the services of gypsies?"

He told her, in detail—chapter and verse.

She had to admit that, in doing so, he managed to avoid sounding superior, which, in the circumstances, was no mean feat.

By the end of his lesson, she was sincerely grateful. "Thank you—for the information and for stepping in and ensuring Robbie didn't succeed in sending the gypsies away." *That* would have been a disaster; she was already well aware of the limited manpower available on the estate.

Christopher studied the fascinating Miss Martingale, today gowned in a frothy confection of white-spotted pink poplin adorned with yards of cherry-red ribbons, with a plethora of tiny ribbon rosettes affixed to the scalloped frills at neckline, sleeve, and presumably hem. He'd noted the widening of her eyes when he'd walked into the room and the telltale way her fingers had twined and gripped, until she'd focused on the matter of the gypsies and her skittishness had subsided.

He would wager she was as aware of the visceral connection that had sprung to life between them as he was. Yet while he was intrigued by it—he'd never felt its like, not in terms of intensity—she seemed determined to ignore the spark, to pretend it wasn't there.

He suspected she would very much rather he stayed far away.

Too bad.

Now he'd met her brother—Sir Humphrey's heir—a few pieces of the jigsaw of the true state of affairs at Bigfield House had shifted, revealing a problematic hole.

Christopher looked at Robert. "I wonder if I could trouble you to check on the goat pen? Just to make sure the goats haven't escaped. Now the hops are coming into full flower, I find I'm a touch nervous over the whereabouts of your uncle's herd."

Robert grinned and all but sprang to his feet. "Nothing easier—I was intending to check on them later today." He flung a smiling glance at his sister. "I'll go now." With a nod in her direction and another to Christopher, Robert strode from the room.

Hiding a satisfied smile, Christopher watched him go, then returned his gaze to Ellen Martingale.

She was watching him through flinty, narrowed eyes. "You haven't a nervous bone in your body."

He held her gaze for a second, then tipped his head in acknowledgment. "I do, however, have several questions that I would rather not ask in Robert's presence."

She stiffened.

Before she could summon every last possible defense, he continued, "Such as, when does Robert reach his majority? By that, I mean the age stipulated in Sir Humphrey's will."

Her eyes locked with his. She blinked, once, stared at him as the seconds ticked by, then pursed her lips as if holding back the answer.

When he didn't shift his gaze or make any further comment, she huffed and rather grumpily admitted, "Twenty-five."

"I believe you mentioned that he's only just twenty."

She nodded. "Five years to go."

"So"—and here was the crux of it—"if Sir Humphrey is no longer able to make decisions—as you, I, and, I assume, Vickers know is the case—then who has the legal right to act for the estate?"

She stared at him. The fingers of her left hand restlessly picked at the papers on her desk. "Legally?"

He shot her an exasperated look. "To be clear, I agree that you and your brother—being Sir Humphrey's closest blood relatives, with Robert being his legal heir—have a moral right to make decisions for the estate. I'm not questioning that. But it must have occurred to you that, over the next five years, it's possible that your right to act in Sir Humphrey's stead might be challenged."

Ellen glared at her discombobulating interrogator. "Of course that's occurred to me—and to Vickers, too!" She flung up her hands. "Why do you think we're trying so hard to keep Uncle Humphrey's condition a secret?"

Christopher-aggravating-Cynster tipped his head appeasingly. "Indeed, but do you know of any particular issue that's likely to arise in managing the estate that will expose the fact that the estate is standing on shaky legal ground?"

She compressed her lips and studied him. She tapped one fingertip on the desktop while she considered how much to share. Eventually, she admitted, "Vickers and I discussed it. As matters stand, the only challenge we could foresee was if any of those agents with long-standing contracts for the estate's produce push to renegotiate. We'd have to fob them off, because not even Vickers can act for my uncle with regard to such contracts."

Somewhat to her surprise, Cynster nodded decisively. "That's what I assumed." He caught and held her gaze. "I wanted to assure you that, if you and Vickers find yourselves facing any challenge over your—or your brother's or even Vickers's—right to act for the estate, then in view of the long-standing connection between Bigfield House and Walkhurst Manor, the long association between my parents and Sir Humphrey, the Cynsters stand ready to discourage anyone who might feel inclined to take advantage of the situation."

She blinked, hesitated, then bluntly said, "That's a very bold claim— to be able to act in such a fashion." She arched her brows. "Can you actually do so?"

His smile was all teeth. "Oh yes."

Confidence rang in his tone.

When she continued to look questioningly at him, he smiled more gently and went on, "The Cynsters wield a great deal of influence in many spheres. I'm not talking solely of my parents but of the wider ducal family. We stand together—that's something of a family badge of honor. If you take on one of us, you will be facing the might of the entire clan." He paused, then lightly shrugged. "As it happens, any agents used by Sir Humphrey are likely to have contracts with us as well. Even if they don't, a quiet word from us would cause serious problems for any agent wishing to do business in Kent, certainly enough to dissuade any agent from attempting to make the situation here difficult—more difficult than it already is."

She heard the simple honesty in his tone, saw it in his expression, and reluctantly rejigged her opinion of him.

He appeared to be the quintessential London rake, possessing every telltale attribute, such as the way he walked into a room and instantly became the focus of attention, such as his invisible cloak of arrogant confidence, and the way he made women—even women like her—forget their names. Yet despite all such evidence, he wasn't a typical member of the fraternity. He actually cared about what went on in this little pocket of the world.

He was offering her—and her brother, the estate, and most importantly, her poor uncle—a shield, a protection against the worst of her imagined and feared scenarios.

"Thank you." The words fell from her lips without conscious direction; there really wasn't anything else she could say.

As if he understood that, his elusive smile returned, lifting the corners of his mobile lips. He inclined his head to her. "If anyone causes problems, send word, and I'll come, and we can discuss how best to keep the wolves from the door."

She had to smile at that, yet the relief she felt was very real.

He considered her for a second more, then uncrossed his long legs and rose. "I'd better be getting on."

She got to her feet, grateful he wasn't seeking to prolong his visit. She could keep her mind on practical matters and away from dwelling on him for only so long.

He turned toward the door, and she fell into step beside him.

As they walked along the corridor to the front hall, he glanced at her. "As with the gypsies, if you stumble across anything about local farming practices that you don't understand or are unsure of, don't hesitate to ask. I'll be fixed at the manor for the foreseeable future, and as I've mentioned, I and my family consider ourselves beholden to Sir Humphrey —we'll happily do everything we can to ease any difficulties arising from his decline."

Even if she hadn't already decided that he was a great deal more reliable than she'd first assumed, that speech would have set the seal on it.

They reached the hall, and looking toward the open front door, he added, "And unlike your brother, I've been trained to manage estates such as this since I could walk."

He halted before the doorway, and she stopped beside him. He turned to her and smiled—an entirely genuine and utterly charming expression.

Because it seemed the obvious thing to do, she returned the smile and held out her hand. "Thank you."

His fingers closed around hers—and she very nearly startled.

His eyes locked on hers, and something shifted in the moss-and-caramel depths.

Her senses sparked, and her wits skittered; before she could summon sufficient will to reorder them, he raised her hand and, with his gaze holding hers, brushed a kiss—the faintest whisper of a teasing kiss—over her knuckles.

Heat flared; a frisson of sensation danced up her arm, and she felt distinctly giddy.

He smiled—a knowing smile, this time—then released her hand, nodded gracefully, turned, and walked out of the door.

Christopher descended the steps feeling thoroughly satisfied with the outcome of his visit.

A groom held Storm's reins; Christopher accepted them, swung up to the saddle, and found himself battling a ridiculously pleased grin.

Pride came before a fall; he reminded himself of that. And there was little doubt that Miss Ellen Martingale wasn't—even now—about to succumb to his charms.

She was quite remarkably resistant—far more so than any lady he'd previously encountered—especially given the intensity, the shocking power, of what had sparked to life between them.

As he turned Storm down the drive and urged the big gray into a canter, he reviewed all he'd learned about the situation at Bigfield House.

One particular conclusion stood out from all the rest.

It was one he found more and more intriguing.

Ellen Martingale might live her life weighed down with ribbons and rosettes, but beneath her frivolous attire, she was anything but a frivolous female.

After quitting Bigfield House, Christopher resumed his interrupted ride around the manor's far-flung fields. It was late afternoon when he finally walked into the manor's front hall and found Pendleby, the butler, hovering.

"Mr. Toby has arrived, sir. He's waiting in the library."

Christopher widened his eyes, then turned toward the library. As far as he knew, after the Summer Celebration at Somersham Place, his cousin Toby had headed back to Newmarket. With Pru now in Ireland, Christopher's uncle, Demon Cynster, relied on his sons, Nicholas and Toby, to manage the famous Cynster racing stable and breeding stable respectively. Christopher couldn't imagine any horse-related matter bringing Toby into the Weald of Kent.

Curious, Christopher strolled into the library, which also served as his study. It was a comfortable room, lined with bookshelves packed with leather-bound tomes and boasting a large fireplace before which were gathered numerous large armchairs and a long, well-padded sofa.

Toby was slumped, eyes closed, in one of the armchairs.

Christopher grinned. He saw Toby's long fingers, spread on the chair's arm, twitch; his cousin was awake. "That tiring?" Christopher asked.

Toby opened his eyes and met Christopher's gaze; Toby's gaze was distinctly jaundiced. "Working for Drake usually is."

"Ah." Christopher sank into the armchair opposite, then frowned. "But why has Drake conscripted you as, I assume, a messenger?"

"Because"—Toby sat up and stretched—"he wanted to be sure the message reached you, and I was the only Cynster or Varisey he could lay hands on." Toby looked at Christopher. "Drake has everyone he trusts out and about, running hither and yon, collecting information on his latest problem. I was in town to check on some sales at Tattersalls—he saw me and tapped me on the shoulder." Toby sighed and leaned back. "You know how it is—Drake's summonses really aren't the sort one can refuse. Especially when his brothers and several of our cousins are already involved."

Christopher humphed in understanding. Drake's summonses invariably involved working for, as the saying went, queen and country. Drake, otherwise known as the Marquess of Winchelsea, had largely taken up where his father, the Duke of Wolverstone, had left off—managing a string of secret agents on foreign soil and generally stepping in whenever matters concerning the Crown or national security required investigating.

Given their fathers had all fought at Waterloo, the current generation, when called on, viewed assisting Drake as, in effect, their turn to volunteer and do their part in defending the realm.

"So what's the message?" Christopher asked.

Toby took a moment to order his thoughts, then said, "Counterfeit notes have started appearing, not in London but scattered here and there across the country—even into Scotland. Not many—just a handful here, a few notes there. Drake believes that what he's seeing is the result of trial runs testing a distribution system. Thus far, the number of fake notes surfacing isn't large enough to create a serious problem, but assuming these are just trials, then subsequent releases are likely to be much larger—"

"And *that* would be a problem."

Toby nodded. "So far, Drake's managed to keep everything quiet—he, or more specifically the banks, can't afford a panic. That's why it's taking so many of us to follow up where the fakes have come from. All inquiries have had to be made very quietly, so that even those being questioned weren't aware of the true nature of our interest. However, through the combined efforts of many, Drake has established that all the fake notes that have appeared to date have come from the pockets of young, well-to-do gentlemen." Toby paused, then clarified, "By young, we're talking of twenty or so—thus far, the oldest found to be involved is twenty-two."

Christopher frowned. "Where are they getting the fake notes? And if they're not aware of being questioned, I assume they're unwitting pigeons."

"Exactly. The interesting point—and the reason I'm here—is that all these unwitting pigeons who've been sent into the wild with counterfeit banknotes in their pockets have one, and seemingly only one, recent activity in common. Every man involved has visited Goffard Hall over the past two months. It seems the lady of the place, which is apparently near here, runs card parties for her younger cousin, and he invites his friends, and many of them bring their friends—you know how it goes."

"Goffard Hall?" Christopher pulled a face. "I know where it is—and yes, it's not far—but I've never had anything to do with the family there, and I don't think the parents have, either."

"Be that as it may," Toby said, "Drake's asked if you can see what you can learn, but—and I'm supposed to stress and underline this for all I'm worth—whatever you do, don't alert anyone to your interest in the place, much less the card parties."

Christopher arched his brows. "Why such secrecy?"

"Because Drake being Drake, he has his eye on whoever's behind the scheme. As far as I can make out, he's hoping to pick up the trail at Goffard Hall and, in one way or another, follow it back to whoever is taking the money the counterfeit notes are substituted for. He's assuming —for what reasons, he didn't share—that the principal purpose of this racket is not to destabilize the currency and the country so much as to simply make money."

Slowly, Christopher nodded. "All right. All I know about Goffard Hall is that it's not an estate—a landholding. It's just a large house—not even a particularly old one—set in its own grounds. The owner is a Mr. Kirkpatrick, an older gentleman who made his fortune in the City and bought the place about six years ago. As far as I know, he has no roots among the local families, no deeper connections within our county circles." He grimaced. "Mama would likely know more, but she isn't here, and in terms of Drake's investigation, she's not really contactable—not in time."

"What about the staff?" Toby asked.

"That's a thought." Christopher rose and tugged the bellpull.

He returned to his chair and, when Pendleby arrived in answer to the summons, asked, "What can you—or any of the senior staff—tell me about the family at Goffard Hall?"

Sadly, Pendleby's answer added nothing to what Christopher already knew. "And I'm sure," Pendleby said, "that Mrs. Marsh and the others know no more. We sometimes encounter the Hall staff, of course, but they don't tend to talk of the family—just as we don't talk about the family here."

Christopher acknowledged that with a grunt and thanked Pendleby, then looked at Toby. "You'll stay the night?"

Toby nodded. "Please." He grinned at Pendleby. "Dinner and a comfortable bed would be nice."

Pendleby rose to the challenge. "Mrs. Marsh has already prepared your usual room, sir, and Mrs. Hambledon said she can be ready to serve dinner whenever it's called for."

Christopher caught Toby's gaze. "You're in the country now—half past six?"

Toby inclined his head. "My stomach thanks you."

Christopher gave the order, and Pendleby left to ferry it to the dragon who presided over the manor's kitchen.

Christopher sank back in the chair. After several moments of cogitation, he said, "It might pay to ask Montague for his opinion of Mr. Kirkpatrick of Goffard Hall."

Toby dipped his head. "If you write a letter, I'll take it with me when I hie back to town tomorrow. Then, after I drop in on Drake and confirm you'll be investigating down here, it's back to Newmarket for me."

Christopher leaned forward. "These young gentlemen—are they noblemen's sons or…?"

"Or," Toby said. "According to Drake, all those he's thus far identified as passing fake notes have been of the gentry. None have been aristocrats—and given aristocrats dominate at card parties in the capital, I suppose that fits with the sort of young gentlemen who would gather at card parties in the wilds of Kent."

Christopher nodded.

When Pendleby returned and announced dinner, Christopher rose and ambled beside Toby to the dining room. He'd been thinking of Robert Martingale and that, as far as he recalled, the Bigfield House estate backed onto the plot of land on which Goffard Hall stood.

As he and Toby entered the dining room, Christopher said, "Regarding the card parties at Goffard Hall, I might know someone who —possibly—might know a lot more."

When Toby looked his question, Christopher waved him to the table. "Leave it with me—I'll see what I can learn and let Drake know."

CHAPTER 3

*C*hristopher rode up the drive of Bigfield House, well aware it was his third visit in as many days. He had his excuse prepared, a reasonable query to disguise his true intent, which was to extract from Robert what he knew about the Goffard Hall card parties.

He halted Storm before the front steps, handed the reins to the groom who came running, then, on impulse, instructed the groom to take the horse to the stables. "I don't know how long I'll be."

"Aye, sir." The groom knew him; he snapped off a salute and turned away, leading a faintly disgruntled Storm.

Christopher trod up the steps, conscious of a certain eagerness that had nothing to do with pursuing Drake's investigation. In the wake of the liberty he'd taken yesterday, he was keen to see how the discouraging Miss Martingale would respond to him this morning.

Kissing her fingers had been an impulse he hadn't been able to resist. Just to see. Just to sense what her reaction would be.

Now he'd confirmed beyond doubt that the visceral attraction he felt toward her—beribboned frills notwithstanding—was fully reciprocated, he felt he stood on firmer ground.

At least he knew and recognized the landscape in which he—they—stood.

Regardless of what she thought of that.

He walked through the open front door, halted just inside, and scanned the front hall, but Partridge was nowhere in sight. Christopher hesitated, then surrendered to the impulse to see Miss Martingale again; it would, after all, be wise to establish his reason for being there before hunting down Robert. He headed for the study, his bootheels ringing on the hall's black-and-white tiles.

"Mr. Cynster!"

The hail brought him to a halt. He swung to his left to face the drawing room, the doors of which, he now realized, stood propped wide, and saw three older ladies beaming in welcome. Two he recognized; Mrs. Carstairs of Benenden Grange and her dearest friend, Mrs. Folliwell, were seated on a long sofa. The third and oldest lady sat in an armchair facing the sofa; her faded doll-like features bore a more-than-passing resemblance to Ellen Martingale. He recalled she'd mentioned an aunt.

It had been Mrs. Folliwell who had called him; she grinned in expectant delight.

Mrs. Carstairs, also smiling delightedly, beckoned imperiously. "Do join us, Christopher. This will save us from having to call at the manor—we had you on our list to speak with next."

Wishing he'd seen them before they'd seen him, he reluctantly obeyed. Mrs. Carstairs and Mrs. Folliwell were grandes dames of the local social circle, together with his mother, to whom they were close. Despite escalating wariness, he plastered on an easy expression and walked into what his instincts were insisting was a lionesses' den.

He stepped into the room before realizing there was a fourth occupant. Ellen Martingale sat in an armchair angled to face all three older ladies. Focused as he had been on the source of impending danger, he'd missed seeing her—which was remarkable considering her pale-green gown, liberally endowed with frills edged with lace and forest-green ribbon. More ribbons and lace had been wound through her golden curls, leaving her looking distractingly pretty, but utterly doll-like.

As his feet carried him toward the older ladies, with her rosebud lips pressed tight, Ellen caught his eye. Her eyes widened fractionally, the appeal in them crystal clear.

For God's sake, save me!

He looked at the three older ladies and wasn't at all sure he would be able to save himself.

With faint and desperate hope, Ellen watched Christopher greet Mrs. Carstairs and Mrs. Folliwell, with whom he was plainly acquainted.

Mrs. Carstairs promptly introduced him to Ellen's aunt Emma. "Since losing her husband many years ago, Mrs. Fitzwilliam lived with her late sister, young Mr. Martingale's and Miss Martingale's mother, in London. But after Mrs. Martingale's passing, Mrs. Fitzwilliam and her niece and nephew came to live here and keep Sir Humphrey company."

Mrs. Carstairs beamed; Ellen suspected the lady's joy was in large part fueled by the expectation of having two new candidates—herself and Robert—to add to the local matchmakers' list.

That was certainly the impression she'd been receiving.

She watched as Christopher did the pretty with practiced ease, bowing over the ladies' hands, exchanging words of greeting, and welcoming her aunt to the area. Despite the country setting, to Ellen's eyes, he still looked like a London wolf; he wasn't even bothering to adopt a disguise —to veil his nature in any way.

She inwardly humphed. She supposed honesty was a point in his favor.

It was, she told herself, ridiculous that she was even noticing.

On the thought, the skin over the knuckles of her right hand heated, brushed by phantom, too-well-remembered lips. She fought down a reactive shiver. *Really?* She'd hoped she would have got over that moment by now.

The truth was she'd never been so afflicted by a man as she was—so effortlessly—by Christopher Cynster; she was starting to comprehend that meant she couldn't predict how she would respond to any future interactions.

She'd tried to tamp down her instinctive responses to him and failed.

She'd tried to ignore those instinctive responses, to pretend they weren't occurring. She'd failed in that, too.

If she'd been able, she would have moved to block all future interactions between them...only she couldn't afford to cut him, to turn her back on the assistance he could give, to jettison the shield he'd willingly offered.

Her primary, overriding aim was to protect her uncle, her brother, her aunt, and all the staff and workers who depended on the Bigfield House estate. That was her principal duty, her responsibility, and she took it seriously. It currently ruled all her decisions and actions.

And that meant she couldn't run from or ignore Christopher Cynster.

Life would be so much easier if I could.

Emma had been exchanging pleasantries with their unexpected visitor; now she waved at Ellen and smiled. "And this is my niece, Ellen. She's been terribly busy helping Sir Humphrey over recent months, but we"—Emma's wave included Mrs. Carstairs and Mrs. Folliwell—"are determined to prevail on her to join the festivities this Monday evening."

Christopher turned to Ellen. His eyes met hers; amusement lurked in their depths as he half bowed, then informed the others, "Miss Martingale and I have met."

"Oh?" came from Mrs. Folliwell in interrogatory tones.

"Indeed." Christopher's smile didn't falter as he moved to claim the armchair beyond Ellen's, nearer the door. "You might say Miss Martingale and I met over goats."

"Ah." Mrs. Carstairs nodded in understanding. "Sir Humphrey's pets, I take it."

"Just so. They were attracted to the scent of ripening hops and thought to take a wander in the manor's fields."

"Such smelly things, goats." Mrs. Folliwell waved the distraction aside and focused once more on the matter the three ladies were determined to prosecute. "We've just been telling Miss Martingale of the summer evening party Mrs. Carstairs will be hosting on Monday."

"It's just my usual event," Mrs. Carstairs informed Christopher. She paused, then added, "Of course, as you're usually gadding about the country, you might not realize that, but Mr. Carstairs and I hold it every year. A summer get-together for all the local families—with dancing, too."

"Gives everyone something to look forward to in what is otherwise a rather slow season, socially speaking," Mrs. Folliwell added.

"It does seem a wonderful idea," Emma chimed in. She looked longingly at Ellen. "I do hope, dear, that now everything about the estate is running so smoothly, you'll be able to attend."

Until now, she'd managed to avoid the local matchmakers—no mean feat given they'd arrived at Bigfield House in October the previous year. She'd ducked and dodged and slipped through the nets they'd cast, but it appeared her luck was about to run out.

"And you, too, Christopher." Mrs. Carstairs directed a pointed look at him. "I understand your brother is off somewhere—gadding as you used to do, no doubt—and of course, your sister is with her family in the north, but you are here, in residence and remaining so, and I'm quite sure your mother would urge you to attend."

" *Expect* you to attend," Mrs. Folliwell put in.

A wise man knew when he was outgunned. Christopher glanced at

Mrs. Fitzwilliam and realized she was looking from her niece to him and back again, a very faint hope in her eyes.

As for Ellen Martingale, her attitude suggested she'd been backed into the same corner he had, and she was no more enamored of that than he.

Perversely, that realization made him smile. He turned that smile on Mrs. Carstairs and inclined his head. "I will be honored to attend, ma'am." He recalled Drake's investigation and smoothly added, "Unless some unavoidable emergency calls me away, I'll be there."

"Excellent!" Mrs. Carstairs nodded approvingly, then turned her bright eyes on Ellen. "And you, Miss Martingale?"

Christopher heard her sigh, but she found a smile and inclined her head with acceptable grace. "An evening party with dancing—how could I resist?" She tipped her head toward her aunt. "I will accompany Aunt Emma and Robert."

"Wonderful!" Mrs. Folliwell boomed.

Having achieved all—and rather more—than they'd expected, given they hadn't known they would catch Christopher there, with gay farewells and satisfied looks, the two local grandes dames took their leave of Christopher, Ellen, and Mrs. Fitzwilliam.

Christopher remained standing with Ellen in the drawing room while Mrs. Fitzwilliam showed the other ladies out. All three bustled into the hall, busily discussing the plans for Monday's event.

He and Ellen waited in silence as the trio moved toward the front door and the porch, and their chatter faded.

Finally, Ellen huffed and, her gaze on the doorway, asked, "What unavoidable emergency will occur on Monday evening to keep you from Benenden Grange?"

He arched his brows. "I haven't really thought of it."

"When you do, please endeavor to have this emergency involve Bigfield House in some way, so that I can escape the ordeal, too."

He chuckled. "It's only a summer evening party." He glanced at her. "You must have attended any number of garden parties in town."

"Which is why I know I won't enjoy this one."

He shrugged lightly. "The country's different—and there'll be dancing!" He grinned. "You never know, you might find yourself swept off your feet."

She gave vent to a disgusted—and disbelieving—sound.

Christopher decided that was challenge enough.

Almost as if she could read his mind, she fixed him with a narrow-eyed look. Then she blinked and frowned. "Why are you here?" She hurried on, "Don't tell me those wretched goats have got free again."

"No." Recalled to his purpose in coming to Bigfield House, he replied, "I came to consult about when you—Bigfield House—are likely to need the gypsies. We usually work out a roster so they know which estate needs their assistance on any given day."

"Ah—I see." She thought, then waved him to the door. "Come to the study—I have the estimated harvest schedule Hopper prepared in there."

He followed her across the hall and down the corridor to the study.

As usual, she took the chair behind the desk, and he lounged in the armchair angled to face it.

"It's here somewhere." She flipped through a pile of papers stacked to one side of the desk, then pulled out a sheet. "Here it is."

After studying the sheet, she held it out to Christopher. "How do we go about this? What do we need to decide?"

From his coat pocket, he drew out his own notes, leaned forward and took the sheet from her, then laid the two side by side on the desk. "I mentioned that three other estates in the vicinity use Aaron's men as well, but only the manor and Bigfield House grow hops, so when the hop harvest starts, the gypsies divide their time between us."

He ran a finger down the dates listed beside each hop field on her list, then on his. She folded her arms on the desk and leaned over them to look.

"These," he explained, "will be Hopper's best estimates of when each of your fields will be ready, and these are my man Radley's estimates for the manor's fields. There's a week or more leeway in when, exactly, the hops need to be brought in, but these estimated dates give us a reasonable order from which to plan. For instance"—he tried not to notice the upper swells of her breasts that, with her leaning forward as she was, were now on display, and tapped a particular entry—"this field of ours, which is farther east, comes into flower first every year, so it will be the first to be harvested. But after that—see here and here—it will make better sense for Aaron and his lads to switch back and forth across the lane."

"I see." Her attention was wholly focused on the sheets. She reached with one hand to point to several dates—and he nearly closed his eyes and groaned. Oblivious to the insight she was affording him into how well-endowed she was, she blithely continued, "Then, I suppose, the gypsies move here and then to here."

"Exactly," he croaked.

She sat back, sitting straight once more, and he breathed again. "Should I speak with the gypsies directly?" she asked. "Or...?"

He cleared his throat and said, "We both should meet with Aaron, but I suggest we wait until the first field is ready. By then, we'll be more certain of the order in which the other fields will peak and can be more definite in our decisions regarding to what schedule Aaron's troop should work."

He picked up his estimates and pushed the sheet containing the Bigfield House dates toward her.

He glanced up and saw she was frowning.

She met his eyes. "So we don't need to decide anything now." There was the faintest hint of not so much suspicion as question in her tone.

"No." He tucked his list into his pocket. "I just wanted to make sure you were aware of how we'll need to deal with the gypsies over the next weeks."

Her lips formed an "Oh," but he wasn't sure she believed him. *Time to move on.* "Is Robert about? I wanted to ask him how he's been finding the shooting hereabouts."

She widened her eyes. "I don't know that he's taken a gun out recently, but regardless, he's not at home."

"Oh." He managed not to grimace.

"He's driven out with several local gentlemen his age—to Tunbridge Wells. I understand they intend to make a day of it."

So Robert Martingale had, indeed, fallen in with the local young gentlemen. Chances were he would know of or even had attended the Goffard Hall events.

Pleased to have at least that much confirmed, Christopher refocused on Ellen and discovered she now looked troubled. "What is it?"

She met his eyes, then lightly grimaced. "I'm happy Robert has made friends among the local young men and is now invited to the usual events with which that group entertain themselves. And while I hope there's no reason to be concerned about a visit to Tunbridge Wells, there are other entertainments—well, one sort primarily—about which I entertain significant reservations."

She couldn't mean... "Which particular entertainment is causing you concern?"

She studied him for only a second before replying, "I'm not sure if you're aware, but there are card parties held at Goffard Hall"—she waved to the west—"specifically for young gentlemen. Actually, *exclusively* for young gentlemen—no one else is invited. Over the past months, the parties have been held every two weeks—every second Friday."

At her inquiring look, he admitted, "I haven't spent much time in the locality over recent years. Although I know of Goffard Hall, I can't recall meeting any of the family. And being no longer classed as a 'young gentleman,' I haven't heard anything about these card parties."

"I thought perhaps your brother..."

"Gregory is only a year younger than I am. He wouldn't have been invited even were he here, which, as you heard earlier, he isn't."

She sighed, then shook her head. "I have a bad feeling about those parties."

"What do you know about the household?"

"Not a great deal. As you doubtless gathered from our interlude in the drawing room, socially speaking, I've been playing least in sight over the months since we arrived. Nevertheless, I understand that the Kirkpatricks of Goffard Hall are not particularly active in local circles. Not so much recluses as not often seen at local events. I gather Mrs. Kirkpatrick—she's Mr. Kirkpatrick's second wife—prefers London society."

Ellen sat back, brooding on what little she knew of the Goffard Hall household. "From what Emma and the local ladies—like Mrs. Carstairs and Mrs. Folliwell—have let fall, it seems they don't think much of Mrs. Kirkpatrick, but that might be because she turns up her nose, albeit elegantly, at their company."

"Who else is in the household?"

"Mr. Kirkpatrick, of course, but socially, he's seen even less than his wife, although he and Julia, his daughter by his first wife, often attend Sunday service at St. George's in the village."

"If I recall correctly, Kirkpatrick's first wife died some years ago."

She nodded. "I gather he remarried about three years ago." After a moment, she stirred and went on, "But you asked about other members of the household. In addition to the Kirkpatricks and Julia, Mrs. Kirkpatrick has invited two young cousins to stay, it seems more or less permanently —Matilda Fontenay, known as Tilly, who I've heard is eighteen, and her older brother, Nigel, who is much of an age with Robert."

"Is Nigel a member of the group of young men with whom Robert associates?"

"I believe so." Ellen brooded some more, then sighed in frustration. "I've even asked the staff here what they know of the Goffard Hall house-hold, but while they do occasionally meet the Goffard Hall staff out and about, they say the Goffard Hall people are very reticent over gossiping about the family."

Christopher studied her expression, noting the concern and the intelligence he could now clearly see. After a second, he asked, "Putting together all you've gleaned, if you were forced to render an opinion about the members of the Goffard Hall household, how would you describe them?"

Behind her doll-like façade, she was observant and shrewd about people; he honestly wanted to know what she thought.

She pressed her lips together, then shot him a look. "If I had to say...I think Mr. Kirkpatrick and his daughter, Julia, are reserved and honestly retiring in character. They are not the sort to do anything to invite attention. In contrast, Mrs. Kirkpatrick is a sharp and grasping lady, one who demands attention as her due and goes her own way in pursuing her desires. Nigel and Tilly are of much the same ilk, cut from the same cloth, and, I suspect, have been invited to stay to support Mrs. Kirkpatrick in her pursuits." She paused, then went on, "I don't know why these card parties of hers—limited to young gentlemen—are so important to her, but they seem to be an event she's been very keen to establish and continue."

She frowned. "I suppose that—not understanding why she's so set on these card parties—is part of what's feeding my unease over Robbie attending them."

Christopher straightened. "Very likely." She wasn't just intelligent, she had sound instincts.

"I can't even protest about his losses," she grumbled. "Although he participates and takes his place at the tables, it seems he hasn't—yet—lost enough to make any serious dent in his allowance." Lips tight, she shook her head, setting her curls bouncing distractingly.

After a second more of patently unhappy introspection, she sat up. "Well, regardless of my thoughts on the matter, the next card party is tomorrow evening, and there's no argument I can legitimately advance to dissuade Robbie from attending." She met Christopher's gaze and lightly grimaced. "And no, I'm not so silly as to try. A meddling older sister has no chance whatsoever of reining in a young gentleman of twenty."

Christopher grinned. "I've only got one younger sister, but she was quite bad enough."

Ellen huffed, then looked directly—measuringly—at him. "Actually, I was wondering... If you have the time, could you stay for luncheon? Believe it or not, Uncle Humphrey remembered you'd called, and yes, he remembered it was you and not your father. In the present circumstances, he doesn't get to see many others beyond the family, the staff, and Vickers—he would, I'm sure, be glad of your company."

Christopher smiled with entirely genuine pleasure. "I would be delighted to stay for luncheon."

"Excellent." She rose, and he came to his feet. She waved him to the door. "The gong will sound soon. If you'll join Uncle Humphrey in the conservatory, I'll tell Partridge there will be one more at table."

"Thank you," he said and meant it. He followed her from the room.

After a pleasant if occasionally conversationally challenging lunch, Christopher strolled to the Bigfield House stable. He'd parted from Ellen, as she'd finally invited him to call her, in the conservatory, where, between them, they'd settled Sir Humphrey in his wicker chair. Ellen had sat beside him, holding his hand and listening as he'd started telling her something about his goats, only to ramble off into some story that had no relevance to Ellen, Christopher, or even the goats.

She'd signaled that Christopher could leave, and he'd nodded and departed. But he was pleased he'd been able to keep Sir Humphrey's mind on track for most of the time they'd been at the table.

At least he'd done that much for the old man, contributed that much to Ellen's and her aunt Emma's peace of mind.

After chatting with the head stableman and reclaiming Storm, Christopher turned the gray's head north and made his way between the fields and eventually around to cross onto manor lands. While he rode, he reviewed the results of his morning's endeavors. Despite having fallen victim to the machinations of the local grandes dames, despite having failed to speak with Robert Martingale, overall, he felt singularly pleased with what he had achieved.

He'd taken the first steps toward finding the answers Drake wanted. "Now for the next stage."

At ten o'clock the next evening, Christopher was silently making his way beneath the trees bordering the lawns of Goffard Hall.

Giving Bigfield House a wide berth, he'd ridden over the fields and had arrived half an hour earlier. Glad that the moon wasn't full and what there was of it was partially obscured by clouds, he'd slipped from shadow to shadow, circling the house, checking the layout of the place—the relative position of the stable and other outbuildings and all exits from the main house.

Guests had still been arriving, rolling up in curricles and gigs; while taking care not to be seen, Christopher had watched long enough to confirm the narrow age range of the arrivals and the singular lack of females.

Now, having gained a reasonable idea of where the main reception rooms were in relation to all else—and also having noted a light burning in a well-proportioned study on the far side of the house and glimpsed an older gentleman, presumably Mr. Kirkpatrick, working behind a desk there—Christopher made his stealthy way toward the sound and light emanating from the large reception room in which the card party was being held.

Ballroom or drawing room, he couldn't yet tell, but when he crouched in the bushes on the outer edge of a stretch of manicured lawn and set eyes on the terrace abutting the middle section of the long room, he grinned.

It was high summer, and the evenings were mild. With all the bright lights plus the crowd in the room, the French doors to the terrace had, unsurprisingly, been left open. Even better, the gauzy curtains hanging over the doors and the windows along the flagged length hadn't been pulled aside; shifting and rippling in the faint breeze, they created a filmy, diaphanous veil that would obscure all details of the night-shrouded garden and the shadowy terrace from those inside.

Christopher was too old—too experienced, too patently aware—to attend the card party himself. Even if Toby, twenty-five to Christopher's thirty-one, had remained to assist, he wouldn't have passed muster, either, even if he'd tried to pretend he was twenty-one or -two. No matter how vague Toby sometimes appeared, as soon as anyone looked into his eyes, the caliber of the mind behind those eyes became obvious.

Assuming the Kirkpatricks were passing counterfeit notes through their card parties, having Christopher or Toby turn up on their doorstep requesting admission would have sounded a loud and strident alarm—the very last thing Drake, and therefore Christopher, wanted.

The best he could do was covertly observe and see what he could discover.

The terrace—largely draped in shifting shadows courtesy of several nearby trees—provided the perfect position from which to do so. Indeed, there was a patch of deeper shadow engulfing one end, and the curtains of the nearest window didn't quite meet. Through the resulting gap, he would be able to get an unobstructed view of the action inside the room.

Silently, he crept forward, making for the steps at that end of the terrace while keeping an eye on the open doors. But it was early yet; he doubted any of the young men whose hazy outlines he could just discern inside the room, gathered in clumps here and there, possibly around card tables, would yet have reached the stage of desperately needing fresh air.

He reached the steps, went swiftly up them, turned to the shadow-drenched corner—and froze.

Someone was already there.

No—not someone. Ellen Martingale.

Her curls, the silly feathered hat she wore, and the frills on her riding jacket and skirt that concealed her curves all screamed her identity.

With her gaze and her attention locked on what she could see through the gap in the curtains, she hadn't noticed his approach.

As silent as the surrounding shadows, he prowled closer, until he was standing less than a foot behind her. Ready to slap a hand over her lips if she screamed, he bent his head and, in decidedly clipped accents, whispered, "What the devil are *you* doing here?"

He'd underestimated her; she startled, but she didn't scream. Instead, after a tense moment when he sensed she concentrated on forcing her lungs to draw in air, she turned her head and, over her shoulder, cast him a narrow-eyed glare.

Ellen held him silent with her eyes while she waited for her senses to settle enough to trust her voice. She'd nearly swallowed her tongue in her desperation to mute her entirely understandable shriek. Compounding her difficulties, every nerve she possessed was ridiculously aware of him standing so close—mere inches away.

Far too close, but asking him to step back—even reaching out and pushing him back—would only draw his attention to her ridiculous susceptibility. If at all possible, she wanted to avoid that. So she gritted her teeth, waited for her reaction to subside, then looked back at the scene inside the Goffard Hall drawing room. "Your questions about Goffard Hall," she murmured. "About the household and these card parties. They started me thinking." She nodded at the activity on the other side of the glass. "There's something wrong about this, isn't there?"

If she'd harbored any doubt as to the validity of that conclusion, the sudden silence that greeted her words settled the matter.

After too long a pause, he asked, all level tone and idle curiosity, "What makes you think that?"

She cast him a glance that was just a touch contemptuous. "Why are you here?"

Christopher muted a snort.

Having successfully rebutted any argument he might think to make, she returned to surveying the room.

Jaw clenched, he looked over her shoulder.

After a moment, she added, "Besides, if there's anything untoward going on, it's my brother—my innocent and entirely unsuspecting brother—who's involved."

He grimaced lightly. He had to grant her that. Had their positions been reversed...

He focused on the gathering inside the brightly lit room. The chandeliers blazed. Even heard through the window, the rowdy chatter was loud, yet with so many speaking at once, it was difficult to make out specific words, much less follow any conversation.

But the card tables scattered about the room required little explanation.

"It seems to be mostly vingt-un," Ellen murmured. "At least at the tables I can see."

"Hmm." He hadn't watched for long enough to be sure but suspected she was right.

She ducked a fraction closer to the window—peering at something—and put up a hand to brush back the fall of the feathers on her hat, only to have a knot of ribbon adorning the end of her sleeve tangle with the feathers. She hissed, straightened, and tugged to free her arm.

"Here—let me." It took him a second to free the feathers.

"Stupid things!" She thrust back the offending feathers.

He blinked, then ventured, "Why do you wear them, then?"

"Not by choice!" Her tone suggested he was a fool for even thinking such a thing.

"Why, then?" He was far too fascinated to let the subject slide.

She sighed. "It's Aunt Emma's idea of how I should look." She flipped a hand at her face, her figure. "You have eyes—you can see. Emma was widowed young. She never had children. She came to live with Mama and Papa, and when I was little, Emma and my mother took great delight in dressing me in ribbons and lace and frills. Just like the doll I looked like. You can imagine it, I'm sure." Her tone was decidedly dry.

After a second, she went on, "As it happens, I really don't care all that much what I look like. I seem to have misplaced that ladylike trait. So if dressing me in ribbons and lace made Mama and Aunt Emma happy, that was all right with me. Sadly, as I grew older, even when Mama became less fixated on the latest style of frippery, Emma remained set on ribbons and lace—and feathers and frills and all such adornments. You should see some of my evening gowns. Sequins everywhere!"

She fell silent, and he waited, then quietly prompted, "And now?"

"And now that Mama is gone, overseeing and adding to my wardrobe remains one of Aunt Emma's favorite pastimes. It's an activity she shared with my mother—her sister—and…I think it's something she clings to. A task that, at least in her eyes, makes her feel she's still doing her best for me."

Christopher didn't break the ensuing silence. Although they both kept their gazes glued to the scene beyond the glass, tracking the young men who wandered back and forth and the frenetic activity around those card tables they could see, for his part, his mind was elsewhere.

In fact, his mind slid back to a moment in May, when he'd stood at the side of the ballroom in Glengarah Castle and, commenting on the relationship between his cousin Pru and her new husband, had somewhat waspishly observed: *It must be nice to be the recipient of that degree of devotion.*

Never again would he view the ribbons and frills on Ellen's dresses in the dismissively censorious way he had.

She knew perfectly well that they made her look silly—a grown woman dressed like a doll—but she bore with them for another reason. A deeper, entirely laudable purpose.

Out of devotion to an old lady who had cared for her for all of her life.

Without warning, Ellen jabbed her elbow into his ribs. "There!" She pointed across the room. "That's Mrs. Kirkpatrick. She must have given up on further arrivals and come to mingle."

He refocused and saw a lady of about his own age, with dark hair and a voluptuous figure, gowned in what his educated eyes identified as a creation from one of the ton's foremost modistes. The lady appeared gay and carefree and was plainly set on dazzling her young guests.

After a moment, Ellen snorted softly. "She's not truly set on seducing them, is she?"

"Not in the usual sense of the word." Of that, he was quite sure.

Ellen threw him a glance over her shoulder, but apparently decided not to inquire how he knew.

Her look prodded his more-reckless self, and he lowered his head and whispered, "Trust me—she's not looking to lure any of these aspiring rakes to her bed. However, she is looking to ensure they return here again and again."

After watching Mrs. Kirkpatrick's performance for several more minutes, Ellen conceded, "I see what you mean. She's feeding their egos —making them feel important and older than they are."

Cynically, he remarked, "Young gentlemen are sadly suggestive and very easily led. Very easily duped."

A second later, he heard the frown in her voice as she asked, "But what is she duping them about?"

He was forced to admit, "As to that, I'm not entirely sure."

Half a minute later, Ellen's elbow came into play again, and he looked where she pointed. "That's Tilly Fontenay," Ellen whispered, "Mrs. Kirkpatrick's young cousin."

He watched a very young lady with coppery curls, who had appeared from somewhere to their left, pause by Mrs. Kirkpatrick and murmur something in her ear.

Christopher noted a hard glint in the older woman's eyes as she nodded. Then, with her expression softening once more, she turned back to the bevy of eager young gentlemen she'd been entertaining. She spoke, and in short order, several of the young men obediently trailed off in the same direction—to Christopher's and Ellen's left—in which the girl, Tilly, had retreated. The young men's eager expressions and their attempts to mimic a more adult sangfroid only underscored how immature and easily influenced they were—putty in Mrs. Kirkpatrick's hands.

"That man there"—Ellen pointed across the room again—"the one with the gray silk cravat, is Nigel Fontenay, Tilly's brother."

Christopher eyed the young man assessingly; he appeared a hail-fellow-well-met sort, but shifty characters usually wore a disguise. "Presumably, he's another of Mrs. Kirkpatrick's helpers."

"So it seems." After a moment, Ellen asked, "Other than Robbie, do you recognize any of the young men?"

He hadn't been taking note of identities. Now, he looked anew and was rather shocked by what he saw. "I can see young Huntly and the Entwhistles' son and also Henry Dalton. They're all local, from estates within easy reach." Theirs weren't the faces that bothered him. After a moment, he murmured, "There are several others who hail from London and even farther afield." Young men of good families...what the devil were they doing deep in rural Kent at this time of year?

Nigel Fontenay had taken up dealing at a card table across the room. Christopher mentally shook his head at the visors several of the players had donned, as if that somehow signaled they were experienced gamblers.

Trapped in front of Christopher, Ellen shifted restlessly. She'd had enough of feeling the heat of his large body seeping through the layers of her clothes. Let alone the moments when he bent his head to whisper by her ear; the waft of his breath over her sensitive skin... She couldn't bear it any longer.

She eased out from between him and the curtained window; to her relief, he stepped back to let her pass. In reply to his plainly questioning look, she whispered, "I'm going to see what I can glimpse from around the corner. There should be a window on that side. Robbie went that way, following Tilly—I want to see what she's about."

She didn't wait for any agreement but went quickly down the terrace steps, skirted the lawn, then followed a grassy path between beds that eventually led her around the corner of the building.

Sure enough, a window blazed on that side of the house. Even better, the sash had been raised to allow cool air to waft inside—and sound to roll out.

Below the window, the lawn extended to the wall of the house, allowing her to silently approach and stand to one side of the frame.

This window wasn't curtained, but ground level was significantly lower than the terrace; she was only just tall enough to see over the lower edge of the window.

She'd been careful to approach the window from one side; no one had seen her slip into position. And no one noticed when she peeked in.

A few feet inside the room, Tilly stood with her back angled to the window, facing an oval card table at which she was plainly dealing. She remained on her feet, as did the young men crowding around the table. Four young gentlemen were seated in an arc facing Tilly, and their peers pressed close, watching the play and, in the way of young men every-where, egging the players on.

Ellen was relieved to see Robbie merely looking on. His face was flushed, and he was grinning inanely, but he didn't seem inebriated. The same could not be said for several of those around him, who appeared distinctly glassy-eyed.

Ellen watched Tilly shuffle the cards, get one of the players to cut the deck, then deal. After a few minutes, Ellen had confirmed that the game was, as at the other tables, vingt-un.

Given the wide popularity of the game, it was a fair bet it was one most of the young men attending would know—and, very possibly, consider themselves expert in.

She'd just reached that conclusion when she felt a now-familiar heat —no less disconcerting because of that familiarity—settle all the way down her back.

Damn! He followed—and he's even closer now than he was on the terrace!

Jaw set, she slanted a glance sideways as his face appeared over her shoulder. His concentration seemed absolute, locked on the scene playing out before them.

Deciding she would have to grin and bear with his presence—she wasn't moving from this very revealing spot—she gritted her teeth and returned her gaze to the cards Tilly was holding.

The ace of spades and the king of diamonds.

Ellen wasn't surprised to hear Tilly blatantly flirting and encouraging the players to increase their wagers. From what Ellen could hear of Tilly's prattle, she was pretending to be an easy mark when, in reality, she was going to win and clean the gullible fools out.

Ellen watched the little drama unfold, sure of its inevitable end…only to blink and stare when, instead of laying her cards face up and claiming the wagered tokens, Tilly dropped her cards face down and pouted, then, smiling to show there were no hard feelings, she pushed a small mountain of tokens toward one of the seated young men. Elated, he crowed and gathered in his winnings…

With her elbow, Ellen nudged her companion and incredulously breathed, "Did you see that?"

Christopher blinked and briefly met her gaze. "No." He'd been too distracted by the perfume rising from her hair; he hadn't been focusing on anything in the room.

Her eyes sparked, and she all but hissed, "Watch Tilly's cards—not her."

He bit his tongue; he hadn't been watching Tilly at all.

Obediently, he focused on the next hand, but saw nothing odd.

When he glanced at Ellen and arched a brow in question, she shook her head and ordered, "Keep watching."

He did—and eventually saw what she already had. Tilly folded a clearly winning hand and claimed her luck had deserted her. "Huh." After a moment of thinking, he murmured to himself, "So *that's* how it's done."

Ellen cast him a sharp glance. "How what's done?"

He pressed his lips together, and she glared.

"Later," he murmured and returned his gaze to the scene inside the room.

They watched Tilly throw two more winning hands, then Ellen stirred and breathed, "I'm going to go back to the terrace."

He nodded and stepped back, allowing her to lead the way. When she halted on the path through the flower beds, swung around, and glared at him, he waved her on. "I want to scan the room again and take more definite note of those I recognize." Drake would have to be told.

They returned to their previous vantage point at the end of the terrace. Shadows still shrouded the spot, but the moon had shifted, and the engulfing darkness wasn't as dense as it had been. Regardless, the position was the best for their purpose, affording as it did a decent view across the central section of the room.

Ellen slipped into the corner by the wall, from where she could see through the gap in the curtains; as before, Christopher stood behind and a little to her right and looked over her head into the room.

He was busy memorizing names when three of the guests walked out of the room through the open French doors.

All three young men became entangled in the gauzy drapes, which caught on their heads and clothes. Laughing, they swatted and peeled the clinging material away.

The fleeting seconds of their distraction was all the time Christopher had to conceal Ellen and himself—or at least concoct an excuse for their presence.

She stood frozen in shock, her eyes wide.

He seized her waist, backed her against the wall, raised a hand, framed her face, and tipped it upward as he bent his head and sealed her lips with his.

CHAPTER 4

Sensation streaked through them both. She tensed, rigid as a poker. Her hands had flattened against his chest; along with her arms, they firmed, preparing to push him away.

He broke the kiss enough to breathe, "Play along."

Her lips parted—either in shock or on a protest. He seized the chance and plunged back into the kiss.

A kiss—and luscious, delectable lips—that had his inner wolf slavering.

From behind his back came a chuckle.

"I say—what's this, then, heh?"

Drunken cackles replied.

Christopher retained enough sense to lift a hand from Ellen's waist and, behind his back, signal to the inebriated three in a gesture that unequivocally stated *Go away!*

More chuckles ensued, then one said, "Lucky devil—I suppose we should leave them to it."

Yes!

"Half his luck." From the shuffling sounds, the three were turning away.

"Who is he, anyway?" one asked, purely curious as the trio stepped back through the doors.

"No idea, but more to the point, where did he find her? I haven't seen any maids about, have you?"

The last comment that drifted back as the three moved into the crowded room was "Funny sort of gown for a maid."

He could stop kissing her now. He should; they should stop and retreat to safety now the men had gone.

But the temptation to linger just a little bit longer—to explore the delights of her lips, her mouth—was difficult to resist. In that moment, he didn't want to resist; the allure of Ellen Martingale, of kissing her and drawing her to him, held sway over him, a powerful compulsion he couldn't turn away from.

And then, as if the retreat of the three men had removed all threat, all sense of danger, she softened against him. No melting, no sense she was swept away. Instead, through the gentle pressure of her lips against his, moving not so much tentatively as exploratively, he felt her curiosity reaching for him.

He met it—carefully; he didn't want to startle her into drawing back.

Ellen wasn't thinking; it was such a strange sensation, to know her wits were whirling, disconnected, and not to care.

For her, this was a first and, therefore, an experience to savor. The first kiss she'd ever experienced that was neither a demand nor a passive brush of lips.

This was something else.

Something she could enjoy, something she could participate in and delight in—a simple pleasure.

She'd never realized a kiss could be so…mentally consuming.

His lips were warm, resilient, and giving, yet even as she pressed her lips to them, molding hers to the sculpted curves, she sensed the strength behind his kiss—the leashed power.

Yet the glide of his tongue over hers was neither aggressive nor possessive but tantalizing, a subtle beckoning toward deeper intimacies, luring her into a tactile game.

A sophisticated seduction.

From him, she would have expected no less.

And regardless of the time and place, regardless of their precarious position, she wanted more, would have sued for more…but then she sensed him drawing back from the exchange.

Suddenly unsure, she pulled back, too.

Their lips parted, and he raised his head. She blinked up at him. The moonlight had strengthened, but his dark eyes remained nothing more than shadowed pools in his pale face.

But she saw his jaw firm, his lips tighten, then he said, "I didn't have a choice."

The words sank in, and her wits wrenched back into place. *No choice?*

Presumably, he meant that as his excuse for kissing her—because, of course, he'd needed an excuse...

The prick of hurt was unexpected. "Yes, of course," she all but snapped.

He stepped back, and she looked down and, entirely unnecessarily, shook out her skirt. She straightened and turned toward the steps. "I suggest we leave before those three idiots mention the kissing couple on the terrace and others come to look."

He nodded curtly and waved her on. She hurried down the steps, wishing she could put real distance between them; her unruly senses were still responding to him, all but reaching for him, craving his nearness despite her building temper.

Naturally, he fell into step beside her as she slipped through the shadows bordering the lawn and struck deeper into the surrounding shrubbery.

"I presume you rode over. Where did you leave your horse?"

She didn't trust herself to speak; she gestured ahead, toward the Bigfield House boundary.

She was, she decided, furious—with the situation and how it had played out, with him, and even more with herself. She'd had no business responding to that kiss as she had. She had no excuse; she should simply have endured it...as she would have had it been any other gentleman kissing her in such circumstances.

But no, she'd enjoyed it, and where was that leading her?

He might not have said he was sorry for kissing her, but his words had made it plain that he'd only kissed her to conceal their true purpose in being on the terrace. Perfectly understandable—so why was she reacting as if his words constituted the greatest insult she'd ever received?

Because you enjoyed it, you liked it, and you would kiss him again in a heartbeat.

She considered that lowering truth, then mentally humphed and stuffed it to the back of her mind.

He accompanied her to where she'd left Nelly, her piebald mare, tethered beneath a tree in the corner of one of Bigfield House's westernmost fields, one planted with damson plum trees.

She had to grit her teeth and allow him to lift her to her side-saddle, another novel experience that left her nerves leaping.

As she drew in a tight breath and gathered the reins, he said, "I left my horse in the next field. Please wait while I fetch him, and we can ride back together."

He hesitated, waiting, but she made no reply. Eventually, with a nod, he strode away.

Perched on Nelly's back, she watched him cross the field, then climb over a stile and disappear.

A few minutes later, he came soaring over the hedge on the back of a powerful gray hunter.

She was a competent horsewoman, but she would never have attempted that hedge.

Without waiting for him to reach her, she tapped her heel to Nelly's side and steered the mare along the path that followed the field's western boundary, then turned onto the wider path that ran between the trees down the middle of the field.

Her nemesis brought his gray up to pace alongside. In silence, they rode under the light of the moon, all the way back to the Bigfield House stable yard.

By then, she'd reviewed the happenings of the past hour and remembered his apparent understanding of what was going on at Goffard Hall and his reluctantly whispered "later."

Later, to her mind, was now.

She ignored the mounting block in the corner and drew rein on the cobbles before the stable door. A sleepy groom came to take Nelly's reins; she had informed the stablemen that she was riding out and expected to return after a few hours at most.

As she'd hoped, Christopher felt obliged to dismount and come and lift her down. She steeled her senses against the moment, yet the sensation of being swung through the air as if she weighed next to nothing still stole her breath.

So annoying!

To gain a few seconds, she glanced at the groom, now leading Nelly into the stable, then with grim determination, she focused her wits, faced Christopher, and locked her gaze on his face. "I believe you have information to share regarding what's happening at Goffard Hall."

The look she leveled at him stated very clearly that she was not going to let him escape before he'd told her all.

His jaw tightened. "I'll call around tomorrow—"

"No." For a second, she let the steadfast refusal stand unsupported, then went on, "If there's anything that threatens Robbie and therefore this household, I deserve to know of it. If it wasn't for me, you would have missed what Tilly was doing. I deserve to be told why she was deliberately losing."

She held his gaze tenaciously and refused to back down.

She looked so fierce, standing there in the moonlight, dogged and determined, her steely temper and adamantine will so very much at odds with her appearance.

It must be nice being the recipient of that degree of devotion. Christopher's words of months ago echoed again in his head.

He looked at her and saw so much that he wanted.

He inclined his head. "Very well." Faintly exasperated with his capitulation, he reminded himself that he—and Drake—couldn't afford to have her asking anyone else. Or at this stage, even trying to rein in her brother. Explaining what she'd seen to Robert and having the news circulate through the fraternity of young male guests...that was an outcome he had to avoid.

Resigned, he glanced around. "Not in the house." That would be stretching propriety until it snapped. He looked back at her. "Is there somewhere we can sit and talk in assured privacy?"

Her gaze grew distant for a second, then she refocused. "The rose garden. It's a warm enough night, and there's a bench at the far end." She turned and led the way.

He fell in beside her. Propriety-wise, sitting together in the rose garden unchaperoned at this hour was only marginally better than being alone in a room inside, but in reality, who was to see them? He seriously doubted she'd told her aunt that she planned to go riding about the neighborhood at night.

The rose garden proved to be a relatively small one, sunken and surrounded by high stone walls. At present, the old bushes were a riot of blooms, and their combined scent lay heavy on the air, even in the cool of the night. She led him along the central path to a stone bench, placed to allow occupants to look up the length of the garden toward the house, a section of which was framed by the entrance arch.

With a swish of her heavy skirts, she sat. Although the moonlight washed out colors, he thought the riding dress was a deep forest green with bronze ribbons and frogging. The offending feathers and ribbon rosette on her deep-green hat were also bronze.

She looked up at him, interrogatory inquiry in her expression.

He considered her, then turned and sat beside her. He leaned forward, resting his forearms on his thighs, and stared up the path while he weighed how much—or rather, how little—he could get away with telling her.

She didn't speak, just waited.

Eventually, he asked, "Did you notice the guests were using tokens to wager?"

"Those little round discs?"

He nodded. "What that means is that, for instance, when your Robbie arrives at the house, he exchanges money—real money—for the tokens, buying however many he wishes to risk in wagering over the evening."

From the corner of his eye, he saw her frown. "Some of those young men had small mountains of tokens lined up on the tables before them."

"Indeed. Some will wager much more than others. However, that's not the point."

"It isn't? I thought losing money was the point of gambling."

He dipped his head in acknowledgment. "Generally, that's the case. The thing about what's happening at Goffard Hall is that the guests losing and the house winning isn't what they want at all." He glanced sidelong at her, unsurprised to find her frown had darkened. "You saw Tilly deliberately lose, not once but several times. I think we can be fairly certain Nigel was playing in the same way, as well as Mrs. Kirkpatrick herself—she'd sat down to act as dealer for another group."

Slowly, Ellen nodded. "Is that why Robbie hasn't lost much?"

"I suspect," Christopher said, "that if you counted up his gains and losses over all his evenings at Goffard Hall, you might well discover that he hasn't lost at all."

"But why, then, are the Kirkpatricks holding these card parties? Purely to entertain all those young men?" She gave a cynical snort. "I would never have credited Mrs. Kirkpatrick with such an altruistic motive."

It was too dangerous to keep the truth from her. If she made a comment to the wrong person, it might well reach the Kirkpatricks and warn them of the authorities' interest. Christopher didn't know enough to predict what the Kirkpatricks and the man they were presumably working for might do.

Suppressing a sigh, he said, "The authorities believe that the Kirkpatricks' card parties are being used as a way of passing counterfeit banknotes into the hands of gullible young men, who then proceed to spread the notes hither and yon throughout the country."

She swiveled on the bench and stared at him. "What?"

"At the end of the evening, when the guests exchange their tokens for banknotes, some of the notes they'll receive will be very good fakes."

When she didn't immediately say anything, he glanced at her face. He watched her expression as she worked out how the Kirkpatricks' system worked.

Then she blinked and caught his eyes. "How do you know about the fake banknotes?"

He'd hoped to avoid explaining that, but like a dog with a bone, she kept her questions coming until he'd answered every one. He even had to explain who, exactly, Drake was and what he did, not something Drake would be happy about.

Let Drake deal with her.

Indeed, by the time she finished wringing information from him, Christopher would have paid money to see what she would make of England's spymaster.

Finally satisfied, as well she might be—Christopher didn't think there was any fact or suspicion about the situation she'd failed to drag from him—she sat back and, apparently, thought. Then, faintly puzzled, she asked, "Why are the Kirkpatricks involved?" She glanced at him and met his eyes. "What do they gain from the arrangement? It would have to be something fairly major, surely, to lead them to become involved in such a crime."

He arched his brows. "Money, I suppose."

"From what little I've gleaned, Mr. Kirkpatrick is considered a very warm man."

That tallied with what he'd heard as well.

"Perhaps," she went on, "he's not involved. He wasn't in the drawing room tonight."

Christopher straightened, recalling a sight he'd forgotten. "Kirkpatrick was working in his study, which is on the opposite side of the house from the room where the party was held—while I was checking around the house, I saw him behind his desk."

Ellen nodded. "And he didn't appear at the party, at least not while we were watching."

Studying Christopher's face, she saw his jaw harden and quickly stated, "We'll need to learn who at Goffard Hall is involved in this scheme." She paused, but he didn't react adversely to her "we," and she rolled on, "But I think the most pressing question before us is: How do these counterfeit banknotes reach Goffard Hall? If they're brought in by smugglers, then to whom and how are the notes handed on? We suspect Mrs. Kirkpatrick and Tilly are involved, but who else is? Is Nigel definitely in on the scheme? What about the staff?"

Christopher nodded. "Those are excellent questions. How to learn the answers…"

Ellen thought, and she was sure he did as well, but neither came up with any brilliant way forward.

Eventually, Christopher glanced at his fair companion, saw she was still cudgeling her brains—and realized the danger. He drew in his legs and rose. "So now you know all, and I hope I don't need to stress how important it is that you don't share the information with anyone else—not even Robbie."

She looked up at him and frowned, then rose to stand beside him. "I suppose he's in no actual danger, is he?"

"No." He tipped his head. "Indeed, he might end in greater danger if you warn him about the Kirkpatricks' scheme—he would likely behave differently, and that might alert them to him knowing, which might not end well." It was the best deterrent he could think of to dissuade her from warning her brother, and judging by the way she faintly grimaced, she'd accepted the argument.

Thank heaven.

Bad enough that he'd had to tell her his secrets.

They walked together up the central path.

Impulse struck—powerful enough to suborn his better judgment. At the end of the path, he paused under the arch, and instinctively, she halted beside him. When she looked up inquiringly, he bent his head and kissed her.

Again.

Not such a long engagement this time, but even sweeter as—it seemed entirely against her better judgment, too—she rose on her toes and, gripping his sleeve, met his lips with hers.

In a delicate, almost languid exchange—one of honey and moonlight and the wreathing scent of roses.

One of open curiosity on both their parts—an innocent inquisitiveness on her account, a more nuanced and experienced one on his.

He didn't prolong the exchange; the trick to successful seduction was to hold back and let anticipation build.

Let desire bloom.

He raised his head and, when her lids lifted, saw the first faint glimmer of wanting in her lovely eyes.

Too wise to linger, to allow her time to reassemble her wits, he stepped back and raised a hand in salute.

"This time," he said, holding her gaze, "not because I had no choice."

She blinked, then her eyes widened even more.

He turned and strode toward the stable yard, smugly pleased to have been the cause of the starstruck look in her eyes.

The following morning, Ellen stood beside her aunt in the small haberdashery-cum-milliner's shop in Benenden village and pretended to pay attention to the discussion raging between Emma and the little milliner, Mrs. Rollins.

Emma had dragged Ellen to the shop in search of new lace with which to refurbish Ellen's favorite evening gown, a creation in turquoise silk that had managed to remain sequin-free. Not, however, lace-free.

The upcoming summer party at Benenden Grange gave Emma all the excuse she needed to insist on new lace. "You won't want to appear shabby," she'd insisted.

Ellen really didn't care; her mother's and aunt's constant embellishing of her wardrobe had long ago deadened her sartorial senses. Yet she could never forget just how much love Emma had lavished on her and Robbie throughout their lives; if her aunt now wished to drape Ellen in new lace, she was entirely willing.

That said, today, Ellen's interest in fashionable adornment was even more spurious than usual. She stood by Emma's side, her gaze on the lace Mrs. Rollins was displaying, but her mind was far away.

The kisses of the previous night—not just the first but even more the second—were blazoned on her memory. Even now, thinking of those moments, she could feel, if not the actual physical contact, then certainly her responses to it.

Even becoming aware of the blush that rose in her cheeks wasn't enough to stop her thinking...trying to extract every last iota of experience and understanding from the utterly unexpected and unprecedented exchanges.

Once she'd watched Christopher ride away, she'd gone up to her room and had fully expected to lie awake for the rest of the night, dwelling on those illicit moments. Instead, she'd drifted off to sleep, albeit with the phantom sensation of his lips moving on hers...

It was inexplicable, the effect those two simple kisses had had on her —and how distracting those moments continued to be. It wasn't as if she hadn't been kissed before, multiple times.

But never like that.

Never with that degree of...connection.

She was back again, standing under the archway to the rose garden, captured and held purely by the touch of his lips on hers...

"Ellen? Stop woolgathering, dear. What do you think of this pattern?"

She blinked and, with considerable effort, shook off the continuing distraction and refocused to see Emma holding up a swatch of delicate lace.

"It's peonies, see?" Emma went on. "It will be just the thing to brighten up your turquoise silk."

Ellen had to admit the lace looked both unusual and very fine. She reached out and ran her fingertips down the edge of the length; the smoothness confirmed the lace was of extremely high quality.

Surprisingly high quality, given they were standing in a small village shop.

"It is very beautiful." She caught Mrs. Rollins's eye and smiled. "The quality is impressive—I admit I wouldn't have expected to find such lace in the Weald of Kent."

Mrs. Rollins took the compliment as it was intended and preened. "My husband fetches it from London," she confided. "He travels there every few weeks to fetch goods from the warehouses, and over the past months, he's occasionally been able to lay his hands on this lovely lace."

Eyeing Ellen, then Emma, shrewdly, Mrs. Rollins leaned forward and said, "I've been warning my ladies that I can't say how long the supply will last—not of this quality at this price."

"What is the price?" Emma inquired.

When Mrs. Rollins named her figure, Ellen blinked. "That really is... an excellent price."

In truth, it was ridiculously cheap. Ellen didn't need to tell Emma so;

they were both accustomed to London prices, and this was barely half of what they would have expected to pay for lace of such exceptional quality.

While Emma discussed lengths and completed their purchase, Ellen looked at the other laces displayed. Only a few were of similar quality, but judging by the prices inked in tiny figures on the reverse of the boards on which each type of lace was wound, those lengths were also being sold at bargain prices.

How odd.

In London, lace of such quality would command a premium price. Ellen found it curious that Mr. Rollins had managed to buy such lace from a London warehouse so cheaply.

Emma tucked the package of lace into the basket on her arm, and with smiles all around and a hope expressed by Mrs. Rollins that she would see Ellen and Emma again soon, Ellen followed Emma out into the village street.

As they walked toward the Bull Inn, where they'd left the gig, Emma leaned close and whispered, "That would have cost so much more in London."

"Indeed." Ellen could only conclude that the London lace sellers were making a very much greater profit than Mrs. Rollins was.

That said, Ellen was woefully aware she had very little head for business. It was assuredly not her strong suit. Even after months of dealing with the estate accounts, she still struggled every week to make her numbers add up and, even then, was usually successful only after the intervention of Hopper or Mr. Vickers.

As they neared the inn, she shrugged aside the mystery of the Rollinses' cheap lace and, refusing to indulge in further contemplation of anyone's kisses, determinedly turned her mind to the more pressing issue it was doubtless her duty to help resolve—that of the criminal and potentially treasonous goings-on at Goffard Hall.

At the end of the service on Sunday morning, Christopher walked with the rest of the congregation up the long nave of the village church.

He'd been baptized at St. George's, and despite his years in London, whenever he was in residence at the manor, he made a point of attending Sunday service.

Today he'd had an additional motive in sitting through the sermon; he'd remembered Ellen's comment that Kirkpatrick and his daughter frequently joined the congregation.

Christopher finally gained the porch.

Reverend Thornley—tall, thin, with tufts of white hair circling his bald pate—was, as always, pleased to see him. He shook Christopher's hand with obvious pleasure. "Good to see you, my boy. Have you heard from your parents yet?"

Christopher smiled. "Not yet. I imagine they're rather busy."

"And they know the manor is in good hands, I'm sure!" The good reverend asked about Gregory and, after Christopher confirmed his brother hadn't yet returned to Kent, consented to let Christopher go.

A quick scan of those gathered on the lawn revealed Ellen, her aunt, and her brother chatting to a local couple, the Cummingses; Christopher stepped off the porch and headed in their direction.

The Cummingses moved on before he reached the Bigfield House party, and Ellen's aunt turned to him with a sweet smile. "Mr. Cynster. It's a pleasure to see you, sir."

Smiling affably, he took her hand and half bowed. "Mrs. Fitzwilliam. I can see you're well."

"Indeed, I am." Ellen's aunt blushed faintly. "I have to admit that after living in London for so long, I did wonder if the country would suit me, but it seems I worried for naught." She beamed at him as he released her hand. "A lovely sermon, wasn't it?"

"Reverend Thornley is very reliable in that respect." Christopher nodded in greeting to Robbie and reached for Ellen's hand—which she hadn't extended but now yielded, accompanied by a distinctly wary look.

For the first time since their kisses in the night, their gazes met and held. In hers, he detected a certain tension, a watchful defensiveness ready to spring to life if he stepped over any line. Nevertheless, her lips curved slightly, and she inclined her head as he gently pressed her fingers, then eased his grip.

He wasn't such a fool as to discombobulate her in public; as experienced as he was, he knew well enough to bide his time. While he couldn't —yet—swear to the nature of what was evolving between them, he was certain that the possibility of a connection of a type he hadn't before encountered was there. Consequently, when she made no move to retrieve her hand, he continued to lightly grasp her slender digits.

Despite her defenses being fully engaged, Ellen was utterly distracted by the feel of his fingers, warm and strong, gently clasping hers. Why the simple gesture, a normal courtesy between gentleman and lady, felt different when he was involved—warmer, more meaningful, more intimate—she couldn't fathom.

She knew he wouldn't kiss her fingers, much less her lips, in the churchyard in full view of the assembled congregation, yet that knowledge hadn't saved her; her lungs had tightened, and her wits and her senses were locked on him.

Her gaze lowered from his faintly amused and inviting brown eyes to his lips and lingered.

Then she realized what she was doing. She felt a blush heat her cheeks as she forced her gaze elsewhere and belatedly reclaimed her hand.

Luckily, no one else seemed to have noticed, although she felt perfectly certain he had.

Now that the initial impact of the kisses they'd shared had faded, her mind had fastened on the underlying and, to her, more pertinent issue. She understood why he'd kissed her the first time, on the terrace at Goffard Hall; that had been a piece of quick thinking that had saved them both from exposure.

But why had he kissed her under the rose-garden arch?

The possible answers kept circling in her brain, as if he'd become a giant puzzle, one she absolutely had to solve.

Distraction wasn't the half of it.

Dragooning her wits into order, she refocused on the conversation Robbie had initiated by asking whether the gypsies ever attended church.

"I've never seen them at St. George's," Christopher replied, "but I believe Aaron's group is Catholic and observe a form of mass within their own band. I've known them to join with other bands to celebrate major religious days."

"Well," Emma stated, "at least they're Christians, which is comforting to know."

As if sensing Ellen was finally paying attention, Christopher turned her way. His eyes quizzed her. "I take it the goats are behaving themselves?"

"Thus far," she replied, "their newly strengthened pen has repelled all attempts to escape and head over to your fields."

Smiling, he looked at Robbie. "Your own hop fields will be flowering any day, then they'll be at risk, too."

"Hopper swears the new fencing will keep the animals in," Robbie said. "To be perfectly honest, I have no idea why Uncle Humphrey is so keen on the beasts."

Christopher knew the answer. "Your uncle bought a breeding pair on a whim and grew attached to them and they to him. The nanny and billy used to follow him around when he was walking in the garden—it was quite a sight, especially as the pair didn't take to anyone else. Then, of course, the pair started dropping kids, and Sir Humphrey wouldn't hear of any being sold, much less eaten, so the herd swelled to its current size."

"Huh." Robbie slid his hands into his pockets. "I suppose that explains things."

"I wonder," Ellen said, "if perhaps Uncle Humphrey would enjoy being taken to see the goats." She arched a brow at Christopher. "Will the beasts still remember him?"

He nodded. "I'm certain they will, and indeed, it would do him good."

The Waltons, a local family with two young unmarried daughters, approached, and Emma and Robbie—the Waltons' primary target—turned to greet them.

After exchanging nods and smiles—and thereafter, being redundant to the ongoing conversation—Christopher and Ellen both glanced around, then Ellen put her hand on Christopher's sleeve.

He reined in the instinctive impulse to cover her hand, possessively anchoring it on his arm, and glanced at her face.

Without meeting his eyes, with a tip of her head, she directed his attention to the church porch, where an older man with a young lady by his side was chatting with Reverend Thornley. "That," Ellen informed Christopher, "is Mr. Kirkpatrick, and the young lady is his daughter, Julia."

Christopher studied Kirkpatrick, who was, indeed, the gentleman he'd glimpsed in the study at Goffard Hall. Kirkpatrick appeared exactly as might be expected of a City financier. He was a large man, now slightly stoop-shouldered, yet he didn't lean on the cane in his hand and still exuded an impressive presence. He was expensively dressed in a gray suit that, to Christopher, screamed Savile Row, and his thick silver hair was fashionably styled. In contrast to such polish, his craggy face bore deep lines, and his features reminded Christopher of nothing so much as weathered stone—sharp edges worn away by age and experience.

Even while Kirkpatrick exchanged pleasantries with Reverend Thornley, Christopher got the impression Kirkpatrick's mind was elsewhere, thinking of weightier things.

For her part, Miss Kirkpatrick seemed to cling to her father's shadow. Although stylishly gowned, she projected the aura of a quiet yet attentive, restrained, and proper miss.

Christopher dipped his head closer to Ellen's. "Julia Kirkpatrick seems rather reserved."

Ellen nodded. "She is." After a second's thought, she added, "I'm not sure if that's her natural character or a reaction to her stepmother's personality."

Christopher considered the epitome of appearance-belying-reality before him, then suggested, "It would be helpful if we could engineer a meeting with Mr. Kirkpatrick. I've never met the man—if you could introduce us...?"

Ellen dipped her head in ready agreement.

At that moment, the Kirkpatricks farewelled Mr. Thornley and stepped onto the path leading to the lychgate. Simultaneously, the Waltons made their excuses and moved on.

Ellen looped her arm in her aunt's and captured Robbie's gaze. "Time to head home."

Christopher hid a smile and fell in beside Robbie as Ellen steered her aunt on a course designed to intercept the Kirkpatricks. Apparently entirely accidentally, the two groups met before the lychgate.

Without prompting, Ellen's aunt beamed and held out her hand. "Mr. Kirkpatrick! How lovely to see you again, sir."

Kirkpatrick halted, took the proffered hand, and bowed. "Mrs. Fitzwilliam—a pleasure, dear lady."

Greetings were exchanged between Ellen and Robbie and both Kirkpatricks, then Ellen gestured to Christopher. "I'm sure you will have heard of the Cynsters of Walkhurst Manor. This is Mr. Christopher Cynster, who is currently managing the estate."

Christopher's "I'm delighted to meet you, sir" and his offered hand conveyed politeness but no eagerness, something that would have triggered Kirkpatrick's defenses. As Christopher smiled amiably and gripped Kirkpatrick's hand, he took due note of the shrewdness behind the man's gray eyes.

Kirkpatrick inclined his head. "I'm happy to make your acquaintance, Mr. Cynster. I have met your parents, but only in passing..." He glanced around. "As it happens, on the lawn here."

Christopher seized the opening. "We've lived here for several genera-tions, so are regarded as fixtures locally. But I understand your family are relatively recently come to the area."

As he spoke, he smiled and half bowed to Julia Kirkpatrick.

Sober and rather poker-faced, she nodded back. "Mr. Cynster."

Planting his cane before him and folding his hands over its head, Kirkpatrick responded to Christopher's implied question. "I bought Goffard Hall...it must be six years ago, now. I felt it was time to find a place in the country in which to put down roots and spend my latter years." Kirkpatrick glanced fondly at his daughter, and she smiled sweetly back.

Kirkpatrick went on, "My first wife was alive then, and she enjoyed the country air. But sadly, she passed away, and thereafter, I must confess, I buried myself in my financial pursuits, which center on the City. Although I've drawn back somewhat, I'm frequently called to town and end staying at my club. Such a lifestyle is not conducive to making connections locally. Consequently, I make every effort to attend service here whenever I'm at the Hall."

Christopher shifted his gaze to Julia. "And you, Miss Kirkpatrick? Do you travel up to London with your father?"

A slight smile curved her lips, an attempt at politeness, yet genuine enough. "No—like my mama, I prefer the country." She glanced at her father. "So I remain here"—her smile faded as she added—"with my stepmother."

Kirkpatrick cleared his throat. "I remarried a few years ago."

Ellen promptly asked, "I do hope Mrs. Kirkpatrick is well?"

Kirkpatrick looked faintly embarrassed, and Julia's lips tightened.

"I'm afraid," Kirkpatrick said, and Christopher saw the man's hands tighten on the head of his cane, "that my wife adheres to London hours, even in the country. She rarely rises before noon and so, sadly, misses Reverend Thornley's excellent sermons."

Judging by the glint that briefly sparked in Julia Kirkpatrick's eyes, she was of the opinion that her stepmother would profit from hearing those sermons.

Both Ellen and her aunt leapt in with requests to have their good wishes conveyed to the absent Mrs. Kirkpatrick.

Under cover of the exchange, Christopher noticed that Robbie's atten-tion was firmly fixed on Julia. On closer inspection, she struck Christo-pher as a clear-eyed young lady of significant backbone, definitely no ninnyhammer and highly unlikely to be anyone's pawn—certainly not her stepmother's. On the subject of the current Mrs. Kirkpatrick, Julia radiated silent yet nevertheless palpable disapproval.

During the ensuing exchange of local news, driven by Mrs. Fitzwilliam, ably supported by Ellen, and to which Kirkpatrick responded readily enough—information, even of such local sort, being a financier's stock-in-trade—Christopher noted the lack of mention of Mrs. Kirkpatrick's young cousins, Tilly and Nigel.

Then beneath the chatter of the other three, Christopher heard Robbie, who had edged closer to Julia, say, "I was at Goffard Hall on Friday evening—I asked after you, and Mrs. Kirkpatrick said you'd been invited, but had chosen not to come down."

The implied query wasn't exactly a complaint but raised the question of what had truly taken Robbie to Goffard Hall the previous Friday.

"I fear," Julia replied, keeping her voice low, as Robbie had, "my stepmother's events are not the sort of entertainments I favor." The words were priggish, contemptuous, and distinctly repressive.

Robbie all but squirmed, but came back with, "They're not that bad—nothing untoward happens. It's just all of us who know Nigel having fun. It's not as if any of us lose much—it's all about the play."

Christopher pricked up his ears at the words "none of us lose much." Just how pervasive was the dealers' throwing of hands—their reverse cheating, as it were?

Julia shrugged, to all intents and purposes giving Robbie's comment short shrift. "There's nothing that attracts me in such entertainments—I would much rather spend the evening reading a good book, which was what I did on Friday."

Christopher was getting the distinct impression the pair had met several times before. Robbie frowned. "Truth to tell, I'm not all that enamored of the card games myself."

Julia shot him a swift glance. "Why do you attend, then?"

It seemed to Christopher's experienced ear that she truly wanted to know.

Robbie's expression changed to that of someone stating the obvious. "Because Nigel's an acquaintance and a neighbor, and as I was invited, it's the done thing—the right thing—to attend. But that doesn't mean I'm drawn by the gambling—I'm no gamester and have no ambition to become one."

Christopher suspected Ellen would be very glad to hear that little speech and would wholeheartedly approve, not only with regard to Robbie's professed lack of gambling ambition but also over his notion of doing "the right thing." The concept was, in Christopher's view, deeply entrenched in the Martingale psyche. That trait was what had driven Ellen herself to shoulder the burden of managing the Bigfield House estate, apparently without argument.

Julia studied Robbie's face, then made an equivocal sound and looked away, as if she was reserving judgment. In Christopher's opinion, that was a sensible response.

He refocused on the wider conversation as Julia added a comment, and Robbie, too, joined in. Mr. Kirkpatrick directed a query at Christopher regarding the upcoming harvest, to which he readily responded. By unspoken consent, their combined company walked on through the lychgate. In the lane beyond, they parted, the Kirkpatricks going left to their carriage while the Bigfield House party turned right.

Christopher had left his curricle and horses at the Bull Inn. He strolled beside Ellen toward the Bigfield House landau. Robbie had given his aunt his arm, and the pair were walking ahead of Christopher and Ellen.

He glanced at her. "Thank you for facilitating that encounter."

"Don't mention it." Her gaze was locked on the pair ahead. A heartbeat later, she murmured, "Far better Julia than Tilly."

While mildly impressed that, while maintaining a conversation with Kirkpatrick and her aunt, Ellen had simultaneously monitored her brother's interaction with Julia, given what Christopher had seen of Tilly Fontenay on Friday evening, he couldn't agree more.

Ellen saw the landau ahead, in the line of carriages drawn up before the church. Robbie assisted Emma up, then glanced her way, smiled, and climbed into the carriage, consigning her to being helped in by her nemesis.

Quite why she felt Christopher qualified as an agent of her downfall, she couldn't have said, yet her instincts saw him as someone fated to have a serious impact on her life.

As they neared the carriage, she glanced sidelong at him and decided that the "downfall" part might simply be her overactive imagination.

All he'd done was kiss her twice—which, she reflected sternly, was quite bad enough!

Swallowing a disgruntled humph—he distracted her even when he wasn't trying—she rapidly canvassed her options, hoping to find one that would enable her not to give him her hand, but there simply wasn't any way around it.

Steeling her nerves, she reached the open carriage door and turned to him with an outwardly serene smile.

He met her gaze, his eyes heating just a fraction, enough to set her pulse tripping even as she offered him her hand. "I bid you good day, Mr. Cynster. Until next we meet."

He smiled, and her hold on her wits started to unravel.

He gripped her fingers, and her senses whirled. "Allow me to help you up."

She clung to her mask of serenity, inclined her head, and gathered her skirts in her other hand—then she felt his hold on her hand firm, curled her fingers about his palm, and sensed the steel in the arm that steadied her as she climbed the steps into the carriage. She withdrew her hand and, with what grace she could muster, subsided onto the seat beside Emma, the one nearest the door.

"Thank you," she managed in a reasonably even voice.

He shut the door, and she met his eyes and saw faint amusement lurking—as if, despite her façade, he knew perfectly well the effect he had on her.

Drat the man!

His smile widened as he took a step back, directed a farewell nod at Emma and Robbie, and finally, saluted her. "I hope," he said, "that you'll save me a dance tomorrow evening."

Her eyes flew wide. Before she could reply, he tapped the side of the carriage, and their coachman gave the horses the office, and the landau jerked and drew out of the line and into the lane.

He'd timed his request perfectly, giving her no chance to make any excuse.

Ellen stared straight ahead, even when Emma patted her hand and congratulated her on having caught Mr. Cynster's eye.

If anyone was caught—captured—it was her; her wits, senses, and imagination were utterly snared by the prospect that, tomorrow evening, she would be whirling around the Benenden Grange drawing room in Christopher Cynster's arms.

The only rational thought to pop into her head was that she would have to tell her maid, Missy, to hunt out her evening fan.

CHAPTER 5

*A*t nine o'clock on Monday evening, Christopher found himself going down a country dance with Ellen Martingale.

He wasn't entirely surprised to discover that the dance she'd consented to grant him was one during which they remained at arm's length, with no opportunity for any closer contact and absolutely no chance of sharing any private remarks.

Any unsettling, discombobulating remarks.

As they whirled at the end of the twin rows of dancers, grasped hands, then bent and rushed beneath the archway formed by the other dancers' arms, he flirted with the idea of telling her that the more she resisted—the more she ran—the more avidly he, in certain circles known as a wolf of the ton, would chase her.

He was, he'd realized, definitely pursuing her. And given their positions in society, there was only one possible conclusion to such a chase.

Given his nature inclined him more to action than dwelling overmuch on outcomes, the inevitable end of his pursuit of Ellen Martingale was something he wasn't inclined to brood about. He knew it, acknowledged it, and that—as far as his inner self was concerned—was enough.

About them, the music emanating from a small country ensemble struggled to rise above the noise of countless conversations. Knots of guests thronged the edge of the impromptu dance floor created by clearing much of the furniture from the Benenden Grange drawing room. That left those not dancing to cluster around the edges of the room and spill into the adjoining parlor, where the older members of the company had found chairs and were holding court.

Those idly observing the dancers from the sidelines were dividing their attention equally with their neighbors, exchanging comments, remarks, and tales, tall and otherwise. Among the gentlemen, discussion of the coming harvest dominated, while between the ladies, the age-old obsessions with fashion and matchmaking held sway.

Meanwhile, the breadth and depth of the younger generation of the local gentry families whirled around Christopher and Ellen. Everyone was smiling, and many were laughing, each enjoying the moment in much the same way as Christopher and his however-initially-unwilling partner.

The spontaneous smile that lit her face assured him of that.

He couldn't help smiling back.

Tonight, she was clad in a turquoise-silk gown—a very pretty color on her—but inevitably, the neckline, sleeves, and hem were heavily adorned with flounces of gathered lace a handspan wide. The upper edge of the lace was bound with satin ribbon of a darker yet similar hue to the gown and further embellished with ribbon rosettes placed every two inches along the beribboned edge.

Two narrow ribbons dangled from every rosette.

As for her hair, the golden curls, already bouncing loose from the topknot someone had endeavored to create, were tangling with a profusion of the same satin ribbon that had been bound about the knot, to which several ribbon rosettes had been pinned.

At least the ivory lace was of a pretty pattern, and the colors didn't clash.

And as usual, Ellen appeared utterly uncaring of her sartorial image.

Somewhat to his surprise, he was starting to disregard it, too.

Possibly because, courtesy of those two kisses and her character, he had started to focus far more intently on the woman beneath the gowns.

Apropos of which...

They'd swung into the last phase of the long dance, the only section during which they danced purely with each other, hands linked, arms held high as they stepped back and forth, then circled and repeated the back-and-forth maneuver.

He caught her gaze. "This part of the dance strikes me as a metaphor for our interaction thus far."

She frowned, thought, but eventually tipped up her chin and inquired, "How so?"

"Stepping closer"—he demonstrated, moving in the prescribed pattern of the dance—"then stepping back." He did so. "Then circling..."

His eyes held hers as they did. "Gradually moving closer, until the burning question in both our minds becomes 'Where will we halt?'"

His timing was perfect; on the words, the music ended, and along with the other dancers, they halted, facing each other with less than a foot between them.

Filling that space, pure anticipation quivered in the air.

Unable to breathe—again!—Ellen stared at him, lost in the inviting warmth of his gaze.

Is this what being seduced feels like?

Hard on the heels of that question came another: *Is he serious?*

The second question was the one she needed to answer.

People shifted around them, pushing past; the brush of a shoulder against her back jerked her from her oblivious state. She blinked, belatedly bobbed a curtsy, then forced her gaze from the distraction standing directly before her. Searching for her bearings and some semblance of safety, she looked for Emma in the surrounding throng.

He'd straightened from his brief bow. Now his lips quirked up at the ends, and he shifted to stand beside her. "Your aunt is over there."

Before she could move, he claimed her hand and wound her arm in his.

As under his direction they started through the crowd, she fought to suppress a glare—a glare a part of her felt he deserved—yet the greater part of her mind was intrigued; curiosity and fascination twined and combined, urging and nudging her into following his lead.

She wasn't sure she trusted that impulse, and her wits remained distracted by the sensations occasioned by his nearness, yet with wholly assumed calm, she moved with him across the crowded room.

She, Emma, and Robbie had arrived nearly an hour ago, entering the Grange with a bevy of other guests. Christopher had arrived later; as far as she'd seen, he'd made a beeline for their party.

Of course, he'd insisted on claiming his dance. To her relief, it had been a country dance; she wasn't sure she could have weathered a waltz.

Mrs. Carstairs had succeeded in enticing virtually all the surrounding families to her summer party. Although Ellen had done her best to avoid the larger social gatherings during the months she'd been in Kent, courtesy of Emma's insistence, she'd attended enough functions to be able to recognize the faces around her and put names to most. The guests were chatting in groups that, every now and again, broke up and re-formed as people mingled. The atmosphere was light-hearted, with an impossible-to-mistake undercurrent of matchmaking intent. The sound of many voices speaking at once swirled around them as Christopher guided her toward the side of the room where Emma was chatting with the Waltons.

They were several yards short of their goal when the stir of a late arrival had her glancing toward the main doorway. She gripped Christopher's sleeve and stopped walking.

He halted and looked at her inquiringly.

She briefly met his eyes, then, with her gaze, directed his attention to the newcomers. "Mrs. Kirkpatrick, Nigel Fontenay, and his sister, Tilly." All three were dressed to the nines in expensively fashionable and overtly sophisticated attire.

"And there's Julia Kirkpatrick bringing up the rear." Christopher lowered his head and murmured, "She looks as if she wants to hide in the shade of the others' flashy presence."

"Very likely." After a moment, Ellen met Christopher's eyes. "Do you think Julia and Mr. Kirkpatrick are involved in the scheme?"

Christopher studied the lady he'd last seen encouraging gullible and malleable young gentlemen to wager in her drawing room. Tonight, Mrs. Kirkpatrick hadn't come to cozen anyone; she'd appeared to reinforce the image she transparently wished to project to the surrounding gentry—that she, and by extension Nigel and Tilly, were accustomed to inhabiting more refined social circles but, tonight, were graciously stooping to honoring Mrs. Carstairs and her guests with their presence.

Aloof superiority dripped from all three.

Christopher hid a cynical smile. Several of those present, himself included, would, socially speaking, outrank Mrs. Kirkpatrick, a fact of which she had to be aware. Her bold and arrogant façade suggested an underlying insecurity.

He realized Ellen was frowning slightly at him and recalled her question. "I would be extremely surprised if either Julia—who seems a sensible young lady with her feet firmly on the ground—or her father knows anything about the true purpose behind Mrs. Kirkpatrick's card parties."

Ellen studied his face, his eyes, then said, "I can understand absolving Julia—she's always struck me as rather strait-laced and very definitely not given to silliness, much less anything illicit. But why are you so ready to discount Mr. Kirkpatrick? Just because he didn't attend the party doesn't mean he doesn't know about the fake notes, and if you think about it, his presence at the event would almost certainly have acted as a dampener—a depressive counter to all Mrs. Kirkpatrick's hard work."

They'd been standing still for too long; Mrs. Fitzwilliam and Robbie had moved on. Instead of pursuing them, Christopher drew Ellen toward the wall, to where, in the lee of a towering palm, they would be out of the path of the circulating guests.

"All you say is true," he conceded as together, they turned to face the room. "But Mr. Kirkpatrick is a financier. To such as he, especially those who operate in the City, the very existence of counterfeit banknotes is anathema." He paused, his gaze on Mrs. Kirkpatrick and her party, now being greeted by Mrs. Carstairs. "If it became known that Kirkpatrick was involved in passing counterfeit notes, his business would be ruined, his reputation in tatters."

"That," Ellen observed, "is assuming both business and reputation are in good order."

"I asked Montague—he's man-of-business to all the Cynsters—for his opinion of Kirkpatrick and received an immediate reply. Kirkpatrick is well known to all those at the top of British finance and universally viewed as a stalwart if conservative money man. His reputation is unblemished, with nothing adverse known about him, and on the personal side, he's considered to be flush with funds." He shifted his gaze from Mrs. Kirkpatrick to the much more alluring vision beside him, ribbons, rosettes, and lace notwithstanding. "Frankly, I can't see Kirkpatrick risking all that—his ongoing business and unsullied reputation—for an outlandish, illicit, close-to-treasonous scheme that will likely generate a profit much smaller than the investments in which he regularly deals. It makes no sense for Kirkpatrick to be involved."

Puzzled, Ellen raised her gaze to his face. "But if the Kirkpatricks are flush with funds, why is Mrs. Kirkpatrick engaging in a scheme that, by your reckoning, will result in only minor profit compared to her husband's wealth..." Her eyes widened, and she looked at Mrs. Kirkpatrick, who was moving through the crowd on the opposite side of the room. "Oh."

He allowed a cynical smile to twist his lips. "Indeed. I suspect the answer is because Kirkpatrick is no fool, certainly not about money. He knows the value of it. I daresay he makes Mrs. Kirkpatrick an allowance—"

"And she's his second wife," Ellen put in. "Very likely he allows her a similar amount to what he gave his first wife, and by all accounts, she was a quiet lady who preferred to live in the country."

"It's not difficult," he said, "to imagine that Mrs. Kirkpatrick might not be satisfied with what her husband allows her. For instance, the gown she has on would have cost a pretty penny, and she was wearing one similar on Friday. It seems likely that her spending is rather more profligate than her husband will bear."

Still on the opposite side of the crowded room, Mrs. Kirkpatrick had noticed Christopher and was staring assessingly.

He looked through her as if he hadn't seen her, then glanced at Ellen. "Let's hypothesize that Mrs. Kirkpatrick likes expensive things. In the first quarter of their marriage, she burns through her allowance, appeals to her new husband, fully expecting him to stump up the ready without any great fuss—"

"And instead, he refuses to pay such extravagant bills and tells her she'll have to put the modistes off until the next quarter." Ellen met his eyes. "I could readily imagine a scenario like that."

Christopher nodded. "So she wheedles and tries all the tricks she knows to persuade Kirkpatrick to loosen his purse strings, but he stands firm—as a gentleman of Kirkpatrick's vintage and caliber would. The new Mrs. Kirkpatrick retreats and broods, then looks about her for some way to supplement her allowance, for some other source of funds."

He glanced over the crowd, locating Mrs. Kirkpatrick's dark head; the lady appeared to be tacking through the crowd in their direction. "From what little I've gleaned of her character thus far, I suspect that situation would make her an easy mark for the counterfeit gang. They would have been scouting around, searching for someone able to move the fake notes into circulation in a way unlikely to alert the authorities. For their purposes, Mrs. Kirkpatrick would have seemed a godsend."

Ellen tipped her head consideringly. "Do you think her card parties are that successful in spreading the counterfeit notes?"

"I think"—he caught her hand and twined her arm with his, drawing her fractionally closer—"they could well be. Thus far, she's exchanged only small numbers of fakes, yet they've surfaced in country towns all over England—which is exactly what the counterfeit gang wants."

He eased her back into motion, threading at a languid pace through the knots of guests. "It's telling that none of the fakes have been discovered in the City or in any of the major financial institutions."

Old Mr. Scott ambled by; both Christopher and Ellen exchanged a smile and a nod with the elderly gentleman, then Christopher quietly continued, "Instead, the fakes have been circulating beneath the notice of all the major banks, including the Bank of England. That's part of what's driving the authorities' concerns—via her card parties, Mrs. Kirkpatrick has established a particularly efficient means of distributing fake notes far and wide that isn't dependent on the usual institutions. If, through her, the gang successfully distributes a large quantity of such notes, the status of the currency will be at risk, and the public furor will shake the country's foundations."

"I see." Ellen pondered that, then let the subject drop.

They paused to chat with several other guests, then moved on again.

"I have to admit," she said, "that Mr. Kirkpatrick seems singularly unconnected with his wife's social life. He hasn't accompanied her here tonight."

"Perhaps he's back in London. Or like Julia"—Christopher nodded to a group ahead—"he would prefer not to be seen as a part of his wife's entourage."

Ellen looked and saw Julia standing beside Mrs. Carstairs, with Mrs. Kirkpatrick nowhere near.

Tilly, however, had attached herself to Julia. Then Robbie approached, bowed, and eagerly solicited Julia's hand for the next dance. As Ellen watched, Robbie spoke again, and Julia smiled her sweet-but-fleeting smile.

Beside Julia, Tilly scowled, clearly unhappy over Robbie preferring Julia's company to hers.

His gaze on the tableau ahead, Christopher murmured, "It certainly appears that Julia wishes to distance herself from her stepmother and the other two, even though the latter are about her age. It might pay to keep an eye on her and confirm that's not an assumed attitude."

"It's not," Ellen confidently returned. "According to Aunt Emma, who is surprisingly insightful in such matters, how Julia appears to us is how she's always been seen by all the ladies here." As they neared the group, she continued sotto voce, "Her reserve alone would make her keep her distance from her stepmother's activities, and to be candid, I've always sensed that Julia has never approved of her stepmother. Regardless of her reasons, that dislike—and it is, frankly, dislike—will ensure Julia gives Mrs. Kirkpatrick and all her works a wide berth."

Christopher smiled at her. "You appear to have taken Julia's cause to heart. I wonder why?" He arched a brow at her.

In reply, she opened her eyes wide.

His lips quirked upward, and with a gentle nudge, he steered her away from the clearing dance floor.

Ellen pretended not to notice as Robbie, beaming proudly, led Julia past.

Then Christopher murmured in her ear, "Let's sit this dance out, so to speak, and instead, be sociable."

When he set course for a cluster of older guests, she cast him a side-long glance. "Don't you want to speak with Mrs. Kirkpatrick—to see what we can learn?"

"I do, indeed, but all in good time."

When she widened her eyes in question, he smiled and replied, "I see no reason to approach her—I would rather she came to me."

Ellen dwelled on that rather enigmatic reply as they paused beside the first group of guests, chatted for several minutes in amiable and relaxed fashion, then moved on, circumnavigating the room in an anticlockwise direction, exchanging greetings, comments, and observations with all those they encountered.

From the corner of her eye, she kept Mrs. Kirkpatrick in sight. The other lady had scanned the room several times, and each time, her gaze had found and locked on Christopher. She'd definitely noticed him—indeed, it appeared she'd set her sights on him. As they continued to move unhurriedly through the assembled throng, Mrs. Kirkpatrick circled in clockwise fashion, putting her on a collision course with them.

Ellen took stock of the other woman. She was, as Christopher had noted, dressed in the height of fashion in a beautiful gown of amber silk, finished at neckline and hem with a single row of gold braid. A long strand of pearls was looped about her throat, and larger pearls bobbed at her ears. Her dark-auburn hair was expertly styled in gleaming waves that highlighted her pale complexion.

With a jolt, Ellen realized that Mrs. Kirkpatrick was much of an age with Christopher. And the woman was definitely stalking them—him—through the crowd. Anxiety of a sort she'd never felt before flared. She glanced at him.

He caught her eye and faintly arched a brow, a devilish glint in his brown eyes. He knew Mrs. Kirkpatrick was nearing; he was waiting for her to reach them.

Irrationally calmed by that knowledge, Ellen faced forward. Well, then—she, too, would play her part.

She glanced at the dance floor; sets were forming for another dance, and Tilly and Nigel had joined in, partnered by others their age. A dark-haired gentleman—a Mr. Denton, if Ellen remembered aright—stepped into Mrs. Kirkpatrick's path and asked her to dance, but she summoned a thin smile and made some excuse, her disinterest in dancing made plain.

Ellen shifted her gaze to Mrs. Folliwell as Christopher drew her to join the group in which that good lady was holding forth about the local hunt. At the same time, Mrs. Kirkpatrick came up, trailed by Mr. Denton. The circle adjusted to accommodate the four of them, with Mrs. Kirkpatrick insinuating herself into the place at Christopher's side while Mr. Denton took station beside her.

Ellen had to acknowledge the insinuating had been smoothly done.

Mrs. Folliwell leapt into her role of secondary hostess and made the introductions. Ellen was acquainted with everyone there, except for Mrs. Kirkpatrick; she nodded to Denton, who she had met before, then touched fingers with Mrs. Kirkpatrick when that lady, with overt graciousness, extended her hand.

"We are delighted to see you among us, Mrs. Kirkpatrick," Mrs. Folliwell boomed. Archly, she continued, "Dare we hope this won't be the last time we'll see you at one of our functions this year?"

Mrs. Kirkpatrick smiled. "As to that, I cannot be sure when I will be in residence at Goffard Hall. As you know, I'm accustomed to spending much of my time in London, but of course, in this season..." She raised her hands in a helpless gesture.

"Oh, indeed," chimed in Mrs. Cummings. "The country air is much preferable to London's heat. You must find it so. Why, our son, Gibson, cannot bear the capital's miasmas—he's somewhat delicate, you know."

"Nonsense!" Mr. Cummings said. "Gibson just dislikes all the noise and grime—never hear him coughing in the country, and he's a fine little rider as well."

"Indeed, George." Mrs. Folliwell nodded in agreement. "At the last meet, he went over the fences in excellent style."

Ellen bit her lip. From the look on Mrs. Kirkpatrick's face, she hadn't imagined being upstaged by a child, delicate or not.

As if sensing that, Mr. Cummings fixed Mrs. Kirkpatrick with a shrewd look. "But how do you find the prospects at Goffard Hall, ma'am? Lively enough for you?"

Mrs. Kirkpatrick smiled tightly and stated she made her own entertainment.

Before she could elaborate—had she meant to do so—she was subjected to a barrage of comments, remarks, and reminiscences, liberally laced with questions, many of which bordered on the impertinent, from Mrs. Folliwell, Mrs. Cummings, and old Mrs. Garland, aided and abetted by their spouses.

Ellen struggled to hide her smile. She watched Mrs. Kirkpatrick attempt to deflect the inquisition and had to wonder if that lady realized that the smothering interest was driven by rampant curiosity.

Probably not. From her haughty performance, Mrs. Kirkpatrick appeared to consider the interest of others her due.

Increasingly, however, Mrs. Kirkpatrick's tactics shifted to appealing to Christopher for assistance; soon, she was patently throwing lures his way.

Ellen gritted her teeth and pretended not to notice, instead encouraging little Mrs. Cummings, who was always ready to talk about her three children and prattled on happily while Ellen kept her ears attuned to Christopher's deep voice.

His responses to Mrs. Kirkpatrick's forays—depressingly vague and distant—did much to bolster Ellen's temper; it was a relief to realize he was, apparently, impervious to the lady's advances.

Relief?

She inwardly frowned, but couldn't deny that was what she felt.

She told herself it was solely because the matter of the counterfeit notes would be so much more difficult to deal with if Christopher proved susceptible to the lady's charms.

Just as well he wasn't. Ellen glanced at Mrs. Kirkpatrick and caught a hint of frustration in her eyes. It seemed even Mrs. Kirkpatrick had started to realize that.

Christopher had found Mrs. Kirkpatrick much as he'd anticipated; underneath the sophisticated glamour, behind the charm she turned up and down like a lamp, she was a hard, distinctly predatory female.

While he abhorred silly flibbertigibbets, he'd never classed them as dangerous. In contrast, he'd soon determined that Mrs. Kirkpatrick was the worst sort of tonnish female—a viper one should never turn one's back on.

How had Kirkpatrick got caught in her coils?

Presumably because he'd been older, a widower who had lived a simple and happy personal life, and therefore had been inexperienced in seeing through the sophisticated façade deployed by the lady who'd sought to ensnare him.

Christopher now accepted that Kirkpatrick had been caught and trapped and that the man had subsequently realized that. Such a situation would only underscore Mrs. Kirkpatrick's need for a secondary source of income, one independent of her husband.

Kirkpatrick had probably already moved to ensure his wife would not be able to lay her fingers on his wealth, even were he to die.

Kirkpatrick is no fool.

Nor was Christopher, especially not when it came to feminine dangers lurking within the ton.

He'd been keeping surreptitious track of the efforts of the musicians. Choosing his moment, across Mrs. Kirkpatrick, he spoke to Denton. "Still hunting over the fields down here?"

Barabas Denton, a handsome, athletic sort with dark hair and dark eyes, was the same age as Christopher; he had always viewed Christopher as a rival, especially when it came to ladies and most especially those few local young matrons inclined to dalliance.

Denton's amorous hunting ground—the one to which Christopher was referring—had remained largely local, while Christopher's had generally been the ballrooms of the haut ton; their paths had crossed only rarely, yet Denton still smarted from those instances in which he'd lost out.

Denton's gaze sharpened. "Indeed. Unlike some, I find more challenge and excitement in local pursuits."

Out of sight of Mrs. Kirkpatrick or Denton, Christopher closed his hand around one of Ellen's; he felt her start, then her fingers relaxed in his. Reassured, he caught Denton's eye and smiled, then as a violin screeched, widened his eyes. "Is that—"

Denton took the bait and bowed to the lady between them. "My dear Mrs. Kirkpatrick, I beg you'll grant me the honor of this dance."

Before Mrs. Kirkpatrick could even glance Christopher's way, he turned to Ellen. "Miss Martingale—dare I hope I can persuade you to the dance floor?"

She met his eyes, understanding gleaming in hers. "You may try, sir."

He chuckled and twined his arm with hers, bestowed a general nod on the others in the circle, and steered her toward the clearing space. He didn't glance back to see if Denton got what he'd wanted.

As they neared the floor, Christopher realized Fate was smiling; the dance was to be a waltz. He turned to Ellen and took her into his arms, the music swelled, and they stepped out.

For several revolutions, pure sensation consumed his awareness. She was light on her feet, gliding effortlessly under his direction through the swirling patterns of the dance. The supple flex of her back beneath his hand, the light pressure of her fingers across his palm and also on his shoulder were their only physical connections, yet to him it seemed that the synchronicity of their movements, the web of togetherness woven by the dance, cast a significantly more powerful net, binding them via their senses.

For long moments, he allowed himself to wallow in the simple pleasure of having such a perfect partner in his arms. As far as he could tell, from the faraway look in her eyes and her somehow softer expression, she was doing the same. But eventually, reluctantly, he forced his mind to refocus.

Unsurprisingly, it focused on her.

There was no denying she was an accomplished dancer, moving easily and confidently to match his stride. The realization prompted him to ask, "You lived in London. Did you move among the ton?"

Her eyes met his; she studied him measuringly, as if assessing why he'd asked.

He smiled. "I wondered where you learned to waltz so well."

"Ah." She glanced aside as they whirled through a turn, then brought her gaze back to his face. "The answer is yes. I made my come-out four years ago and had a second Season the following year. Shortly after that, Mama took ill, although she lingered for over a year before she passed away." She met his eyes in her usual direct fashion. "That rather curtailed my time in the ton, and then, when we came out of mourning, Uncle Humphrey and Vickers urged us to sell up and come down to Bigfield House. All three of us—Emma, Robbie, and I—were happy to embrace a change of scenery. For us, the house in Belgravia had come to hold too many sad memories, so we fell in with Uncle Humphrey's plan."

He tipped his head, his eyes holding hers. "Two seasons and no suitors?"

Her lips curved, rather smugly. "If you must know, I had several perfectly eligible gentlemen vying for my hand, but I had already inherited a comfortable fortune from two great-aunts and felt no pressing need to take a husband purely to secure my future."

"Ah." He nodded sagely. "You're a lady of substance."

"An *independent* lady of substance." She quirked a brow at him. "According to my mother, acquiring wealth made me picky."

He'd learned what he'd wanted to know; it was time to move on— before she wondered too much about his motives. They turned again, swinging past Robbie and one of the Walton girls; even while he waltzed, much to his partner's chagrin, Robbie was trying his best to keep an eye on Julia Kirkpatrick, who was waltzing with Alex Huntly.

"It occurs to me," Christopher murmured, drawing Ellen just a tad closer and pulling her attention from her brother, "that this is a venue at which we should see if we can't confirm the answers to some of our questions."

Obligingly distracted, she looked at him. "Which questions?"

"I think we should see what we can glean about Tilly and Nigel Fontenay."

Ellen was grateful to have a definite topic on which to focus her attention and her wits. She'd waltzed with gentlemen times without number, yet waltzing with Christopher was an entirely different experience. There was an elegant strength in him that became particularly evident while dancing; waltzing with him had fascinated and enticed her and absorbed every iota of her awareness. She'd barely registered the others around them; even the sight of Robbie had been insufficient to break the hold of the moment.

As if on cue, the music drew to a close, and they swirled to a halt. Christopher released her, and she curtsied while he bowed. She straightened, scanned the room as best she could, then smiled and looped her arm with his. "This way."

She led him to where Tilly was standing, patently bored, with a group including the Entwhistles, their son Tolliver—who had been dancing with Tilly—as well as three other young gentlemen, all of whom were vying for Tilly's smiles.

The way Tilly's eyes lit when Christopher appeared told its own tale.

Confident in Christopher's social skills, Ellen engaged the Entwhistles, asking about the local plum harvest—a subject likely to appeal to local landowners; courtesy of her work with her uncle's estate, she was well versed in such topics.

The younger men took that as their cue to redouble their efforts to fix

Tilly's attention, but the girl's sharp eyes had latched, gimlet-like, on Christopher.

For his part, Christopher divided his attention between the Entwhistles and Ellen, contributing several comments to the discussion.

Predictably, Tilly didn't like being ignored by a London swell. Brazenly, she attempted to draw Christopher's interest with an overloud comment regarding the lack of experienced dance partners.

When all that gained her was a sharp glance from Mrs. Entwhistle and a depressingly dismissive look from Christopher, Tilly sulked.

Eventually, she allowed the still-eager young gentlemen to distract her.

Ellen viewed Tilly's petulant performance for another minute, then excused Christopher and herself and moved on to pause beside a group of young men gathered about the Walton sisters. Nigel Fontenay was holding court.

Ellen drew the attention of Parthenope, the elder sister, complimenting her on her gown. She continued chatting with the girl—a sensible sort—leaving Christopher, who remained beside her, his arm looped with hers, to listen to Nigel's boasting of his exploits on the hunting field, his prowess with the whip, and his plans to attend an illegal boxing match to be held on the Downs in a few weeks' time.

Several of the other young men made various comments about the latter, to which Nigel replied in sharp and dismissive fashion.

Then Henry Dalton obligingly remarked, "Not a bad evening last Friday." Henry grinned. "I came away quite happy."

Displeasure flashed in Nigel's eyes. "No need to be so smug—not if you want an invitation to the next evening."

Over Parthenope's shoulder, Ellen saw Nigel's gaze shift pointedly to Christopher, who had kept his gaze on Ellen and Parthenope rather than attempting to engage the younger men.

"Oh." Henry's face fell. "Yes—of course. I didn't realize..."

"I've told you before," Nigel went on, his tone rather nasty, "we're keeping things *exclusive*."

The implication that loose-lipped acquaintances like Henry might find themselves excluded in future was plain.

Ellen brought her exchange with Parthenope to a close, releasing the girl to return to the group. With a vague smile at the others in the circle, Ellen steered Christopher on.

Once they were out of earshot, Christopher lowered his head and murmured, "Both Tilly and Nigel are as sharp as tacks. I've met their sort before—they're out to get what they want, regardless of what that might involve. I believe we can conclude that neither is Mrs. Kirkpatrick's *unwitting* pawn."

"No, indeed," Ellen murmured back. "Both are very much wide awake."

They fetched up beside a group of older guests anchored by their hostess. Mrs. Carstairs smiled and turned aside to speak with Ellen and Christopher. A certain hope gleamed in her eyes. "I'm delighted to see you entertaining each other. I hope the evening has lived up to expectations thus far."

They assured her it had.

Christopher had known Mrs. Carstairs—and she, him—all his life; he seized the opportunity to state his pleasure at catching up with so many local acquaintances he hadn't seen in recent times. He glanced back at the group he and Ellen had just quit. "And, of course, meeting the more recent additions to the local circles." He looked at Mrs. Carstairs, met her blue eyes, and arched a brow. "I hadn't met the Fontenays before."

Mrs. Carstairs primmed her lips, then shot a glance at Ellen and moved conspiratorially closer. She lowered her voice. "Mrs. Kirkpatrick is one thing—despite her snide comments and observations, she walks an acceptable line. But those two—Tilly and Nigel." Mrs. Carstairs gave vent to a derogatory sound. "They are unbecomingly grasping and forever giving themselves airs. As for their tongues, someone needs to blunt them."

She shook her head, and her corona of gray curls bounced. "If they are examples of London's younger generation, then I don't know what society is coming to. At their age, they should be enjoying life and gratefully accepting all that comes their way, not constantly on the lookout to advance their own cause." She paused, then humphed defiantly. "At least, that's the way they strike me."

Christopher murmured, "That's much as we found them, too." He paused, then ventured, "We"—he nodded at Ellen—"have heard about the card parties Mrs. Kirkpatrick holds at Goffard Hall. From all we've gleaned, the events are restricted to younger gentlemen. That seems a rather odd undertaking for such as Mrs. Kirkpatrick—certainly as a regular happening."

"Oh, those." Mrs. Carstairs flapped her hand. "Apparently, Mrs. Kirkpatrick dotes on Nigel and is happy to host the card parties as a way for him and his friends to have fun. From what I've heard, even his most distant acquaintances are invited, and they do seem to flock to the Hall." Mrs. Carstairs's eyes narrowed, and the shrewdness born of age infused her expression. She leaned in and lowered her voice further. "Between you and me"—she included Ellen with her gaze—"I'm not entirely sure that it's solely for Nigel's benefit that Mrs. Kirkpatrick hosts those card parties, although I understand it is, indeed, only his peers who are invited."

Her lips setting primly, Mrs. Carstairs straightened. She caught Ellen's gaze, then Christopher's, then gave a sharp nod. "But enough of that. Now!" She beamed, then reached out and patted both their shoulders. "Off you two go—and enjoy yourselves!"

They smiled, half bowed, and duly moved into the crowd.

CHAPTER 6

*R*esettling Ellen's hand on his sleeve, Christopher murmured, "I hadn't imagined Mrs. Kirkpatrick as a cradle snatcher."

"Neither had I," Ellen admitted. "Yet I can see why Mrs. Carstairs might think that to be the case."

"Despite Nigel's fond imaginings, it seems the existence of the card parties is common knowledge." Christopher scanned the company. "I find it odd that, so far, we've encountered no dismay, disapproval, or disapprobation regarding the events. It might be worthwhile to see what we can learn from those couples with sons Nigel's age."

Frowning slightly, Ellen nodded. "One would think they would be concerned over their sons attending."

As she had been over her brother's involvement. Christopher nodded and steered her toward the group about Mrs. Folliwell, which included the Entwhistles and the Daltons; both couples had sons who were acquainted with Nigel.

The group had been chatting in relaxed fashion and readily welcomed Christopher and Ellen, smiling and shuffling closer to include them in the circle.

With everyone knowing everyone else, it wasn't difficult for Christopher to swing the conversation to the schedule of local events, such as the Harvest Ball later in the season and, from there, to ease into mentioning the recent addition of card parties at Goffard Hall. "Although I understand attendance is restricted to younger gentlemen."

He met the Entwhistles', the Daltons', and Mrs. Folliwell's eyes with easy, open curiosity. "Having recently returned to the manor and heard about the card parties, I own to being curious." He allowed faint puzzlement to color his expression. "It sounds rather rum. Surely local families can't be all that pleased to see their sons lured into gambling."

The Entwhistles and Daltons nodded with ready understanding.

"Oh, we all had reservations, dear—at first," Mrs. Entwhistle said.

"We thought just as you do." Mr. Dalton tipped his head in acknowledgment.

"Definitely had our suspicions, what?" Mr. Entwhistle put in.

"But as it was Mrs. Kirkpatrick's event, we felt we couldn't simply put our foot down and say no," Mrs. Dalton said. "Not the first time."

"But you may be sure we watched," Mr. Dalton said.

"And," Mrs. Entwhistle concluded, "while one can't approve of gambling per se, as things have panned out, having these local card parties has proved something of a boon."

Christopher didn't have to fabricate his surprise. "A boon? How so?"

He slanted a glance at Ellen; her puzzlement, too, was entirely genuine. What had he and she missed?

"Well, you see," Mr. Dalton explained, "none of our youngsters have lost more than a few pounds, yet to them, they're gambling."

"They're experiencing the thrill, but without much risk," Mrs. Dalton added.

"Exactly!" Mrs. Entwhistle nodded. "As Mrs. Kirkpatrick said when we broached the matter with her, the card parties allow our sons to indulge in an activity they want to plunge into regardless, and with her parties, they can do it locally, without having to travel to London and being at the mercy of the card sharps there."

"If they go to London, they'll be fleeced!" Mr. Entwhistle declared. "But instead, playing at Goffard Hall... Well, they're really not doing too badly, all in all."

"There's no rum customers allowed," Mr. Dalton said. "And so far, there's been no great losses."

" *And*," Mrs. Entwhistle said, "Mrs. Kirkpatrick assured us that other than Tilly, who helps at the events, and possibly Julia, there are no young women invited or allowed at all." Mrs. Entwhistle nodded approvingly. "That might not be to our sons' tastes, but we appreciate Mrs. Kirkpatrick's sense in forbidding any other temptation."

The other three parents and Mrs. Folliwell nodded sagely.

Christopher summoned an expression of enlightened relief. "You've set my mind at ease. Clearly, there's no reason for concern over these card parties."

The group, Mrs. Folliwell included, assured him that was so, then Ellen stepped in with a question about the local markets, diverting attention from Goffard Hall.

Soon after, Christopher excused Ellen and himself, and they strolled on.

Once they'd been swallowed by the crowd and could no longer be seen by those they'd just left, he shook his head. "You'd think the fact that their sons—all of whom are wet behind the ears—haven't lost more than a few pounds would raise their suspicions, but apparently not."

Ellen softly snorted. "They probably fondly imagine that their darlings are becoming dab hands at gambling and developing wise heads into the bargain." She glanced at him. "It's human nature to believe the best of one's children."

"I don't have children, but I do have numerous younger cousins, and I can assure you that, except in rare cases, the house always wins significantly, even over just one night."

"Not everyone has your experience to draw on," she dryly returned. "Besides, in this instance, the house isn't interested in winning. It's all about exchanging the notes, and when you think about it, not allowing any young man to lose too much is a sure way of ensuring they come back."

He huffed. "That's a stark contrast to the more usual reason of going back in a desperate attempt to recoup steep losses. In this case, I suppose they return more for the company and, as they would term it, the sport."

"Hmm. And perhaps that accounts for the large stakes we saw being wagered by some of the young men last Friday. If they'd previously won small amounts, they might think to win more by wagering more—"

"Along the way, giving Mrs. Kirkpatrick and her helpers the opportunity to exchange many more notes." Christopher halted; when Ellen glanced at him, he grimaced faintly and said, "One has to admit that the way the card parties are being run is really very clever. Mrs. Kirkpatrick has thought through her part in the scheme very thoroughly. Her guests will continue to roll up, drawing in more and more of their friends, all eager to play for the highest stakes they can manage, thus giving her maximum opportunity to substitute fake notes for real ones and have the fakes distributed far and wide."

Ellen nodded. "It's ingenious."

A sudden buzz among the guests was followed by a general exodus into the adjacent dining room. After looking over the heads, Christopher returned his gaze to Ellen. "Supper is served." He waved toward the dining room. "Shall we?"

They joined the flow of guests into the cramped chamber. With many others, they hung back, allowing the elderly still mobile to serve themselves and retreat, and for the relatives dispatched by the older guests ensconced in the parlor to discharge their duties.

Finally, Christopher and Ellen moved forward and filled their plates, then took refuge in a quiet corner to wield the tiny supper forks and sample the delicacies the Carstairses' staff continued to ferry out.

To Ellen's surprise, Mr. Denton appeared and glibly asked, "May I join you?"

She cut a glance at Christopher; when he simply stared assessingly at Denton, she inclined her head politely. "Of course, sir."

Denton shifted to stand beside her.

For several seconds, they continued eating, then Denton remarked, "I haven't seen you at such events previously, Miss Martingale. Dare I hope you intend to delight us with your presence more often?"

Ellen swallowed and lightly shrugged. "As to that, sir, I really can't say. Much of my time is taken up with household matters."

"Be that as it may," Denton persisted, "I hope we can persuade you to join our company more frequently. I understand you're relatively new to the area. If I might suggest, a picnic on the Downs is a pleasant way to see more of the county. If you're interested, I would be happy to arrange a party of like-minded souls to make the most of the day."

"I fear, Mr. Denton, that at present, my time for such excursions is limited."

"Oh, come now, Miss Martingale. All work and no play—"

"Denton."

Ellen's blinked at Christopher's low growl.

Sadly, Denton appeared impervious; he arched his brows haughtily and met Christopher's gaze. "Yes, Cynster?"

Ellen looked from one to the other.

"There you are!" Mrs. Kirkpatrick swanned up, a plate in her hand. She halted beside Christopher and, smiling, met his eyes. Then, belatedly, she let her gaze drift to Ellen and Denton. "I must admit I hadn't expected such a crush in this backwater. So difficult to find those one wishes to speak to with so many crammed into such small rooms."

The relief Ellen had felt at the interruption evaporated, but before she could think of a rebuttal for the idle insult to their hostess, another thought struck. "Actually, Mrs. Kirkpatrick, I was hoping I would have a chance to speak with you."

Mrs. Kirkpatrick's perfectly arched eyebrows rose. "Indeed, my dear?"

Ellen ignored the insufferably superior tone and plowed on. "Although I've been at Bigfield House for several months"—she glanced at Denton, smiled slightly, and prayed he would remain silent—"as I was just discussing with Mr. Denton, I haven't yet had much chance to look about the neighborhood and assess its amenities." She schooled her features to an expression of innocent inquiry and looked at Mrs. Kirkpatrick. "However, I understand you've lived at Goffard Hall for several years, and I was hoping you might share with me the places you deem worth visiting and, of course, which towns have the better shops—Hastings? Rye? Tunbridge Wells, perhaps? Oh, and I've heard of Romney Marsh—do you think it worth a visit? Do you know anything of it?"

Keeping her eyes innocently wide, Ellen willed Mrs. Kirkpatrick to answer, thus revealing with which of the local areas she was familiar.

Instead, that lady laughed dismissively. "My dear Miss Martingale, when it comes to the locality, I have absolutely no information to share. While I have lived at Goffard Hall for over two years, I continue to shop in London and, occasionally, Paris, of course." She, too, opened her eyes wide. "I haven't even stopped in Tunbridge Wells, much less towns farther south—exploring provincial regions has never been of interest to me."

Pretending to be oblivious to the lady's barbs, Ellen heaved a disappointed sigh. "I used to live in Belgravia and grew accustomed to having nice shops all around. I suppose I just assumed there would be shops of similar style somewhere near here."

This time, Mrs. Kirkpatrick's laugh was brittle and distinctly cynical. "No, my dear—none, not one, I do assure you. For London quality, you need to go to London."

Ellen recalled the lace adorning her gown, but held her tongue on that subject and, with every appearance of resignation, inclined her head. "Thank you for the advice—at least I won't waste precious time searching for what isn't there."

Mrs. Kirkpatrick's lips quirked, making it plain she hadn't intended to be helpful. With the distraction of Ellen dealt with, she turned to Christopher.

Only to discover he was reaching to relieve Ellen of her now-empty plate. "Your aunt just signaled from the parlor—I believe she wishes to speak with you."

"Oh, thank you." Ellen watched him add her plate to his and deposit both on the tray of a footman he'd summoned with a look.

Mrs. Kirkpatrick blinked, faintly nonplussed.

"Permit me to escort you to your aunt." Christopher offered Ellen his arm.

She took it and smiled easily at Mrs. Kirkpatrick, then at Mr. Denton. "Pray excuse us."

With a nod to Mrs. Kirkpatrick and a curter one to Denton, Christopher bore Ellen away.

As he guided her into the parlor, she asked, "Is Aunt Emma really looking for me?"

"No," he admitted, "but I'd had enough of Mrs. Kirkpatrick's company. I can bear with Denton for at least ten minutes, but the lady wears out her welcome remarkably rapidly."

Ellen smiled.

In the drawing room, the dancing was starting up again, but only the younger guests were taking part in the country dance. Their elders were, by and large, sitting in the parlor, fanning themselves.

The drawing room had heated, and the parlor was almost as bad; even though the windows had been opened, there was not a breath of cool breeze to be had. Other couples had ventured onto the terrace, seeking relief in the moonlit night.

Christopher steered Ellen toward a spot by the parlor wall. "Reviewing our conversations, we've learned quite a lot. I'd like to revisit the facts and fix them in my mind." The better to craft his report to Drake.

From her beaded reticule, Ellen extracted a fan, predictably composed of feathers tied with ribbon. She wielded it energetically. "It's terribly warm in here."

"And insufficiently private to risk a discussion of our observations." He knew the house. He debated, then said, "There's a small conservatory —we can reach it via the door in the corner."

She looked at him—once again in that measuring way—then asked, "Does this conservatory have openable windows?"

"From memory, yes."

"In that case"—she snapped her fan closed—"lead on."

He guided her across the room, then lowered his arm, closed his hand around hers, opened the narrow secondary door, and led her through. The short corridor beyond was unlit, but at its end, the door to the conservatory stood open, and silvery moonlight lit the space.

He shut the door behind them, then hand in hand, they walked on and into the conservatory—into blessedly cooler fresh air. The windows were open and, on this side of the house, caught a slight breeze. No lamps had been left burning, but the moonlight streaming through the glass panes of roof and walls provided more than enough illumination for their purpose.

As they strolled down the center aisle between rows of potted plants, Ellen looked down and observed, "The tiles must help to keep the place cool."

However it was achieved, the atmosphere was a great deal more comfortable, propriety be damned. At the end of the aisle, before an open window, stood a white-painted wrought-iron seat. Christopher led Ellen to it. He released her hand and waited while she turned, drew in her wide skirts, and sat, then he sat beside her.

He leaned forward, resting his forearms on his thighs, the better to study her face as she sighed and said, "I'd hoped by luring Mrs. Kirkpatrick into revealing her knowledge of the area to gain some idea of where she might go to fetch the counterfeit notes, but it seems she eschews all country towns." She met his eyes. "I'd assumed she would visit some town—for instance, to buy hats or gloves—and that would be the area she would choose to meet with whoever delivers the notes from the smugglers—perhaps the smugglers themselves."

He nodded. "It was a good idea to ask, but if she's to be believed—and I rather suspect she spoke the truth about never visiting local towns..." He broke off, then after a second, said, "The surest way to check will be via the coachmen." He met Ellen's eyes. "The coachmen of the local houses have shared a drink once a week at the Bull Inn for as long as I can remember. They'll confirm if Mrs. Kirkpatrick travels anywhere other than London."

She inclined her head. "For now, let's assume she spoke the truth. That means the fake notes make their way to her—that they're delivered by someone, either to Goffard Hall or somewhere close by."

He considered that. "So the notes are delivered to her—by whom?" He remembered Drake's injunction against tipping anyone off. "If we're to unravel how this scheme works, first to last, then we'll need to learn how the fake notes get into Mrs. Kirkpatrick's hands. Who brings them to Goffard Hall or its environs, and who in that household receives them? Is it Mrs. Kirkpatrick herself, or for instance, does Nigel play a part?"

Ellen frowned. "I can't see Mrs. Kirkpatrick trusting Nigel that much. Can you?"

"No." After further cogitation, he went on, "So let's hypothesize that the notes are delivered directly into Mrs. Kirkpatrick's hands, either at the Hall or close to it, by…either someone who receives the notes from the smugglers or, as you said, by a member of the smuggling gang."

"Is there some way we can learn who that person is?"

They fell silent, both, Christopher assumed, turning that problem over in their minds.

After several minutes, the pervasive silence impinged, and he glanced at the door. He'd expected others to have joined them by now, but it seemed everyone else had overlooked the existence of the conservatory.

They were entirely alone and, apparently, forgotten, at least for the moment.

Hands loosely clasped between his knees, he turned his head and looked at Ellen. The moon was high; its silvery light slanted across her features, gilding the smooth curves of her cheeks, the crescents of her long lashes.

The delectable curves of her rosebud lips.

He seized the moment to study her face and pay visual homage to her exquisite features.

She'd grown accustomed to him being near, physically close. Despite the mere inches between them, she was totally absorbed with her thoughts and, at least in that moment, oblivious of him.

His impulses jabbed, prodding, poking, and urging him on—down a reckless path. He knew what his instincts were pushing him to do, yet…

What am *I doing?*

Where is my interaction with Ellen Martingale leading me?

Even as the question formed in his mind, he knew the answer. Very likely, he had known it from the first—from the instant she'd run into him in the corridor at Bigfield House.

He'd expected to feel something akin to panic—some degree of shying away. But no.

This, apparently, was how it felt when the Cynster curse, as he'd long termed it, struck.

No quarter. No option at all. Only one way forward—at least if he wanted to seize the future he'd already acknowledged he wanted.

Well, then.

Her continued obliviousness was a prick to his ego, and his thoughts only spurred him on.

To act rather than dwell on things was his habit. Eschewing further thought, he raised one hand and ran the back of one finger down her silken cheek.

He'd thought she would startle, but instead, as his finger hovered by her jaw, she turned her head and looked at him.

Openly, directly, without the slightest guile.

Her eyes had widened, the bright hazel gleaming in the moonlight.

Gruffly, he confessed, "I've been wanting to do that for days."

Her eyes widened further, but she said nothing. He sensed she was barely breathing as she sat there, all frivolous fancy, and stared at him as if he was a strange and unpredictable species.

Then her gaze lowered to his lips and steadied, fixed.

When the tip of her tongue appeared and, transparently without thought, she ran it over the plump fullness of her lower lip, he almost groaned.

"Don't look at me like that." The words were a growled plea.

She blinked, raised her eyes to his, and after a fraught second, breathlessly asked, "Like what?"

"As if you want me to kiss you again."

She hesitated for a telltale second, then up went her chin, and she declared, "You're imagining things."

No, he wasn't—or rather, he was, but his imagination stretched much further than just another kiss.

More, her eyes, full of curiosity and more than a hint of anticipation, contradicted her words.

She was, in her way, challenging him to take the next step. To persuade her, to seduce her.

He straightened and swung toward her, raised his other hand, gently gripped her chin, and turned her face fully to his—so he could capture and hold her gaze.

Then, excruciatingly slowly, he leaned closer—acutely aware of how her breath grew shallow, still shallower, then suspended. How her gaze fell to his lips as, with bated breath, she watched them near.

He was conscious to his bones of the softness of her skin, the tempting lushness of her lips as, inexorably, they drew nearer his. More than anything else, he was aware to his soul of the vibrancy, the untapped energy, that infused her slender body and that not even by a tensing of muscles had she given any sign of wishing to avoid the kiss.

When a bare whisker separated his lips from hers, he let his gaze fall to the luscious curves and breathed, "I don't think so."

Then he sealed her lips with his, fused his to her softer curves. He kissed her invitingly, imploringly...and after a mere heartbeat of hesitation, her lips softened, then molded to his.

Melded with his as, on a rush of exultation, he sank into the kiss and drew her with him.

She readily followed where he led, seeking, he sensed, to know, to explore.

Then dispensing with all restraint, she leaned into him—into the kiss.

He'd been waiting for that—for that quintessential moment of surrender. Not to him, but to her own wanting.

Experienced as he was, he knew *that*—her desire, her need—was what he wished to foster. To encourage and nurture and grow. So he kissed her with his own passion held firmly in check, and with temptation on his tongue, he deepened the kiss, degree by degree, until it transformed into an invitation as old as time and as potent as the sun—an unshielded enticement to engage and indulge with him.

He sank his heart and soul into convincing her to accept. His lips supped at hers, then firmed and possessed, and she answered his call, meeting and matching him and, ultimately, making her own demands— embarking on her own forays within the seductive and enthralling engagement.

Somewhat to his surprise, it took effort on his part to maintain control of proceedings; she was neither meek nor mild nor, in this sphere, completely untried and naive.

Ellen couldn't stop kissing Christopher. Their lips melded, their tongues tangled, and she couldn't get enough of the fascinating, riveting exchanges. The kisses they'd shared previously had hinted that there was more to explore, that under his direction, the simple art of kissing would be elevated to an entirely new plane of sensation.

He and his kisses—these increasingly avid and hungry kisses they were so utterly engrossed in sharing—hadn't disappointed.

In light of her less-than-enthralling London experiences, she'd long wondered at the whispers shared by other young ladies of the delights they had found... Now, she knew the fault for her earlier disappointments lay with those gentlemen with whom she'd engaged.

When it came to the art of kissing, compared to Christopher, they had had no clue.

Firm and tantalizing, his lips moved on hers with a subtle pressure that had effortlessly ensnared her wits; now, along with her senses, they followed every shifting sensation, cataloging the nuances and the resulting small pleasures.

With his clever lips and educated tongue, he orchestrated a symphony of those small pleasures, and her senses waltzed to his tune.

It was that straightforward—that clear-cut. For her, with respect to her appreciation and pleasure, Christopher's kisses were the epitome of perfection.

He'd drawn her closer, the hand initially at her jaw lowering to span the back of her waist and urge her to him. All the way against him; her bodice was pressed to his chest, and most peculiarly, her breasts felt swollen and the peaks ached, oddly pleasurably.

The solid contact was another source of engrossing sensation.

He seemed intuitively to know what she wanted—for what she was seeking—and time and again, he redirected the engagement to deliver it. To let her see, know, and if she wished, explore.

Yet the most enthralling, fascinating, deeply satisfying feature of their exchanges was that he was every bit as engrossed as she. That he found her and her responses as utterly enthralling as she found him and his.

Tit for tat, perhaps; balance, most definitely.

The thought gave her the confidence to fully engage and press him to go further—to extend her horizons.

They were immersed in a scintillating duel of tongues when abruptly, the sounds of hooves and wheels on gravel and calls of farewell erupted beyond the conservatory windows.

They both started and drew apart—for one giddy instant, they stared into each other's eyes, and both knew unquestioningly that neither had wanted the heady, all-consuming exchange to end. Then the unmistakable sounds of departures had them turning their heads to look out. Beyond one side of the moonlit lawn—which, thankfully, remained deserted—guests were climbing into their carriages while others took their leave of their host and hostess.

"Good Lord!" she exclaimed. "How long have we been..." Faint color rising to her cheeks, she looked at Christopher.

He continued to stare across the lawn. His lips—those tempting, tantalizing lips—firmed into a line. "Obviously, far longer than either of us realized." He met her eyes. "Too long for safety." He rose and, capturing her hands, drew her to her feet. The instant she was upright, he set one of her hands on his sleeve and urged her toward the door. "We need to rejoin the others before anyone truly misses us."

She fervently hoped no one had. She hurried beside him into the corridor and on toward the parlor, surreptitiously tweaking her bodice straight.

Together, they slipped through the door into the rear of the parlor. She was relieved that he had taken charge; her wits were still reeling giddily, and she feared that, if left to herself, she would fail abysmally to adequately conceal their recent endeavors.

Luckily, it seemed that no one had noticed their joint departure, absence, or return; as Christopher insinuated them into the body of guests moving slowly toward the Grange's front hall, she dragooned her wits into order, ready to deflect any arch or pointed questions, but none came.

Christopher clung to his relaxed, sophisticated persona, the one he habitually displayed to those gathered at the Grange, and smoothly guided Ellen to her aunt's side, then, after they'd tendered their thanks and made their farewells to the Carstairses on the front porch, he walked beside Robbie as they escorted Ellen and Emma to the Martingale carriage.

When they reached the landau, Robbie gave his aunt his hand and assisted her up the steps, then followed.

Christopher offered Ellen his hand. She laid her fingers across his palm and raised her eyes to his face, waiting to see…

He smiled and, manfully resisting the urge to raise her fingers to his lips, instead helped her up the steps and to the seat beside Emma.

She watched him almost warily, waiting to draw back her hand.

He gripped her fingers and held her gaze for a heartbeat too long, then with his smile deepening, he lightly squeezed her fingers, released them, and stepped back.

Her eyes narrowed.

He grinned and saluted her. The carriage drew away, and he stood by the side of the drive and watched her golden curls, rendered silver by the moonlight, until the carriage had passed out of sight.

Christopher looked down, unseeing, at the ground while he examined his reaction to the evening. It seemed telling that he couldn't seem to banish the smile interacting with Ellen had left on his face. He felt buoyant, uplifted. Certainly happier than he would have expected to feel after a summer party—even one with dancing.

Smiling still, he swung on his heel and made for where a groom stood holding the reins of the chestnuts harnessed to his curricle.

Christopher hadn't expected to find Toby waiting for him in the manor's library.

Alerted by Pendleby, Christopher strode into the room to see his younger cousin sprawled half asleep in an armchair.

At the sound of the door closing, Toby roused. He stared blearily at Christopher, then sat up and ran both hands over his face. From behind his palms, he mumbled, "What time is it?"

Christopher glanced at the clock on the mantelpiece. "After one o'clock." He looked at Toby and arched a brow. "What brings you back so soon?"

Toby snorted. "Drake, of course, and this infernal mission." Slumping in the chair, Toby waited until Christopher sank into his usual chair opposite, then explained, "Matters are proceeding at a faster pace than Drake or anyone else anticipated. Drake's agents in Paris located and seized the counterfeiting plates, but unfortunately, they were too late to prevent a very large shipment of fake notes being dispatched for England's shores."

Toby paused, plainly ordering his thoughts. "Drake's minions seized the counterfeiter—a Belgian, well known within the fraternity. His work is considered top-notch, meaning the notes he produces will fool most people unless they know what flaw to look for. There always is some tiny flaw, and with these notes, it's the lower curve of the g in England. It's not quite exactly right but close enough to pass a cursory inspection."

Toby went on, "Drake and his men persuaded the counterfeiter to tell all. Or at least all as pertains to this caper. Apparently, they didn't have to persuade too hard—by all accounts, the counterfeiter was disgusted with himself for becoming involved. His opinion of the man behind the scheme is not high, but more on that later. The first bit of pertinent news is that the counterfeiter confirmed that the earlier, smaller shipments of fake notes were intended to test the distribution system on this side of the Channel. More importantly, the very large shipment that's presently on the way was intended to be the last, at least for now, the plan being to use the established and proven distribution system to exchange the fake notes for real ones, with the fakes being subsequently dispersed throughout the country."

Christopher frowned. "Any chance of halting the large shipment on the Continent?"

Toby shook his head. "By the time Drake's men seized the plates and the counterfeiter, the network used to move each shipment to the coast—presumably into the hands of French smugglers who would run the notes across the Channel—had completed the task, and those involved had scattered. There was no one to ask, no trail to follow."

Christopher settled in the chair and stretched out his legs. "I assume Drake wants this large shipment found and seized. What's known of the route by which the notes enter Kent?"

"Not a lot," Toby replied. "All the counterfeiter had heard was that the notes would come in via the southeast coast. Drake's men narrowed it as much as they could, but the best they could manage was somewhere between Hastings and Deal."

Christopher snorted. "That's a lot of coast, and all of it the home of longtime smuggling gangs, even if, in recent years, they've been inactive."

"Given that last, Drake is hoping you'll be able to pick up whispers of which gang has come to life again. It seems likely one of them will have."

Christopher nodded. "Difficult to see how else French smugglers would find the right sort of helpers on this side of the Channel, and it isn't that long ago that the gangs in Kent were still active—there are many around who remember the old routes as well as their erstwhile connections with the French. No reason the French side wouldn't have approached the same group they worked with in the past."

"So everyone thinks." Toby's expression suggested he was reviewing all he'd said. "While the counterfeiter couldn't give us more details about the shipment other than confirming the size of the threat, his other unwelcome revelation concerns the man Drake has labeled the mastermind—the man behind the scheme. He personally recruited the counterfeiter, who had been quietly enjoying a well-funded retirement."

"Did the counterfeiter know who the mastermind is?"

Toby sent Christopher a long-suffering look. "When are Drake's missions ever that easy?"

Christopher had no answer to that.

Toby went on, "Firstly, as Drake had suspected but had hoped wouldn't be the case, the counterfeiter is prepared to swear that the mastermind is an Englishman. The counterfeiter met him, but only in poorly lit surrounds—the counterfeiter couldn't give any better visual description beyond tall, dark-haired, and well-dressed. But as to voice, the counterfeiter was certain—the man was fluent in French, but with an accent and idiosyncrasies that, to a French-speaking Belgian, marked the man as unquestionably English."

Toby grimaced. "Bad enough, but from the counterfeiter's description of the man's clothes, the degree of his fluency in French, and several accessories—a signet ring and a crest on the head of the man's cane, although the counterfeiter saw neither clearly enough to describe in detail —it seems fairly clear that our Englishman is a member of the haut ton, possibly even from one of the noble houses."

"Ah," Christopher said. "And now Drake's after him in earnest."

Toby nodded. "I'll leave it to Drake to explain when he gets down here, but the chance that the mastermind hails from society's upper echelons makes it even more imperative that whatever you do here in tracking and seizing the notes in no way alerts those further along the chain, or else our mastermind—and Drake didn't choose that moniker without cause—will vanish into thin air, leaving alive the possibility of him emerging with a similar threat at a later date, or so Drake fears."

"Presumably with good reason—I seriously doubt there's all that much that Drake fears."

Wearily, Toby grinned. "Except, possibly, his wife's temper."

Christopher chuckled. "He is a wise man." Sobering, he reviewed Toby's news, aligning it with the information he'd compiled.

Toby studied his face. "Have you got anywhere regarding the inhabitants of Goffard Hall?"

Christopher arched a supercilious brow. "As it happens, I have. The principal agent in the distribution system operating via the Goffard Hall card parties is Mrs. Kirkpatrick, the lady of the house."

Toby's brows rose. "Not the husband?"

"No. He appears to be a solid sort—a financier, what's more." Succinctly, Christopher summarized their findings regarding the Goffard Hall household.

Toby looked impressed. "That was quick. It's less than a week since I set you on the trail."

Christopher felt forced to admit, "I had help in the form of Miss Martingale, the niece of our longtime neighbor, Sir Humphrey Martingale of Bigfield House."

Toby stared at Christopher. " *Miss* Martingale?"

Ignoring Toby's stunned expression, Christopher explained, "Miss Martingale's younger brother, Robert, regularly attends the card parties, and naturally, Miss Martingale was concerned. We essentially joined forces in furthering our knowledge of the family at Goffard Hall."

The clocks throughout the house struck twice.

Toby smothered a yawn. "Two o'clock, and my bed calls. But before I collapse, I need to convey just how adamant Drake is that, while exerting every effort to locate and seize the incoming shipment of fake banknotes, we absolutely must not show our hand. Or Drake's hand, as the case actually is."

Christopher frowned. "Based on what we know to this point, I'd say we need to lay hands on the fake notes before Mrs. Kirkpatrick receives them."

"Before she has a chance to stuff them into the pockets of gullible young gentlemen." Toby nodded and yawned again.

"If Drake wants the mastermind, then it's possible Mrs. Kirkpatrick knows who he is."

"But if she doesn't..." Toby pushed to his feet. "Given how careful this blasted mastermind has been to this point—leaving nothing by which he can be traced—"

"Then," Christopher said, standing as well, "unless we follow the trail of the notes—be they fakes or real ones exchanged for the fakes—all the way to the mastermind, we'll likely never identify him, which is probably Drake's worst nightmare."

"Exactly." Toby turned to the door. "Drake said he'll be down here as soon as he can manage it. He wants you to focus on locating the notes, but if at all possible, to wait until he arrives before seizing them."

Christopher strolled beside Toby; together, they made for the stairs. As they climbed, Christopher glanced at his cousin. "Can you stay and assist?"

Like Christopher, Toby had spent a great deal of his life in the country; he was comfortable moving among country folk and the gentry of county circles. Drake possessed a similar background, but not all of his occasional agents—most recruited from the ranks of the sons of the nobility—did. "For this investigation," Christopher said, "we need those who can slide effortlessly into county society, from the fields to the ballrooms."

"Well," Toby said, "it seems I'm your man. I sent word to Nicholas before I left London. He'll cover for me until I get back."

They reached the head of the stairs, and Christopher clapped Toby on the shoulder. "Good man. Now let's get some sleep. I suspect tomorrow —no, it's now today—is going to be hectic."

CHAPTER 7

At nine o'clock the following morning, Christopher stood behind his desk, poring over a map of the immediate locality. Flanked by Pullman, his groom, Granger, the manor's head stableman, Radley, the estate manager, and Toby, he was exploring the logistics of setting up an around-the-clock watch on Goffard Hall.

"The critical point," Toby stressed, "is that we have to be certain of seeing anyone who arrives—or any of the household who leaves, for that matter—but we absolutely must not be seen ourselves."

Pullman and Granger grunted.

His arms crossed, Radley tugged at his lower lip. "Using field glasses, we can watch their boundaries from the cover of various copses." He leaned forward and pointed. "For instance, here and here."

"Mind you," Pullman said, "we'll have to let the Bigfield House staff know what we're doing, or they'll see us slinking about their fields and wonder."

"Getting the Bigfield House staff's support won't be difficult," Christopher said. "We can count on Miss Martingale to smooth our way. In fact, we can ask the Bigfield House staff to monitor their shared boundary. That'll leave *us* with fewer fences to watch."

"It's the front of the house that'll be the problem," Granger said. "That and keeping an eye on the lanes leading away to either side. Spotting our men lurking about the hedgerows would look odd to anyone, even city folk like the Kirkpatricks."

"Indeed." Christopher straightened. "That's why I've asked Aaron"— for Toby's benefit, Christopher added—"the leader of the band of gypsies that helps with our harvests, to join us."

Sounds of an arrival reached them. "I expect," Christopher said, "that will be Aaron now."

The door opened, and Pendleby entered to announce, "Mr. Aaron Codona and Mrs. Gracella Codona, sir."

Christopher blinked, then stepped past Granger and went to greet Aaron and the matriarch of the Codona clan.

Gracella offered her hand, and Christopher bowed over it. "We're honored by your presence, ma'am." He viewed Aaron as shrewd, but Gracella was shrewdness personified.

"My grandson"—Gracella indicated Aaron with a wave—"informed me of your request for assistance. The Cynsters have always been good friends to the Codonas. Of course we will help."

Christopher inclined his head and waved Gracella and Aaron to the armchairs.

Sinking into the chair facing the one Christopher moved toward, Gracella took note of the other men. She exchanged nods with Pullman, Granger, and Radley. Her gaze lingered on Toby. "This is another Cynster, yes? I do not know him."

Somewhat warily, Toby came forward and bowed. "I'm Christopher's cousin, Tobias Cynster, ma'am, but everyone calls me Toby."

Gracella eyed him assessingly. "That is wise—you are much more a Toby than a Tobias. But it is good that you are here helping, too." With her curiosity satisfied, she turned her gaze on Christopher. "Now, what is this thing you wish the Codonas to help with?"

Christopher explained that he needed to keep a covert watch on Goffard Hall with a view to intercepting an illegal delivery and stressed the need for secrecy.

Gracella nodded her understanding, and when Christopher suggested they rise and study the map, she waved at Aaron to do so.

The assembled men were once more poring over the map, with Gracella looking on, when a tap fell on the door and Pendleby appeared. "Miss Martingale, sir."

Surprised, Christopher looked up; he hadn't expected Ellen any more than his men had.

Toby brightened and looked interested, as did Aaron and even more

Gracella. The latter swiveled in the armchair, the better to study the newcomer.

Ellen walked in; today, she wore a leaf-green walking dress adorned with the inevitable ribbons and rosettes, this time in shades of white, pale pink, and darker pink.

She reminded Christopher of an apple tree in blossom. He realized that was possibly her aunt Emma's intention.

Ellen showed no surprise at finding so many gathered there; instead, she looked inquisitively at the faces, then at the map on the desk. "I wondered what was afoot."

Christopher stepped around the desk to meet her. He waved at his staff and introduced them; she bestowed a smile and a nod on all three. "And this is my cousin, Toby Cynster, who I believe I've mentioned."

Ellen held out her hand and smiled warmly. "Mr. Cynster. It's a pleasure to make your acquaintance."

Smiling delightedly, Toby took her hand and bowed over it. "Miss Martingale. The pleasure, I assure you, is all mine."

Ellen's smile grew rather more amused. Withdrawing her hand, she turned to Aaron and Gracella.

Gracella rose, and Christopher made the introductions.

Gracella returned Ellen's smiling nod with a distinctly regal inclination of her head. "You are the sister of the young man who thought we shouldn't camp on Sir Humphrey's fields?" A note in Gracella's voice signaled combative readiness.

Ellen either remained oblivious or chose to ignore it; Christopher suspected the latter. She stepped closer to Gracella, so when she spoke, it seemed more personal, more open and direct. "I'm so very sorry about Robbie's misunderstanding." Although her gaze included Aaron, Ellen spoke primarily to Gracella. "Neither Robbie nor I have lived in the country before, and there aren't any gypsies in London, not traveling about as you do. Robbie had no notion of the previous arrangements, but as matters stand, with Sir Humphrey temporarily indisposed, Robbie has assumed responsibility for Bigfield House, and he takes that very seriously. When he saw you and your people about to move into the field, he made an incorrect assumption, albeit from worthy motives." She smiled, transparently sincerely. "I do hope you and your son and the other members of your group can see your way to accepting Robbie's and my heartfelt apologies."

For a long moment, Gracella studied Ellen's earnest face. Christopher held his breath.

Then Gracella nodded. "You, I approve of. And your brother was willing to learn and change his position when informed of his error. That is also a trait to be encouraged." Gracella swiped a hand through the air in a negating gesture. "All is forgiven. You will come and take tea with me soon, yes?"

Ellen smiled warmly. "I would be honored."

Aaron caught Christopher's eye and arched a faintly amazed brow.

Christopher smiled, glanced toward the desk, and saw Toby staring assessingly at Ellen, patently impressed. Deciding that reasserting control of the situation would be wise, Christopher turned to his unexpected visitor. "But what brings you here?"

She glanced at the desk. "I was exercising my mare and checking the repairs to the hedgerow where the goats got through, and saw Aaron and Gracella walking up the manor drive." She flashed a smile at the pair, then looked at Christopher. "I assumed you must be planning something." Her gaze moved to the map on the desk, and she walked across to study it.

Christopher inwardly sighed and followed; better he tell her what was going on than risk having her act on her own. "We're organizing a watch on Goffard Hall."

The others gathered around again, and Gracella joined them as he refocused the group on how best to keep track of all comings and goings at Goffard Hall.

Toby, meanwhile, was taking careful stock of the most recent arrival. To his experienced eyes, despite her frilly and distracting appearance—and he had to wonder if the distraction was intentional—Miss Martingale ranked as a formidable lady. She didn't look like one, not in the least, but he knew too many members of the sorority to be fooled.

The more intriguing observation was that Christopher knew the same formidable ladies, yet there he was, accepting Miss Martingale's interest in their mission, effectively including her in it.

Toby concluded, and he felt sure he was correct, that Miss Martingale was Christopher's lady. The one he'd chosen…or at least, had fixed upon.

Toby wondered if he should write to his elder sister, Prudence, and inform her that her fear that Christopher would end his days a crusty old bachelor was likely to prove groundless.

As if Christopher could hear his thoughts, he cast Toby a narrow-eyed glance, then returned to finalizing their plans for mounting the necessary watch on Goffard Hall.

Toby wasn't surprised to hear Miss Martingale as well as the gypsy matriarch put forward suggestions as to how their watchers might conceal themselves, in some cases in plain sight.

Christopher accepted and incorporated Ellen's and Gracella's ideas, such as Ellen pointing out that given the gypsies' history in the area, no one would think it strange to see several of their number trimming hedgerows or wielding scythes to neaten the edges of fields. "Any of those little tasks that, I'm reliably informed, estate managers would like to see done, but often have to let slide."

Gracella added, "We could send some of the younger ones—those too young to be included in the work teams that help the farmers. They have sharp eyes and ears, and they will think it a lark—a game to play—and so concentrate all the more."

Ellen nodded. "They would very likely be the most effective watchers."

All agreed that with the help of the gypsies, mounting a tight watch on Goffard Hall would be relatively easily accomplished.

After specific men were assigned to each observation point and period of the day, with the gypsies taking responsibility for monitoring the front of the house day and night, the meeting finally broke up. As the others left, Christopher asked Ellen to remain, then went out to farewell Aaron and Gracella.

On returning to the library, he discovered Ellen and Toby sitting in the armchairs, with Ellen explaining where she lived and how she had come to meet Christopher. He closed the door with a definite snick, attracting their attention.

Ellen smiled at him; Toby grinned and quirked his brows in a knowing way.

Christopher would have scowled at his cousin, but then he would have to explain that reaction to Ellen. Instead, he walked to the armchair next to hers, drawing her gaze from Toby, sat, and said, "There's been a development."

She arched her brows. "One that necessitates placing a watch on Goffard Hall?"

"Indeed." Briefly, Christopher explained about the large shipment of counterfeit notes presently on its way. "Ultimately to be delivered into Mrs. Kirkpatrick's hands."

"I see." She fell silent for several moments, then said, "I'll speak to Hopper about keeping watch along our shared boundary. I'm sure that won't be a problem." She met Christopher's eyes. "But in return, I would ask—"

Christopher steeled himself to reject any suggestion of her joining the watchers.

"—that you keep me apprised of any result—of whoever is caught with the notes." She held his gaze in a forthright way. "My brother is one of the young gentlemen being taken advantage of by this scheme. I would like to know if there's liable to be any developments that might pose a danger to him."

Given what he'd imagined she would ask for, Christopher was happy to agree. Having done so, he looked at Toby, who had been listening to the exchange all too avidly. "So it seems we have the most critical point in the distribution of the notes covered."

Toby's gaze shifted to Ellen.

When Toby arched his brows, Christopher followed Toby's gaze and saw that Ellen was frowning. "What?" Christopher asked.

"It's just that"—she grimaced faintly—"it's ten days to the next card party." She glanced at Toby. "Mrs. Kirkpatrick has been holding them every second Friday, and the most recent was last week." She returned her gaze to Christopher. "There's nothing to say that the notes will be delivered to Mrs. Kirkpatrick soon. Depending on the arrangements in place, whoever currently has the notes might hold back until closer to the date. As that person is presently unknown to us and has no reason not to believe themselves safe, there's no need for any urgency on their part to pass on the notes, is there?"

Christopher was forced to concede the point with a reluctant nod.

Toby looked thoughtful. "You're right."

"So..."—Ellen drew out the word—"while maintaining the watch on Goffard Hall, what else can we do to locate the smuggler or intermediary who, according to your information, currently holds the counterfeit notes?"

Christopher registered her use of "we," and if the smile Toby tried to suppress was any guide, so had he.

"That," Toby said, "is an excellent question." He looked pointedly at Christopher.

Ellen also fixed her gaze on his face.

He met her eyes, then Toby's, then reluctantly admitted, "I know people we can ask about any recent smuggling activity."

Ellen beamed. "Excellent!"

Toby grinned.

~

Seated beside Christopher in his curricle, Ellen smiled delightedly as they bowled down the Bigfield House drive.

It was early afternoon, and the sun was shining, the air redolent with the scent of hay being scythed in nearby fields.

Christopher slowed as the mouth of the drive drew near, and expertly turned the carriage right. He drove his pair—two gorgeous chestnuts—at a smart clip down Walkhurst Road, toward Benenden village.

Ellen lifted her face to the light breeze, closed her eyes, and all but floated on contentment. She was pleased to have been included in the planning session that morning and even happier to have been able to contribute useful suggestions.

Still better had been the decision for her and Christopher to drive out in a first foray to see what they could learn regarding any recent smuggling activity. Toby had volunteered to hold the fort in terms of the watch on Goffard Hall; it had seemed wise to leave him to oversee that task, just in case anyone suspicious was sighted.

Yet the most potent source of her contentment, her happiness with her lot, was her memories of the kisses she and Christopher had shared in the Benenden Grange conservatory.

Kisses that had had no reason for happening other than that he—and she—had wished them to.

And now she had another kiss to add to the list.

When she'd woken that morning, she'd wondered how, given those kisses in the moonlight, Christopher would react when next they met. For her part, she'd been eager to learn what might happen. She'd waited through the meeting, but all the others had been there, and he and she had kept their minds on organizing the surveillance of Goffard Hall.

Once the others had gone, Toby had remained, gooseberry-like, until she'd excused herself to return to Bigfield House for luncheon.

Christopher had walked her to the stable, and while they'd been waiting for her mare to be saddled, he'd reached for her and stolen a very thorough kiss—to which she had enthusiastically responded.

Only when they'd heard the clop of approaching hooves had they stepped apart.

She let the remembered warmth flow through her, but, she reflected, kisses weren't everything.

Admittedly, Christopher's kisses were impressive, but the fact that she was where she was, sitting beside him as they embarked on the next phase of this investigation, spoke to some other, deeper and equally important need.

She couldn't predict how the interaction between them would evolve, nor could he. They would have to see, but meanwhile, they had smugglers to find.

She opened her eyes as the curricle rolled past a gap in the hedge to her right. Through it, in the distance, she glimpsed Bigfield House. She'd missed luncheon in order to cram all the tasks for her day into the few hours before Christopher came to fetch her; she hadn't completed absolutely everything, but hopefully, she'd done enough.

"I'm sure they can manage for one afternoon."

Christopher's dry comment had her facing forward. After a second, she replied, "We'll see."

Their destination was Hastings, where Christopher hoped to find men he knew who used to run with the local smuggling gang.

She wondered how he'd come by the acquaintance, but before she could ask, he slowed his horses to a walk and turned right, into one of her uncle's fields. She blinked. "Did you forget something?" Was he intending to turn his horses?

"No." He nodded ahead. "The gypsies are camped farther down the meadow, and Aaron, Gracella, and their band have just finished traveling and working through the Weald east of here." Christopher met her eyes. "Gypsies have a very efficient communication system, so before we go rattling off to Hastings, it won't hurt to ask if they've heard any relevant whispers. They might be able to pinpoint the area in which it would be most profitable to search."

Thinking of the earlier meeting, she frowned. "You didn't tell them that the contact we're hoping to identify by watching Goffard Hall might be a smuggler?"

He shook his head. "The point didn't arise, and regardless, I wouldn't want to direct our watchers to think it was only smugglers—people who look like smugglers—they need to watch for. We don't know who might turn up with those notes."

Ahead, Ellen saw ten gaily painted wagons drawn up in an arc above the stream. Her curiosity reared its head, and she returned an amenable "Ah—I see."

She was more than happy to visit the gypsy camp. Besides, Gracella had invited her to take tea.

Christopher halted his pair twenty yards from the nearest wagon. Several children came running up. After greeting him and Ellen politely —the children already knew their names—the two oldest boys offered to hold the horses.

After descending and handing over the reins, Christopher rounded the curricle and gave Ellen his hand.

She'd been studying the girls, who had congregated on her side of the carriage; they'd been unabashedly examining her, transparently fascinated by her ribbons and rosettes.

Ellen gripped his hand and descended. While she twitched her skirts straight, he looked at the oldest girl. "We would like to speak with Mrs. Codona and Aaron."

Although patently reluctant to cut short her scrutiny of Ellen, the girl nodded, turned, and ran to the wagons.

The other girls pressed close about Ellen: one, greatly daring, put out a finger and touched one ribbon rosette. The girl smiled up at Ellen. "They are pretty—and you are pretty, too."

Ellen smiled. "Thank you." She considered the rosettes around her hem, then confessed, "My aunt likes to see me in ribbons and bows and frills." She lightly shrugged. "I don't mind."

The girls grinned, as if mention of an aunt had struck a chord.

Christopher offered his arm, Ellen laid her hand on his sleeve, and they set off across the grass with the gaggle of children as escort.

The oldest girl had vanished around the wagon Christopher knew was Gracella's and Aaron's; before he and Ellen had reached the first wagon in the arc, the girl came racing up.

She halted before them. "Great-grandmama says welcome and please come to her wagon."

The red-and-gold-painted wagon sat in the center of the arc, its steps facing the distant gate. Several yards before the wagon's steps was a ring of stones enclosing a large fire pit in which a small fire licked the base of a kettle hung over it.

Gracella sat in state in a wicker chair set before the fire. Stools of various shapes and sizes ranged to either side.

Ellen was looking about her, curiosity stamped all over her face. As Christopher led her forward, the children danced around them, chattering, laughing, and staring, then two boys ran ahead to place stools for the visitors to either side of Gracella's throne.

Christopher halted before Gracella and half bowed. "Mrs. Codona. Thank you for seeing us."

Gracella favored him with a nod, but immediately, her bright eyes moved to Ellen, and a smile wreathed her face. "I am pleased you have come—you will take tea, yes?"

Ellen darted a swift glance at Christopher and answered, "With pleasure, ma'am."

Gracella waved them to the stools the boys had arranged and rattled off a string of orders to the older girls. They dashed off, climbing the steps into Gracella's wagon in search of the requirements to make tea.

"Now"—Gracella looked from Ellen to Christopher—"while the young ones are preparing the tea, you can ask me what it is you wish to know."

Christopher wasn't surprised by her directness. "While the others are keeping watch on Goffard Hall, we thought to see if we can learn who is ferrying the illegal package from the coast to the Hall. We believe a smuggling gang is involved. Before we"—with a tip of his head, he included Ellen—"head to the coast and start making inquiries, I thought to ask if you, Aaron, or your people had heard any whisper of recent smuggling activity in the areas through which you've traveled this season."

He'd forgotten that Aaron and most of the other adults would be out working, but if any of the band had heard anything, Gracella would know.

She looked mildly intrigued, but shook her head. "No—of that, we have heard nothing. In fact, I would say we have not heard of any smuggling in these parts, in this county, for…perhaps as many as ten or twenty years. Not since Aaron was a small boy and my husband was leader of our group."

Christopher tipped his head in thanks. "It was a long shot, but I would have felt foolish had I driven to the coast, only later to find that you already had the answers."

Gracella nodded regally. "It was wise to check, and besides"—she turned her smile on Ellen—"now we may have our tea."

The girls bustled around, setting out glasses and an ornate teapot on a lacquered tray. After carefully pouring boiling water from the kettle into the pot, they carried the tray to Gracella.

She inspected their efforts, then nodded approvingly, poured the rose-colored tea into the small glasses, doctored each with a dollop of honey and stirred it in, then indicated that the girl holding the tray should offer glasses to Christopher and Ellen.

Once they each had a glass, Gracella accepted the last and dismissed the girls, commending them on their performance, bringing relieved and happy smiles to their faces.

She waved the bevy away. "Off now and let us have some peace."

In a swirling horde, the group ran off toward the stream.

Ellen noticed Gracella's gaze following the children. She sipped, then couldn't resist asking, "Are they all related to you?"

Gracella glanced at her, then smiled. "In one way or another." After a second, she went on, "We Romany travel in bands, and at least in this country, the members of each band are more or less family." She tipped her head toward the children. "Five of the eleven are my great-grandchildren, and the others are great-nephews or great-nieces. It makes it natural for me to watch over them while their parents are working in the fields. The children pay me all due attention, and the parents know I will not fail them—they are my flesh and blood."

Ellen looked around. "So this"—she waved at the gathered wagons —"is really a big family community, much like many large farms or tiny villages. The only real difference is that this one moves every month or so."

Gracella grinned and nodded. "This is true. We are just like any other family."

"Perhaps bigger than most," Ellen said, "but people are people, so the same rules apply."

Gracella switched her gaze to Christopher. "This one is wiser than most. She does not leap to judge, but she looks, and most importantly, she sees."

Christopher met Ellen's eyes and smiled. "Indeed."

Blushing, Ellen raised her glass and sipped.

They drank their tea and talked of the harvest and the state of the farms around about. Ellen noted that if Christopher wanted to know how his neighbors' crops were faring, all he need do was ask the gypsies; they missed nothing—not even the repairs to the Bigfield House goat pen!

Once they'd finished their tea, she and Christopher rose, and she thanked Gracella for her hospitality. "The tea was delicious, and I'm glad to have seen your camp for myself."

Gracella smiled contentedly and graciously waved them on their way. While walking to the curricle, Ellen glanced back and saw Gracella strolling toward the stream, resuming her eagle-eyed supervision of the children.

Christopher handed her up to the seat. She was pleased to note that her previously ridiculously leaping nerves had steadied; while they still tensed in anticipation of his touch, now, when that touch came, their reaction was more like a happy purr.

He reclaimed the reins from the boys, tossed them a penny each, then climbed up and set the chestnuts walking out of the field.

"If I've understood correctly"—still curious, she glanced one last time around the camp—"this band moves around the county as the harvest and the consequent need for their labor dictates."

He nodded. "I'm not sure where this group winters these days, but in this area, we see them first for the cherry harvest in July. Then they move to a few other areas and return about now as the hops, and then the apples, and eventually the plums ripen."

She arched her brows. "We don't grow cherries." She glanced inquisitively at him. "Does the manor?"

He shook his head as he guided the horses out of the gate and into the lane. "We specialize in hops and apples. Bigfield has some hops, lots of apples, and a damson orchard, but the damsons won't be ready to harvest until at least the end of September, after the hops and most of the apples are in."

"That's a relief! Before the gypsies arrived, I was wondering how we were going to manage just to harvest the hops, never mind all the rest."

He'd set his horses trotting freely, and the curricle was once more bowling along. "We—the manor and Bigfield House—usually pool our workers for the harvest. Normally, the manor's crops are ready a few days before yours, so we combine your workers and Aaron's band with our men and get the job done, then we all head across the road and get the Bigfield House crop in." He shrugged. "It's been that way for decades, at least since I was a boy."

"That sounds an eminently sensible approach." She glanced at his face. "I hope we can continue the tradition."

He briefly met her eyes and smiled. "If you and your brother agree, I see no reason why we can't."

She smiled and looked ahead. The news that the entire harvest would occur more or less by rote was a significant relief.

Christopher returned his gaze to his horses. "Incidentally, Sir Humphrey always loved to see his hops brought in." He glanced fleetingly her way. "You might think about bringing him down to the fields on one of the days we're harvesting. I'm sure he'd enjoy that."

"That's an excellent idea. Poor Uncle Humphrey doesn't get out enough—I'll get Partridge to organize it. Perhaps make a picnic of it."

Christopher slowed his horses as they reached the village and found themselves facing the Bull Inn. He turned the chestnuts left, onto the main village lane but heading east, away from the village. He set the horses trotting quickly along the better-surfaced lane, which afforded a fairly straight run between ripening orchards and fields to the town of Rolvenden. There, he turned south, onto the Hastings Road.

With smooth macadam beneath the wheels and the way ahead clear, he let the chestnuts stretch their legs, and they fairly flew along.

The wind ruffled his hair and tugged determinedly at Ellen's bonnet.

She clutched it to her head, then grasped the dangling ribbons and tied them beneath her chin. "At least these wretched ribbons can be useful for something other than just bouncing about my ears," she muttered.

He laughed and let the horses race on.

An hour later, he tooled the curricle down the last stretch of the London Road toward the Hastings seafront and turned in under the arch of the Royal Sussex Arms, one of the better coaching inns.

In the yard, he gave the reins into the care of an attentive groom with orders to feed and water the chestnuts, then rounded the curricle and helped Ellen down.

Predictably, she was looking about her with open curiosity, transparently interested in all she could see. He took her arm, steadying her over the cobbles as he guided her back through the archway to the street. He halted on the pavement in front of the inn; while Ellen looked interestedly up and down what was one of Hastings's busiest streets, he wondered how best to handle the situation—meaning manage her.

In the end, when she glanced at him and arched a brow, patently inquiring as to what came next, he opted for the unvarnished truth. "I need to go to a tavern by the waterfront." He tipped his head toward the end of the road, beyond which lay the sea. "At this hour, the men I know should be there, but the tavern—that whole area—is a rough sort of place.

Definitely no place for a lady, and I wouldn't be at all comfortable taking you there."

He steeled himself for her arguments—that she could come and wait in the street, watch through a window, or some such notion.

Instead, she smiled quite happily. "That's all right—I'll amuse myself by looking in that shop." With one gloved finger, she pointed to a haber-dashery on the other side of the street. "And once I finish there"—she glanced at the inn—"I'll order some tea and wait in the inn's parlor until you return."

She lifted wide, golden-hazel eyes to his face. "If that will suit?"

Ellen registered Christopher's surprise at her sudden interest in frip-peries, but it would take too long to explain what lay behind it, and it was hardly a topic a gentleman would be interested in. So she waited, and eventually, he dipped his head in acceptance.

"Very well. That seems…sensible."

He sounded distinctly suspicious, which made her smile all the more. Really, what did he think she was going to get up to in a haberdashery?

He continued to hold her arm as they crossed the busy street and halted before the haberdashery's door. Releasing her, he caught her eye. "I'll be back, certainly within the hour, but most likely earlier."

She continued to smile brightly. "I'll be waiting, sipping tea in the inn parlor."

With that, she opened the shop door and stepped inside, leaving him, apparently still suspicious and faintly befuddled, on the pavement.

Christopher eyed the door she closed behind her, then shook his head, turned, and strode rapidly down the street. The faster he dealt with his inquiries, the sooner he could return and learn what she was up to.

The Old Dolphin Tavern in George Street was exactly as he remem-bered it, with low beams across the ceiling, smoke-stained walls, and a long, well-worn, highly polished bar counter.

He leaned on the counter and, while the barman tended to another customer, squinted through the fug of tobacco smoke that wreathed the taproom. He spotted his quarry in the far corner, hunched over a table.

The barman came up, and smiling, Christopher ordered three pints of the tavern's ale. After paying the barman, he hefted the three large mugs and made his way between the intervening tables to the far corner.

As he neared, the pair of ancient mariners seated at the table looked up, eyes narrowing in suspicion and distrust—then they recognized him, saw what he was carrying, and their faces split into wide grins.

"Christopher, old son!" Old Edgar reached out to claim one of the pints Christopher set down. "You're quite a sight for these old eyes of mine."

"Aye." Cam, Edgar's younger brother, reached for a mug. "A reminder of the good ole days and all." As Christopher pulled up a chair, Cam raised his mug to him. "Here's to you, matey!"

Christopher grinned, sat, and raised the third mug.

After a suitable pause for refreshment, Edgar lowered his mug with a satisfied "Aah." He focused his old yet still bright eyes on Christopher. "So what brings you here, heh?"

Christopher set down his mug and met Edgar's gaze. He'd spent long minutes during the drive deciding on the best way to broach his subject. "There have been suggestions, you might say from on high, that at least one of the old smuggling gangs has started up again."

The brothers pulled surprised faces and looked at each other, then Edgar said, "Haven't heard anything about that."

Christopher arched his brows. "No whispers of any activity around Hastings?"

"Nope." Edgar shook his head definitively. "Ain't none of us plying that trade these days. Not for the past ten years and more. Besides"—shrewdly, he studied Christopher—"what would anyone be smuggling?"

Christopher grimaced. "I'm not free to answer that, but I can say that anyone becoming involved in this latest sort of trade would be very ill-advised."

"Hmm." Edgar slowly nodded. "I'll pass that on, but truth be told, there's not anything going on around here."

Christopher accepted that with a tip of his head. Edgar was the oldest representative of the erstwhile smuggling fraternity, and if there was anyone—no matter who they were—running goods in through Hastings and the beaches around the town, Edgar would know of it.

"Only cargo we run these days is fish," Cam said. "And let me tell you, there's no excitement in that!"

Christopher grinned and spent the next twenty minutes chatting about others—including his brother, Gregory, and several well-heeled friends who had run with the gang years ago—and reliving close escapes from the local excisemen.

After buying the old sailors another round, Christopher left them deep in reminiscences and walked back to the Royal Sussex Arms.

There, exactly as she'd said she would be, he found Ellen in the inn's parlor, sipping tea and staring meditatively out of the window at the haberdashery across the street.

He sat in the chair opposite, drawing her gaze. He arched his brows. "Did you find what you wanted?" He could see no sign of any purchase.

She smiled and lowered her cup. "I did, as it happens. I wanted to compare the price of something I'd seen in the shop in the village." She waved dismissively. "Pure curiosity." Her eyes met his, and her smile deepened. "As you've probably noticed by now, curiosity is my besetting sin."

He arched his brows cynically and allowed her to pour him a cup of tea.

Ellen waited until they were bowling along, heading toward Benenden once more, before she asked, "Did you locate the men you'd hoped to find, and if so, what did you learn?"

"I found them, but they were very sure there's been no smuggling activity of any sort around Hastings and environs recently."

She considered, then asked, "How reliable is their information?"

"If Old Edgar says there's been no activity on what was—and arguably still is—his patch, then there hasn't been."

Curiosity jabbed and jabbed, until she asked, "How did you come to know them—Old Edgar and whoever else was there?"

His lips quirked in a wry smile. He whipped up his horses, took a rising curve in style, then eased the pair to a steady pace. "When we were younger, my brother and I joined the Hastings smuggling gang."

"The gang this Old Edgar ran?"

"Along with his brother, Cam." He paused, then went on, "We only went on two runs. It was brandy they still smuggled in those days, but even then, smuggling was a dying trade—nothing like it used to be in the glory days of Edgar and Cam's youth."

"Was it exciting—being on a run?"

He shrugged. "Exciting enough, but a liking for being involved in illicit endeavors wasn't what drew us—it was more peer pressure of a sort. Back then, as it had been in my father's day, joining a smuggling gang and going on a few runs was a rite of passage for the local young men of the aristocracy or gentry families hereabouts."

He drove on for several moments, she sensed in reflective mood.

Eventually, he added, "As far as I know, although we all participated, none of us were ever more than hands on a few runs." A rueful grin on his lips, he glanced fleetingly at her. "In reality, the experience wasn't as thrilling as our imaginations had painted it."

She arched her brows. "I suspect that's the case with most of the larks young gentlemen get up to."

He smiled and dipped his head. "Touché."

They bowled along at a cracking pace. Ellen sat back, hearing the wind rush past her ears, and thought of the logical next steps. "There are other towns along this coast that are home to smugglers, aren't there?"

He nodded. "And yes, we'll have to check there."

"Where is 'there'?"

"The information we have is that the French delivered the package of notes somewhere between Deal and Hastings. For various reasons, not least of which is increased naval activity, Deal is unlikely these days, and we now know that Hastings isn't involved. Logically, the next place we should investigate is Rye. As you travel around the coast, Rye is roughly halfway between Hastings and Deal, and it's also a town with a long history of smugglers."

She recognized a farmhouse; Rolvenden was not far ahead. A short while before, she'd heard a church clock strike five times; they would soon be home and parting for the day. "So," she said, "Rye tomorrow."

She made it a statement, not a question, and didn't look his way.

Nevertheless, she felt his gaze touch her face, then he looked back at the road. Several moments ticked past before he capitulated. "If we go tomorrow, we should set off in the morning, just in case we turn up nothing at Rye and need to cast our net farther."

She caught his gaze as he glanced her way. "And where is 'farther'?"

He smiled and looked ahead. "There are marshes beyond Rye— Walland Marsh to the east and, to the north of that, Romney Marsh itself. Along the Kent coast, the marshes arguably have the longest and oldest association with smugglers."

"Do you know people there you can ask for information on smuggling activity?"

He nodded, then amended, "Or more correctly, I know *where* to ask."

To be able to leave in the morning, she would have to cram all her day's duties into a couple of hours, but his suggestion of leaving then made sense. Regardless, she wasn't about to let him go alone. "All right. Shall we say ten o'clock?" When he tipped his head in agreement, she added, "I'll do what I can to placate everyone in time to leave then."

Christopher glanced at her, saw the expression of concerted plotting that had overlaid her delicate features, and accepted that she'd meant her last comment literally. He was starting to suspect that, beyond her attempts to keep reasonable order and have everything rolling on as it should on the Bigfield House estate, she'd become the lynchpin that held the household together in the face of Sir Humphrey's decline.

"Let's make it ten-thirty," he said. That would give her a little more time. "I need to discuss things with Radley before absenting myself for another day."

Not entirely true—George Radley was reliable capability personified —but not a complete lie, either. While he was in charge, Christopher liked to keep his finger on the pulse of the estate.

Unsurprisingly, Ellen readily agreed to the later time.

While slowing to negotiate the streets of Rolvenden, then the turn to Benenden, Christopher made a mental note to have a quiet word with Robbie. In Christopher's estimation, Robbie was quite old enough to start actively taking on some of the responsibilities that currently rested squarely on his sister's much slighter shoulders.

CHAPTER 8

At eleven-thirty the next morning, Christopher tooled his curricle at a spanking pace down the road to Rye. Despite the lack of progress yesterday, he was in a buoyant mood.

He glanced at Ellen as she sat alongside him, her face tilted up to the breeze. It was another fine day, with the sun shining brightly out of a clear blue sky, and she was smiling.

He was, too. He looked forward, glad that he'd seized the chance that had offered yesterday, after he'd dropped Ellen off at Bigfield House; he'd been heading out along the drive when he'd spotted Robbie riding in the field alongside. He'd halted his horses, hallooed, and waved. Robbie had seen him and come riding over.

A short discussion of how matters were playing out at Bigfield House had convinced Christopher that Ellen's brother was no less capable than she, but until now, Robbie had lacked positive encouragement to take on more of the managerial tasks beyond those Ellen assigned him.

Christopher hoped he'd remedied that. Although both he and Robbie acknowledged the necessity for subtlety and tact in gradually transferring the weight of the estate from Ellen's shoulders to Robbie's, they now had a plan and some hope of a favorable outcome. Christopher had parted from Ellen's brother with a reassurance that if Robbie needed advice at any point, he should feel free to call at the manor. Christopher had confirmed he expected to remain in residence for the foreseeable future.

"I meant to ask"—Ellen swiped back the loose tendrils of hair plus ribbons that had blown across her cheek—"has anything occurred at Goffard Hall?"

"Nothing unusual, just deliveries from the local butcher and fishmonger, which our staff assure us are regular events." Christopher grimaced. "Not that I would imagine a butcher or fishmonger the sort of tradesman likely to be asked to ferry counterfeit notes, but regardless, we had people close enough to view through field glasses what was handed over at the back door, and no package that might have been notes was passed on."

She leaned back against the seat. "So our journey today might yet yield useful information."

"Indeed. The possibility is definitely worth our time."

Ellen stared down the road. Initially, they'd taken the same road as yesterday, but south of Newenden, they'd turned east for Rye. She'd never visited the town, but deciding she would see it soon enough, rather than asking for any description, she turned her curiosity in another direction. "You've mentioned your brother, Gregory, and a sister who I take it is married. Do you have any other siblings?"

Christopher shook his head. "Only those two—Gregory and our younger sister, Therese."

"How much younger?"

"She'll be twenty-eight later this year."

"And she's married?"

"Yes, to Devlin Cader. He's the Earl of Alverton."

"An *earl*?"

At her exclamation, Christopher glanced at her, mildly amused. "Despite not being lords and ladies, we are part of a ducal dynasty, so yes, Therese married an earl."

She frowned and tried to hold back the words, but they tumbled from her lips. "Does that mean you're expected to marry"—she gestured —"some noble lady?"

He was silent for a moment, and her heart—stupid thing—sank. Then he tipped his head pensively. "I suppose others in like circumstances might have such an expectation thrust upon them, but I'm a Cynster, so such considerations don't apply."

What does that mean? She told herself that she shouldn't have asked the first question; she couldn't possibly be so lost to all propriety as to ask the second.

While she was debating—wrestling with her ever-unruly curiosity, given extra strength where he was concerned—he said, "So tell me about your life prior to coming to Bigfield House. You lived in London, in a house in Belgravia, I think you said. Did you always live there?"

She nodded. "That was the house Robbie and I were born in, and we lived there, in London, until we moved down here. That's why Robbie and I have no real idea of country ways. Prior to our relocating here, the only places outside London we'd visited were Bath and Cheltenham, and when we were young, Brighton and, once, Margate." She huffed. "Not by any stretch of one's imagination could such visits be considered appropriate preparation for the challenges of managing the Bigfield House estate."

Christopher looked at her and smiled encouragingly. "Given such a background, you're both managing well. I haven't heard any complaints from the Bigfield House people."

"They're very loyal and therefore ready to support us come what may and to excuse our failures."

"I seriously doubt you've had any real failures," he said bracingly. "Perhaps a hiccup or two, like the goats getting free."

They drove on for a moment, then, with his eyes on the road ahead, he mused, "I have to admit I can't really imagine not knowing the ins and outs of country life. I was born at the manor and spent all my early childhood there. London was a place we visited often—my grandparents have a house in Berkeley Square. And of course, later, I spent the Seasons in town, but most of every year would be spent in the country, not always in Kent but hunting, shooting, fishing with friends, visiting relatives, that sort of thing." He paused, then said, "In short, I'm more country-bred than town-bred." Briefly, he glanced at her. "You might be town-bred, with scant previous experience of the country, but you've lived at Bigfield House for the past ten or so months. If, now, you were given the choice of living in the country or living in London, which would you choose?"

She expected to have to think, to consider, but to her surprise, the answer sprang, immediate and definite, to her tongue. "I'd rather stay here. I might not have previously experienced country life, but now I have...well, even with the pressures of managing the estate and shielding Uncle Humphrey, I would still choose to live here."

She drew breath and acknowledged the truth of that statement. Wonderingly, she went on, "It's the...rhythm of things, of the seasons, I think. I've experienced a full cycle now, from autumn to summer, and there's something reassuring and settling about having a known, predetermined progression of events that happen every year, like the harvests, the pruning, the tilling and sowing." She glanced at him. "London has seasons, but none of the regimen of seasonal tasks to mark them. That makes a difference, at least to me."

He nodded. "Those seasonal tasks are what connects us to the land. Town dwellers lack that."

She nodded emphatically. "Exactly."

Cottages appeared along the sides of the road. She looked around. "Is this Rye?"

"The outskirts. We'll be in the center soon."

While his passenger looked curiously about her, Christopher steered the chestnuts to the Old Bell Inn. After consigning the horses into the ostler's care, he handed Ellen down and escorted her into the inn.

He guided her to a table by the window in the main taproom. With her eyes, she was drinking in all the features of the inn—the low beams, the horse brasses, the rows of tankards on a shelf. The "old" in the inn's name wasn't an affectation; the place was genuinely ancient.

She sat and brought her gaze to his face; he'd remained standing by the table. "Is this the inn where you're going to ask about smugglers, or is that a different place?"

"No, this is the place." He glanced around. "In times past, this was a notorious smugglers' den. Excisemen raided it innumerable times, but it never shut down. Even now, with smuggling all but dead, as you can see, the place has survived and appears to be thriving." He met her eyes and grinned. "That's probably due to the landlord's ale."

She threw him a look, but then eagerly asked, "So who are we here to see?"

"The old man behind the bar. He hasn't seen me yet, but once he does, he'll recognize me."

She looked at the wizened figure, head down behind the bar as he busily polished glasses. He'd barely cast them a glance when they'd entered. "Can I come and listen?"

"He won't talk as freely if you're beside me." Christopher smiled. "You'll distract him." She unquestionably would. Today, her bonnet was festooned with bronze ribbons and ostrich feathers, and more feathers and ribbons adorned the fake lapels of her neatly fitting carriage dress. "But if you stay here, you'll be able to hear what we say quite clearly. The sound carries in funny ways in this place."

She nodded in reluctant agreement. As he turned away, she folded her hands on the table and pretended to look out of the window.

Christopher made his way to the long bar counter and leaned on the polished surface opposite the old man. "Good morning, Sam."

Sam Winkle looked up, blinked, and peered myopically, then his face cleared. "Mr. Cynster, as I live and breathe!" Sam's gaze cut to the figure at the table by the window. "What's brought you this way, sir?"

"This and that, but how's tricks with you, Sam?"

"Oh, I can't complain, sir—the inn keeps me busy, and the missus keeps me in line. Did you hear the Mermaid's under new management, as they say?"

"Indeed?" Christopher paused, then asked, "Given the connection, will that make any difficulties for you here?"

"Oh, I doubt it, sir—the new folk there seem just as keen to make the most of our shared past. We're talking of running tours through the tunnel and all—dress things up a bit and make it exciting. Plenty of folks want to know about smuggling, these days."

"Is that so?" Christopher wondered if there was more to that remark than the obvious. "I was over at Hastings yesterday and caught up with Old Edgar and Cam."

"Oh, aye, and how're they keeping?"

Christopher replied and used the answer to lead to his reason for being there. "I went to Hastings to ask Edgar and Cam if they'd heard of any recent runs or any whispers of any of the old gangs becoming active again."

Sam blinked. "Really?" He continued to slowly polish a glass. "Wouldn't have thought there'd be enough profit in it, these days. That's why we all disbanded years ago."

Christopher nodded. "The authorities have started asking questions because someone told them a dangerous cargo is or recently has been run in via the Kent coast." He pinned his gaze on Sam's face. "So I've come to ask you as well, Sam—have you heard any whispers of any sort at all about a recent run? One recently completed, in progress, or anticipated?"

Sam's lips pursed, and he shook his head. "I haven't heard a single whisper." He met Christopher's eyes. "And that's God's truth, sir. I don't want no excisemen turning up here again—it's bad for business."

Christopher read Sam's eyes and accepted that as truth. "If there had been a run anywhere near, you would have heard, wouldn't you?"

Sam hesitated, but then nodded. "Aye—anywhere from Camber

around to Winchelsea Beach, and I'd've heard. And any run west of Winchelsea, Old Edgar would know about."

Christopher nodded. "I'll let those asking the questions know that from Hastings to Camber is clear."

"Aye," Sam said. "Whatever it is that's being run, we're not involved."

"I'm glad." Christopher straightened and glanced at Ellen, who was doing her best to look disinterested in their exchange. "I'll have a pint of your ale, Sam, and perhaps a half of cider for the lady."

Sam moved to the taps. "We've a nice drop of cider from up your way. Think she'll like that?"

"Let's see. And have a pint yourself as well." Christopher scanned the blackboard listing the inn's fare for the day. When Sam set the two glasses on the bar, Christopher nodded at the board. "What do you suggest?"

"The missus's game pie can't be beat."

Christopher picked up the glasses and tipped his head toward Ellen. "I'll see what she thinks."

When he set the glasses on the table, she peered at the one before her, then raised her eyes to his face in question.

"Cider," he confirmed, claiming the chair opposite hers. "Try it."

Obediently, she sipped. Then she sipped again and smiled. "That's very pleasant."

He grinned and sampled his ale, then said, "You can't live in Kent and not drink cider." He set down the glass. "Did you hear?"

"Yes. Surprisingly well." She directed a curious look at Sam. "Did you run with these smugglers as well?"

"No. But Gregory and I used to come here of a winter's evening, along with many other young men of the same age, and listen to Sam's tales. He was the leader of one of the largest and most active gangs in his day, and the stories he told were…well, for us, utterly riveting."

Christopher read the open interest in her eyes and grinned. "For instance, that tunnel Sam mentioned."

She nodded eagerly. "In connection with the Mermaid Inn—perhaps literally?"

"Indeed. Both the Old Bell and the Mermaid Inn were known haunts of the infamous Hawkhurst gang. The Mermaid lies a block south of here, and there's an underground passage that links the Mermaid's cellars to the cellars here. That passage was often used by smugglers to escape raids by the authorities and also to move contraband. Because the excisemen never had enough men to mount raids on both inns simultaneously, if they raided the Old Bell, the smugglers would escape via the passage and through the Mermaid and vice versa."

"Ha!" Ellen sat back and looked about her with newfound appreciation. "So this place is steeped in smuggling history." She refocused on Christopher. "And old Sam there would have heard if there'd been any recent activity nearby."

Christopher nodded decisively. "He most definitely would have."

A young barmaid approached to ask if they wanted to order any food. Christopher mentioned the game pie, and nothing loath, Ellen agreed.

The girl whisked away and promptly returned with two steaming servings.

Ellen nibbled at her first bite, then smiled and dug her fork deeper. "This is delicious."

"Mmm" was all the reply Christopher made.

They chewed, swallowed, and sipped, then pushing away her empty plate, Ellen sighed and smiled. "You're introducing me to new experiences—drinking cider and eating game pie in a smugglers' den in Rye."

He grinned. "We have to get you acclimatized to living in rural Kent."

With their meal finished, they rose. Christopher paused by the bar to pay their shot and make his farewells to Sam, then side by side, they walked out into the sunshine.

Ellen halted on the pavement and looked at Christopher. "Now what?"

He was looking across the street. "Let's take a walk." He caught her hand, twined her arm in his, and started them across the road. "There's a place nearby from which we can see the surrounding countryside laid out before us. In the interests of furthering your education into the wonders of Kent, from there, you'll get an unparalleled view and an excellent notion of the lie of the land, especially with regard to the marshes."

He didn't volunteer anything more, and she didn't ask. She and her curiosity trusted he would deliver on his promise.

They climbed a sloping street, which led to a church—St. Mary's—and to her surprise, Christopher led her inside to the bell tower and urged her up the stairs.

Holding the front of her skirts high, she climbed, wary of her footing on the narrow stone steps. "I'm surprised the tower's left open."

"It's always open." Christopher was following close behind. "If there's a ship in trouble or any emergency along the coast, someone will come running up here to look."

They walked along an enclosed corridor, past the large bells, then had to negotiate a short ladder. On reaching the top, they emerged onto the tower's roof, and she immediately understood why he'd brought her up there.

The view was utterly breathtaking.

"That's Rye Castle." He pointed to a collection of pale stone towers a short distance away. "And that's the river leading to the sea." The silvery ribbon snaked away into the haze obscuring the Channel.

Ellen halted before the stone parapet. The town clustered all around, a skirt of warm red bricks and tiles. Beyond the town's boundaries, the fields were largely flat, except for the rise of an escarpment to the north.

Christopher waved toward the distant rise. "That's the southern edge of the Weald."

She looked to the south, then scanned the landscape around to the east. At that height, the wind was stronger and whipped her bonnet ribbons about her face. She raised her voice to ask, "Are those the marshes?" The land was flatter than any stretch she could remember seeing; it appeared to run horizontally into the distant gray-blue line of the sea.

"Yes. And yes, that is the Channel you can see in the distance."

She took her time appreciating the views. He made no move to hurry her; leaning against the parapet, he watched her with a rather smug smile on his face.

Eventually, she returned to stand beside him. "So"—she held back whipping tendrils of her hair—"is there some other town we should visit? It's only just after two o'clock."

They'd heard the town's bells ringing a few minutes before. She'd been glad the huge bells below their feet hadn't joined in.

Christopher looked to the east. "As we've heard nothing thus far—meaning there's been no smuggling of any kind between Hastings and Rye—we should check at Lydd." He caught Ellen's gaze. "It's a tiny place, isolated and surrounded by marshland. It's also on one of the oldest smuggling routes, and if our modern-day smugglers wanted to escape notice, then Lydd is arguably the place with the least number of other people about to see anything at all."

Ellen's chin set determinedly. "Lydd it is, then." She waved at the trapdoor and the ladder leading down. "Shall we make a start?"

Getting down the tower took almost as long as climbing up had;

Christopher insisted on going first down the long stretch of narrow stone steps, in case Ellen stumbled and fell. But eventually, they reached the ground without mishap. After returning to the inn and reclaiming his curricle, he set his pair trotting out of the town on the Ashford Road. On reaching the hamlet of East Guldeford, Christopher turned his horses onto the lane that led to Camber and, ultimately, Lydd.

After the first mile, Ellen had a better understanding of what he'd meant by "isolated." Gradually, the roadway rose higher than the land through which it passed. There were few trees to be seen, and those that clung stoically to life were stunted and bent by the strafing winds. The coarse grass grew in spiky tufts apparently unpalatable to livestock, of which there was a striking lack. Indeed, as they bowled along, everywhere she looked seemed eerily devoid of life. Even in summer, this was a bleak and desolate landscape. In winter... The thought made her shiver.

The lane angled to the sea, passing through a cluster of cottages that Christopher informed her was the hamlet of Camber, before running parallel to the shore for some way. Low sand dunes lay between the roadway and the shore, blocking all sight of the waves, yet affording little protection from the strong sea breeze.

Eventually, the lane turned inland, skirting several small lakes before finally reaching Lydd.

The village was a conglomeration of stone cottages clustered tightly together as if to better withstand the buffeting of the elements. Christopher guided his pair along the narrow cobblestone street toward the village's center, then turned in under the arch of the George Hotel.

Ellen was very ready to get out of the wind. Christopher escorted her to the taproom—a cozy and comfortable space with tables set before windows that looked out on the street, while other tables were arrayed before a presently empty fireplace.

After seating Ellen at a table close to the bar, Christopher went to the counter to order tea—and to fall into conversation with the barman and the three locals propping up the counter, all of whom greeted him by name.

After ordering a tea tray for Ellen, Christopher signaled the barman to supply drinks all around.

While pretending to idly scan the street, Ellen found she could easily listen in to the ensuing exchange.

"Nah," one of two ancients said in reply to Christopher's query about recent smuggling activity. The old man picked up the mug the barman set before him. "And even if someone were to come along with a job, we're all too old for that caper now."

That, Ellen thought, was entirely believable.

Christopher persisted. "You haven't heard any whisper of a run coming through anywhere around here?"

The second ancient, a grizzled, heavy man, took a slurp of his ale and shook his head. "Not a chirp." He looked sharply at the middle-aged man beside him. "What about you, Clyde, m'lad? Any of you younger lot got your sticky fingers into any pies?"

At a guess, Clyde was in his fifties. "Nah, Dave—no sense in it these days." Clyde looked at Christopher. "Though your question makes me wonder what this run you're searching for was ferrying."

From the corner of her eye, Ellen saw Christopher meet Clyde's gaze. "Trust me—that's one of those things you don't want to know."

The tea tray arrived, and she accepted it with a quick smile. She poured herself a cup while continuing to listen to the conversation at the bar.

"Aye, well." The first ancient raised his mug to Christopher. "You're one as has never steered us wrong, so we'll take that as a warning. If we hear anything, we'll send word."

Christopher inclined his head in thanks. He was about to push away from the counter when the barman—who'd been silently listening to the exchange—volunteered, "This might be nothin', but you speaking of runs like used to come through here put me in mind of it. Old Mrs. Withers, she who lives in one of the cottages down by the church and comes in every now and then for a glass of port of an evening, was in here only last Sunday, sitting right there"—the barman nodded to where Ellen sat sipping her tea—"and going on about hearing the clop of ponies in the night, just like when she was a child. She said it gave her a right turn. Well, we all thought she'd been dreaming, although she swore blind she hadn't been."

Dave grunted. "She *was* dreaming, like as not." But after a moment, Dave raised his small, hard eyes and met Christopher's gaze. "But in case she wasn't, we'll ask around the boys, just to make sure no one's tramping through our patch. Still, like Alf said, I can't see any of our lot —nor their sons, either—getting into the game again. Like you said, the stuff anyone would want to smuggle these days is too damned risky."

"And," Alf added, as if setting the seal on it, "not enough profit in it for us."

Christopher thanked all four, paid for another round, then quit the bar for the table where Ellen sat. He drew out the chair facing her. "You heard."

It wasn't a question, but she nodded and drained her cup. "Perhaps we should go and speak to Mrs. Withers."

He grimaced. "I doubt she'll be able to tell us any fact we haven't already heard." He paused, then met Ellen's bright, inquiring eyes. "I was more interested in where Mrs. Withers lives."

Those bright eyes opened wide. "Near the church?"

He nodded. Leaning his forearms on the table, he gazed out of the window as he thought things through. "Churches were often used as temporary stores, and All Saints' Church"—he tipped his head along the street—"in the center of Lydd, was well known as being one such smugglers' storehouse. It's only two miles from the beach—either beach, south or east. The smugglers would meet their contacts on the sands at night, off-load the cargo, then carry the goods to All Saints' and store it there. The cargoes could only be moved at night, so on a subsequent night, the smugglers would return with ponies, load up, and ferry the cargo onward, through Kent and often all the way to London. But each night, they could only go so far, so they needed safe places to store the cargo along the way. They used to swap ponies, too, returning one lot and using different beasts borrowed from farms and estates whose owners turned a blind eye. Often the crypts of churches were used to store contraband cargoes."

Ellen straightened, the light of adventure in her eyes. "So we should investigate All Saints' Church."

Christopher glanced at the bar, only to discover that Dave, Alf, and Clyde had left. "Damn! I should have asked what spot in the church they used."

"Never mind." Ellen gathered her reticule and rose. "Let's go and see what we can find."

There was no holding her back. Christopher didn't try and kept pace beside her as she strode briskly along the pavement to the church, which was a short block away.

She marched through the lychgate, then paused on the path and surveyed the church, which stood directly before them. "Is there a crypt, do you know?"

"I don't know," he admitted, "but there'll be someplace on church grounds that was used by the gentlemen, as they were called."

She huffed and walked on.

The door creaked as he pushed it open, then followed her inside.

A clergyman—the minister, by his appearance—looked up from setting out hymnals in the pews. His face brightened at the sight of Ellen in her gaudy dress. "Can I help you?"

Ellen looked at Christopher.

He strolled forward. "I'm Christopher Cynster, from up near Tenterden." He offered his hand, and the minister gripped it.

"Reverend Alcott. I'm the vicar here."

Christopher glanced at Ellen. "This is Miss Martingale, who has lived all her life in London. I've been telling her about the smugglers who used to haunt this area."

That was all the introduction Ellen required. She leapt in to say, "I was particularly intrigued by the notion that the smugglers used church crypts and the like to store their cargoes." She opened her eyes wide. "I understand this church was often used." She looked around. "Is there a crypt here?"

Alcott was no fool. Christopher sensed Ellen's innocent façade wasn't bamboozling the minister, yet Alcott somewhat carefully replied, "There is—or rather, was—but it's been bricked up. Seepage, I gather—it was before my time."

"Oh." Ellen visibly deflated, then rallied to ask, "I don't suppose there's been any sign of smugglers recently?"

Alcott studied her for a second, then looked at Christopher. "I'm not sure what your interest is, but if you had asked me that last week, I would have laughed and assured you that all smuggling in this area was in the long-distant past. However"—he glanced at Ellen, then turned again to Christopher—"over the past few days, I've noticed a...disturbance around two large tombs in the rear corner of the graveyard. I looked through the notes left by my predecessors and learned that, in decades past, both tombs had been used as smugglers' stores."

Christopher straightened, and all pretense of airiness fell from Ellen like a discarded cloak. "What sort of disturbance?" she asked.

Alcott hesitated, then said, "Frankly, if I didn't know that the smugglers around about have been inactive for decades, I would have thought they'd returned to their old vices and were using those tombs to store contraband again." He shook his head. "But surely that's absurd."

"Speaking in general," Christopher replied, "I would agree. However, there may be a very special cargo being run in as we speak. I've been asked by the authorities to check for any signs of recent smuggling activity along this coast. Can you show us these tombs?"

Alcott eyed him assessingly, then crisply nodded. "Yes, of course." He set the stack of hymnals on a pew and waved them to a side door. "It's faster through the vestry."

Ellen and Christopher followed Alcott through the vestry and into the graveyard. The vicar led them to the rear quadrant of the church grounds, where two massive tombs raised high on plinths sat beneath the spreading branches of a towering beech.

The tops of the tombs, clearly a matched pair—presumably that of husband and wife although the inscriptions had long since worn away— were nearly as high as Ellen's shoulder.

Christopher and Ellen circled the tombs, searching for signs that the heavy stone lids had been lifted.

"Not there." Alcott pointed down, into the narrow passage between the tombs. It was just wide enough for a man to pass through. "See those scrapes on the ground? It's as if those side panels on both tombs had been opened and shut again."

Christopher and Ellen peered at the ground and saw what the sharp-eyed Alcott had spotted. Fresh grooves were cut through the sparse grass, scoring the earth beneath just enough to leave a detectable mark.

"When did you first notice the marks?" Christopher slid sideways into the gap and carefully crouched to examine the side panel on one of the tombs.

"Three days ago, on Sunday afternoon. I walk through the graveyard on my way back to the vicarage, checking that the tombs are as they should be. I noticed the first marks then."

Christopher looked up. " *First* marks?"

Features set, Alcott said, "It rained on Sunday night, and on Monday, still puzzling over the marks, I looked again, and they'd almost washed away. But those marks"—he nodded at the scoring on the ground—"are fresh. They were made last night."

Christopher had been prodding and poking at the panels, to no avail. Now, he straightened and moved out of the gap, rejoining Ellen and Alcott at the head of the tombs. "So the tombs were opened and shut again on Saturday night—and you saw the marks on Sunday, which were subsequently washed away. Then the tombs were opened and shut again last night." Christopher tipped his head at the scored ground. "Leaving fresh marks."

Alcott nodded. "I tried to find the catch for the panels, but had no more luck than you."

Christopher stared at the tombs. "I doubt there's any point in trying to open them now."

"Because whatever was hidden there has been taken away," Ellen said.

He nodded. "Something was delivered here on Saturday night—Mrs. Withers heard the ponies that night. And whatever was delivered was collected last night." He met Ellen's eyes. "Whatever it is, it's started on its journey across the county."

Alcott sighed. "So there'll be nothing there now—nothing to worry about."

"Only old bones," Ellen helpfully remarked.

"So one would hope!" Alcott huffed softly, then met Christopher's gaze. "Have the smugglers started up their trade again?"

"I don't believe so." Christopher held the vicar's gaze. "I've been asking along the coast from Hastings to here, and other than this, there's no indication whatsoever that the smuggling fraternity are thinking of setting up again. In fact, most assured me that, these days, there isn't enough profit left in smuggling to tempt any of them out of retirement."

Alcott frowned at the tombs. "But someone has used the old spot. Someone knew of it and used it again. And you said ponies were heard, too?"

Christopher nodded. "The authorities expect this to be a single event. There were likely some small runs before, but the one that's just come in is expected to be the last."

"Thank the Almighty for that," Alcott said. "I really don't fancy having to guide a flock indulging in the old trade."

Christopher exchanged a look with Ellen, then offered Alcott his hand. "Thank you for being so observant and for trusting us enough to tell us of this."

"Yes, well..." Alcott gripped his hand. "I had a feeling"—he glanced skyward—"that I should."

"In that case"—Ellen smiled and held out her hand—"thank God, indeed."

They parted from Alcott and hurried back to the George.

"Saturday night," Ellen said, as they neared the hotel's stable arch. "Is the timing correct for that to have been the large shipment from France?"

Christopher nodded. "Yes, it fits." He turned in under the arch and signaled imperiously for the ostler to bring his carriage and horses. Halting, he grimly concluded, "If the notes were fetched last night and taken inland, that means they're on their way to Goffard Hall."

"Has Mrs. Kirkpatrick already received them?" Ellen all but jigged with impatience.

Christopher shook his head. "No, not yet." He met Ellen's eyes. "We set up our watch on Goffard Hall yesterday, which as it turns out, was just in time. If the notes were fetched from here last night...the one thing we can state with reasonable certainty is that they haven't yet reached Goffard Hall."

Relief washed over Ellen's face. "So we still have a chance to seize them before Mrs. Kirkpatrick spreads them around."

Christopher nodded. The ostler led his chestnuts out. Christopher helped Ellen up, took the reins, and tossed the ostler a shilling. Then he climbed up, sat beside Ellen, and gave his horses the office. In short order, he turned out of the stable yard into the street.

The instant he had the chestnuts pacing, he glanced at Ellen and met an impatient look. He faced forward. "Let's get back to the manor and see what Toby has to report before we make any further plans."

CHAPTER 9

*A*n hour later, Ellen rushed into the manor's library with Christopher on her heels.

Toby, seated behind the desk, glanced up. At the sight of their faces, he came to his feet. "What's happened?"

"First," Christopher said, striding past the desk to the drawer in which the maps were kept, "has there been any activity of interest at Goffard Hall?"

"No," Toby said. "At least, not that I've heard of. Nigel rode out midmorning. We kept him in sight, but he didn't stop anywhere, just rode around and about the village, exercising his horse." Toby glanced from Christopher, pulling out a large map from the drawer, to Ellen, who was hovering impatiently by the desk. "Why? Should there have been some action?"

"Hopefully not yet." Christopher carried the map he'd extracted to the desk and spread it over the desktop. "But we believe the counterfeit notes came into the country via Lydd churchyard."

" *Something* was delivered into a pair of tombs on Saturday night." Ellen held down the far end of the map.

"And it was retrieved last night." Leaning over the map, Christopher glanced at Toby. "What we've found suggests the counterfeit notes are en route to Goffard Hall." He looked at the map. "The question now is, would one night be enough to carry them to the Hall from Lydd, or would whoever is transporting them have stopped along the way?"

"Here's Lydd." Ellen had been poring over the map and stabbed her finger down on the town.

"And Benenden is here." Christopher set his finger on the spot.

Toby had joined them in studying the map. "Where's the scale?" He located it on a corner of the map, glanced at the two towns, gauging the distance between... "As the crow flies, it would be an easy night's journey, but via the lanes..."

"This"—Christopher traced a route from Lydd to Benenden—"is the most likely route a smuggler would take. The lanes are local, not main roads—unlikely anyone else would be traveling along in the dead of night."

Toby pulled a piece of string from his pocket and laid it along the route Christopher had indicated, then used the printed scale to estimate the distance. "Thirty miles, give or take." Toby met Christopher's eyes. "An easy night's journey for a man on a horse, even leading a pack pony."

Christopher frowned and straightened, releasing the map.

Toby looked from Christopher to Ellen. "Clearly, you found something. Are either of you going to tell me what?"

Christopher waved Ellen and Toby to the armchairs and moved to claim one himself. "As we'd planned, we started in Rye, but there was nothing to be learned there."

Between them, Christopher and Ellen described what they'd discovered in Lydd.

"All right." Toby nodded. "That explains your thinking."

"What I'm thinking *now*," Christopher said, "is that we don't know the actual physical size of this last shipment of notes. Is it a package a lone man on a horse could manage? Or would he need a pack pony—or more than one?"

"Don't forget," Ellen said, "that Mrs. Withers heard hooves on the cobbles on the night the packages were delivered to the tombs. Ergo, a pony—one at least—was needed to bring the packages up from the shore."

"And here's another thought." Toby looked from Ellen to Christopher. "How big were the storage compartments? I know you didn't see inside, but if they were the size of the door and the width of the tomb...?"

Christopher held his hands apart. "That wide." He shifted his hands. "That high. And internally, the tombs must have been at least two feet wide." He looked to Ellen for confirmation.

She nodded. "There were two such spaces, and both had been used."

"From that," Toby said, "I think it's safe to assume that the smugglers aren't transporting this cargo simply as a large packet of banknotes. If they had, I'm fairly certain they wouldn't have needed both compartments—they would have used only one."

Ellen studied Toby. "You think they're concealing the notes in some other cargo?"

Toby pulled a face. "More that they'll have disguised the notes so they don't appear to be banknotes."

Christopher huffed. "If you think about it, transporting fake notes all the way from the counterfeiter in Paris to Mrs. Kirkpatrick at Goffard Hall simply as a packet of banknotes would be stupendously risky. Everyone who saw them—everyone involved on the French side, the crew of the ship that brought them across the Channel, and everyone involved in moving the notes on this side—would instantly guess what the package contained, just from its size, feel, and weight."

"Exactly." Toby nodded. "That would be an open invitation to anyone involved to filch the notes for themselves or—if someone was really clever—to sell the information to someone in authority for an entirely legitimate reward."

They fell silent, cogitating, then Christopher said, "According to Drake, who is rarely wrong about such things, the mastermind behind this scheme has put not a single foot wrong in all his planning. It was sheer luck that Drake and company got wind of the counterfeit notes at all, let alone in time to attempt to stop the scheme from going forward to its ultimate climax."

"I agree," Toby said. "Our mastermind wouldn't have overlooked such a massive and predictable risk. The notes will have been disguised in some fashion—secreted in some other cargo or made to look like something else." His brows rising, Toby looked at Ellen and Christopher. "But what? Accepting that it's almost certainly not a nice, neat package of banknotes, what are we actually looking for here?"

"It would have to be an item that smugglers—who aren't the most trusting individuals—would find plausible as contraband in this day and age." Christopher frowned. "Tobacco?"

"Not from France," Toby stated. "And not via this coast."

Christopher pulled a face. "Finest brandy? Extra special port?"

Toby tipped his head. "That might fool the smugglers, but how would you safely hide banknotes in barrels of liquid?"

After a long moment, Christopher said, "In the middle of last century, there was a time when they smuggled silk, but now..."

"What about lace?"

Ellen's question had both men looking her way. Christopher realized she'd been silent for several minutes, rather unlike her, but clearly, she'd been thinking... He frowned. "I'm not sure, but that might work. What made you think of lace?"

"Remember I went to that haberdashery in Hastings to check the price of something?" When he nodded, she went on, "It was lace. The reason I'd been wondering about lace prices in Kent was because Aunt Emma had insisted on buying new lace for the gown I wore on Monday night—you must have noticed it."

Christopher recalled the copious flounces all too well. He nodded.

"Well," Ellen went on, "that lace is nothing short of exquisite. Trust me. When it comes to ribbons, feathers, lace, and so on"—she gestured to the feathers and ribbons adorning her carriage dress—"I know all there is to know. And I would be prepared to swear that, in London, there's no chance whatsoever of getting such lace at the price the village milliner is selling it—not in any warehouse, not even on the docks direct from the ship."

"The lace is foreign?" Toby asked.

She nodded. "Belgian, almost certainly. They make some of the best."

Toby looked at Christopher. "The counterfeiter was Belgian."

Christopher nodded. "If he wanted to disguise notes he'd produced to pass muster with smugglers, he could well have chosen a product he was familiar with—one that was good enough, highly priced enough, to be a plausible item for smuggling."

"The counterfeiter didn't mention that to Drake's men," Toby pointed out.

Christopher tipped his head consideringly. "It's possible the specific point—how the notes were concealed for transport—never came up. Alternatively, the counterfeiter might simply have handed on the notes, and someone else disguised them for transport."

Ellen put in, "The haberdashery in Hastings was selling lesser-quality lace at a price higher than Emma and I paid in Benenden for lace of exceptional quality, and as I had expected, the price in Hastings was significantly higher than the price we would have paid for that lower-quality lace in London." She looked from Toby to Christopher. "London prices should be the cheapest for legitimately imported lace. Therefore, I suspect that the lace Mrs. Rollins, the milliner in Benenden, is selling isn't, as she truly seems to think, bought by her husband from a warehouse in London."

Christopher looked at Toby. "There were several ladies with fine lace on their gowns at the party on Monday evening." He glanced at Ellen.

She nodded. "I noticed that, too. Mrs. Rollins had several patterns of high-quality lace available, all at that very low price."

Toby leaned forward, focusing on Ellen. "Do you know how lace is transported?"

"In packets." With her hands, she outlined a rectangular shape with a length of two feet and a width of six to nine inches. "The lace is wound around boards about that size."

Christopher narrowed his eyes, imagining it. "How thick is the lace on a full board?"

"Two inches?" Ellen arched her brows. "It might be more."

"That would work." Toby's tone suggested they'd hit on their answer. "The counterfeiter or his immediate contact could have packed the banknotes against both sides of a board, then wound the lace over it, securing the notes and hiding them completely. Four stacks of notes on each board."

"How many boards might that result in?" Christopher asked.

Toby shrugged, but his eyes were alight. "No idea, but at least enough to make up what would appear to be a reasonable cargo of contraband lace."

"But not too large or heavy a cargo, either," Christopher said. "This is sounding like exactly the sort of plan our mastermind would have put into place. He would want the smuggling run to look normal, yet the fewer people involved, the better."

"If the notes were concealed in, say, twelve packets of lace, which seems reasonable, that would explain the need to use both of the tombs in Lydd." Toby looked increasingly excited. "We know they retrieved the packets from Lydd last night. There's no reason they wouldn't have transported it to somewhere near here—not to Goffard Hall but somewhere close. It's only thirty miles or so by the most deserted lanes. Ponies would do that in an easy night."

Christopher agreed. He looked from Toby's eager face to Ellen's. "Clearly, we need to have a quiet word with Mr. Rollins."

~

Christopher was not all that surprised to find himself tooling his curricle down to the village the following morning with Ellen perched beside him.

He, she, and Toby had spent an hour discussing possible ways of approaching Rollins with a view to learning what they wanted to know, namely if he'd received another shipment of lace over the past twenty-four hours and, if so, from whom. Whether Rollins knew about the counterfeit notes—whether he presently held them—was an open question.

Given Ellen was the only one of them with experience of the shop and Mrs. Rollins, let alone any real knowledge of lace, it was inevitable that it was her plan he and Toby had eventually, reluctantly, agreed to. With Drake's injunction against unnecessarily showing their hand high in their minds, he and Toby had been forced to step back and let Ellen lead.

Resigned to his role as supporter, he slowed his pair as they reached the village lane, opposite the Bull Inn, then he turned the chestnuts right, setting them trotting into the village proper.

As they passed the inn, Ellen looked into the trees that clustered alongside, bordering the opening to the lane leading to the church, and glimpsed Toby hanging back in the shadows.

From that position, he had a good view of the front of the millinery-cum-haberdashery and the mouth of the alley that ran down the nearer side of the shop. The Rollinses lived above the shop, and beyond a narrow strip of garden at the rear, the land was heavily wooded; if Rollins left, he would use the front door or the side door that gave onto the alley, which in turn led only to the village lane.

Toby would see and follow Rollins if he shot off to warn anyone while she and Christopher were in the shop.

Christopher slowed, then halted his horses opposite the millinery, where a hitching post provided a place to secure the reins. He stepped down and did so, then came to help her down.

She descended, then released his hand, twitched her skirt straight, and turned determinedly toward the millinery. Mrs. Rollins's creations—bedecked with plumes, lace, and artificial fruit and flowers—made a colorful show in the front bow window.

Schooling her expression to one of expectation, Ellen walked purposefully to the millinery's door. Christopher strolled languidly beside her. He was under instructions to appear bored, and from the corner of her eye, she saw that his expression was conveying disinterest quite effectively.

They reached the door, and he opened it, and she swept inside, a bright smile lighting her face.

From behind her main counter, Mrs. Rollins looked up, saw who it was, and beamed and bustled forward. "Miss Martingale." Then the shop-keeper noted the presence looming behind Ellen and blinked. "Mr. Cynster." Her tone suggested uncertainty.

Realizing that it wouldn't be often Mrs. Rollins had a gentleman, much less one of Christopher's ilk, walk into her shop, Ellen stepped forward and took charge. "Mrs. Rollins, I do hope you can help me. Well," she temporized, "I suppose I should say 'help us.' I'm here on behalf of a friend, you see. She saw the lace my aunt and I purchased from you recently, and nothing will do for it but she wants to use that or similar lace on her wedding gown."

"A wedding?" Mrs. Rollins forgot about Christopher. Her eyes lit. "Will it be here or in town, miss? The wedding, I mean."

"In London—I believe at St. George's in Hanover Square. It will be a major social event, and my friend, Miss Hargraves, is absolutely certain she wants your lace for her gown."

"And I'll be very happy to supply it, miss." Mrs. Rollins looked as if all her Christmases had come at once. "Will she want to see samples? How much does she need?"

"Twenty yards," Ellen replied. When Mrs. Rollins looked stunned, she explained, "The entire gown will be formed from cascading flounces of lace. Nothing but lace from shoulder to hem—that's why she needs so much."

"I see." Mrs. Rollins looked torn, but as Ellen watched, the little milliner's chin firmed, and she smiled more confidently. "I'll have to check with my husband, miss—to make sure I can supply such a length, all in one pattern."

"Yes, well, it will need to be all in one pattern, I'm afraid." Ellen smiled encouragingly. "Could you, perhaps, speak with your husband now? I need to let Miss Hargraves and her mama know if you can't supply the lace to give them time to look elsewhere."

"Oh," Mrs. Rollins hurriedly assured her, "I'm sure we'll be able to get the lace in. But I will just check." She pointed toward the curtained doorway leading to the rear of the shop. "Hector's just upstairs. As I think I mentioned the other day, he brings the lace from London. I'll just fetch him."

Mrs. Rollins hurried out; they heard her footsteps patter up the stairs.

From above their heads, the murmur of voices reached them, followed by an exclamation that subsequently gave rise to a muted argument.

Christopher looked at Ellen, met her eyes, and arched his brows. Thus far, her plan had worked like a charm; the next bit would be the tricky part.

Seconds later, the argument ended, and they heard heavy footsteps descending the stairs, closely followed by the lighter patter of Mrs. Rollins's feet.

Christopher watched as a short, rather rotund man of unprepossessing mien emerged from behind the curtain, looking faintly harassed.

Ellen's smile brightened. "Good morning, Mr. Rollins! I do so hope you can oblige my friend by supplying the lace for her wedding gown."

"'Morning, Miss Martingale." Rollins bobbed his head, then squinted at Christopher. Plainly surprised, he nodded warily. "Mr. Cynster, sir." Rollins shuffled sideways behind the counter, apparently prodded by his wife, who had followed closely and was directing a pointed glare his way. Rollins glanced at her, then cleared his throat and addressed Ellen. "As to the lace for your friend's gown, Miss Martingale, laying hands on twenty yards...well, it's not that easy, you know."

Mrs. Rollins uttered a soft gasp; the look she turned on her husband was shocked and not a little outraged. "But you can get more from where you got it before in London, can't you, Hector?"

"Twenty yards," Ellen said, "is likely not much more than four or five packets. Surely you can manage that?" She glanced at the wide counters arranged to either side. "Why, when I was here with my aunt, you must have had almost that much then."

Subjected to a direct look from Ellen's fine eyes, and a muted glare warning of incipient doom from his spouse, Rollins shifted uneasily, then glanced again at his wife. "I...ah..."

To say the man had grown nervous would have been an understatement.

Then he looked at Ellen and, in the manner of a drowning man seizing a lifeline, gabbled, "I'll need to check with my source." Realizing that was a response both women would have to accept, Rollins drew in a breath, raised his head, and reiterated, "Yes, I'll have to check with him. Mayhap we can get in that quantity." After a swift glance at his wife, he hurriedly added, "We'll certainly do our best, miss."

His wife was placated; she eased back from her threatening stance.

Ellen widened her eyes in consideration, then nodded. "Very well."

She smiled approvingly at the milliner, very much woman-to-woman. "I'll call back early next week. Miss Hargraves will be waiting to hear, but I'll explain and put her off until then."

"Thank you, miss." Mrs. Rollins came out from behind the counter. "You may be sure that if it's possible to lay hands on that lace, we'll get it for you."

Ellen smiled and turned to leave.

Rollins remained behind the counter as if his feet were glued to the floor. In contrast, his gaze had grown distant—calculating, Christopher suspected.

He stepped back and allowed Mrs. Rollins to escort Ellen out of the shop, then, with a nod to Mrs. Rollins, followed Ellen into the lane.

As he fell into step beside her, still clinging to his utterly disinterested façade, he caught her eye. "Now to see if he takes our bait."

Ellen smiled brightly, transparently pleased with herself. He helped her into the curricle, retrieved the reins, then settled beside her and drove on through the village, circled, drove back, and turned right onto the branch of the lane that ran around the triangular green. The church stood at the apex of the elongated triangle, but Christopher halted the curricle outside the vicarage, which stood nearer the main lane.

They left the horses tied there and walked through the gate, as if they were visiting the vicar. Instead, once they were out of sight of the lane and anyone who happened to be walking along it, they followed the path through the vicarage's shrubbery to the church, rounded the tall edifice, and continued circling the far side of the graveyard until they reached the wood at the rear of the inn.

A minute later, they joined Toby where he stood just inside the tree line, keeping watch on the front of the Rollinses' shop.

"How did it go?" Toby studied their faces. "Do you think he'll run off to his source?"

"I think," Ellen smugly replied, "that we can count on Mrs. Rollins to ensure he does. She got stars in her eyes when I asked for twenty yards of lace."

Christopher nodded. "I can't see Rollins being allowed to dally for too long—Mrs. Rollins will be at him to contact his source and get an answer as soon as possible. So if the source of that lace is anywhere near, Rollins will go to speak with him, if nothing else to escape the edge of his wife's tongue."

Toby looked at the shop. "While you were inside, I took a quick look down that alley. There's definitely no way out other than via the lane."

"Good." Christopher settled beside Toby. "So now we wait and see whether we were, in fact, as successful as we think."

Ellen shifted her weight from one foot to the other. Time ticked past —a minute, then more.

She'd almost attained a somnolent state when Rollins appeared at the mouth of the alley. He barely paused to check the lane was clear before striding across it, heading to his left.

Toby straightened. "He's heading for the inn."

Christopher frowned. "For lunch?"

"Or because his 'source' is someone who works there?" Toby glanced at Christopher in question.

"It's too early for lunch," Ellen pointed out.

Meeting Toby's gaze, Christopher tipped his head toward the inn. "Rollins might get suspicious if he sets eyes on us. You'll have to go and see who he speaks with."

Toby saluted, stepped out of the shadows, and swiftly strode for the inn's front door, which faced the lane.

Ellen frowned, then wrinkled her nose. "I don't suppose we can go and peek through the front windows?"

"No." Christopher grimaced as well. "We'll have to let Toby play this hand alone."

∼

Inside the inn, Toby glanced around the deserted entry hall, then ducked under a low lintel and entered the taproom. After a cursory glance around the long room, he ambled to the bar.

Rollins, thank God, wouldn't know him from Adam. Confident in his anonymity, Toby walked up beside the man and lounged on the bar a few feet away, patently waiting to be served.

He was in time to hear Rollins ask the barman, "Where's your father, Shep?"

"He's in the office." Bending to lift bottles from a crate he'd just carried in, with his head, Shep indicated some area deeper in the house. "Want me to tell him you're wanting a word?"

"Yes." Rollins was nervously tapping a finger on the bar. He glanced sidelong at Toby, then leaned back and surveyed the other occupants of the taproom—three laborers gathered about a table and two old codgers in the inglenook. Rollins turned back in time to catch Shep's eye as he moved toward the swinging door giving access to the inn's nether regions. "Tell him I'll wait at the front desk."

Shep saluted, then said to Toby, "Back in a moment, sir," and lumbered off.

Toby leaned on the counter; he didn't look as Rollins left the taproom, presumably to wait at the reception counter at the rear of the entry hall.

Toby was grateful that Shep didn't dally on his errand. He was back in less than a minute and happy to provide Toby with a pint of ale.

After handing over the required coins, Toby picked up the tankard and turned; he pretended to survey the available seats before heading for the table by the window just inside the taproom's doorway. He slid onto the bench seat fixed to the wall separating the tap from the entry hall, then raised the tankard and sipped.

From the corner of his eye, he could just glimpse Rollins, obviously nervous, still waiting before the reception counter.

Toby was careful to keep his head bent, his gaze apparently on the tankard.

Then the door behind the reception counter swung open, and a tall, heavyset man walked through. He nodded at Rollins and halted behind the counter. "'Morning, Rollins. What can I do fer you?"

Rollins leaned on the counter and lowered his voice. "It's about that last shipment of lace."

Toby blessed the acoustics of the entry hall; he could hear Rollins well enough to make out his words.

Behind the counter, the publican's expression grew stony. "Yes?" Wariness had seeped into his tone. "What of it?"

"My wife has a customer who wants to buy a ruddy great amount of it —twenty yards! That's more than double what we got last time." Rollins paused, apparently searching the publican's face. "I don't suppose there's any chance of you laying your hands on more?"

The publican visibly relaxed. "Well, old son"—the man smiled as if at some private joke—"as it happens, you're in luck. I had another shipment come through just last night. A big one. I checked it over, and to my eyes, the stuff's every bit as good as the last batch. Might be a different pattern, mind, but you know I know next to nothin' about lace." He paused, as if debating, then said, "I'm supposed to move most of it on to London, but I can let you have what you need, I'm sure."

Rollins all but slumped with relief. "Good." His voice gained in strength. "Excellent!" Then he recalled this was business and belatedly asked, "The same price?"

The publican pursed his lips and tipped his head from side to side before saying, "Well, this is between friends, right? So yeah—I can let you have it at the same price per packet as the last lot."

Rollins straightened. "In that case, I'll take however much you can give me."

The publican thought, then said, "How about I let you know tomorrow how many packets I can slide your way, heh? I can tell you that it'll be something like three times the last load. Like I said, it was a large shipment."

Rollins was so delighted he forgot to lower his voice. "Excellent! Mrs. Rollins and I appreciate your help, Hardcastle."

Hardcastle shot a glance toward the taproom; Toby felt it and kept his head down, staring into the tankard he was cradling between his hands, for all the world as if his thoughts were fixed on some far-distant imagined vista.

When he sensed Hardcastle's attention leave him, Toby glanced sidelong and saw Hardcastle lean over the counter and quietly tell Rollins, "Just remember, old son, keep everything about our arrangement to yourself."

A menacing quality had insinuated itself into Hardcastle's tone.

Rollins took a step back, hands raised and waving in assurance. "Of course. Of course! I haven't even told my old lady where I come by the goods."

Hardcastle studied Rollins for a second, then nodded and straightened. "You come back tomorrow, afternoon sometime, and I'll tell you how many packets I can let you have." He started to turn toward the swinging door, then paused to tell Rollins, "One thing—this'll be the last shipment, at least for a while. I haven't heard anything about another but"—Hardcastle shrugged—"who knows, heh?"

Rollins didn't look happy at that news, but having unexpectedly had his most pressing need met, he raised a hand in farewell, turned, and walked out of the inn.

Hardcastle lingered, watching Rollins go, then snorted somewhat contemptuously, pushed through the door, and disappeared.

Toby remained sitting, staring at nothing while he unhurriedly finished his pint. Then he pushed away the empty tankard, rose, and strolled out of the inn.

He slid his hands into his pockets and ambled around the side of the inn. One glance informed him that Christopher and Ellen weren't in the trees where he had left them. He raised his gaze and saw them sitting in the shadows of the lychgate all the way across the village green. They'd seen him but, wisely, made no move to attract his attention.

He set off along the narrow lane bordering the green. It led him to the church, and he walked along beside the front wall, eventually drawing abreast of the lychgate. He met the others' eyes, a warning in his, dipped his head in polite greeting, but didn't pause his ambling stride. "I don't want to risk being seen with you two. I'll meet you back at the manor."

Without waiting for any response, he strolled on, past Christopher's curricle tied up outside the vicarage, eventually circling around to where he'd left his horse in a copse opposite the inn. He was mounting up as the curricle rattled past.

Toby grinned and set off across the fields for the manor.

Christopher and Ellen were seated in armchairs in the library, waiting impatiently, when Toby walked in.

"Well?" Ellen demanded. "Who did Rollins see?"

Toby's grin stated he knew the answer. He dropped into the armchair facing Christopher. "I bet Rollins was smiling when he returned to the shop."

Christopher nodded. "He was. So cut line—who did he speak with?"

"The publican."

Christopher arched his brows. "Hardcastle?"

"Tall heavy man of middle years. Looks fairly fit."

Christopher nodded. "He's relatively new to the village, but not, I believe, the area. He took over as landlord of the inn about two years ago, but I heard he hails from somewhere around Battle."

"So"—Toby leaned forward, resting his forearms on his thighs—"not that far from Hastings. He could have connections to the old smuggling gangs."

"Possibly," Christopher conceded. "And two years is enough time to discover that being landlord of a small village inn isn't any path to riches."

"Indeed. So despite living here, buried in the Weald, if someone made inquiries in Hastings, they might have been steered Hardcastle's way," Toby theorized. "And if Hardcastle was looking for some way to supplement his income, he might well have been ripe for recruiting by our mastermind."

"So it appears," Christopher said.

Ellen looked from one to the other. "But what about Mr. Rollins? Is he involved, too?"

Toby pulled a considering face. "I honestly don't think so—I think he's a dupe." He recounted all he'd heard of the exchange between Hardcastle and Rollins. Toby shook his head. "It seemed to me that Rollins has no inkling whatsoever about the notes. He thinks Hardcastle is smuggling high-quality lace into the country, ultimately for delivery to someone in London, and that Hardcastle is being neighborly in letting Rollins have some packets on the side at a bargain price. But in reality, Rollins and his wife and their shop are Hardcastle's way of disposing of the lace after he's extracted the notes from the packets."

"Hmm." Ellen frowned. "I suppose a publican wouldn't want to have packets of lace piling up in his cellars."

"That would be difficult to explain if the gentlemen from Customs and Excise came calling," Christopher drily remarked.

"It's also," Toby said, "another way for Hardcastle to make money from this scheme. He might be letting Rollins have the lace at a 'bargain price,' but Hardcastle will have paid nothing for it—what he gets from the Rollinses is pure profit."

Christopher refocused on the most important aspect. "You said Hardcastle received the lace yesterday and has already checked it?"

Toby nodded. "I take that to mean that the notes have been extracted from the packets of lace, counted, combined, and wrapped in whatever way they need to be, and are now ready to be passed on to Goffard Hall." He tipped his head. "However, when, exactly, the handover will occur is, at present, anyone's guess."

"Was Hardcastle unsettled at all by Rollins's sudden demand for more lace?" Ellen asked.

Toby snorted. "Not in the slightest. Hardcastle isn't the sort to unnecessarily get the wind up." He paused, then added, "That said, based on the way he pounced on Rollins and dinned into him the need for continued secrecy, I would wager that Hardcastle's not the sort to take any risk, not if he can avoid it."

"Regardless," Christopher said, "Hardcastle has had the notes for close to twenty-four hours and as yet has made no move to pass them on. He hasn't sent a message or contacted anyone from Goffard Hall, nor has he gone out that way."

"So if we leave things as they are," Ellen said, "Hardcastle will follow whatever procedure was established during the earlier test runs—whatever steps he's supposed to follow to pass on the notes to Goffard Hall."

Silence fell as the three of them contemplated the current situation.

"We need to confirm who at Goffard Hall receives the counterfeit notes," Toby said. "We've assumed it's Mrs. Kirkpatrick, but it might, for instance, be Nigel, and Mrs. Kirkpatrick is merely working to some notion he's planted in her head."

"Or vice versa," Ellen said. "Nigel might not have a clue what's going on." She grimaced. "I might not be able to imagine that, but we can't just assume—we can't be certain."

Christopher shifted in his chair. "Potentially the easiest way to learn who at Goffard Hall is involved is to follow the notes from Hardcastle into the hands of whoever receives them." Christopher pulled a face. "Unfortunately, that runs the risk of something unforeseen happening and the notes slipping from our grasp. According to Drake, we shouldn't risk that."

"On top of that," Toby added, faintly disgusted, "we aren't supposed to let any of the villains guess the authorities are on to them, so Drake can follow the notes all the way back to the mastermind."

"Hmm." Ellen's expression mirrored Toby's. "So what *can* we do? What should we do?" She looked from Toby to Christopher, plainly inviting enlightenment.

Christopher sat up. "I think we should keep our watch on Goffard Hall in place—our arrangements for that seem to be working well."

Toby nodded. "The gypsies are a find—they're very inventive when it comes to obvious reasons for their presence in the lane within sight of the front of the Hall."

Christopher nodded. "We'll leave them and the others involved to continue the watch there, but we also need to mount a similar watch on the inn." He met Toby's gaze. "We can't predict who will come to whom. We need to be in place to witness the notes being handed over regardless of whether it's Hardcastle taking the notes to Goffard Hall or someone from there coming to him."

Toby nodded, rose, and stretched his arms above his head. Lowering his arms, he said, "I'll take first watch on the inn until you can send down more men, and I'll take one of your grooms with me. I'll be in those woods where I was earlier, keeping watch on the rear of the premises. I'll station your groom opposite, just up the lane, so he'll have a clear view of the front."

Christopher nodded and rose, too. "I'll sort out a roster of watchers for the inn—and I'll also send an urgent message to Drake to shake his stumps and get down here." Christopher glanced at Ellen, meeting her eyes, then he looked at Toby. "The mastermind's pawns are moving, and we need to know how Drake wants to play this game."

CHAPTER 10

*E*llen returned to Bigfield House to see how the household was managing in her partial absence, only to discover that there were no impending dramas to defuse, no disasters to avert.

Indeed, everything appeared to be running reasonably smoothly. She was particularly pleased to find Robbie and Hopper working together in the study; the pair were poring over harvest forecasts and planning a timetable for various relevant works.

After she blithely inquired how things were going and Robbie, frowning, replied that he rather thought he was finally getting a handle on things, she cocked a brow at Hopper, inviting his assessment.

Somewhat to her surprise, the often gruff and abrupt man, his gaze on Robbie's downbent head, slowly nodded. "Time the young master learned the ropes, and he's not doing badly—not at all."

"Excellent." She was truly glad to hear that.

She hesitated. Previously, she would have sat down with them, asked to be shown all, and then joined in the forward planning, but if Robbie was finally picking up the reins…

And she did have other matters—potentially more pressing and threatening matters of wider import—to deal with.

"In that case"—she infused believable brightness into her voice—"I'll leave you to your endeavors."

Hopper nodded in taciturn approval. Robbie grunted and didn't look up.

After checking on her aunt and her uncle and, later, lunching with the family, she debated having her mare resaddled, but as the day was gloriously fine, after tying on her bonnet, she opted to walk to the manor via the path she'd noted during her recent excursions. Commencing in the shrubbery, the path crossed the Bigfield House fields to the lane, reached via a stile, then another stile opposite gave access to the extension of the path that ran along the edge of a field, past an orchard, ultimately to the manor's shrubbery. The path appeared to be the most direct route between the two houses.

She set off at a good pace, delighting in the pleasant day. She clambered over the stiles without mishap and arrived at the manor in time to hear Toby report. He'd just returned from watching the inn and, over a late luncheon taken in the dining room, advised her and Christopher that, other than to receive a delivery of beer, neither Hardcastle nor any of his family—who apparently acted as staff—had left the inn.

"According to Pendleby, Hardcastle has two sons and two daughters who act as barmen and maids, and his wife is the cook. The Bull Inn is a family enterprise, but Hardcastle himself is very definitely in charge." Toby reached for the mug of ale before him. "So at this point, Hardcastle appears to be sitting tight."

Christopher sat back in the carver at the head of the table. "The watchers about Goffard Hall reported no sign of unusual activity. Nigel rode out, exercising his horse again—"

Toby waved his fork. "I saw him ride into the village and around the green, then off and away."

Christopher inclined his head. "Other than that, no one's arrived, and no one's left."

Toby pushed aside his empty plate, and they all sat back and considered that.

A minute later, Pendleby came in, bearing a tea tray that he placed before Ellen. She thanked him with an absentminded smile, then lifted the pot and poured.

Toby stared at the teapot, then looked pointedly at Christopher.

Christopher pretended not to notice either Toby's stare or the fact that his butler, the head of the manor staff, had just treated Ellen as if she were mistress of the house.

Hmm.

When Toby continued to stare, eyes widening, Christopher shot him a sharp glance.

His younger cousin held up his hands defensively and, blessedly, said nothing.

Busy filling three cups, Ellen hadn't noticed the byplay.

She set down the teapot, passed Christopher and Toby their cups, picked up her own, sipped, then said, "Which is higher on this Drake person's list of desires—seizing the counterfeit notes or identifying the mastermind regardless of whatever risks that might entail?"

That was an excellent question. Christopher exchanged a long look with Toby.

Eventually, Toby said, "Knowing Drake, he'll want both—the notes and the mastermind—equally."

"And," Christopher drily added, "he'll expect us to deliver accordingly."

"Be that as it may," Ellen persisted, "it seems to me that allowing the notes to slip through our fingers is the more immediate and potentially wide-reaching—Empire-shaking—danger." She looked at Christopher, then Toby. "What if the mastermind realizes your Drake is aware of his scheme, and the mastermind decides to contact Hardcastle directly? What if, while our attention is focused on a contact from Goffard Hall, the mastermind arranges to pick up the notes himself, then vanishes?"

Toby grimaced and met Christopher's eyes. "Sadly, that's entirely possible, especially given not even Drake has any idea of who the mastermind is. He could be high enough in Whitehall to be aware of Drake's activities and to be keeping a quiet eye on them. At present, hardly anyone but us down here know of Drake's interest in Goffard Hall, but it's possible the mastermind might, by now, have learned about the action against the counterfeiter. That was in Paris and would have involved more than just Drake's men."

"So the mastermind might guess that investigations into smuggling gangs in Kent might already be under way." Christopher compressed his lips in thought, then added, "If the mastermind is as clever as Drake paints him, if he gets any hint that Drake knows of his scheme...then the most obvious way to salvage what he can from the current situation is for him to arrange to collect the fake notes and stash them away, to be used at some future date. That would be the worst outcome for Drake and the authorities—they would have lost the fake banknotes *and* the mastermind and gained nothing in terms of reducing the threat to the realm."

"That's what I keep coming back to," Ellen said. "Aren't we risking losing *both* the items, if you will, that Drake and the authorities desperately want to secure—the counterfeit banknotes *and* the mastermind—by failing to seize the fake banknotes now that we know who has them?"

Toby looked at Christopher. "I can't—don't—disagree."

Christopher wrinkled his nose. "Neither do I. It feels like tempting Fate, knowing that Hardcastle has the notes and making no push to seize them."

"The only flies in that ointment," Toby cynically said, "are Drake's insistence on not alerting the mastermind to the authorities' interest and keeping the way clear to use the notes to ultimately lead to the mastermind."

During the moments of cogitation that followed, Ellen checked the teapot, then refilled their cups. After setting down the pot, she suggested, "Perhaps we should think through how matters might progress if we step in and seize the counterfeit notes from Hardcastle." She looked invitingly at Toby and Christopher. "Once we have the notes, what then?"

Toby promptly replied, "We persuade Hardcastle to tell us to whom at Goffard Hall he delivers the notes and how he arranges to do so."

Ellen nodded. "And then?"

"Then," Christopher took up the exposition, "we do whatever we need to do to mimic Hardcastle's meeting and pass on the notes to whoever from Goffard Hall comes to pick them up."

"Do we allow the Goffard Hall person to take the notes and continue unsuspecting," Ellen asked, "or do we seize them and the notes again?"

"The latter," Christopher and Toby replied in unison.

Christopher continued, "If we're going to follow such a path, we need to keep our hands on those notes."

"Agreed," Toby said. "And the next step would be to convince those involved at Goffard Hall to continue the charade that all is proceeding as the mastermind has arranged." He paused, then observed, "Until we know more about how the mastermind interacts with his contact at Goffard Hall, we won't be able to make further plans."

"True"—Christopher inclined his head—"but we'll have time to deal with that, because the mastermind won't be looking to make contact—presumably to pick up the legitimate banknotes for which the counterfeit notes will have been substituted—until after the last card party Mrs. Kirkpatrick needs to hold to exchange all of the notes."

"She won't be able to swap a large number of notes during just one card party." Ellen looked at Christopher. "We saw how many guests and tables she had at her last party. She would need to hold multiple parties—five, six?—to exchange a large number of notes."

Christopher nodded. "And she's presently holding parties every two weeks. Her part of the scheme might take months—time enough for us to construct a solid trap for Drake's mastermind."

"All right." Looking considerably more energized, Toby looked from Ellen to Christopher. "I take it this means we're going to go after Hardcastle and the notes."

Christopher took a moment to think things through, then looked at Toby and Ellen. "Given Drake isn't here, leaving us to chart the best way forward, then, bearing in mind Drake's injunctions about not alerting the mastermind and also eventually trapping him, seizing Hardcastle and the notes now, rather than risking any occurrence that might see the notes slip out of our reach, seems the course of wisdom."

Toby looked keen, and Ellen brightened.

"It's more than a week to the next regular card party," Ellen said, "and we have no reason to suppose Hardcastle will arrange to pass on the notes today or even tomorrow rather than closer to the date of the next party."

Toby shifted. "Hardcastle almost certainly has the notes stashed away in his cellars somewhere. With days to go before they're needed, the notes would be safer at the inn than at the Hall. Unless Mr. Kirkpatrick is involved—which you consider and I agree is unlikely—the notes wouldn't be able to be placed in any safe or strongbox. They'd have to be locked in a drawer or some such place, and with a houseful of staff, that would constitute a significant risk."

Ellen was nodding. "Something might happen, a maid come across the notes, take them to Kirkpatrick, and that would be the end of the scheme."

"I agree." Christopher straightened in the carver. "It's only Thursday—those involved at Goffard Hall probably won't expect the notes for another week."

"That means," Ellen pointed out, "that if we move to seize the notes now, we only have to deal with Hardcastle."

Christopher nodded.

Toby did, too. "So"—Toby looked from Christopher to Ellen—"how are we going to put the wind up Hardcastle and make him scurry to lay his hands on the notes?"

Christopher wasn't surprised—and he didn't think Toby was, either—that it was Ellen who came up with the perfect plan to spook Hardcastle into rushing to move the notes from wherever he'd hidden them. Admittedly, he and Toby tweaked, embellished, and adjusted the details, but the idea was Ellen's. He was fast learning to respect her insights into how people would behave; even if she hadn't had much to do with country folk, people were still people, and her grasp of human nature was sound.

They all agreed that it was best to strike now, before Hardcastle got around to even thinking about passing the notes on to Goffard Hall. The manor's clocks were chiming for four o'clock when they quit the house and, co-opting Granger and two stable lads, rode down to the inn.

At that time—after the lunch crowd, but not yet dinnertime even by country hours—the inn would be relatively quiet.

They dismounted in a clearing in the woods behind the inn and joined the watchers, who confirmed Hardcastle hadn't left the inn, nor had anyone from the Goffard Hall household visited.

"Right, then." Christopher looked around the circle of eager faces. "This is what we're going to do."

Ellen listened while, between them, Christopher and Toby outlined the plan. She shifted from foot to foot, increasingly frustrated over having no role in what was, in essence, her plan. Still, she could hardly go with them into the inn; that wouldn't be believable at all. The most she could do was stay with the watchers stationed in the woods at the rear of the inn so she would be on hand when Christopher and Toby brought Hardcastle out.

Most of the manor's male staff used the inn as their local drinking place; when Christopher asked, the men confirmed that Hardcastle, as publican, was occasionally absent, traveling to arrange deliveries from breweries and the like, and during those times, his family carried on and the inn operated as usual.

"So," Toby concluded, "if we nab Hardcastle, most likely his family will assume he was called away unexpectedly, and they'll carry on without fuss, thinking he'll return."

"And"—Christopher met Toby's eyes—"given we're talking about mere days, it's unlikely Hardcastle's absence from the inn will even register with those at Goffard Hall."

Everyone hoped that would be so; that went without saying.

"All right." Christopher nodded at the assembled men. "We each know what we're supposed to do." To those remaining in the woods behind the inn, he said, "We're hoping Hardcastle will grab the fake notes and leave the inn with them—certainly, that will be his first and hopefully overriding impulse. I seriously doubt he'll leave by the front door. He's much more likely to come out this way, into the woods—if he does, we'll allow him to walk out, into your arms, so be ready."

Granger, who had joined that group, nodded grimly. "Never fear. We'll grab and hold him until you get here."

Christopher cast a last glance over the men. His gaze came to rest on Ellen, standing a few paces behind the cordon and looking distinctly disgruntled. He smiled faintly, then, sobering, looked at Toby. "We're as ready as we can be."

"Excellent!" Toby's eyes lit. "In that case, let's go."

They returned to their horses, mounted up, and rode via the side lane to the front of the inn. After leaving their horses with the young ostler, they entered the inn through the front door and strolled into the taproom.

Hardcastle was presiding behind the bar, which was a relief; that was a crucial requirement for their plan that they hadn't seen any way of ensuring.

Hardcastle recognized Christopher and gave him a deferential nod. Hardcastle's beady eyes moved on to Toby, where they paused assessingly, before Hardcastle fractionally dipped his head in acknowledgment.

The only other occupants of the taproom—two old men in the inglenook—raised a hand to Christopher, and he smiled genially and nodded back.

Giving every appearance of having nothing better to do, he and Toby slid onto stools at the far end of the bar.

Once they'd settled, Hardcastle lumbered up. "What can I get you, gents?"

They ordered pints of ale and, once the tankards arrived, leaned on the bar and sipped. Taking the coins Christopher pushed his way, Hardcastle retreated to his position in the middle of the long bar, about two yards distant. He picked up a rag and returned to his, it seemed perennial, occupation of polishing glasses.

Minutes ticked by, then Toby sighed and stared into his half-empty tankard. "I hope this isn't going to take too long. I was planning to meet some friends in Tenterden."

Christopher hauled out his fob watch, consulted it, then tucked it back into his pocket. "They said they'd be here sometime in the next half hour." He raised his tankard, sipped, then, lowering the mug, murmured, "You don't have to stay. They requested my presence as a witness representing the local landowners—you're just here for the excitement."

"Well," Toby returned, "it's not often these days one has the chance to witness such an action." Toby was angled toward Christopher, who was sitting farther from Hardcastle.

They were both careful not to look at the publican, but from the corner of his eye, Christopher noted that Hardcastle's polishing had slowed. Although his gaze remained on the glass in his hand, the man was listening for all he was worth.

Toby leaned closer to Christopher and whispered, "Do you have any idea what they're expecting to find? I mean, I thought smuggling had died off years ago, yet here *they* are nosing about in deepest Kent."

With a warning look at Toby, Christopher repressively said, "They didn't say. For all I know, this is just some exercise." He lowered his voice still further. "I can't imagine there is any contraband about. Not these days."

Before Christopher had finished speaking, Hardcastle set down the glass he'd polished to a high gleam. Without glancing at Christopher or Toby, Hardcastle pushed open the swinging door behind the bar and called, "Shep?"

"Yes, Pa?" The barman Toby had seen that morning appeared in the doorway.

Hardcastle thrust the polishing cloth at his son. "Take over. There's something I have to see to."

Shep did as ordered, replacing Hardcastle behind the bar, while Hardcastle vanished through the swinging door.

Christopher and Toby waited until the door ceased swinging, then drained their tankards and, with a nod to Shep, left the taproom.

In the entry hall, Christopher signaled Toby to silence and led him around the reception counter to the door leading deeper into the inn. Christopher eased the door open enough to look past, then opened it and slid silently into the corridor beyond.

Toby was a ghost on his heels.

They crept forward. Straight ahead, at the corridor's far end, lay the inn's rear door. To the left was an open archway that gave onto the busy kitchen, while to the right, set in the stone wall, a door normally secured with a heavy padlock gave access to the inn's vast cellars.

As Christopher had hoped, the padlock hung open and the cellar door stood ajar. To follow Hardcastle, all they needed to do was to slide through the gap before anyone in the kitchen spotted them.

Toby tapped Christopher's shoulder and held up a hand with four fingers raised. Christopher nodded. Hardcastle's wife, two daughters, and younger son were preparing the evening meal.

As if in confirmation, a woman called, "Jed, Mary—get over here and help me with this pot. And Polly—don't you take your eyes off that gravy!"

"No, Ma."

A flurry of footsteps on the flags signaled the two summoned were rushing to their mother's aid. "Right, then," she said. "On three. One, two—"

Christopher and Toby walked quickly forward and, without glancing into the kitchen, slipped past the open cellar door. They found themselves on a narrow wooden landing. They paused, but no shouts came from the kitchen.

Toby nudged Christopher and held up a hand.

Dangling from Toby's long fingers was the padlock he had lifted from the door latch. Christopher nodded and faced forward. The narrow beam of light striking past the edge of the door illuminated wooden steps leading down.

Gradually, their eyes adjusted enough to attempt the steps; they couldn't risk a light. Christopher cautiously started down. When they stepped off the wooden stairs onto the cellar's beaten-earth floor, they saw the glow of a lantern issuing through an archway to their right.

The sudden clatter of wood striking stone came from the same direction.

Stepping carefully, avoiding kicking or bumping into anything, they made their way across the first large chamber, passing between rows of ale barrels—perfect for hiding behind when Hardcastle made his way back. Given he would be carrying the notes and doubtless would be focused on removing them from the inn with all speed, with any luck, he wouldn't notice the missing padlock, or if he did, he would leave it to deal with later.

Getting the counterfeit notes out of the inn before any excisemen arrived would be his overriding priority.

They reached the archway. From beyond came the sounds of wood shifting. Flattening themselves against either side of the arch, Christopher and Toby craned their necks and peered into the next chamber.

Hardcastle had set his lantern atop a wooden crate and was delving into another that he'd plainly just opened; the discarded lid was dumped on the floor on his other side, and on it, he'd stacked several packets of lace, loosely wrapped in thin paper.

After a moment, Hardcastle grunted, straightened, and placed a pile of notes, neatly banded into inch-high stacks, beside the lantern.

He turned back to the open crate, reached in, then rose with more notes to add to the pile.

He glanced around, causing Toby and Christopher to reflexively pull back. When they looked again, Hardcastle was holding a large piece of ordinary wrapping paper. He dumped the lace back into the open crate, lifted the lid and dropped it into position, then spread the paper on the top of the lid.

They watched as Hardcastle carefully wrapped the notes in the paper, then secured it with a string he drew from one pocket, resulting in a package about twelve inches long and nine inches high.

Christopher caught Toby's eye and, with his head, signaled that they should retreat to hide among the ale barrels. Soundlessly, they did and waited for Hardcastle to return to the steps.

Barely breathing, they waited, their eyes now well-adjusted to the gloom.

Then Christopher realized the light from Hardcastle's lantern was fading.

He glanced at Toby, then they both rushed silently back to the archway.

Only to see the light from the lantern receding, moving steadily away from them.

"Damn!" Toby hissed, and searched frantically in his pockets.

Grimly, Christopher said, "There must be another way out of the cellars—Hardcastle's not going to risk coming back this way and running into excisemen with counterfeit notes in his hands."

"Indeed." Toby managed to light a lucifer, just as the lantern ahead of them swung to the left and vanished.

"He's turned a corner." By the flickering light of the match, Christopher strode through the archway and started after Hardcastle.

Toby stuck to his heels, holding the match high to light their way.

They reached the end of the tunnel down which Hardcastle had gone and turned left as he had—into another tunnel. They continued as fast as they dared. The tunnel wasn't straight, but although it wended back and forth, its direction remained more or less the same.

"We're heading toward the woods, right?" Toby whispered.

"Yes. Thank God we left our men waiting there."

They continued on; a minute later, a much less comforting realization struck. "Damn!" Christopher muttered. "This goes farther than the woods."

His face grim, Toby nodded. "The church?"

"Must be." Christopher broke into a run. "Come on. We have to catch him."

They glimpsed a faint glow ahead and redoubled their efforts to close the distance.

Ellen was doing her level best to possess her soul in patience.

When Christopher and Toby had ridden off, she'd taken up a position three yards behind the line of Christopher's men, folded her arms, and tried to imagine what was happening and what would happen next.

As she stood, silently tapping her toe on the dead leaves, she had to wonder why she felt so…anxious.

She recognized the feeling; it was how she often felt over Robbie. Over his exploits and the possible dangers they might expose him to.

Now here she was, feeling exactly the same way over Christopher. For some reason, she was perfectly certain Toby would emerge unscathed, but Christopher…?

She frowned. It wasn't that she considered Christopher any less able than his cousin. Quite the opposite, truth be told. Yet regardless, it was Christopher and his safety that currently sat uppermost in her mind, sharp and clear, riveting her thoughts, her emotions, her feelings.

One other feeling that was making itself known was the need to relieve herself.

"Blast!" she murmured. "I shouldn't have had that second cup of tea. Given the one I had at lunchtime, that was actually my third."

Regardless, she'd swallowed the tea, and now…

She focused on the men, all of whom had their attention locked on the rear of the inn. She took a step back, but none of them noticed; none turned around to see what she was doing.

She took that as a sign, turned, and quietly retreated into the woods, farther back to where the trees were older and the bushes between them grew thickly.

She found a suitably screened spot; two minutes later, she emerged, feeling much better.

She shook her skirt straight—

Screech!

She whirled, almost slapping her hands over her ears as the horrible grinding of stone sliding on stone continued, then abruptly ceased. The sound hadn't come from the inn, nor from the church itself, but from nearer at hand. Searching for the source of the sound, she realized her quest for privacy had taken her to within a yard of the wall around the graveyard.

Curious, she crept closer.

The sound of stone shifting resumed in short, sharp bursts.

Where the graveyard wall backed onto the woods, a section had crumbled; she hiked up her skirts and clambered over to stand in the ankle-high grass that grew between some of the older graves, tucked against the wall.

She brushed down her skirt and stared toward the source of the noise—and saw that the flat rectangular stone lying atop a grave had swiveled almost a full ninety degrees from its normal position. As she watched, a hand emerged from the darkness beneath.

She swallowed an instinctive gasp, but this was no specter arising from the grave; even from where she stood, she could see that the hand and the burly arm it was attached to were solid and real.

"It has to be Hardcastle," she muttered. "He's come through a tunnel from the inn's cellars."

After administering a last shove to the rectangular stone, the arm retreated, and a second later, a head emerged.

Ellen had never met the publican, but she had no difficulty believing the heavyset man was he—especially when, as he climbed out of the hole and stepped over the stone lip of the grave, she saw the paper-wrapped package he was carrying under one arm.

Hardcastle hadn't seen her; she was standing unmoving in the shadows cast by one of the huge old trees. He turned to face the open grave, paused as if to catch his breath, then set down the package and reached for the swiveled stone.

Christopher and Toby must be down there.

Ellen didn't stop to think further. She marched forward. "You, sir! Just what do you think you're doing?"

She'd used her best "how dare you" tone and had exclaimed as loudly as she could, hoping that Granger and the watchers behind the inn would hear and come running.

Hardcastle leaped back from the open grave and swung to face her.

She halted; now she was closer, she realized how powerfully built the publican was. But she was committed to keeping him there until help arrived. She planted her hands on her hips and, in strident tones, informed him, "You have just desecrated a grave! That's a terrible sin!" Every word was uttered at the top of her lungs.

Hardcastle wasn't a fool; his eyes narrowed. His gaze darted to either side, then returned, assessingly, to her. Slowly, he bent, reaching for the package lying at his feet.

She had to distract him. Maintaining her belligerent stance, she pointed imperiously at the package. "What's that? It wouldn't happen to be counterfeit notes, by any chance?"

Hardcastle's eyes flew wide. He swiped up the package and took half a step back, then his features turned to stone. He tucked the package under his arm and strode toward her.

She didn't wait for him to reach her; he was heavy and lumbering— she was sure she would be faster. She shrieked and raced along the waist-high graveyard wall, keeping a row of substantial monuments between her and Hardcastle.

He swore and started after her. She heard his boots thumping on the ground and chanced a glance back, only to discover he was faster than she'd expected. She shrieked again—entirely in earnest—and fled out of the grave-yard and across the open lawn beside the nave, parallel to the wall that ran all the way to the lychgate. She shrieked again and prayed the others would look and see her, then she swung under the lychgate and out into the lane, intending to race back toward the wood behind the inn and the men waiting there.

She glanced up just in time to see Hardcastle leap over the low wall and land less than two yards away.

He'd dropped the package of notes somewhere; both his hands were free as he lunged for her. "Come here, you doxy!"

Ellen didn't have breath left to shriek. She skidded to a halt; just avoiding Hardcastle's grasping fingers, she pivoted and plunged back under the lychgate. Praying that Christopher and Toby had by now reached the end of the tunnel—that they had, in fact, followed Hardcastle as per their plan—she raced straight ahead, desperately making for the west end of the church.

The graveyard lay to the east; she hoped to lead Hardcastle back to where he'd emerged from the grave.

She was perhaps ten feet ahead as she ran along the path parallel to the nave on the south side of the church—and she'd been right. She was faster than he was on the flat; he wasn't gaining on her.

She risked a glance back, saw his features contorted with fury, and promptly faced forward again.

Her breath sawing in her lungs, a stitch starting in her side, she rounded the northeast corner of the church and looked toward the open grave.

She nearly sobbed with relief when she saw Christopher standing beside it and Toby climbing out.

She didn't have breath left to call; she gasped and rushed on. Christopher heard her footsteps and, instantly alert, swung her way.

His eyes widened as she staggered into his arms.

"Hardcastle!" She managed to wave behind her—just as the publican came roaring around the corner.

Ellen found herself thrust at Toby; he grabbed her arms and dragged her aside.

She twisted to look back and saw Hardcastle skid to a halt.

His eyes wild, Hardcastle raked the scene. He took in Christopher, who was quickly circling to block Hardcastle from fleeing to the south.

"Stay there!" Toby pushed Ellen down to sit on the top of an undisturbed grave.

She was too winded to argue and, struggling to catch her breath, all but wilted on the grave top.

Toby stalked forward between the graves, together with Christopher slowly closing in on Hardcastle.

Ellen heard footsteps and voices approaching as the watchers in the wood came running.

Hardcastle saw them. He was trapped and about to be taken.

He snarled, reached into his jacket, and whipped out a long, wicked-looking knife.

The sight of it—Ellen was pleased to note—caused Christopher and Toby to pause and take stock.

Then they started forward again, moving to trap Hardcastle between them.

Horrified, Ellen sat up. Her eyes felt as round as they could get as she watched Hardcastle swing the knife point first toward Toby, then toward Christopher.

Back and forth, Hardcastle went, then he lunged at Toby, but it was a feint.

Hardcastle swung and flung himself at Christopher—who was standing between him and his only possible route to freedom.

Faster than Ellen had thought possible, Christopher sidestepped, flung up his forearm, pushing aside the knife, and jabbed a vicious punch into Hardcastle's chest.

Hardcastle huffed and staggered.

Christopher tripped him and helped him on with a two-handed shove.

The publican went sprawling, plowing almost headfirst into the side of a monument.

Stretched full-length, Hardcastle abruptly deflated; he lay facedown between two graves, plainly struggling to breathe, while the men from the wood ran up.

Granger had brought rope. He and the other watchers swiftly tied Hardcastle's hands, then hauled the man—still wheezing—to his feet and dragged him toward the woods and the horses.

Toby called back two of the grooms, and together with Christopher, they slid the top stone over the open grave, sealing the tunnel once more.

Straightening, Christopher and Toby dusted their hands. The grooms, dismissed, hurried to catch up with their fellows.

Toby glanced at Christopher, then at Ellen, still seated on the monument where Toby had left her. He grinned and saluted her. "That was quick thinking."

She huffed, still faintly breathless. "Just as well I'd dropped back in the woods and was close enough to hear him open the grave." She looked out across the village green. "It seems no one else heard my shrieking."

"Indeed." Toby exchanged a glance with Christopher, who remained distinctly tight-lipped. "Despite our plans taking an odd turn, it seems we've succeeded in securing both Hardcastle and the notes." With his head, he indicated the package, lying in the grass near the graveyard wall, and started for it. "I'll take this back to the manor, along with Hardcastle." He bent and picked up the package, then looked at Christopher and Ellen. "We'll get him settled in the manor's cellar, then we can see what he has to say."

Christopher managed a terse nod. "I'll see you back there."

Ellen looked from Toby to Christopher, then back at Toby. "I'll be there, too."

Toby waved, stepped over the low wall, and headed off after the other men.

Ellen swung to face Christopher and leveled a distinctly challenging look at his uninformative, not to say stony, visage. "I believe that as I was instrumental in apprehending the man, I have a right to be present and hear what he says."

Christopher stared at her. Inside, a whirlwind of emotions and fears raged, buffeting him and rattling the very foundations of his control. Eroding it.

He stalked toward her; as if from a distance, he heard himself ask, "How did you come to be chased by Hardcastle?"

She pushed off the monument and rose to her feet. "I saw him come up out of the grave—I realized you and Toby would be following him, but then he bent to push the stone back into place. I had to distract him, so I marched out and upbraided him about desecrating a grave, but he wasn't going to wait meekly until you came, and the others were too far away, so I asked him if the package contained counterfeit notes. He picked up the package and came for me, but I knew I was faster than he was, so"—she shrugged—"I shrieked and ran, and of course, he followed."

He frowned. "How far did you run?"

She pointed. "Along the wall to the lychgate, through it, but then he leapt over the wall and nearly caught me, and I pelted back around the church"—she transcribed the route with her finger—"and around to here, and thankfully, you and Toby had arrived." She blinked at him, her gaze untroubled, as if such a performance was commonplace and not to be wondered at.

Christopher felt something inside him rupture. He seized her arms, held her before him, and exploded in the equivalent of an icy roar, "Don't you ever— *ever*—put yourself in danger like that again!"

Her level gaze turned to a glare. "I beg your pardon?"

"You heard!" He couldn't seem to rein in the force that was driving him; he met her glare for sizzling glare. "You must not, ever again, put yourself in danger."

She frowned. "Why?"

"Because..." He gritted his teeth against the words, but they forced themselves through. "I can't bear it."

Because I've fallen in love with you.

But he couldn't say that. Instead, he ground out, "Not here, not now—not on my watch." He saw anger cloud her eyes, only to be dissipated by suspicion. One part of him prayed she would guess all he hadn't said, while the rest of him cringed at the possibility.

Her lips had set as if she was about to hotly argue, but now, the luscious curves eased, and she tipped her head and eyed him assessingly. After another moment of searching his eyes, she drew in a short breath and said, "You have to understand that I find this"—she waved a hand between them—"quite odd. No one has ever really worried about me—I'm the one who worries about everyone else." She paused, then, her gaze still locked with his, evenly said, "I really can't see why you're so upset. I'm safe, you're safe, Toby's safe, and everything has turned out as we wished."

"No! Not as I wished." He released her and clutched at his hair. His swirling emotions were making him giddy. He reiterated, "You were in danger. *Real* danger! What if Hardcastle had caught you? The devil had a knife!"

The words reminded her of his earlier clash with the publican; her gaze deflected to his left arm, and she saw the gash in his sleeve.

Her face transformed into a mask of concern. "My God—he cut you! How badly is it bleeding?" She hauled his arm down and tried to examine the wound.

He couldn't worry and react, but she could?

He uttered a sound he would never have thought he might make—that of a man pushed beyond the limits of frustration—gave up all pretense, hauled her to him, and crushed his lips to hers.

He raised a hand, gripped her jaw, and kissed her ravenously, letting free all the pent-up emotions the past half hour had sent raging through him.

For all of one second, she was passive in his arms, then she pushed both hands up, over his chest, framed his face, and kissed him back.

Passion, desire, and so much more collided and erupted in a maelstrom of need. A need for reassurance at the most primal level—a hunger that could only be assuaged by the heartbeat and the heat of the other.

By the feel of her in his arms, by the thunder of her heartbeat when his hand fell to her throat and his thumb came to rest on the pulse point at its base.

She pressed against him, demanding more, inciting, inviting, and as lost to the moment as he.

As caught in the turmoil of the unruly, untamable emotions caring for another—loving—evoked and brought so powerfully to bear.

This—precisely this—had driven his resistance to marrying, given that, for him, marriage meant falling in love and developing a suscepti-bility to the mindless panic and desperation that had pierced him with icy claws when he'd realized just how much danger she'd courted.

How close she'd come to harm.

Yet they were mutually afflicted, it seemed, both subject to the same pressures, the same unavoidable, overriding fear.

If she could manage, could weather the storm...

One thing she couldn't manage was this raging, out-of-control kiss.

That, he accepted, fell to him.

It took every ounce of his willpower to ease them both back from the beckoning conflagration. Even then, he gave thanks when she—finally—consented to follow his lead and ease back from the all-consuming, avidly greedy exchange.

Now was not the time; doubtless, she realized that as well as he.

Their lips finally parted.

He looked down, into her face, framed by the curved edge of her bonnet, into her eyes, pupils wide. Her lips were rosy and swollen.

He ached to consign the rest of the world to oblivion and kiss her again...but he couldn't.

They couldn't.

Not yet.

He read that understanding in her hazel eyes as awareness returned and her wits realigned.

Still holding her against him, her gaze trapped with his, he quietly stated, " *That's* why you can't put yourself in danger."

She blinked, then her eyes widened as his words and their underlying meaning sank in. "Oh." She searched his eyes. "I see."

Gently, he set her on her feet, but she didn't step away.

Instead, she held his gaze and told him, "You do realize that argument works both ways, don't you?"

It was his turn to blink, to read in her eyes what she intended him to comprehend. "Does it?"

The words, along with an undercurrent of vulnerability, slipped out before he could muffle them.

She returned his faintly questioning look with a very direct look of her own. "Yes, it does."

The sound of hooves clopping up the lane had them both turning.

One of the manor's grooms was riding toward them, leading their horses.

Christopher caught the glance Ellen threw him and waved her toward the lychgate. "We'd better get back, or Toby will start questioning Hardcastle without us."

She huffed, but said nothing more as, side by side, they strode for the gate.

CHAPTER 11

*I*n a room off the manor's kitchens, they set about convincing Hardcastle that the very best thing he could do at that point was to tell them everything they wanted to know.

Initially, perhaps unsurprisingly, Hardcastle was surly and resistant to all overtures, refusing to answer any question, even the most obvious, such as to whom he was to have delivered the fake notes.

Apparently comfortable and relaxed, Christopher and Toby sat behind a narrow desk while before it, Hardcastle shifted his bulk on a hard, straight-backed chair. His hands, bound together, lay in his lap, and the grooms who had brought him to the room had also tied him to the chair.

Ellen, meanwhile, had chosen to stand, or rather, with her arms crossed, to pace slowly and consideringly—distractingly—around the tableau created by Hardcastle, the desk, and Christopher and Toby. Her gaze remained trained on Hardcastle, as if seeking some chink in his armor.

Hardcastle glowered at Christopher and Toby, but the occasional glances he threw Ellen were more wary. Regardless, he clung doggedly to silence.

Eventually, Toby, with his forearms on the desk and his hands clasped before him, ventured, "Perhaps we should explain what will happen if you continue to refuse to cooperate. Shortly, others will arrive, and if you fail to talk, you'll be taken to the Tower."

Shock froze Hardcastle's expression, and Toby grimly nodded. "Yes, the Tower, because engaging in spreading counterfeit notes in such quantity used to be classed as treason. Many still consider it a most heinous crime." Toby paused, then arched a brow. "I believe hanging will be the least of what you can expect."

Although Hardcastle had paled, he continued to stare truculently at them, his jaw set like an iron trap.

Ellen paused by Christopher's chair and artfully sighed. "Such a waste of a life. I've always thought hanging peculiarly gruesome, especially with the crowd baying for blood. And just think of your poor wife and children having to watch—because of course, they'll feel they should be there."

Hardcastle's eyes flared.

Ellen noticed, but pretended she hadn't; clasping her elbows, she shuddered evocatively. "Such a horrible experience—let alone the stigma they'll have to live with for the rest of their lives. They might even have to leave the Bull—or feel they have to because everyone hereabouts will know. Even though they're entirely blameless…" She frowned and focused on Hardcastle. "Or are they accomplices? Do they know about the counterfeit notes?"

Hardcastle's lashes flickered, and he straightened. "No," he growled. "None of them know a damn thing—you leave them out of it."

Christopher leapt in to say, "The authorities are more interested in laying hands on those who organized the scheme rather than minor players along the way, such as you, let alone your family." He caught Hardcastle's gaze. "If you cooperate and, by so doing, assist the authorities in catching the people they're after, we can ensure that the worst you'll face will be transportation rather than an appointment with the hangman. At best…?" Still holding Hardcastle's gaze, Christopher shrugged. "Who knows? Depending on how helpful you are, it's possible the authorities will turn a blind eye to your involvement."

"That," Toby quietly said, "is something we can arrange *if* you cooperate with us."

Hardcastle shifted on the chair. His gaze flicked from Toby to Christopher, then he looked down at his bound hands.

When the silence stretched and Hardcastle didn't look up, Ellen wondered if he was ready to talk but didn't know where to begin. She started pacing again; passing behind Toby's chair, she asked, "How did you know about the old smuggling routes?"

Hardcastle raised his head, stared at her, then moistened his lips and replied, "My father used to run with a smuggling gang, back in the old days. Out of Lydd. I'd grown up hearing all the tales, all the stories of how things were done, and my father had shown me the hidey holes they'd used, back when I was a nipper." He transferred his gaze to the desk.

When Hardcastle again fell silent, Toby caught Christopher's eyes and arched a brow.

Christopher mouthed, "Wait."

Several seconds later, Hardcastle shifted awkwardly again, then looked up and met Christopher's and Toby's gazes. "You've got the notes, but you already knew I had them. You knew about the notes themselves, and you knew I had them stashed somewhere in the inn. All that palaver about a raid was a trick to make me rush and get the notes to move them, wasn't it?"

Christopher held the publican's gaze, then nodded once. "Yes."

Hardcastle gave that due thought. "Sounds like you already know how the notes got to me, then."

"We have some notion," Toby admitted. "Why don't you tell us, to make sure we've guessed correctly?"

Hardcastle narrowed his eyes at Toby, then looked at Christopher, but the man's belligerence was fading. "I was a fool to get involved, but...I just wanted the money. Not the counterfeit stuff, the real money the lady paid me for delivering the notes to her."

Before they could ask which lady, Hardcastle said, "I don't want my family dragged into this. They know nothing at all about any of it. If I tell you all I know..." He looked at them questioningly.

Brows rising, Christopher looked up at Ellen.

She nodded and, halting behind Christopher, met Hardcastle's eyes. "Regardless of what happens to you, we'll do what we can to ensure your family doesn't suffer for your sins."

Hardcastle studied her, then looked at Christopher, searching his face. Eventually, Hardcastle nodded. "All right."

Toby leaned forward. "Start at the beginning. Who first approached you?"

"I was in Rye, picking up supplies from the warehouse there. I'd stopped at a tavern on the docks for a quick pint before starting home, and I heard this fellow, a Frenchy by his accent, asking about the old smuggling routes." Hardcastle huffed. "He was asking in the wrong tavern—no one there had any connections. Well, except for me, and after paying for a month's worth of spirits, I'd just been worrying about how little I was making at the Bull... Anyways, I tipped the fellow a wink and met him outside. He explained he needed a sure way of carting a package from the coast to a place up in the Weald."

Hardcastle paused, clearly thinking back. "He and I, we went round and round, neither trusting the other first off. Eventually, I told him I knew of ways it might be done, but I'd want the cargo to come ashore about two miles west of Dungeness. That suited him fine—he got quite excited and told me the destination was a place near St. George's Church in a village called Benenden. Well, it seemed like it was meant, didn't it? I told him I knew the place—that it wasn't far from where I lived. I didn't want to tell him the church was next door, but that seemed to settle it for him. We went into a coffeehouse and sat and worked it all out—how the cargo, which was really a bundle of counterfeit notes, would come across the Channel stuck inside packets of lace. Me and a mate would pick up the packets on the beach, direct from the boats, and cart them to Lydd. We would hide them in the tombs in Lydd churchyard—you can never be sure of exactly what time of night a boat will beach, so to make sure we never got caught out by the dawn and no one ever saw us carting strange packets about, we left the packets in the tombs, rode home, then came back the next night or a few nights later and picked up the stuff."

Now he'd started talking, Hardcastle rolled on without prompting, "The man said the first three runs would be small—just four or so packets —to make sure the entire system was working. After that would come larger loads. A message stuck in with the fake notes would tell me by what date I was expected to hand the notes on."

Hardcastle looked at Christopher and Toby.

Christopher asked, "Who were you told to pass the notes to?"

"And how," Toby asked, "were you to let them know you had notes to pass on?"

Hardcastle pulled a face. "Even now, I don't know who, exactly, comes and gets the notes. The Frenchy—Millais, his name was—asked me if there was a gravestone in St. George's churchyard, an old one, one no one ever put flowers on. I told him the grave of old Jeremiah Walkhurst had a big old headstone, and there were no Walkhursts in the district anymore. So Millais told me that after I'd picked up the first run —which turned out to be four packets—to pull the notes out from the lace, check what date I was to deliver them by, wrap the notes up in a neat bundle, all tied up, then early one morning, on or before but close to the delivery date, put flowers on old Jeremiah's grave. He told me I'd get a note in reply, left with the flowers, telling me when and where to meet the person who would take the notes and pay me. I'd get ten pounds per packet of lace, on top of the lace itself, which I'd be free to sell on." Hardcastle shrugged his beefy shoulders. "That was good money for doing very little, and it seemed like no real risk, either." He met Toby's eyes. "No skin off my nose if some of the notes going around aren't from the Bank of England."

Toby only shook his head.

"So what happened the first time you left flowers on the grave?" Christopher asked. "Who contacted you?"

"I left the flowers like Millais said, then checked back late in the afternoon and found a note tucked in with the flowers. It said to meet in the woods to the west of the lychgate at midnight that night—and to burn the message, which I did." Hardcastle shrugged again. "So I took the banknotes and went, and there was a woman there, cloaked and veiled, waiting for me. I told her I had the notes from four packets of lace, and she said, "Correct," and handed me the money—forty quid, just like Millais had promised."

Hardcastle stared at the desktop, a faint frown on his face. "She told me leaving the flowers on Jeremiah's grave was to be our signal. If I left them, she would be there at midnight to pick up the notes, and if she wanted to contact me, she'd put flowers on the same grave, but later in the morning." Hardcastle glanced at Christopher. "She's never done that."

"Who is she?" Christopher asked.

"I don't know, do I?" A touch of Hardcastle's earlier truculence resurfaced. "I've met her three times now, and the second and third time, she said nothing at all."

"But you heard her speak the first time," Ellen said. "How did she sound? A lady or a maid or...?"

Hardcastle looked at Ellen; his expression grew distant, as if he was replaying the moment in his memory. "Fact is," he eventually said, "she sounded a bit like you. Wasn't you—I do know that—but similar. Cool and collected and sure of herself. Perhaps a bit more haughty-like." He paused, then said, "I always thought she was a lady, but which lady and from where, I haven't a clue. She was always there ahead of me, and she waits until after I slope off before she leaves. I don't know how she gets there or from which direction she comes or in which direction she leaves, so it's no use asking me."

Christopher exchanged a glance with Toby. The arrangement matched what else they'd learned of the mastermind's scheme. Each person involved knew very little about the next cog in the mechanism. Or the previous one, come to that.

Toby returned his attention to Hardcastle. The publican's shoulders had gradually slumped as he'd told his tale; his belligerence had evaporated, and he looked sober and increasingly anxious. Toby asked, "What date were you given for your next delivery?"

Hardcastle blinked. "By next Monday. That means Monday midnight at the latest."

Christopher rapidly reviewed all they'd learned. He met Hardcastle's eyes. "Rollins—does he know anything about the notes?"

"Nah. I just used him to off-load the lace once I'd taken the notes out of it."

"What about your mate who helped collect the packets?" Toby arched his brows. "Does he know what was hidden in the lace?"

Hardcastle shook his head. "No. The Frenchy—Millais—harped on about that. Only those who needed to were supposed to know about the fake notes. I paid me old mate two pound per packet, brought up and stashed in the inn's cellars, and he was happy with that. He knew well enough not to ask questions."

And Hardcastle saw no reason to give them his mate's name; Christopher didn't bother to ask for it.

"Right, then." He pushed back from the desk and rose. Toby did the same.

With the first hint of desperation creeping into his expression, Hardcastle looked from one to the other. "So you'll make sure I don't swing?"

Christopher joined Ellen and urged her toward the door. "If all you've told us proves true, our agreement will stand, and at worst, it'll be transportation for you."

Hardcastle grimaced, but remained slumped, resigned. He didn't watch as Christopher guided Ellen out of the room and Toby followed.

Christopher paused to give the grooms waiting outside the door orders to transfer Hardcastle back to the cellars, where there was a cell-like room they could hold him in. "He's been cooperative, so make sure he's got decent food and some ale and a pallet and blanket for tonight. I'm not sure how long we'll have to hold him, but it'll likely be several days."

The grooms nodded and went in to fetch Hardcastle.

Christopher followed Ellen and Toby along the short corridor that led from the kitchens to the door at the rear of the front hall.

Ellen spoke over her shoulder. "Hardcastle was foolish to get involved, but for all that, he seems to have a certain sense of honor. He didn't want anyone else to be blamed for things they didn't know about."

Head down, his hands sunk in his pockets, entirely sober, Toby said, "He's a perfect example of just how clever the mastermind has been—he's had his agents hunt and search to find just the right sort of people to run his scheme for him."

Christopher nodded. "Capable people who have a weakness—in Hardcastle's case, a desire for more money, possibly to help keep the inn afloat."

Ellen sighed. "I just hope his family can manage without him."

Christopher grimaced. "Eventually, we'll have to tell them where he's gone and why, but for now, given he's been in the habit of going off for days every now and then—"

"And," Toby broke in, "he told his son there was something he had to see to."

Christopher nodded. "Given that, let's leave his family to manage for now. For them, any bad news can wait."

They emerged into the front hall to discover an arrival in progress. Several trunks and hatboxes along with two suitcases stood in a clump in the middle of the floor. Mrs. Marsh was directing two footmen over which rooms to cart everything to, while Pendleby was bowing and attempting to usher the not-entirely-unexpected guests into the drawing room.

Christopher and Toby spotted Drake's dark head and strode forward with considerable relief, even while their gazes settled on the second dark-haired guest—Louisa, Drake's wife.

Toby and Christopher had met the couple at Somersham Place only a few weeks before; Louisa was expecting the couple's first child, albeit with some months yet to go, but not even the skills of London's best modistes could conceal her burgeoning figure.

Louisa's green eyes locked on the three of them. "There you are, Christopher. And Toby, too." Louisa smiled delightedly at Ellen. "And who's this?"

Christopher shot Drake a look, along with a thank-God-you're-here-and-about-time nod. He was a trifle surprised Drake had allowed Louisa to accompany him into the country on a critical mission which might yet prove dangerous, but then again, this was Louisa; Christopher had never known anyone able to rein her in—except, sometimes, Drake. Clearly, her husband had elected to choose his battles.

After welcoming Louisa with a suitably cynical "What a lovely surprise!" and bending and bussing her cheek, Christopher stepped back and allowed Toby to greet her.

Ellen had halted a few paces from the group.

Smiling encouragingly, Christopher captured her hand and drew her forward as Louisa, her expression alight with curiosity, stepped past Toby. Christopher glanced at Louisa. "Allow me to present Miss Ellen Martingale of Bigfield House, which is just across the lane. Ellen—this is a cousin of sorts, Louisa, Marchioness of Winchelsea."

Ellen's eyes widened, and she dropped into a curtsy. "My lady." As she rose, she glanced sharply at Christopher, then, her own habitual curiosity surfacing, regarded Louisa. "It's a pleasure to meet you, ma'am."

Louisa hadn't missed the swift look Ellen had cast him. "Please, no ma'ams! Just Louisa." She reached for Ellen's hand and, as she shook it, smiled with smug delight. "Indeed, I'm exceedingly glad to make your acquaintance."

Louisa undertook to introduce Drake, and to Christopher's eyes, Ellen's curiosity only grew.

With the social niceties dealt with, Christopher caught Drake's gaze. "You've arrived earlier than I anticipated. Did my latest message reach you?"

Drake nodded. "I'd already made arrangements to come down, and we were on our way. When we stopped to change horses at Sevenoaks, Louisa recognized your man in the inn yard. He gave us your message, and I told him to return here at his own pace. He'll be somewhere behind us—we didn't dally."

Knowing the sort of horses Drake favored, Christopher wasn't surprised that his man hadn't yet reached the manor.

"Just as well you're here," Toby said. "We've had to take the first steps without you, and we'll need your input over how to go on."

"Indeed." Louisa looked from Ellen to Toby and Christopher. "We're here to work on this business at Goffard Hall." She returned her gaze to Ellen. "Have you been assisting, too?"

Drake's expression stated that he wanted to know the answer to that question as much as his wife did.

Christopher replied, "Ellen has been an active party in our investigations."

"Excellent!" Louisa looped her arm in Ellen's and turned toward the drawing room. "So we can all go into the drawing room—and to please my husband, I'll put my feet up—and you three can tell us what's been going on down here, and then we can decide what we, as a group, need to do next."

Louisa was poised to sweep an unresisting Ellen through the open drawing room door when Pendleby cleared his throat and shifted as if to intercept them.

"My lady." He bowed, then cast a look at Drake. "My lord. If I might suggest, the hour is somewhat advanced, and you might wish to retire to your room and refresh yourselves before dinner."

"Good gracious!" Louisa swung around to regard her menfolk. "Is it really that late?"

"Country hours, my dear," Drake smoothly said. "So yes, it truly is time we went up."

Pendleby bowed again. "Mrs. Marsh"—he indicated the housekeeper —"and I will be happy to escort you to your room."

Their luggage had already vanished up the stairs.

"Yes, of course." Louisa sounded deflated, but she knew the ropes of a household such as this.

"Perhaps"—Drake looked at Christopher, then transferred his dark gaze to Ellen and arched a brow—"Miss Martingale—"

"Ellen, please, my lord."

Drake smiled, "Only if you call me Drake."

Ellen smiled back. "If you wish."

"I was going to suggest," Drake continued, including Louisa, Toby, and Christopher with his gaze, "that if Ellen would remain for dinner, Louisa and I could hear all your reports at once."

Brightening again, Louisa took her husband's arm. "And afterward, we could make the necessary plans all together."

Ellen felt her spirits rise; Louisa's inclusive attitude was heartening. "As Christopher mentioned, I live across the lane. I can easily send a message that I'll be dining here."

Drake smiled. "Good—so that's settled." He looked at his wife. "Come, my dear, and let's dispense with the dust of the journey."

Louisa smiled benevolently at Christopher, Toby, and Ellen and announced, "For the record, I am not dressing for dinner."

Christopher tipped his head in acknowledgment, while Toby muttered, "Thank God."

Louisa briefly arched her brows at Toby, then allowed her husband to lead her up the stairs in Pendleby's wake, with Mrs. Marsh bringing up the rear.

Christopher glanced at Toby, then looked at Ellen. "We may as well take refuge in the library. You can write your note, and I'll get a groom to run it across to Bigfield House."

Ellen smiled and acquiesced with an inclination of her head. As she walked with the men to the library, she considered her initial assessment of the newcomers. Drake was tall, dark-haired, dark-eyed, and much like Toby in build, projecting a sense of steely, whiplike strength, all under perfect control. In contrast, Christopher was more the strong, solid sort—more rocklike than whiplike. Yet Drake possessed an aura of power beyond what either of the other men wielded; Ellen found such overt political and social pre-eminence a touch unnerving.

She wasn't surprised that Louisa, for her part, patently took all that Drake was in her stride. Indeed, she matched him, for Louisa—also dark-haired yet with unusual pale-green eyes and what must, initially, have been a neat, petite figure—possessed a similar, perhaps complementary inner strength and assurance. Indeed, assurance, confidence, and certainty in her ability to achieve whatever she set her mind to...that, for Ellen's money, described Louisa's character to a T.

They reached the library, and Ellen preceded the men into the room. Christopher waved her to his desk and settled her behind it with paper and pen. She drew the paper to her, dipped the sharpened nib into the inkwell, and started to craft a short note for her aunt.

That endeavor didn't take long. While she waited for the ink to dry, her mind returned to the recently arrived couple. Both Drake and Louisa hailed from the very highest echelons of the ton, which emphasized the fact that Christopher and Toby did, too. Yet all four were quite unlike any of the nobility she'd previously met, not that she'd rubbed shoulders with dukes and duchesses, yet she'd observed and met many who inhabited such circles during her years in London society.

The Cynsters—and apparently those they associated with, like Drake —were...

As she glanced at her note and realized the ink was dry, it struck her what the difference was. Christopher, Toby, Louisa, and Drake didn't care what circle of the ton she, or anyone else, inhabited; they knew she was of "good family," and that was enough. They didn't need to bolster their own standing with that of their friends.

Or their connections?

She was careful not to frown as she folded her note and inscribed her aunt's name on the front. In following the path she had, hand in hand with Christopher, she hadn't really thought of where, exactly, that path led—was leading, if where she thought they stood at the moment was in any way accurate. Yet there was no denying that Louisa's and Drake's acceptance of her presence and her continuing inclusion in their group was...

At the very least, it was encouraging rather than discouraging.

Christopher had been seated in an armchair chatting with Toby about the woods to the west of the lychgate; on seeing Ellen set down the pen, he rose and went to her side. "Let me have that." He held out a hand for her note. "I'll send a groom to deliver it."

She looked up, smiled, and surrendered the note. "Thank you."

While he tugged the bellpull, then went to the door, she rose and claimed the armchair beside his. He intercepted Pendleby and consigned the note to his care.

Christopher had only just resumed his seat when the door opened and Louisa looked in. Seeing them, she smiled and walked in, Drake at her heels. "I thought you'd be here." She sank onto the sofa facing the armchairs. She waited until Drake subsided onto the leather beside her, then fixed her pale-green gaze on Christopher. "You said in your message that the mastermind's pawns were moving—in what way?"

"At that point," Christopher said, "we'd learned that the latest batch of counterfeit notes had been brought into the country last Saturday night, and we'd guessed the notes were secreted in packets of contraband lace, which had been hidden in tombs in Lydd churchyard. Subsequently, two nights ago, on Tuesday night, the packets were moved to somewhere near here."

"Lace!" Louisa's eyes widened, then she tipped her head. "I suppose there might be profit to be made by smuggling the high-quality stuff."

"Enough," Christopher agreed, "to allow it to be a believable cargo. We realized they were using lace"—he glanced at Ellen and smiled—"because of Ellen's experience when her aunt insisted on buying some from the village millinery-cum-haberdashery."

When Drake's and Louisa's eyes swung her way, Ellen explained the oddity of finding such lace at such a low price in a small village shop.

Louisa asked the price, and when Ellen told her, her brows flew high. "Yes, indeed—that's quite astonishing."

"Quick of you to make the connection," Drake said approvingly.

"Because of that," Christopher continued, "we decided to pressure the milliner's source, which was her husband, using a ruse of wishing to purchase a great deal of lace."

"Enough for a tiered wedding gown," Ellen put in.

"Yards and yards." Louisa nodded. "So what happened?"

"The first thing that became clear was that the milliner herself knew nothing about the true source of the lace—she thinks her husband purchases it from a warehouse in London."

Louisa shook her head. "Would that were possible, but it isn't."

"So Ellen assured us, and when she pressed for more lace than the milliner had on hand, the husband was pushed into consulting *his* source, who proved to be the publican of the local inn."

The door opened, and Pendleby appeared. "Dinner is served, sir. My lord, my lady."

"Thank you, Pendleby." Christopher pushed to his feet and gave Ellen his hand. As she gripped it and rose, he said to Drake, "We can continue this over Mrs. Hambledon's roast."

They settled about the dinner table, with Christopher at the head, Drake at the foot, Toby and Ellen on one side, and Louisa facing them.

They'd consumed the soup and Pendleby had removed the plates before Drake looked up the table and asked, "Did you pressure the milliner's husband today, or was that yesterday?"

"This morning—we got back from Lydd too late to take any further action yesterday." Christopher picked up the knife and fork Pendleby had placed beside him and commenced carving the sizeable haunch of beef that had been placed ceremonially before him.

"It's been a busy day." Toby took up the tale to allow Christopher to concentrate. He summarized how they'd identified Hardcastle, the publican, as the receiver of the lace-bound notes and how, subsequently, they'd prodded him to rush to move the notes out of the inn.

"What a brilliant plan," Louisa said, and Drake inclined his head in approbation.

Toby grinned and looked at Ellen. "That was another of Ellen's ideas. And," Toby continued, with a sideways glance at Christopher, "if it hadn't been for her hanging back in the woods, closer to the church, Hardcastle might well have escaped with the notes."

"As it was," Christopher said, sawing at the roast as if that required all his attention, "Ellen ended up throwing herself into Hardcastle's path and getting him to chase her all over the churchyard until Toby and I emerged from the tunnel Hardcastle had taken from the inn and saved her."

He glanced up, and he definitely wasn't smiling as he looked pointedly at Ellen. After a second, he switched his gaze to Drake. "In the end, however, in very large part thanks to Ellen, we caught Hardcastle and succeeded in securing the notes."

The change in Drake was marked enough for them all to notice. "Good work!" While the words were mild enough, the emotion behind them was anything but. "I'm exceedingly glad that we have the counterfeit notes in our hands." As Pendleby halted beside Drake to offer the platter of roast beef, Drake arched a brow at Christopher. "Where are the notes at present?"

"In the safe here."

While they ate the main course, then moved on to desserts of pudding and trifle and platters of cheeses and fruits, Christopher, Ellen, and Toby recounted what they'd learned from Hardcastle.

Drake concluded, "He's revealed less than we would have liked, yet enough for us to move forward."

"Speaking of moving." Louisa set down her napkin. "As we've finished doing justice to Mrs. Hambledon's fare"—she smiled at Pendleby—"and do pass on our compliments, Pendleby—then perhaps you gentlemen can take your brandies or whiskies in the drawing room so we can continue our discussion in greater comfort."

As Louisa pushed to her feet, Drake leapt to draw out her chair.

Ellen watched as the patently powerful nobleman hovered over his, relatively speaking, diminutive wife, and battled to hide a smile.

With Christopher and Toby flanking her, she fell in behind the couple as they led the way to the drawing room.

Once settled in the more comfortable chairs, with Louisa semi-reclining on the sofa, her feet resting in her husband's lap, they returned to the matter at hand.

"This mastermind of yours"—Christopher stretched out his long legs and crossed his ankles—"has been remarkably careful over who knows what."

Drake nodded. "That's been our problem all along—even when we ran the counterfeiter to earth, he had no real idea of the identity of the man who'd hired him. And although we suspect that someone at Goffard

Hall is involved in distributing the notes via the card parties, as yet we have no firm evidence as to who, exactly, is involved."

Drake's dark gaze fixed on Christopher, then shifted to Toby and Ellen. "The link via the French smugglers to Hardcastle and from him to a lady who presumably hails from Goffard Hall is our only solid evidence tying a particular person from the Hall to the mastermind's scheme. Your efforts thus far have put our investigation on much more certain ground in terms of taking the next step and identifying and capturing the contact at Goffard Hall.

"However," Drake said with a sidelong glance to meet his wife's eyes, "before we start discussing how to take that next step, I should explain why I'm so set on using the trail from Goffard Hall onward to trap the mastermind himself."

Louisa nodded decisively. "Indeed, you should. Explain, I mean. Otherwise, it sounds as if you've simply got a bee in your bonnet over hunting down the mastermind, especially now that we have the counterfeit notes in hand."

Drake faintly grimaced and looked at the other three. "The authorities —by which, in this case, I mean me, two of the more senior Whitehall mandarins, the Prime Minister, three of his senior ministers, and last but by no means least, the Queen and the Prince Consort—are severely exercised by the likelihood that the mastermind is a peer. Even if he isn't quite that, from the description we have, it seems likely he's highly placed in society. Just how high he and his connections lie is the principal source of anxiety."

Christopher frowned. "I'm not sure I follow. Yes, it's regrettable, but we've had bad apples high on the tree before."

Drake inclined his head. "However, in this case, our bad apple—the mastermind—has, whether he's aware of it or not, put himself in the hands of those who command various criminal enterprises on the Continent. It was through them that he learned of, and was put in contact with, the counterfeiter. He—the counterfeiter—was one of their best, indeed, *the* best. That alone testifies to the level of interest the mastermind's scheme held for the criminal families of Europe. Now, however, from the point of view of those underworld lords, through my men following the mastermind's trail and seizing the counterfeiter, the mastermind has cost them a prized asset."

"Ah," Toby said. "They won't be happy."

"No, they aren't. But the men in charge of the Continental crime families didn't get to their present positions by acting rashly. Our information is that they have already had reports on the outcome of the mastermind's first trials in passing counterfeit ten-pound notes. Those men in charge are watching, learning, and also looking for other advantages they can exploit."

Drake paused, then went on, "The fear is that, if the mastermind escapes us, regardless of whether his present scheme comes to fruition or not, the crime families of Europe will have a hold on him—a secret he dare not allow them to air, especially given his likely social and potentially political prominence."

"You fear blackmail," Christopher said.

Drake nodded. "And it might not end solely with the mastermind himself. Given the names of some of those we know to have passed fake notes during the trials—even though they themselves were unaware of it —coupled with indications that the European crime lords are particularly interested in learning who those young men are, then if the mastermind's scheme succeeds at any level, the government might be left with...very few people they can trust, even among their own ranks."

Toby arched a brow. "Using the sins of the sons to influence the fathers?"

Louisa nodded. "Precisely. And we all know that at our level of society, that sort of blackmail has a good chance of working."

"But," Ellen said, frowning slightly, "now we've seized the main shipment of counterfeit notes, surely the latter threat is...well, defusable?" She looked at Drake. "You say you know who passed fake notes during the initial runs. Surely you or someone from the government can, later, quietly tell those young men that they are not at risk of being taken up for passing counterfeit notes."

Drake inclined his head. "With the main shipment in our hands, if all goes smoothly, that or something similar is what will ultimately occur. However, we may need to risk at least some of the fake notes to lure the mastermind into our net—and if anything goes wrong and he slips past us, the latter threat might yet come into play. Regardless, the threat personified by the mastermind himself will continue until we have him." He looked at the others. "I wanted you to know why, despite securing the notes, it remains essential that we apprehend the mastermind."

"So even with the bulk of the counterfeit notes in our hands," Christopher said, "as a result of this scheme, the country still faces two significant threats. One is the mastermind himself—and in order to nullify all future threat from his direction, he must be identified and caught."

Ellen was nodding. "And the secondary threat is that of something going wrong and counterfeit notes being deliberately put into the pockets of young men from families of high social and political standing."

"That"—Drake half bowed to them—"is precisely what we need to keep in mind."

Toby nodded. "All right. Now we all know how matters truly stand, what ought to be our next steps? How, exactly, are we going to move forward?"

CHAPTER 12

They spent the next hour thrashing out the outline of a plan. Sadly, once they'd agreed on the major points—all those they could predict—they were flagging and agreed it was too late to do any more detailed plotting.

Louisa swung her feet to the ground and prepared to push upright. "Regardless, you"—she looked at Toby and Christopher—"can get the ball rolling at first light by putting a handful of wildflowers on that grave."

Drake rose, took her arm, and helped her stand. "We can work on putting all else in place once that's done." He looked at Christopher and Toby. "We can reconvene over breakfast."

Turning toward the door, Louisa arched her brows. "I believe I'll join you over the breakfast cups."

"Not me," Ellen said.

Christopher would have felt relief if he'd believed she wouldn't expect to play an active role in whatever plan they finally hatched.

Indeed, as they followed the others into the front hall, she met his eyes and smiled. "I'll come over after breakfast and see how far you've got." She caught Louisa's eye. "I'll be here by nine o'clock."

Louisa nodded. "I'll keep them in line until then." She waved and headed toward the stairs. "I'm for bed. Drake?"

Drake nodded elegantly to Ellen, cast a warning look at Christopher and Toby, then called "I'm coming" and went after his wife.

Toby held back until the pair were out of earshot, then chuckled. "How the mighty have fallen." With a cheeky look at Christopher, Toby saluted Ellen and ambled toward the stairs.

"Come." Christopher waved Ellen toward the front door. "I'll drive you home."

He opened the door, and after collecting her bonnet and her reticule from the hall table, she preceded him onto the front porch. He followed her gaze as she looked up at the stars; the night sky was the color of midnight silk with diamonds scattered over it by a generous hand. There were no clouds to veil the moon, over half full and riding high.

She raised her face to the gently riffling breeze. "It's almost balmy, and there's enough moonlight to see." She glanced at him. "Rather than disturbing your grooms, we could walk. If we go via the direct path rather than the drives, it's really not that far."

He arched his brows. "I haven't walked that way since I was a boy."

He waved her on, and they descended to the forecourt, then veered toward the shrubbery. Instead of donning her bonnet, Ellen held it by its ribbons; after looping her reticule cord over her left wrist, she allowed the purse to ride in the bowl of her bonnet as she walked along. "Did you often go over to Bigfield House when you were a child?"

He grinned. "I did—or rather, we did, Gregory and I, and Therese often tagged along as well."

Ellen glanced at him; his expression suggested he remembered those excursions fondly.

"As Humphrey and Maud didn't have children, we more or less had the run of the place as well as the manor." Through the shadows cast by the shrubbery's high hedges, he met her eyes and smiled. "Maud always had boiled sweets for us."

They emerged onto the stretch of path that bordered one of the manor's orchards. Blossom time was over, yet the perfume seemed to linger, with just a hint of the tart sharpness of setting fruits creeping in.

Christopher's hand found hers; their fingers twined, then held.

She smiled and walked on, content in the moment.

Somewhere, someone had cut hay, and as they neared the lane, the tang of clipped grass and the elusive perfume of the hawthorn hedge mingled with other night scents and washed over them in a soothing, strangely anchoring wave.

Words seemed superfluous. The night was quiet and still about them as they crossed the lane. Christopher climbed over the second stile, then gave her his hand and helped her up.

Balancing on the narrow top rung, she looked down, into his face, and he smiled, reached up, grasped her waist, and swung her down. The seconds of being suspended in midair stole her breath.

He set her down before him; she knew she should smile, thank him, step away, and straighten her skirt, but she couldn't find the will to move —to end the moment.

A magical moment in which they stared at each other, communing without words.

He bent his head, and she shifted nearer, lifting her face.

An owl swooped and hooted mere yards away—they started and looked up, and the moment was lost.

They exchanged a resigned smile, then he held out his hand and she took it, and they set out again, strolling between the moonlit fields, with her swinging her bonnet by its ribbons.

For once in his life, Christopher wasn't sure of his next step. While his ultimate goal grew increasingly clear, the path to achieving it with the least possible angst remained shrouded and hazy.

He knew what he wanted, but the intrusion of the mission created a distraction and, simultaneously, heightened the need—his need, anyway —to secure his ultimate goal with all speed. The exigencies arising from dealing with the threat represented by the notes and the slippery mastermind acted as spurs, elevating his awareness of the emotions that trailed in love's wake.

Love. Despite being someone who had avoided even thinking the word for most of his life, he was increasingly at ease invoking the emotion and laying outcomes at its feet, at least in his thoughts.

Regardless, at moments like this, it was probably wise to think of something else. He glanced ahead and saw the dark shape of Bigfield House looming between the surrounding trees. "Given you've been spending recent days assisting the investigation, how are the household here"—he nodded toward the house—"managing?"

"Better than I thought they would." She sounded quite pleased. "Robbie has stepped up—or perhaps more accurately stepped into my shoes..."

When she didn't continue, he glanced at her face.

With her fine features gilded by moonlight, she met his eyes. "Robbie can't 'step into my shoes' if I'm already standing in them." When he arched his brows, she looked at the house and, after a moment, continued more definitely, "I want Robbie to take over managing the estate, but if I'm there, he'll defer to me. That's second nature for him—if I'm present, he'll step back and let me lead. It's been that way all his life, so..."

Seconds later, her chin firmed, and she tipped her head Christopher's way. "I realize, now, that if I want Robbie to step up to the challenge and take on the management of Bigfield House, I need to keep away—at least away from the study. When I checked this morning, Robbie and Hopper were getting along quite well. Hopper knows how things should be done. *He* can teach Robbie, and, I now realize, *I* can't. If I try, Robbie will assume I'll do whatever needs to be done." She frowned. "I see that now."

Christopher broke the ensuing silence to say, "In that case, perhaps it's just as well that this business with the counterfeit notes has taken you from the house and effectively dumped into your brother's lap the tasks that, until now, you've dealt with. From what you've said, he appears to be managing well enough—I agree that's a sign he's ready to meet the challenge, and you need to leave him to find his way."

She continued to frown as if visualizing some scenario, but then her face cleared, and she nodded. "You're right." She cast him a sidelong glance. "That leaves me free to devote my time to assisting with Drake's mission."

Christopher wasn't sure that was an ideal outcome. However... "We'll have to see what tomorrow brings."

As far as the first steps in their plan for the next stage went, neither she nor Louisa were directly involved.

The sculpted hedges of the Bigfield House shrubbery rose ahead, almost black in the silvery light. They followed the path through an arch and eventually ambled into a grassed courtyard surrounding a long, stone-edged pool.

The water shimmered blackly under the teasing fingers of a barely there breeze, the glassy expanse interrupted by the spreading pads of water lilies, the fat buds of their flowers, furled for the night, held high on thin stalks.

Another owl hooted, more distantly this time, and even farther away, a fox barked.

Through the arch at the other end of the courtyard, the gravel of the drive glimmered palely under the stark light, and beyond, the mellow walls of Bigfield House rose. They'd almost reached the side door.

Their footsteps slowed.

She turned to him and tipped back her head to look into his face. "Thank you for walking me home."

He looked into her eyes, and even in the moonlight, her gaze remained open, direct—and expectant.

Between them, the specter of their earlier kiss in the churchyard and the pressure of unfinished business rose and swelled, potent prods re-evoking the roiling emotions that, in that earlier setting, had driven them both.

They hadn't had a chance to address what that interlude had revealed. Now...

She waited, and neither slowly nor hurriedly, he reached for her, and as his arm encircled her waist, she boldly stepped forward.

As she stretched up on her toes, he bent his head, and this time, when their lips met, the caress was one of mutual deliberation and unabashed need. The need to seize this—the opportunity, the prospect, the promise—and go forward and see what might be.

A simmering hunger that wouldn't be denied sparked to life at the first firm touch, the first sliding, gliding melding of their lips. Then she parted hers and invited him in, and he gathered her to him and settled to plunder. To appease the need that, even now, still prowled beneath his skin.

Fearlessly—when had she ever behaved otherwise?—she met him and matched him, then pressed her own kisses, her own caresses, on him. She, he realized, had her own agenda—her own quest to pursue—one that largely mirrored his, at least in intent, in desire and in need.

They moved closer, indulging all their senses in the increasingly passionate embrace. Her breasts, swollen and peaked, pressed against his chest, her hips molded to his thighs, and the softness of her belly cradled his erection.

They reveled, each in the other; openly and without reservation, they set their senses free.

Even in that, there was a togetherness, one he hadn't expected—hadn't known might be.

He held to it, wrapped that subtly intimate closeness about him—about them—like a cloak, and let their rising passions lead them on.

Ellen danced, waltzed, and rejoiced in the sensual symphony of her senses; delight fizzed just beneath her skin, warming and enticing.

Through the kiss, she endeavored to assure him of her agreement, her wish to take this further, wherever further led. Of her unfettered need to have more.

Her senses swirled in pleasured delight, then he raised one hand and swept her bobbing curls aside, and long fingers traced, with exquisite slowness, down the line of her throat. The touch set an ache pulsing beneath her skin—a need, a want, a desire to be touched.

More. She said it with her lips, with her tongue, and was confident he heard her plea.

His fingers slid lower, to trace the curve of her breast, firm and warm beneath the constraint her bodice had become. Her senses leapt, and his blunt fingertips continued to explore—until ultimately, at long last, he cupped the firm mound, and she sighed into the kiss. Gently, inexorably, he closed his hand, and pleasure swelled and flowed through her.

He played; that was the only way she could describe the knowingness behind his touch. He knew how much she grew to crave the delight his caresses sent surging through her, tangling and jangling her nerves until she couldn't focus on anything else.

Until craving transformed to yearning, then to need, and eventually to unadulterated desire.

He plucked at the tight peak of her breast, and she gasped. He closed his hand and kneaded, and it was all she could do to remain upright.

But then his caresses slowed. The pressure of his lips eased, drawing her—unwilling, yet unable to forge on without him leading the way— back to the world of moonlight and shadow in which they stood.

At last, his hand fell from her breast, and he raised his head.

To her relief, he still held her close. She'd dropped her bonnet and reticule, and her hands had been gripping his shoulders. She relaxed her fingers, raised both hands, and laying her palms on either side of his face, searched his shadowed eyes. "Why have we stopped?"

The question amused him; the line of his lips curved. But then he swallowed and said, his voice low and gravelly, "Because we need to talk about...this." His gaze traced her features, then his jaw firmed. "However..."

"There's so much else going on." She finished the sentence for him, certain that was what was in his mind.

He nodded. "And this, between us, is not something we should rush." He paused, then added, "I hope you agree that what comes next deserves our full attention, which is more than either of us can presently give."

She searched his eyes, his features, felt the warm pressure of his hands at her waist, and knew that he, no more than she, had wanted to call a halt. Yet he was unquestionably correct, and the fact he'd drawn back was surely the clearest assurance she might want that he saw what was evolving between them as both serious and worthy of their unwavering focus.

He didn't want to get it wrong.

Neither did she.

She drew in a tight breath and nodded. "You're right. And we have time—will have unlimited time once this business with Goffard Hall and the mastermind is dealt with."

He sighed. His expression wryly self-deprecating, he murmured, "I was fairly sure you'd agree."

With mock haughtiness, she arched her brows at him.

Christopher smiled, bent his head, and kissed her once—gently—then raised his head, released her, and stepped back. He bent, picked up her bonnet and reticule and handed them to her, then tipped his head toward the house. "I expect I'll see you tomorrow."

"Indeed." She bent a smiling look on him. "You may count on that."

After holding his gaze for a moment more, she turned and walked through the archway cut in the final hedge.

She passed out of his sight, and he listened to her footsteps crunch on the gravel, then she stepped onto stone, and he heard a faint click.

A second later, he sensed she was gone.

He stood silent and still in the lengthening shadows of the shrubbery and wondered how he truly felt about what had just passed between them.

Eventually, he realized that a smugly satisfied smile had taken up residence on his face—which, he supposed, was his answer.

Sliding his hands into his pockets, he turned and headed back to the manor.

At first light the following morning, Christopher placed a small bunch of wildflowers on the plinth below the once-impressive headstone of Jeremiah Walkhurst's grave.

The Walkhursts had owned the manor in the distant past, before Christopher's grandfather had bought the property from the estate of the last of the tribe.

There was barely light enough for Christopher to pick his way between the graves. He quit the churchyard and slipped into the wood that pressed close on the graveyard's eastern boundary. Deep in the trees, he joined Toby, Granger, and two of the manor's younger grooms, brought along in case, while maintaining the watch to see who took note of Hard-castle's signal, they needed to send a runner with a message to the manor.

The five of them found comfortable positions on the thick blanket of leaf mold beneath the trees and settled to wait.

An hour, then two went by without anyone venturing even close to the church.

Eventually, Granger grunted softly, rose, stretched, and ambled off toward where they'd tethered the horses, well back in the woods. When he reappeared, the others discovered that Granger had had the foresight to bring a sack of bread and cheese. He passed the contents around, and having missed breakfast, they all tucked in.

Another hour dragged by, then soft footsteps reached their ears, approaching through the woods. Startled—they hadn't expected their pigeon to come from that direction, much less on foot—they peered through the trees, wondering whether to leap up and hide, only to spot Drake making his way toward them.

Relieved, they relaxed. They'd ended sitting in a semicircle, propped against the boles of trees, each with a clear view of the graveyard, that side of the church, and part of the green with the vicarage on the opposite side. No one could approach Jeremiah Walkhurst's grave from the right angle to see the small bouquet without being in their sight, but courtesy of the heavy shadows deep in the wood, the chance of anyone spotting them was negligible.

Drake halted between Christopher and Toby and, hands on his hips, surveyed the scene. "I take it no one's appeared."

"No," Toby replied. "Speaking of which…"

When Toby made a great show of looking beyond Drake—patently searching for someone following him—Drake sent him a warning look. "Louisa's gone to call on Ellen at Bigfield House."

Toby looked at Christopher, then back at Drake. "Do we know why?"

"No idea," Drake said. "And no, I didn't ask."

Toby's expression suggested that might have been a mistake.

Drake crouched, then sat, joining the others in staring out at the graveyard.

Every now and then, Christopher consulted his watch and kept the others apprised of the time. Some minutes after ten-thirty, the crisp clop of hooves reached them. A rider was approaching at a slow trot from the direction of the inn.

Courtesy of the curve in the lane, they couldn't see the rider at first, but then he neared the churchyard and rode into view.

"Quiet," Drake murmured. "Don't move. Let's see what he does." He looked at Christopher, waited until Christopher felt the weight of his gaze and glanced his way, then arched his brows.

"Nigel Fontenay," Christopher whispered.

Drake nodded and returned his attention to the dapper young gentleman clad in flashy riding togs who was perched atop a black hunter.

Nigel slowed the horse to a walk and, apparently idly, scanned the graveyard.

His gaze snagged on the bunch of flowers on Jeremiah Walkhurst's grave.

Nigel stared at the flowers, then grinned.

Smiling to himself, he shook his reins and sent his horse into a canter around the green.

Christopher got to his feet, and the others followed suit. Moving forward to the tree line, they watched Nigel reach the lane and turn in the direction of Goffard Hall.

Christopher looked at Drake. "Message received."

Drake nodded. "Indeed. That also means Nigel Fontenay is no more innocent than his sister. Both are acting as agents in the scheme, even if under their cousin's direction."

"So Nigel will take the news back to Goffard Hall—to Mrs. Kirkpatrick? Or is it his sister who meets Hardcastle in the woods?" Toby asked.

Drake looked at Christopher and arched his brows. "You're the only one who's met both women."

"My money's on Mrs. Kirkpatrick," Christopher said. "But regardless, we'll learn who comes to pick up the counterfeit notes tonight." He waved toward the horses. "Our next step is to return to the manor and get our package of 'counterfeit notes' ready."

Granger and the grooms went ahead. Following with Drake and Toby, Christopher picked his way through the woods to his mount.

They entered the library to discover that not only were Louisa and Ellen there ahead of them, they'd also brought a stack of Sir Humphrey's old editions of *The Times* and were sitting on either side of the desk, busily cutting up the sheets to make stacks the same size as banknotes—counterfeit or genuine.

Finding themselves with nothing to do—the ladies were closing in on the required amount without their help—the three men subsided into armchairs.

"So." Ellen looked up from her industrious snipping and fixed all three with an inquiring look. "Who came? I assume someone did."

"Nigel," Christopher replied.

"He rode up the lane around the green," Toby said, "glanced over the church wall at the graveyard, saw the wildflowers on the right grave, smiled to himself, and rode off in great good humor, apparently straight to Goffard Hall to report."

"We'll be able to confirm his arrival there via the watchers keeping an eye on the place." Drake looked at Christopher. "It would be wise to keep a diary of any movements we see, in case, later, any of the players try to weasel their way out of being charged by claiming they weren't where we say they were."

Christopher nodded. "We've been keeping a record of any sightings, just in case something slipped past us."

"There!" Louisa put down the scissors she'd been wielding and compressed the stack of "notes" she'd assembled on the desktop. "That should do it, don't you think?"

She'd addressed the question to Ellen, who looked, then nodded and glanced at the three other stacks they had ready and waiting. "I think we've actually got more than we need, but better that than less. We'll have to get the counterfeit notes out and match everything up."

"Indeed. And"—Louisa swung to face the men—"that brings us to another thing that will need to match. Namely, Hardcastle. Ellen pointed out that whoever comes to fetch the notes at midnight will expect to see Hardcastle." She eyed the men's faces. "We didn't discuss it last night, but do we want to trust Hardcastle to lure into our net whoever turns up?"

Drake pulled a horrendous face. "No. We don't." He looked at Christopher and Toby. "The ladies are right—no matter how cooperative Hardcastle has been, we can't afford to trust him to act as we need, not at this crucial stage."

Toby arched his brows. "But is it necessary for Hardcastle or anyone to get close to the lady? Surely if a lady turns up at midnight in the place appointed for the handover, that will be proof enough of her involvement."

Drake inclined his head. "Proof enough for us, but not, I fear, leverage enough to pressure her into telling us all she knows, then agreeing to play along and continue with the card parties and so on, until such time as the mastermind shows his face." He paused, tipping his head. "If we're lucky, she might even know who the mastermind is, but without having something unequivocal to hold over her to enforce her cooperation, I suspect that merely catching her at midnight in the woods isn't going to yield what we need."

"For instance," Louisa said, "if we merely catch her there—cloaked and veiled in those woods at midnight—she might claim to be waiting to meet someone quite different, or that she was blackmailed into being there and has no idea what any of it is about, or invent some other story to explain her presence."

"No matter how odd it might be, being cloaked and veiled in a wood at midnight isn't a crime," Ellen pointed out.

"We need," Drake said, steepling his fingers before his face, "to catch her—presumably Mrs. Kirkpatrick—with the counterfeit notes in her hands. At least some of the notes, if not all. That will give us the hold over her we need to set a trap for the mastermind."

Toby grimaced. "I stand corrected."

"All right," Christopher said. "So we're going to have to find someone who can impersonate Hardcastle well enough to pass muster, at least in the churchyard at midnight."

"We can't count on it being cloudy and dark," Ellen said. "It wasn't last night, and the sky is just as clear today."

Drake swung around to look at his wife and Ellen, both still seated at the desk. "You two know what your sex is likely to look for in terms of recognizing someone at night. What characteristics does our substitute Hardcastle absolutely need to have?"

Both ladies frowned in thought.

"Whichever lady comes," Ellen said, "assuming she's the one who came before, this will be the fourth time she's met Hardcastle like this—in the woods at midnight."

"She'll recognize his outline," Louisa said. "And the way he walks."

"Luckily"—Ellen looked at Drake—"after their first meeting, Hardcastle and the lady haven't exchanged words. If they'd been in the habit of speaking, that would have made things difficult."

Drake nodded. "So we need a man with a similar build and gait to Hardcastle, dressed in clothes Hardcastle might wear, with hair and coloring good enough to pass on a moonlit night." He looked at Christopher. "Can you think of anyone who could pass for Hardcastle in build? The other traits can be faked, but build and even gait is hard to alter given we have only hours until midnight."

Christopher's brows faintly rose. "Let me think."

The library door opened, and Pendleby walked in. "Luncheon is served, sir."

"Thank you, Pendleby." Along with the others, Christopher rose.

Ellen and Louisa led the way to the dining room with the three men trailing behind. They arranged themselves about the dining table in an informal pattern, with Christopher, Ellen, and Drake on one side of the rectangular table, facing Louisa and Toby, seated on the other side.

Christopher waited until they'd all served themselves from the platters of sliced meats, bread, and fruits and had settled to eat before suggesting, "The leader of the local band of gypsies, Aaron, has a very similar build to Hardcastle. Similar height, similar stature. In suitable clothes, I think he would pass well enough."

Ellen swallowed and glanced at Christopher. "Aaron's hair is blacker than Hardcastle's, which is browny gray." She looked at Louisa. "But that's easy to fix with a little powder, especially for viewing in moonlight."

Louisa nodded. "But what about hairstyle? Any woman would notice that, even in moonlight."

"That's the best part," Ellen said. "They both have similar, curly hair —much the same length, too."

Drake leaned forward to look past Ellen at Christopher. "Do you think the gypsy will help us?"

Toby waved his fork. "They're already helping us quite significantly with our watch on Goffard Hall."

Christopher nodded. "If we present the role to Aaron in the right way, he'll almost certainly seize the chance—he was always one for a lark."

They discussed how best to approach Aaron and the other preparations they needed to make to ensure the meeting in the woods at midnight went the way they wanted.

In the end, it was agreed that Christopher, Ellen, and Drake would visit the gypsies and use their persuasive skills to convince Aaron to impersonate Hardcastle. Meanwhile, Toby would speak with Hardcastle himself to ascertain the relevant details for the meeting—namely, how many lace packets Hardcastle was expecting to be paid for, what he usually wore, and what route he followed from the inn to the woods.

Louisa undertook to assemble the package their "Hardcastle" would place in the lady's hands. They agreed there was no reason to use all the counterfeit notes; instead, several fake notes would be placed on both sides of the four bundles of "notes" Ellen and Louisa had assembled to replicate the stacks of counterfeit notes that had made up Hardcastle's original package. "Just in case," Louisa said, "the lady thinks to peek inside and check. And later, we might wish to show her what's in the package to stress the seriousness of her situation."

Everyone being in agreement, they pushed back from the table, rose, and dispersed upon their assigned tasks.

To call on the gypsies, Christopher drove himself and Ellen in his curricle, while Drake rode Gregory's horse; Granger had said the beast was eating its head off and needed the exercise. Not that the gypsy encampment was all that far away, but Christopher and Drake both felt that Drake arriving in style—on horseback rather than crammed into the curricle—would be preferable.

According to Toby's schedule of watchers, Aaron would be at the camp that day. Christopher tooled the curricle into the meadow and drew up by the fence above the dip where the circle of wagons stood. He and Ellen climbed down, and Drake halted the horse, dismounted, and tied the beast alongside Christopher's team.

Together, they walked down the meadow toward the wagons—and the gaggle of children came swarming, as they had before. The children recognized Christopher and Ellen and called hellos, while once again, the oldest girl went running toward the lead wagon.

Drake watched, amused, as the children surrounded Ellen, intrigued again by the ribbons, bows, and lace that adorned her walking dress of purply-mauve twill.

Entirely seriously, one round-eyed urchin informed her, "You have a *lot* of ribbons."

Much as if such a number bordered on an affliction.

Ellen smiled. "My aunt buys them for me."

The children's lips formed "Ohs" of enlightenment, then they reached the campsite enclosed by the wagons and saw Gracella, followed by Aaron, walking toward them. Gracella waved a hand, and the children dispersed, slipping away between the wagons and heading for the stream.

Christopher, Ellen, and Drake halted, as did Gracella. She nodded to Christopher, smiled at Ellen, then looked assessingly at Drake. "You," she stated, "I have not met before."

Drake bowed. "I'm Winchelsea, Mrs. Codona. It's a pleasure to make your acquaintance."

Gracella's eyes narrowed. After a moment of staring at Drake, she said, "Winchelsea. You are the son of..." Without taking her eyes from Drake, she tipped her head toward Aaron and demanded, "What is that other one's name?"

"Wolverstone." Aaron's dark gaze was fixed on Drake. "From Northumbria. The Boswells' territory."

Drake's lips twitched, and he inclined his head to both Aaron and Gracella. "You're well-informed. I know Harry Boswell and his band— they camp on my family's lands."

"Humph!" Gracella folded her arms. "It is summer. Why aren't you there, in the north?"

Drake's smile deepened, sincerely charming. "Would that I could be, but sadly, duty calls, and it's brought me here, to Kent, seeking to snare the wrongdoers I gather you and your people are already helping to watch."

"Ah!" Gracella nodded as if that explained everything—and, Christopher thought, given the remarkable knowledge she'd just displayed, perhaps it did.

He decided it was time to state their purpose. "We've come to speak with you and Aaron. It's become vital that we have someone we trust who, at night and without the need to speak, can pass for Hardcastle, the publican of the Bull Inn."

Aaron met Christopher's eyes, his own widening with interest, then he exchanged a swift glance with Gracella and waved toward the stools that, during the short conversation, had been arranged by others before the leader's wagon. "Come, sit, and tell us."

Of course, Gracella insisted on serving them tea, but once they were settled, sipping the rosy liquid from the tiny glasses, she waved at Christopher and Drake. "So the publican, this Hardcastle, he is one of your wrongdoers?"

"He is," Drake confirmed, "but only in a minor way." With a look at Christopher, he added, "Hardcastle is presently sitting in the manor's cellar and has decided to be helpful. He's told us how he hands on coun-terfeit notes he ferries up from the coast. We want to pretend to deliver his latest package—which those further along the chain are expecting—so we can catch the person who receives the counterfeit notes in the act, so that they, like Hardcastle, will have no choice but to help us follow the trail on, eventually to the one who is behind the whole scheme."

Gracella pondered that. After several minutes, she glanced at Aaron, then returned her gaze to Drake. "This is not, strictly speaking, a matter that involves the Romany, yet counterfeit notes will cause strife for all." She transferred her gaze to Christopher. "You and he"—she tipped her head at Drake—"are from families who are longtime friends of the Romany, and as you have come to ask for our help with this"—she swiveled to nod decisively to Aaron—"then it is right that we should assist." Returning her gaze to Drake, Gracella waved. "So ask what it is you came here to ask."

Drake half bowed, then said to Aaron, "I haven't seen Hardcastle myself, but Christopher and Ellen believe you could pass for him well enough for our purpose."

Aaron looked at Christopher. "Hardcastle is older than I am."

Christopher nodded. "But you and he are much the same build."

"And the meeting will take place in a wood at midnight," Ellen rushed to say.

Gracella sat back as, between them, Christopher and Ellen explained to Aaron what their plan required.

Eventually, Aaron agreed to do his best to impersonate Hardcastle and place the counterfeit notes into the mysterious lady's hands. "It will help," Aaron said, "if—as you say Hardcastle is willing to be helpful—I can spend a few minutes watching him walk. Perhaps put the packet in his hands so I can see how he carries it." A hint of cunning showed in the gypsy leader's dark eyes. "Little touches like that are often the things that carry a deception."

Both Drake and Christopher acknowledged that.

"I'm sure that can be arranged," Ellen said.

"In that case," Aaron said, "I will come to the manor at...shall we say ten o'clock? Plenty of time to study Hardcastle and don my disguise before I need to be at the inn."

With that agreed, Christopher, Ellen, and Drake rose to leave. Gracella as well as Aaron accompanied them across the campsite.

Walking beside Ellen, Gracella patted her arm. "It is good that you came. Matters like this, meetings like this, should rightly be attended by both lord and lady."

Somewhat startled, a little unnerved, Ellen shot a glance at Christopher; he was walking on her other side and had heard Gracella—as, no doubt, had Drake, even if he gave no sign of it.

Christopher merely raised his brows at her.

Ellen inwardly humphed and wondered if they—he and she and the understanding evolving between them—were really that obvious.

They parted from Gracella and Aaron beside the last wagon. As they climbed the slope of the meadow to where they'd left the curricle and horses, Drake glanced at Christopher, then looked ahead and asked, "Does Mrs. Codona remind you of anyone?"

Christopher promptly replied, "Great-aunt Helena."

"Hmm," Drake said. "Either Helena or old Lady Osbaldestone. That leaves me wondering if there's some unwritten law that says there has to be one in every tribe."

Ellen caught Christopher's eyes and looked her question.

He squeezed her hand. "You haven't met Great-aunt Helena or Lady Osbaldestone—"

"But you will," Drake put in.

"Inevitably," Christopher admitted. "And when you do, you'll discover that they, like Gracella, are…"

"Perspicacious enough to make every last descendant or connection extremely wary." Drake reached his horse and untied the reins. He met Ellen's eyes and quirked his brows. "Even me." He paused, then added, "And truth be told, my father, which is even more telling."

With that, he mounted, and Christopher handed Ellen into the curricle.

In less than a minute, they were on their way back to the manor, with Ellen wondering just what she might face in pursuing a connection with a family like Christopher's.

However, once at the manor, she had no time to think of anything beyond their plans for the night. They returned to the library to find Toby sitting behind the desk, poring over a map of the village, while Louisa, facing the desk, put the final touches to the package of supposedly counterfeit notes that Aaron, as Hardcastle, would hand over at midnight.

Louisa snipped off the trailing ends of the string she'd tied around the package. "There! That's the best I can do."

Drake paused behind her chair, placed his hands on her shoulders, and when she tipped up her face, bent to place a quick kiss on her lips. Straightening, he released her and studied the package. "That should be perfect."

Ellen sat in the other chair angled before the desk and told Louisa about Aaron coming at ten o'clock to study how Hardcastle walked and carried the package.

"I got the impression," Drake said, dropping into an armchair, "that this won't be the first time Aaron Codona has impersonated someone."

Christopher grinned as he sat. "I certainly wouldn't wager against that."

Toby, who had listened to their news, tapped a pencil on the map of the village. "Hardcastle was as forthcoming as we might wish regarding his route and the clothes he usually wears. As for matching the latter, work boots, heavy trousers, a pale shirt and a loose coat, no waistcoat, and just a neckerchief of any design should suffice."

Christopher frowned, then rose and went to the desk. "I'll send a note to Aaron—he'll almost certainly have clothes like that of his own, and he'll be more comfortable in them."

The note to Aaron was duly written and dispatched via a groom.

"Now," Toby said, once again tapping the map, "as to Hardcastle's route, we need to work out where to station our men to ensure the lady, whoever she might be, has no chance of slipping past us. Given Hardcastle says she waits in the wood until he's long gone, we can't rely on her not taking off in the same direction as he does, meaning toward the inn." Toby gestured with the pencil. "We'll need a cordon around the whole area."

"I wonder how she reaches the spot," Louisa said. When the others glanced at her, she elaborated, "Does she ride or come in a carriage?"

"Good point," Drake said. "Sadly, we don't know the answer and can't take the risk of guessing which."

He rose and joined Christopher and Toby at the desk, and the three began discussing where to site men around the knot of woods to the west of the lychgate.

Louisa and Ellen listened and watched.

Eventually, Louisa reached across and pointed to the east wall of the church. "I think Ellen and I should wait there."

All three men, until then bent over the map, slowly straightened. They stared at Louisa, then Christopher and Toby looked at Ellen.

Eventually, Drake, his voice hard, but his tone careful, said, "I can't see any need—"

"For us to be there?" Louisa's eyes flew wide. "But of course we must —how will you cope if this mysterious lady has her wits about her enough to realize that her captors are all male and"—Louisa held up her hands—"faints?"

"Or dissolves into hysterics?" Ellen added.

"Or simply takes refuge in floods of tears?" Louisa looked pointedly at her husband.

Drake frowned. "We have sisters—that's not going to sway us."

Louisa conceded that with a dip of her head. "Ultimately, perhaps not. But in the interim, such tactics will cause considerable disruption, especially among the other men. Trust me when I say that, once she sees Ellen and I are a part of the company, she—whoever she is—won't try any such tricks."

Toby looked from Drake to Christopher. "I, for one, vote to include the ladies. Hysterics are the very devil to deal with, even if they are all for show."

His lips compressed, Drake looked at Christopher.

After a moment, his expression faintly exasperated but resigned, Christopher said, "Ellen was with me at Goffard Hall last Friday night. As long as they agree to abide by the plan"—he shrugged—"I can't see why they shouldn't be there. And," he grudgingly admitted, "it might, indeed, be helpful if they were."

"There!" With restrained triumph, Louisa smiled at her irate spouse. The message in her green eyes was crystal clear; just because she was significantly pregnant didn't mean she would consent to being left at home with her feet up on a stool. Then she looked at Ellen and faintly arched her brows. "If it will help, Ellen and I solemnly promise to remain at that spot"—she pointed to the east end of the church—"until you three and the other men have this lady captured."

Ellen nodded her agreement.

Drake looked from her to his wife and sighed.

CHAPTER 13

*E*llen returned to Bigfield House not long afterward. That morning, Louisa had driven over in the manor's gig, and later, Ellen had followed Louisa back to the manor in the Bigfield House gig so she could return in good time in case she was needed over anything to do with running the estate or household.

She drove straight to the stable and, while walking to the house, encountered Hopper crossing the yard in the opposite direction. In response to her query, the estate manager was quick to reassure her that all was running "nice and smoothly."

Well and good. Quietly pleased that her recent absences appeared to have created the right opportunity at the right time for Robbie to step into their uncle's shoes, she parted from Hopper and entered the house through the kitchen door.

In the large kitchen, she came upon Partridge, waiting while Mrs. Swanley, the housekeeper, organized a tea tray.

Ellen eyed the tray, which seemed rather more elaborate than usual for just Emma and herself. "How is everything, Partridge? Any problems?"

"No, indeed, miss. Sir Humphrey was asking for you earlier, but Mrs. Fitzwilliam told him you were visiting at the manor, and that settled him down." With his head, Partridge indicated the tray. "And now we have a caller."

"Who?" Ellen had no wish to be captured by Mrs. Carstairs or Mrs. Folliwell.

"It's Miss Kirkpatrick, miss—Miss Julia. She walked across the fields and arrived about ten minutes ago."

"I see." *Now that is interesting—I wonder why Julia's here?* A possible reason struck her. "Does my brother know Miss Kirkpatrick has called?"

"Yes, miss. Mrs. Fitzwilliam sent me to let him know, and the young master joined the ladies in the drawing room straightaway. He's there now."

Ellen smiled. "Excellent. I believe I'll join them as well."

"If you would, miss, please tell Mrs. Fitzwilliam I'll bring in the tray momentarily—we're just waiting on some fresh scones."

Intrigued on several counts, Ellen headed for the drawing room. She stopped in the front hall to remove her bonnet, with its silly ribbon knobs adorning the crown. She paused with the bonnet in her hands, her gaze snagged on the ribbons; the laughter of the gypsy children rang in her ears, and she looked up at her reflection in the hall mirror—at the ribbons wound around the knot of her hair, their trailing ends dangling to either side of her face, bobbing about her ears.

She wondered if Emma would notice if she left off some of the ribbons and bows. She didn't like to think of the picture she must present when standing beside Louisa, the sartorial epitome of the severely elegant. How she looked—how she appeared to others—had never really mattered before, but now…

She grimaced at her reflection, then a light laugh from the drawing room reminded her of her quest, and she set the bonnet on the hall table and walked on.

As she opened the drawing room door, from the corner of her eye, she saw Partridge enter the hall, carrying the laden tea tray. With a bright smile, she swept into the room. "Good afternoon, everyone." Emma was on the chaise with Julia, and Robbie sat in an armchair facing the pair; all three wore easy expressions and, clearly, had been enjoying each other's company. Walking forward, Ellen waved at the open doorway. "Here's Partridge with the tray, so I'm just in time to join you for tea."

All three welcomed her. She shook hands with Julia, then sank into the armchair beside Robbie's.

"Dear Julia walked over to see us." As Partridge set the tray on a low table he stationed before Emma, Emma signaled Ellen with her eyes. "Isn't that a delightful surprise?"

Comprehending that Emma wanted her to encourage Julia, Ellen was only too happy to oblige. "It is, indeed. It's very kind of you to call, Julia —we are, after all, neighbors of sorts."

Julia smiled somewhat tentatively and accepted a cup and saucer from Emma. "It isn't all that far over the fields—and of course, I brought Peggy, my maid, with me. I didn't walk alone."

Accepting her own cup and saucer, Ellen nodded approvingly. "Very wise." Regardless, she was curious as to why Julia had come, especially without her stepmother. Finding no other way to broach the point, finally, she baldly asked, "Has Mrs. Kirkpatrick gone to London, then?" *Is that why you came without her?*

To Ellen's surprise, Julia blushed faintly. She sipped her tea, then lowered the cup and met Ellen's gaze, hesitated, then her chin firmed, and she said, "My stepmother—and her cousin, Tilly—are of the opinion that our neighbors here, in the country, are provincials and therefore not worth cultivating. I disagree, so"—with her free hand, she gestured—"as I'm now of an age to go about by myself, albeit with a maid, here I am."

"And very happy we are to have you call, my dear," Emma promptly reassured her.

"Heavens, yes!" Robbie grinned, encouraging for all he was worth. "You don't need your stepmother or her cousin to call on us."

"No, indeed," Ellen added. "Do feel free to call whenever you like."

Julia's careful nod to propriety notwithstanding, it had taken courage to call on her own.

The next half hour went in easy conversation while Ellen, Emma, and Robbie sought to ease any awkwardness Julia might feel and mounted a concerted mutual effort to ensure she would call again.

Ellen wondered if her and Emma's efforts to further Robbie's cause were as obvious to Julia as they seemed to Ellen, but if so, Julia gave no sign. Instead, gradually, she relaxed and even bloomed, eventually laughing unreservedly at one of Robbie's sallies.

That her brother was captivated was apparent to any who knew him. He barely took his eyes off Julia, not even when tempted by the last scone.

When she smiled, Julia was a very pretty girl, and Robbie could do a lot worse for himself than fix his eye on such a quiet and apparently sensible young lady.

Thinking to further the pair's interaction, Ellen asked, "Do you ride, Julia?"

"I used to, but I haven't for a while." She glanced briefly at Robbie, then looked back at Ellen. "My stepmother and Tilly don't ride, and Papa never has time anymore, so the only one who rides out at present is Nigel." Julia faintly grimaced. "I haven't felt inspired to ride recently."

Ellen caught Robbie's eager eye. "Perhaps," she said, "after church one Sunday, Robbie could ask your father's permission to accompany you on a ride about the lanes, then you could fetch up here for luncheon."

"By Jove, yes!" Robbie looked at Julia with hope in his eyes. "And I would, of course, escort you home later."

Julia looked from him to Ellen to Emma. "That would be…a very kind invitation." She glanced back at Robbie and shyly admitted, "I do love to ride."

"That's settled, then," Emma declared. "We'll consult with you and your father after church this Sunday and see what we can organize." Emma looked at Ellen. "If the weather holds, we might even try for a picnic, and we could invite the folk from the manor as well."

Julia rose to leave soon after. Ellen walked out with Julia and Robbie as far as the entrance to the rose garden, then made her farewells to Julia and let the pair walk on; still chatting, occasionally laughing, they ambled along the path between the fields that would eventually lead to the rear boundary of the Goffard Hall gardens, with Julia's complacent maid trailing a few yards behind.

Exceedingly happy with her afternoon's endeavors, Ellen watched the trio go, then turned and headed for the conservatory to catch up with her uncle.

As she and Christopher had arranged, he met her in the Bigfield House shrubbery, by the pond, at ten-thirty that evening.

The very last of the light had only just faded from the sky when she walked beneath the archway and saw him waiting. With his hands sunk in his trouser pockets, he was standing by the stone coping of the pool; he'd been staring at a clump of water lilies, but as she neared, he looked up.

His gaze roved over her. His brow quirked.

She'd elected to wear a dark-gray walking dress, one she'd kept after her year of mourning her mother. The style of the gown was more severe than any other she owned, with only a single deep ruffle around the hem, a narrow strip of black lace edging the collar and placket of the bodice, and not a ribbon to be seen.

"So I'll blend with the shadows," she murmured and extended her hand.

He humphed and grasped it. They turned to follow the path to the manor, and he looped her arm with his so they strolled side by side.

"I suppose," he ventured, "there's no point attempting to convince you that you don't need to attend this particular event."

She tried to hide her smile. "No."

He sighed.

"Besides"—she raised her chin—"if I don't go, who will keep Louisa company?"

Faintly grimacing, he tipped his head. "There is that."

Apparently accepting the situation, he lengthened his stride, and she kept pace as they left the shrubbery and walked on between the fields.

"Aaron arrived before I left. He's rehearsing with Hardcastle."

"I got the impression he—Aaron—was secretly delighted with his role."

"He is—it's just the sort of ploy, pulling the wool over some haughty lady's eyes, that appeals to him."

Several paces on, she asked, "Do you think he'll pull it off?"

"We have to hope he will. Drake's in his element organizing everyone else. He wants us in place well before midnight."

They reached the manor forecourt to find men milling around several wagons, with grooms holding horses nearby. A palpable sense of excitement blanketed the scene, gripping everyone and heightening the tension.

The sight of the map of the local area—which Drake had spread on the tailgate of a wagon so he could indicate to the various groups of men where he wanted them—reminded Ellen of the information Julia had innocently divulged.

Halting beside the wagon's end, Ellen waited until Drake glanced her way, then said, "I spoke with Julia Kirkpatrick this afternoon—she told me neither Mrs. Kirkpatrick nor Tilly Fontenay ride."

Drake's brows rose, and he looked at the map. "That means she'll arrive at the meeting via some sort of carriage."

Christopher moved around the tailgate and, with his fingertip, traced the lane leading from Goffard Hall to the village. "She'll come this way, but instead of turning in to the village lane, she'll continue straight on, along the lane leading to Iden Green. Then"—he tapped the map—"just here, there's a track that runs east to join the lane around the village green, a little way north of the church. Depending on how large the carriage is and how good her coachman, she might take that lane and stop about here"—he put his finger on the spot—"then make her way through the woods to where the meeting's supposed to take place."

Christopher looked up. "Lipman?" He spotted the manor's coachman among the men who had crowded close to view the map. "What do you think?"

Lipman nodded. "Sounds about right. That lane's passable for a gig or even a smallish carriage."

"Right, then." Drake rapidly redeployed the men he'd previously positioned in that area, then looked at Christopher and Lipman. "Is her coachman liable to hear if, when she's at the meeting point, the lady shrieks or screams?"

Lipman pulled a face. "The spot he'll stop at is about a hundred yards, give or take, from the meeting place, so depending on the wind and how loudly she screams, he might."

"How well do you know the Goffard Hall coachman?" Christopher asked.

Lipman shrugged. "I've known old Ottis for more'n thirty years."

"It might be best"—Christopher caught Drake's eye—"if Lipman is with the men closest to the spot where the Hall coach is likely to stop. Then, once we have the lady secured, Lipman can go and tell Ottis—or intercept him if she screams and he comes running—and explain that the lady has been involved in something illegal and is now in the hands of the authorities."

From her perch on the seat of the wagon alongside, Louisa said, "Lipman should tell Ottis that the lady will be returned to Goffard Hall most likely tomorrow, but in the interim, raising a hue and cry won't help anyone. The authorities will come and speak with Mr. Kirkpatrick tomorrow and explain all. It would be best for everyone, including the family at Goffard Hall, if Ottis drives home and carries on as if nothing unusual has happened."

Ellen nodded emphatically. "As if everything is normal." She, too, met Drake's eyes. "If Ottis drives back and reports the lady missing, the entire household will be in a panic."

"And we don't want that." Drake looked at Lipman. "Can you remember all that?"

Lipman thought, then nodded. "Aye—I've got it." He looked at Christopher. "I'm to wait until the lady's in hand, then go and tell Ottis that she won't be coming back with him but not to worry."

Christopher nodded. He looked at the map, then at Drake. "That's every eventuality covered, I believe."

Drake faintly arched his brows. "Everything we can predict, as least."

The front door opened, and everyone glanced around to see a heavy figure stomp across the porch and come lumbering down the steps.

"And here's our Hardcastle." Christopher had to grin.

Toby scrutinized Aaron, then shook his head in disbelief. "I've seen Hardcastle on several occasions—the lady's eyes will need to be sharper than mine for her to spot any difference." And Toby was known to be acutely observant.

Aaron grinned. "As long as I don't have to speak beyond telling her 'twenty-six'—and I've been practicing that with the man himself—I believe we'll pull this off."

Christopher clapped him on the back, and Drake raised his head and gave the order to mount up or clamber aboard the wagons.

Less than a minute later, their small army rattled and clopped out of the forecourt and headed down the lane to take up their positions in the woods. Ellen sat beside Louisa on the bench of one of the wagons, while Christopher rode ahead with Drake and Toby.

They left the horses and wagons in a clearing at the end of a minor track that ran past the east side of the inn. The clearing lay to the east of the woods from where, earlier, they'd watched the graveyard. From the clearing, the company spread out, quietly making their way through the woods to their assigned positions.

Christopher, Drake, and Toby walked Louisa and Ellen to their chosen spot. A stone bench had been positioned against the east façade of the church to allow parishioners to sit and contemplate the graves of their loved ones. As the spot was protected by the buttresses flanking the church's great east window, it was effectively out of sight of anyone other than their own men waiting in the woods bordering the churchyard.

After the ladies settled on the bench, Drake delivered a pithily worded recommendation that they remain in place until he and the others reappeared with the mystery lady. "We'll march her along the lane on the way to the wagons, so you'll see us and can join us then."

Bright-eyed, Ellen and Louisa looked up at him and said nothing at all.

Christopher inwardly shook his head, while Drake didn't bother to veil his skepticism. But time was running short. With a wave, Drake directed the last of their company into place in the woods along the southern boundary of the churchyard, then he, Christopher, and Toby walked on to take their own positions in the patch of woodland that crept close to the unwalled western edge of the churchyard, not far from the lychgate.

With Drake, Christopher reached the small clearing in which Hard-castle had always met the mystery lady; he found a suitably concealed spot around the perimeter to the south of the mouth of the narrow foot-path from the lychgate, while Drake moved silently to cover the north.

Toby, meanwhile, vanished deeper into the woods. He was one of those Drake trusted to be able to move without sound in woodland and had been assigned to keep watch midway between the clearing and where they thought the Goffard Hall coachman would pull up. In effect, Toby was their lookout.

Christopher sank into his chosen spot. Within seconds, all other sounds of human activity faded as their men did likewise, and all settled to wait.

∽

Seated beside Ellen, Louisa sighed. "I wonder how long we'll have to wait?"

Ellen consulted the timepiece she'd pinned to her bodice. "It's ten minutes to midnight," she whispered.

Louisa leaned forward and peered around the buttress to the north.

Ellen peered as well, but from that spot, they could see only a short stretch of the lane leading to the church and along the church wall a little way, but not as far as the lychgate.

"When is Aaron—Hardcastle—due to come along?" Louisa asked.

"Not until just before midnight."

"I haven't heard any bells. Does he have a watch?"

"Granger is with Aaron, and he does. He'll send Aaron into the lane, as if he's come from the rear of the inn, at the right time."

"Oh. Good."

Louisa lapsed into silence.

Then the hoot of an owl reached them, low and repeated once.

Louisa sat up. "That's Toby's signal. She must have passed him."

Louisa wriggled on the bench, then subsided. "I wonder whether it's Mrs. Kirkpatrick or the younger girl."

"We'll soon know," Ellen murmured back.

Alert and expectant, they sat with their eyes trained on the section of lane they could see.

A few minutes later, Aaron appeared, walking along the lane toward the church. Ellen studied the heavy figure with its rolling gait, then nodded decisively. "He's keeping his head down, but he's making that look natural. As long as she doesn't look closely at his face, he'll do."

Aaron was carrying the package of supposedly counterfeit notes between his large hands. They watched him walk steadily along the lane until he passed beyond their sight.

Louisa muttered a curse, then whispered, "I hate not being able to see what's going on. Do you think we can risk sneaking around this buttress to the next one along, so we can peer along the front of the church?"

"No—we have to stay here." Ellen studied Louisa and shook her head. "If you can see her, she'll be able to see you. And chances are, as she's standing in the woods looking out and you will be lit by the moon, she's more likely to see you while you won't be able to see her. And then what will Drake say?"

"Damn!" Louisa grumbled and subsided once more.

Christopher watched Aaron, in his guise as Hardcastle, lumber beneath the lychgate and emerge onto the lawn, carrying the packaged notes toward the woods and the clearing where a cloaked and veiled lady now waited.

Aaron had done well; if Christopher hadn't known better, he would have sworn the figure stumping forward was, indeed, the publican.

The lady had arrived about five minutes before the hour. She stood silent, upright, and unmoving in the center of the small clearing. Although Christopher had met both Mrs. Kirkpatrick and Tilly Fontenay, in the shadows and with the cloak about her, he couldn't tell which of the two women the mystery lady was.

Aaron approached the clearing in Hardcastle's heavy-footed, stumping walk, the package held before him.

Christopher tensed; the lady had been watching Aaron's approach—

now was the moment, as he drew near, when she might see or sense their deception and bolt.

But Aaron kept his head tipped down as he halted several feet before the cloaked woman and held out the package.

Moving confidently—almost dismissively—she reached out and lifted the notes from Aaron's hands.

Christopher almost sighed with relief. Now the counterfeit notes were in her possession, they had her.

She hefted the bundle and waited.

In a passable imitation of Hardcastle's rumbling growl, Aaron said, "Twenty-six."

She huffed but, cradling the notes in one arm, reached beneath the cloak and pulled out a wad of presumably real notes, which she held out to Aaron.

He took the notes, then paused—clearly wondering if, faced with that quantity of notes, Hardcastle would count them.

"Don't bother," the lady contemptuously advised.

The heavy veil muffled her voice; Christopher still couldn't tell who she was.

"There's twenty-six—two hundred and sixty pounds—as agreed." Her tone grew haughtier, and she raised her chin. "I'm not stupid enough to shortchange you at this point."

Aaron hesitated, but then nodded, thrust the notes into his pocket, and clinging to his role, turned and lumbered off.

Christopher waited, his gaze locked on the woman. Watching Aaron walk away, she remained as still as a statue until he'd disappeared from sight.

Then Christopher glimpsed the flash of a smile behind the veil, and the woman swept around to leave—and discovered Drake immediately in front of her.

She uttered a small shriek and stepped back, then whirled—and Christopher was there, waiting to prevent her from fleeing.

She looked around wildly, then recognized Christopher and all but spat, "Cynster!" Then she focused on Drake. Clutching the package to her chest, she demanded, "Who the devil are you?"

Imperturbably, Drake replied, "Winchelsea. I'm a representative of the Crown."

He reached out. The woman tried to step back, clutching her package even more tightly, but with Christopher there, she had nowhere to go. "No! This is mine!"

"Indeed." Drake hadn't been reaching for the package; instead, he locked his long fingers about the woman's wrists. "I'm so glad you've confirmed that." With a wrench, he tugged the woman's hands apart, forcing her to drop the package. She shrieked in rage and tried to knock the package toward her with her foot, but Christopher, dodging her boot, swooped and picked up the bundle.

The woman's gaze followed the package as he lifted it. "No!" The denial held desperation along with utter disbelief. "You—" Her gaze swung to Drake, then she tipped back her head. *"How dare you!"* she howled to the sky.

Others—the members of their cordon—were closing in. The darker shadows of their men appeared in the trees around the clearing.

Now wide-eyed, the woman saw. Lowering her head, all but vibrating with fury, she drew in a huge breath, as if preparing to blast them all.

Ellen and Louisa rushed up, halting beside Christopher.

Their appearance shocked the woman into silence. Ellen and Louisa stared at her, and she stared back; not even the night shadows of a woodland clearing could hide Louisa's pregnant state, or the instinctive poise and grace and the polished elegance consequent on being a duke's daughter.

"So who is she?" Louisa looked at Drake.

Drake flicked an amused look at Christopher and replied, "We don't yet know. Perhaps you would do the honors."

Louisa didn't wait for any further invitation; with Drake shackling the woman's wrists, she stepped forward, reached up, and caught the dark veil.

The woman flinched backward.

"Oh, stop that!" Louisa chided. "You've been caught with counterfeit notes in your hands, and you're surrounded by a horde of capable men intent on taking you prisoner—there's no use being difficult."

The woman's resistance held for a second more, then palpably dissolved. Triumphant, Louisa drew off the veil, revealing the stony face of a lady of much the same vintage as Christopher.

Drake and Louisa looked at Christopher and Ellen, a question on their faces.

Ellen nodded. "She's Mrs. Kirkpatrick."

Louisa smiled and turned the gesture on their captive. "I thought it would be you."

Toby appeared at Drake's shoulder. "Lipman has squared all away with her coachman. The staff at the Hall are not her greatest fans—he assured us he would say nothing but leave it to us to inform her husband."

At that, Mrs. Kirkpatrick all but snarled, "You can't do this." She tugged against Drake's hold, but it was unbreakable.

George Radley came up, a strip of leather in his hands. Drake forced Mrs. Kirkpatrick's hands together and held them as Radley efficiently lashed her wrists.

"This is *preposterous!*" She continued protesting as Drake released her hands and several of the older men stepped forward.

Drake moved aside, as did Toby, Christopher, Ellen, and Louisa. Drake waved the men on, and two grasped Mrs. Kirkpatrick's arms and propelled her toward the wagon that had just rolled up to halt in the lane beyond the lychgate.

She continued to rail at them, not protesting her innocence but rather questioning their right to act as they were. As Louisa, Ellen, Christopher, Toby, and Drake walked past the wagon into which the men had unceremoniously loaded her, she screeched, "You're kidnapping me!"

Drake paused and met her gaze. "No. By the authority vested in me, I'm arresting you for crimes against the Crown."

Horror finally dawned on Rose Kirkpatrick's face, and she fell silent.

With his fingers twined with Ellen's and accompanied by Toby, Louisa, and Drake, Christopher smiled and walked on.

In quiet triumph, they returned to the manor.

Drake directed that Mrs. Kirkpatrick be shown to the room prepared by Pendleby and Mrs. Marsh. Tucked away behind the scullery, the room might once have been a maid's sleeping quarters, but hadn't been used for years. However, it boasted a large, old-fashioned, very heavy lock.

The room had been cleared of the detritus that had inevitably accumulated and furnished with the bare necessities—a hard cot, a simple washstand, a small table with a single chair and a single candle burning in a plain wooden holder, and a bucket.

Granger and Radley—both large men—escorted Mrs. Kirkpatrick into the room, then Granger produced a knife and sliced through the leather binding her wrists.

Both men retreated immediately, and Pendleby shut the door and locked it.

At Drake's suggestion, they left Mrs. Kirkpatrick to stew—and calm down and stop banging on the door. Ten minutes later, all had fallen silent inside the room.

Drake, who had taken charge of the key, slid it into the lock, turned it, and albeit on guard, swung the door open.

He looked in, then stepped over the threshold, and the others congregated in the doorway, Ellen and Louisa, arms crossed, in front, with Christopher and Toby looking over their heads.

Mrs. Kirkpatrick was sitting on the bed. Her expression was stony, her features set. With her lips tightly compressed, she glared malevolently at them.

Unmoved, Drake stated, "You were found in the woods holding a package of counterfeit banknotes. In the hearing of several witnesses, you declared the package was yours. While dealing in counterfeit currency is no longer deemed to be high treason, it is, nevertheless, considered a most serious offence against State and Crown. As matters currently stand, were we to hand you over for trial, you would be found guilty and sent to the gallows."

Drake paused. Mrs. Kirkpatrick's gaze was now riveted on him. Christopher suspected they would have been able to hear a pin drop.

His tone even and matter-of-fact, Drake went on, "However, like Hardcastle, you are merely a pawn in a larger game. Measured against apprehending the man behind the counterfeit scheme, capturing you is a minor matter—a mere step toward our major goal. Consequently, depending on your willingness to cooperate, thus enabling us to lay hands on the villain behind the scheme, I'm in a position to offer you an alternative to the hangman's noose."

Mrs. Kirkpatrick's eyes slowly narrowed to glittering shards. "You want me to...what? Help you trap him?"

"Yes." Drake studied her, then added, "If you're entertaining thoughts of your husband or, indeed, anyone else rescuing you from your present predicament, I would suggest you think again."

The cold light in her eyes seemed to fade.

Drake waited for a moment more, then turned and waved the others to retreat; they stepped back into the scullery. "Doubtless," Drake said, pacing to the doorway, "your abrupt change in circumstances has come as something of a shock. We'll leave you to ponder your state." He reached for the doorknob. "We'll speak again tomorrow, sometime in the morning, to assess your options."

He shut the door and locked it.

Pocketing the key, he turned to the others. "That, I believe, is it for tonight."

They walked through the deserted kitchens and into the front hall.

Louisa looked weary. She murmured her goodnights, and Drake went with her up the stairs.

Toby smiled at Ellen and Christopher. "A successful evening all around. I'm for bed." He saluted them. "I'll see you in the morning."

They exchanged goodnights, then as Toby climbed the stairs, Ellen looked at Christopher.

He smiled. "I'll walk you home. It isn't far, and after the excitement, I'm still wide awake."

"So am I."

He offered his arm, and she wound hers in his, and together, they strolled out of the front door, into the soft summer night.

A large shape was leaning against the pillar at the head of the porch steps. Aaron straightened as they neared. "All done?"

"For tonight," Christopher said. "Drake hasn't yet told her what he wants her to do—that'll come tomorrow."

"He told her she would hang for her crimes if she didn't agree to help," Ellen said, "and he's left her to ponder that."

Aaron huffed. "I'm very glad," he said as the three of them went down the steps, "that I'm on Winchelsea's side. He doesn't strike me as the sort it's safe to cross."

Faintly amused, Christopher confirmed, "No, he's not."

The three of them made their way to the lane via the shrubbery and the stile.

Halting in the lane, Aaron grinned at them. "I have to say it was fun, impersonating someone at the behest of the authorities—legally, as it were."

"Don't let it go to your head," Christopher cautioned.

"But," Ellen added, "your performance must have been utterly convincing. Mrs. Kirkpatrick showed no suspicion at all that it wasn't Hardcastle who delivered the notes."

"Incidentally," Christopher said, "none of us have let on it wasn't Hardcastle she met tonight."

Sobering, Aaron nodded. "That might be as well." He raised a hand in farewell.

Christopher and Ellen did the same, and the trio parted, with Aaron striding down the lane toward the gypsy camp and Christopher helping Ellen over the stile and onto the path to Bigfield House.

The night air was pleasantly cool, with the occasional rustle of some nocturnal creature and the distant hoot of an owl all they heard.

Eventually, they reached the shrubbery and the water lily pool.

Christopher slowed, and Ellen slowed, too. After all the excitement of the day, she didn't want him to leave. Indeed, quite the opposite. Frowning slightly, she halted and faced him. "I was just thinking…it's early Saturday morning, so the next card party is nearly a week away."

He arched his brows. "Assuming Drake intends the card parties to continue, it might take us that long to get everything in place to ensure that, to all outward appearances, the scheme looks to be going forward as the mastermind originally planned. That will be critical—we'll have to hit all the normal notes, whatever those might be, if we're to convince him that nothing's gone awry."

Christopher studied her face, lit by the silvery moonlight; she wondered what he saw there, even while she registered the way his gaze traced her features. He smiled faintly. "Despite Drake's persuasive skills, convincing Mrs. Kirkpatrick that she has no real option but to dance to his tune will likely take time. I have no doubt that, at this very minute, she's sitting in her cell, trying to think of some way out of the snare she walked into tonight."

How to turn his mind in the direction she wished? She grimaced. "There's also the question of how many card parties will need to be held to believably exchange such a large number of notes." She caught his shadowed gaze. "It might take weeks—even months—before we reach the point of being able to lure the mastermind into the open."

He realized she was trying to steer his thoughts. He tipped his head, searching her face. "And if it does take a month or more?"

She pressed her lips together and stared into his eyes, then she reached up, curled her fingers in his lapels, stepped into him, drew his head down, and kissed him. One hard, deliberate kiss brimming with intent, then she drew back and whispered, "I know we agreed to wait, but I don't want to wait that long."

CHAPTER 14

*C*hristopher's arms had instinctively closed around her, banding her waist.

He knew that propriety demanded he resist. The problem was that, with her eyes on his, honesty was his only option. "I don't want to wait that long, either."

Her expression brightened; her eyes sparkled, and a glorious smile lit her face. "Then I see no reason why we should."

On that confident declaration, she stretched up and set her lips to his again, and it was utterly impossible for him not to respond—not to angle his head and claim all she offered, not to savor the promise of passion and desire she pressed on him, a potent elixir that slid over his tongue and snared his senses, wreathing through his brain and effectively smothering any ability to even think of the doubtless myriad reasons why he ought to exercise restraint—restraint enough for them both.

He couldn't. As he drew her to him, pressing her slender form against his harder, muscled frame, resisting her, her siren's call, was utterly beyond him.

The next minutes in the moonlit garden reminded him forcefully of a racing carriage where the driver had lost the reins; with her pressing for urgency and him responding to her need, desire escalated, fed through every second of their increasingly hungry kisses, then passion ignited—not in a fury but in a slow, steady burn, a conflagration impossible to deny, to extinguish. Impossible to contain.

Then, set on her goal, she pushed back and broke away, seized his hand, and breathless, picked up her skirts and led him—in a somewhat frantic rush—to the side door. She opened it and towed him, unresisting, into the unfamiliar territory of the side hall, waiting only until he closed the door to tug him on and up a secondary stair to the floor above.

Whether it was the need to look about him to fix in his mind where in the house they were or simply his faculties resurfacing from the haze of passion that had erupted between them, the moments spent silently hurrying to her room, tucked away in a corner of the house overlooking the rose garden, allowed him to recall his own goal.

His own ultimate desire.

He wasn't willing to relinquish that—not even to allow it to be pushed aside to be addressed at some later date.

No—he was who he was, and *she* was what he wanted.

She set the door to her room swinging wide, stepped through, and smiling in expectation, drew him with her. He obliged, caught the door, and shut it, but instead of surrendering to her tug to follow her toward the bed, he leaned back against the panels and waited.

Puzzled, she halted and looked at him. She met his eyes, and he said, "There's something I need to say—and something I need to hear you say in return."

She searched his eyes; her expression remained eager and open, her gaze direct, as she tipped her head, inviting him to continue.

He drew in a breath, one more constricted than he'd anticipated. Moonlight poured through the panes of the uncurtained window, gilding everything in subtle silver—as if everything about the moment, everything in it, was precious. "I can't pretend that I don't want you—I do. With every fiber of my being." His voice was low, gravelly, the normally smooth tones roughened by desire. "And because of that, for me, this, now, has to be...forever."

It had never been that way before, but with her, *that* was his reality.

He hadn't rehearsed any speech—hadn't even thought this far ahead. She and he had rushed this fence, and he was flying, soaring without any notion of where or how he might land.

Before she could respond, he went on, "I need you to know and accept that I don't want you for a night—not even for a month of nights. I want you for the rest of our lives."

She'd stilled.

His eyes on hers, he pressed, "Are you willing to give me that? To commit to that? Are you up for placing your hand in mine and taking a leap into the unknown...because that's where going forward as you wish, here, tonight, will take us."

Ellen held his gaze. She sensed, quite unexpectedly, a vulnerability in him—in he who otherwise appeared so invincibly strong. So sure and certain, so confident and assured. She'd assumed that, ultimately, the road they'd been following would, at some point in the not-overly-distant future, lead to precisely the question he'd asked.

To her facing that question and having the answer, ready on her tongue.

She hadn't expected to be facing that question tonight. She hadn't thought...

Something inside her stilled, quietly calm and certain. She looked inward and realized thinking wasn't, in this instance, in this sphere, required. Not at all. Her heart was sure, and her soul was beyond convinced.

Not a skerrick of doubt existed inside her.

She met his eyes, held his gaze, and asked in return, "Are you, here, tonight, offering forever? If I take your hand"—she strengthened her grip on the hand she still held—"and lead you to my bed"—a tip of her head indicated the shadowy four-poster farther down the room—"will you be mine, and will I be yours, for the rest of our lives?"

"Yes." The answer had come without hesitation and with absolute, unguarded honesty.

Christopher stepped forward, away from the door. He gripped the hand holding his, caught her other hand, clasped both between his palms, and raised them to his lips. His gaze locked with hers, he pressed a kiss to her fingers. "If we spend tonight—or any night—together in a bed, if we indulge the passion that's flared between us, if we feed it and allow it to burn, for me, that will signal that we both accept we will live as one for the rest of our days."

He stared into her eyes and forced himself to ask, "What will such an event mean for you?"

Even with the moonlight behind her, he read her answer in her face, heard it, too, in her immediate response of "The same."

But then her eyes narrowed fractionally, and she searched his face; with the moonlight falling full upon him, she could see his features clearly. He shifted, angling them so the moonlight reached her face as well.

Still a trifle breathless, she drew in air and said, "You need me to make a choice—a clear decision. A declaration."

He blinked and realized she was right—that knowing her mind absolutely, being assured of it, was fundamentally important to him.

"So," she continued and tipped up her chin, "here's the decision I've made, the choice I've made. *I choose you.* I choose *us*, here, now, and forever."

That truth shone in her eyes, resonated in her voice.

It freed something—released some emotion—within him; some part of him had been waiting to hear just that from her.

His eyes locked with hers, he again touched his lips to her clasped fingers. "I, too, choose you—choose *us*. Us, together, now and forever, is what I want more than anything else in life." He paused to draw in a deeper breath. "Here, now, I plight you my troth and freely bestow on you my forever."

"I accept, and in return, I pledge the same to you." Her expression radiant, she drew her hands from his, raised her arms, and wrapped them about his neck as she stepped forward—confident and assured—eradicating the last inches of space between them. As his arms tightened about her, she tipped up her face and drew his lips to hers.

They fell into the kiss.

Plunged into the passion that had waited, simmering, to snare them again.

Together, as one, they embraced it.

Yet even while desire whipped and passion thudded like a drumbeat in their veins, both fought the compulsion to rush, to race. Caresses grew ever more urgent, yet the act of disrobing held them both spellbound; neither wanted to miss a moment, a second of the sensuous delight.

He saw wonder light her eyes as she finally drew his shirt from him and let it fall to the floor. With fascination in her face, she stepped closer, splayed her fingers, and ran the tips lightly over his chest and down. He closed his eyes and fought to suppress a sensual shudder.

He'd already stripped her dress, petticoats, and stays from her. Now he drew her to him, and the press of her full breasts to his bare chest, the tight peaks screened only by the fine silk of her chemise, made them both catch their breaths and freeze, just for a second, to savor.

This, their coming together for the first time, was, plainly, to be a seduction of the senses.

Bringing his considerable expertise to bear, he ensured it was.

When he slid the last of the screening silk away and held her, a naked goddess, in his arms, his senses whirled, giddy as they'd never been before. He might be regarded as one of London's wolves, experienced to the point of being jaded, yet in this, tonight, he felt more akin to a stripling exploring a woman's fascinating form for the first time—thrilling to the silk of her skin, to the firm curves, to the rosy flush that tinted her skin as the desire he fanned took hold.

Took hold and built and drove her as well as him.

When, finally, he laid her on her bed, she was heated and wanting—and impatient. She barely waited for him to strip off his breeches before she reached for him, drawing him down beside her.

He went willingly—as eager as that stripling he couldn't even remember being.

Their bodies met, skin to skin along their lengths, and the fire that had warmed them converted to a raging inferno.

Yet even then, they both possessed sufficient strength of will to hold the fiery compulsion at bay; there was so much tactile delight, so much mutual pleasure yet to be enjoyed as they devoted their attention to exploring each other's bodies, learning what most pleased the other and being delighted in return.

Inevitably, their caresses grew more urgent, more intimate, and, at the same time, more laden with meaning. Neither spoke, yet the words were there, carried on each stroking touch, in the pressure of their clutching fingers, and in the long, heated glances they shared through eyes heavy lidded with passion.

Please...be mine.

Yes. I'm yours.

Take me.

Love me.

As I love you.

It was a litany that was repeated, over and over, even as her gasps grew more frantic, and desperation mounted, until he eased into her, then slid home, and they joined.

The moment—not only the spike of pain overridden by pleasure, not even that senses-stealing, breath-stopping pulse of sensual delight when she instinctively tightened about him, but even more the deep and acute realization that they stood on the cusp of true intimacy, a connection neither had ever before known—held them. Shook them. To their souls.

Their gazes met and held.

Then she arched and gasped, and he reacted instinctively, withdrawing only to thrust again, and they plunged into the whirlpool that, denied, had intensified and now seized them, hauling them into its roiling depths and overwhelming their wits with wanting and yearning, with the need to strive for the ultimate in pleasure.

Filled with that burning desire, he rode on and drew her with him.

Ellen had no thought but to follow his lead, to meet him, match him, and glory in the heated, piercingly acute, impossibly intense sensations.

Nothing she had ever known had prepared her for this. For the sheer physicality of their joining, for the mind-numbing pleasure and the searing passion that drove them both ever on.

He was all she'd ever imagined in a lover—caring and as aware of her as she was of him, yet with a potent strength investing every movement, every touch, that fed every fantasy she'd ever had. He moved over her and inside her, and she couldn't get enough.

Her every sense strained as together, they raced on. As their mutual passion raged and waged war on their senses, bombarding them with unrelenting tactile stimulation.

She gasped and clung, dimly aware of a building urgency, yet for all that, the end, when it came, took her by surprise. Her awareness had drawn in and in, locked tight on where they joined, then sensation exploded in an eruption of sharp, incandescent pleasure, shattering her awareness and sending shards of white-hot sensation streaking down her nerves.

She cried out, and he thrust deeply again, and again, and she held him to her as if she would never let him go.

Then he stiffened and groaned, and she felt the warmth of his seed inside her.

Somewhere deep inside, she smiled in simple joy.

Then the rigidity left him, and he slumped. He would have tipped to her side, but she clutched him to her, wanting—needing—to feel his weight upon her, and he grunted softly and obliged as the aftermath of the earlier explosion of her senses dissipated in waves of pleasured warmth, flushing beneath her skin.

She smiled, sighed, and held him in her arms.

Spent, exhausted, they tumbled into sleep.

~

The following morning, Ellen considered riding to the manor, but opted to walk instead. Muscles she hadn't known she possessed felt somewhat tender, and sitting on a saddle, even for a short time, wasn't an appealing prospect.

She reached the manor to find Christopher, along with Toby, Louisa, and Drake, about to go into the drawing room. It was the first time she'd set eyes on Christopher since he'd slipped from her bed just before dawn; she'd wondered if, after their rather lengthy night spent in each other's arms, there would be any awkwardness between them, but other than a deeper warmth in his eyes when they rested on her—an expression she hoped only she could see—there was nothing in his outward manner that signaled the change in their relationship, namely that, in both their minds, they were betrothed.

In the depths of the night, they'd agreed to keep their glad news to themselves for the moment, to be shared at a more appropriate and less fraught time.

After exchanging greetings, Louisa said, "I suggested that having Mrs. Kirkpatrick brought before us while we sat in elegant comfort might underscore her changed situation."

Ellen agreed. "One can only hope the hours spent alone in that cell have improved her temper."

Following her and Louisa into the drawing room, Drake huffed. "I suspect she'll have seen the light—or at least will pretend to have done so while she continues to search for some way out of the mess she's landed herself in."

They reorganized the furniture, then sat—Ellen and Louisa on the long sofa, now with its back to the presently empty hearth, Drake and Christopher in armchairs flanking it, while Toby fetched a straight-backed chair and placed it centrally before them, then moved to lounge in the armchair beside Drake's.

Christopher looked across at Drake. "She does seem the sort to dance to our tune as long as it suits her to do so."

Drake nodded. "Just how much of what she says we believe... As far as possible, we'll need to confirm all she says via others."

Christopher had already sent Radley and two footmen to fetch Mrs. Kirkpatrick from her cell. When Pendleby entered and announced, "The prisoner, sir," then, nose in the air, stepped back, Christopher had to hide a smile.

Radley escorted Mrs. Kirkpatrick into the room. At Drake's order, her wrists had again been tied, but this time, with softer cord. Radley led her to the chair and indicated she should sit.

She did, then stared expressionlessly at them.

At a nod from Christopher, Radley left, closing the door behind him.

They all studied the woman staring at them. Deliberately, they hadn't supplied her with comb and brush, so her hair hung limply, the knot at the back of her head askew. Her walking dress was badly crushed, and her face was pale, washed and now devoid of any cosmetic color.

She looked distinctly bedraggled; Louisa had maintained that denying her the chance of refreshing her appearance—her outward armor—would leave her feeling more vulnerable.

Judging by Rose Kirkpatrick's expression—one that suggested she was uncertain over making any move at all—Christopher suspected Louisa had been correct.

Eventually, Drake said, "Your name is Rose Kirkpatrick." He didn't wait for any confirmation, but rolled on, "You were approached by a Frenchman when you were last in Paris, earlier this year. He offered you a deal, specifically that you would act for his master to distribute counterfeit English banknotes in England in return for money."

Rose's lids flickered; she was surprised by how much Drake already knew.

Drake recaptured her gaze. "Why did you agree?"

She blinked, then frowned; that was clearly not a question she'd expected to be asked. "I…wanted the money."

"Your husband is wealthy," Christopher observed.

She cast him a contemptuous look. "Kirkpatrick is a tight fist. He makes me an allowance that's far too small and won't listen to reason. My clothes cost far more than he realizes, but he's refused to see sense." She looked at them challengingly. "I had to find some way to raise money, and when the Frenchman made his suggestion…"

When she left the sentence hanging, Louisa calmly supplied, "It seemed the answer to your prayers?"

Rose nodded. "Yes."

"It didn't occur to you"—Drake spoke gently, as if he was merely interested—"that passing counterfeit notes was a crime?"

"Of course I realized." She shifted on the chair and resettled her bound hands in her lap. "But I couldn't see that such notes were all that much of a danger—not to me and not to anyone else, either." She scanned their faces. "I was told the notes were excellent replicas and would fool almost anyone." She paused, then, looking down, added, "It didn't seem that much of a risk nor something that would actually harm anyone. They weren't asking me to shoot someone."

"Quite." Still employing his gentle voice, Drake asked, "Having accepted the commission from the Frenchman, how did you set about the task of distributing the notes?"

Drake's nonaggressive questioning—his genuine interest—appealed to Rose's vanity. She explained that she'd maintained contact with her younger cousins, the Fontenays, and had invited the pair to relocate to Goffard Hall and, subsequently, had exploited Nigel's acquaintance to draw young gentlemen to her card parties. "It was really very straightforward, and gentlemen are so gullible and easy to manage at that age."

She seemed quite chuffed with her own cleverness.

Faintly puzzled, Drake asked, "Did you have previous experience holding such events?"

She nodded. "In the years before I met and married Kirkpatrick, I frequently held similar evenings at my parents' houses, both in London and in the country. Of course, my mother was theoretically the hostess, but I was the one who organized everything. I knew exactly what drew young men of the right sort to one's house, and at that time, I had my older brothers' friends to draw in." She shrugged. "It was simple enough to reinvent such events at Goffard Hall, especially as, for the purpose of exchanging banknotes, I didn't have to bother inviting young ladies as well."

Christopher slid a glance at Drake and wasn't surprised when he asked, "Do you have any idea why the Frenchman approached you specifically?"

Clearly, the Frenchman—or more likely, the man behind the scheme—had known of Rose's particular talent.

But she merely arched her brows. "As he—the name he gave was Millais—came up to me outside the shop of one of the best French modistes, and I had been staring through the window, wishing I could order one of her creations, I assumed he'd seen enough to guess that I would welcome extra funds."

Drake dipped his head and let the point go. They already knew that the mastermind was a meticulous planner.

"Very well," Drake said. "Let's move on to how you passed the fake notes into the pockets of the unwitting young gentlemen who attended your card parties." He didn't ask her to tell him but instead told her what they'd pieced together of her modus operandi.

Once again, that they already knew so much about the scheme made Rose wary—especially of lying, given she couldn't tell whether they already knew the correct answers and were testing her.

"You've already exchanged the counterfeit notes from three trial runs," Drake told her. "Once you've substituted the notes and have only genuine notes in your hands, to whom and how do you pass on the takings?"

Rose smiled faintly; she knew from the question that they didn't know the answer. She hesitated, but then dipped her head and replied, "I haven't yet been required to pass on anything."

Drake's brows rose, but he waited in silence for her to explain.

Eventually, she went on, "That was the arrangement I had with Millais. The...profits from the first three runs were to be entirely mine."

"And from the subsequent runs?" Drake prompted.

She clearly debated whether to speak, but eventually said, "From any subsequent run"—she glanced somewhat peevishly at the others—"I was to keep ten percent of the genuine notes and pass on the rest."

Given the value of the counterfeit notes they'd intercepted, even ten percent amounted to a tidy sum.

"To whom and how were you to pass on the rest?" Drake asked—the critical questions.

Rose straightened and arched her brows, rather smugly. "I can't tell you because I don't know."

Toby frowned. "How can you pass on notes without knowing at least how?"

Again, Rose hesitated; again, she finally deigned to answer. "According to Millais, after I successfully converted the notes from the first major run, I would be contacted and told how to pass on the agreed percentage of the genuine notes." She briefly surveyed their faces, then, with a faint smile, added, "So as of this moment, I still don't know, so I can't answer your questions."

Any doubt that the mastermind's plans were exceedingly thorough evaporated.

Although it must have cost him to do so, Drake nodded equably. "In that case, please explain how you planned to exchange the large number of counterfeit notes contained in this most recent run."

She shifted on the chair and lightly shrugged. "In the same way as we switched the notes previously—by selling the young men tokens to gamble with and, at the end of the evening, exchanging the tokens for a mixture of genuine and counterfeit notes."

Louisa spoke, her tone cuttingly haughty. "We are already aware of your methods. What we wish to know is how you planned to adjust those methods to accommodate the larger number of notes." When Rose didn't reply, Louisa arched her brows in weary superiority. "More card parties, presumably. I'm sure we can learn the answer by asking others at Goffard Hall."

Rose studied Louisa through flinty eyes, then, as if the words were dragged from her, admitted, "The arrangements are already in place." She paused, then grudgingly explained, "We—Tilly, Nigel, and I—have been touting a special series of three card parties to be held to celebrate the height of summer. The first will be held next Tuesday, with a second on Thursday and the final event on Saturday. Millais told me that, if all went well, the fourth shipment of notes would be the first large run. He'd given me a schedule, so I knew the notes would arrive by this coming Monday, and we've been assiduously beating the drum about our special event ever since we started the card parties, enough so that it's become a major fixture in the minds of our regular attendees. A number of local young gentlemen are hosting house parties to coincide with the events, essentially structuring a weeklong house party around the three evenings, using our card parties as entertainment highlights."

With a smile of some satisfaction on her lips, Rose revealed, "I've heard that quite a few of the younger London dandies who haven't previously visited Goffard Hall have made plans to be in Kent over the coming week."

"So," Louisa said, "not only are you planning on running three events, you're also expecting significantly more guests over all three evenings."

Rose nodded. "Yes. It will be—" She broke off, looked at Drake, then amended, "Would have been something of a tour de force."

It wasn't difficult to see how perfectly Rose and her plans fitted into the mastermind's scheme.

"As a matter of fact," Drake said, "you were correct in the first instance. You only have one chance to escape the hangman's noose, and that involves ensuring that your special height-of-summer celebration lives up to everyone's expectations."

Rose frowned. After a second, she said, "I don't understand."

"It's simple," Drake said. "Under our direction, with our active assistance, you and your household will host the three card parties in exactly the manner your gullible guests expect. The only alteration will be that, at the end of the evenings, no counterfeit notes will make their way into innocent punters' pockets. However, you and your helpers will otherwise run the tables in exactly the same way as before, manipulating the play to ensure that no one loses any large amount. We will expect you to do everything you can to ensure your three events are the successes you've envisioned."

"And if I don't?"

"The choice is, of course, yours, but be assured that is the only choice you have. If you don't wish to assist, I will arrange for you to be transported immediately to the Tower, and we'll go on without you." Drake paused.

Rose paled as the fact sank in that he wasn't bluffing.

Smoothly, he continued, "Assuming you have the sense you were born with and agree to do as we ask, you can start by listing the various games of chance you intended to offer your guests and how many tables you thought to devote to each game."

After several seconds' absolute silence, Rose commenced enumerating the card games she'd intended to offer.

Between them, Drake, Louisa, Toby, and Christopher drew from Rose every last logistical detail of her planned card parties, down to the arrangement of the tables; it was plain her organization for the three evenings was already well advanced. Ellen contributed by questioning how the household managed the events, eliciting the information that in order to cope with the anticipated larger number of guests, Rose had intended recruiting extra footmen and dealers from certain gambling houses in London.

"But I haven't sent them the signed agreements." She glanced at Drake. "I would have signed them first thing this morning and sent the papers off. It's too late, now, to get extra staff for Tuesday."

Drake smiled. "Not too late for us—we'll have the extra staff, and I assure you they'll be very well-trained."

Ellen glanced at Drake and wondered from where he planned to source such people, although she didn't doubt he could and would.

Once they'd extracted all the relevant information, Drake returned to his earlier point. "You said that once you'd exchanged all the counterfeit notes in this upcoming major run, you would be contacted regarding how to pass on the genuine notes. How was your contact to know when you'd completed exchanging such a large number of notes?"

Rose shook her head. "I don't know." After a moment, she shrugged. "Perhaps unbeknown to me, one of the young men who attends reports to someone."

Christopher suspected that was the most likely explanation.

Drake appeared to agree. He nodded and went on, "So, let's say after the third card party, when it might be thought that you'll have passed off the majority of notes in this latest shipment, your expectation is that you'll receive a note telling you to bring the money to some particular spot."

When he paused and arched his brows, Rose dipped her head in agreement.

Drake smiled faintly, but the gesture held no humor. "One trait we've established in those behind this scheme is unrelenting attention to every detail. You can't expect us to believe that a simple note from anyone at all would be enough to have you deliver what will amount to a small fortune in cash."

Rose stared at Drake as if wondering, again, just how much he knew. Eventually, she opted for caution once more and grudgingly revealed, "Millais gave me a seal—it's actually half a seal, with a design based on a playing card. The note I receive will bear the stamp of the other half of the seal, which should match up with my half perfectly to create the complete design—that's how I'll know the message comes from my contact, whoever that proves to be."

"Where is this seal?" Drake asked.

"I keep it in my jewel case." After a moment, she added, "Millais insisted that I made no effort to befriend the person who delivered the notes to me and that I took steps to conceal my identity from him. I'd been told that, on seeing the signal in the graveyard for the first time, I was to leave a message in the same place, nominating a time and place to meet, but that I should not seek to identify or otherwise meet and speak with whoever turned up with the notes. As it happened, I recognized Hardcastle when he arrived for our first midnight tryst, but I adhered to Millais's orders. I doubt Hardcastle recognized me or realized where I lived." She paused, then looked up and met Drake's eyes. "However, while I wasn't informed that it would be Hardcastle who brought me the notes, whoever contacts me over passing on the notes will have to know who I am." Her lips quirked in self-deprecation. "So they'll know my identity, but I don't—and presumably never will—know theirs."

Drake nodded. "Those organizing the scheme have been extremely thorough in concealing their identities. Consequently, we're having to follow the trail of the notes back to the originator of the scheme. Our need for your cooperation is the sole reason I've offered you a chance to secure leniency with respect to your sentence. I would suggest that, through the next week, you hold that point uppermost in your mind."

Her brows rose. "I take it Hardcastle was swayed by your arguments?"

"I offered him the same deal I've placed before you." Drake held her gaze. "He took it."

Drake waited for a second more, then nodded to Christopher, who rose and went to the door to summon Radley and the footmen.

Rose glanced over her shoulder as the men approached, then stood and looked back at her interrogators, sitting comfortably before her—a calculated reflection of her fall in status.

"Think carefully," Drake advised. "We'll speak with you again shortly."

With an almost haughty nod and a glance that included Toby, Louisa, Ellen, and Christopher as he reclaimed his armchair, Rose turned and, with Radley leading the way and the footmen flanking her, walked out of the room.

After Pendleby shut the door, Louisa said, "She's definitely thinking of self-preservation. As long as she can't escape us, she'll cooperate."

"So I think," Drake said.

The door opened again to admit Pendleby, who announced that a cold collation was awaiting their attention in the dining room.

They repaired to the dining table and settled to eat in unusual silence as they each reviewed what they'd learned from their captive.

At the end of the meal, Drake pushed aside his plate, leaned back in his chair, and looked around the table. "While the secrecy the mastermind has instituted between his pawns makes following the trail to him difficult, such secrecy is also a weakness in that one rarely feels loyal to an anonymous being. That's allowed us to gain the necessary cooperation from his pawns thus far."

The other four nodded, and Drake went on, "In addition to what we need to do to lure him into the open, we should also turn our minds to what evidence we'll require to bring him to justice."

Ellen bent a questioning look on Drake. "You speak of the master-mind as one man—as the tonnish gentleman who hired the counterfeiter. Are you and your people certain it's only one man? Rose doesn't know—all she knows is that there's someone who will fetch the notes from her. There's nothing to say that person will be the mastermind, nor that the mastermind won't prove to be a group of people."

Drake tipped his head her way. "A valid point, but from what the counterfeiter told us and also from the discussions among the European crime families to which we're privy, we're fairly certain there is only one man at the head of the scheme—the gentleman who contacted the European crime lords and subsequently hired the counterfeiter. If there's anyone who pays or directs that gentleman, we haven't caught even a whiff of their existence."

Christopher nodded. "So to the best of our knowledge, we're after one man. Will he be the person who comes to fetch the notes from Rose?"

Drake grimaced. "That would be nice, but I'm not counting on it." He paused, then, his voice hardening, said, "However, we can't disregard the possibility."

"Surely," Toby said, "putting more steps—more people—between him and the real notes doesn't fit his cautious style. More steps, more people—more opportunities for things to go wrong."

Drake inclined his head. "There is that as well."

"All right." Louisa shifted in her chair as if trying to get comfortable. "Let's hypothesize that it's the mastermind who will take the notes from Rose's hands. Is he the one who contacts her?"

"Yes," Drake said, "but the message may not come directly from him. If he's wise, he'll have someone else deliver the note bearing instructions and the imprint of the half seal to Rose. He, however, will be the one she meets."

"Any bets that he'll engineer a meeting where she won't be able to see his face well enough to identify him?" Toby asked.

"I think," Drake drily replied, "we can take that as read."

"So"—Christopher met Drake's eyes—"we'll need to be at the meeting."

Drake nodded. "And as with Hardcastle and with Rose, we'll need to catch him with the notes in his possession." He looked around the table, meeting the others' eyes. "In his case, that will be critical. Given his likely social and even political standing, we need evidence he won't be able to excuse or explain."

They fell silent, all thinking, then Ellen said, "That means we'll need to ensure that the next three Goffard Hall card parties not just occur but meet all expectations."

"Except," Louisa put in, "with no substitution of fake notes for real ones."

She looked questioningly at Drake, who nodded.

"I can't see any way forward," he said, "other than by continuing with the three card parties. Given Rose won't be contacted until those watching from a distance are satisfied she's had time to exchange the majority if not all of the last run, we'll have to give them what they expect to see."

"Lots of young gentlemen leaving Goffard Hall with happy smiles on their faces," Toby said.

"Hmm." Drake narrowed his eyes. "Given that from all we've gleaned, this scheme is about the money rather than an attempt to cause chaos for the Empire, it's unlikely the mastermind is monitoring the appearance of counterfeit notes around the country. That's not his aim—it won't be his focus. So although due to our intervention, no more counterfeit notes will be appearing, I think we'll be safe on that score."

Christopher nodded. "But the card parties have to occur exactly as advertised, so to speak, or he might grow wary and slip away."

Drake wrinkled his nose. "Even though he's now lost the counterfeiting plates and will be leaving a small fortune behind…sadly, I think you're right. If we do anything that raises his suspicions, he'll opt to slip away and start up another scheme rather than pursue this one and risk exposure and all that will stem from that. If things fail to go exactly according to his expectations, he'll deem it too risky and, regardless of his need for cash, slide back into the shadows."

They fell silent again, then Louisa declared, "Well, then! Rose's cooperation notwithstanding, what do we need to run these card parties in a manner that will satisfy not just the guests but our distant watcher, too?"

They tossed around ideas and suggestions, with Louisa's experience in organizing large ton events tempered by Ellen's and Christopher's knowledge of what was available locally. Of particular note was the need for extra staff.

Both Ellen and Christopher volunteered staff from their respective households, but Drake pointed out that most of them would be needed to assist with keeping a tight cordon around Goffard Hall in order to snare the mastermind if and when he appeared. Instead, Drake suggested sending for staff from Wolverstone House, his family's London home. Toby and Christopher promptly volunteered staff from St. Ives House, the principal Cynster London residence.

"That," Drake said, "will give us not just sufficient staff but also people we can trust to keep an eye on Rose, and Tilly and Nigel as well, and to act as extra dealers."

"As these parties have been touted as special," Louisa said, "none of the guests will see anything odd in Mrs. Kirkpatrick having brought in extra staff, extra tables, and more dealers."

Head tilted, Toby asked, "What are the chances, do you think, of our mastermind turning up as one of the guests?"

Drake shook his head. "He's too old—he would stand out, and that's the last thing he would ever risk."

"But," Christopher said, "we mustn't forget that, as Rose suggested, it's likely the mastermind will have at least one of the guests in his pocket. They'll report to him as to how the card parties are going." Christopher looked around the table, meeting the others' eyes. "Throughout the three card parties, our façade will need to be flawless."

"With respect to that, there's something we haven't yet discussed." Ellen met the others' questioning looks. "There are several others whose support we'll need to pull off our charade. For instance, Mr. Kirkpatrick, Julia Kirkpatrick, and my brother, Robbie, who is known to attend the Goffard Hall events."

Louisa was nodding. "And we'll need to have the active support of the Goffard Hall staff as well."

Drake looked at the clock on the sideboard. "It's time I called on Mr. Kirkpatrick and explained where his wife has disappeared to and what she's involved herself in."

Louisa frowned. "It's odd we haven't had some sort of general inquiry —a groom sent to ask if anyone here had seen her."

Ellen shook her head. "I understand Rose doesn't normally leave her room before noon, and it's only just two o'clock."

"Ah—how helpful." Louisa looked at her husband as Drake pushed back his chair and rose.

"I suggest," he said, "that Toby remains here and holds the fort while the four of us"—he included Ellen and Christopher as well as Louisa with a sweep of his dark gaze—"venture to Goffard Hall. With luck, we'll arrive in time to prevent anyone sending for the constable."

CHAPTER 15

They drove to Goffard Hall in Louisa and Drake's carriage, as Louisa put it, the better to make the right sort of entrance. Unmarked though the carriage was, there was no disguising its quality or that of the horses between its shafts.

As the carriage slowed before the Hall steps, Ellen looked out of the window and saw Robbie, Julia, and Mr. Kirkpatrick standing on the porch. All three appeared anxious.

"They've realized Rose isn't here," Ellen told the others as the carriage rocked to a halt.

Christopher got down and handed Ellen out. Immediately, she swept up the steps to greet Kirkpatrick and Julia. Christopher followed at her heels, with Louisa and Drake bringing up the rear.

Kirkpatrick made a visible effort to put aside his distraction and welcome them.

After Christopher had shaken hands with the older man, he introduced Drake and Louisa as the Marquess and Marchioness of Winchelsea to Kirkpatrick, Julia, and Robert.

Although he did his best to maintain an inscrutable façade, Kirkpatrick clearly recognized the name and was surprised. He glanced from Drake to Louisa. "Are you visiting the area, my lady?"

"So to speak." Louisa put her hand on Mr. Kirkpatrick's arm. "But I'm afraid we have some disturbing news. Perhaps we might go inside?"

Kirkpatrick's eyes narrowed, and his lips firmed, but he nodded. "Of course."

As they turned to enter the house with Kirkpatrick, Julia, Louisa, and Drake leading the way, Robbie murmured to Ellen, loud enough for Christopher, walking on her other side, to hear, "They can't find Mrs. Kirkpatrick. Her dresser says she's not in her room, and her bed hasn't been slept in."

Ellen patted Robbie's arm and whispered, "We know. That's why we're here."

Robbie's eyes widened, and with a warning look, Ellen stepped past him to join Julia in entering the house.

In the front hall, Kirkpatrick paused and turned to Julia, clearly intending to suggest she and Robbie wait elsewhere, but before he could speak, Julia fiercely said, "Whatever it is, Papa, I need to know."

For a second, Kirkpatrick wavered, then he resignedly acquiesced with a dip of his head. He turned to Louisa and Drake and gestured to an open doorway. "The drawing room will be best."

They all filed in and settled, with the ladies on the sofa and the gentlemen in various armchairs.

Kirkpatrick sank into a chair. "You'll pardon me, my lord, my lady, if I seem a trifle distracted, and I'm afraid my wife will not be joining us."

His tone grave, Drake said, "We're aware that Mrs. Kirkpatrick is not at present in the house—indeed, that's why we're here, to explain where she is and why."

Kirkpatrick's expression hardened, and he nodded at Drake. "Go on."

Succinctly, Drake outlined what they knew of Rose Kirkpatrick's actions in support of the mastermind's scheme.

Kirkpatrick had paled. "Counterfeit banknotes?"

"Sadly, yes. We witnessed her accepting them from a man she thought was Hardcastle, the publican, who we also have in custody. It was he who ferried the counterfeit notes from the coast to your wife." Drake paused, then went on, "We have also witnessed the active involvement of Mr. Nigel Fontenay and Miss Matilda Fontenay in your wife's illicit endeavors."

Kirkpatrick's features turned stony. "That, I'm sad to say, surprises me not one whit. I wondered why Rose insisted on having them to stay."

Drake went on to describe the card parties Rose had planned. He was frank in elucidating the current situation, the potential threat to State and Crown, and what that required of them all. "Specifically, to have any hope of capturing the mastermind behind this scheme, we need the three card parties to go ahead as intended, as if Rose's plan to exchange the notes is progressing unimpeded."

Slowly, Kirkpatrick nodded. "I take your point." After a moment, he glanced at Julia, then looked at Louisa. "I confess that I realized quite quickly after we wed that Rose wasn't the sort of lady I had thought her. I had hoped to marry a lady to act as my hostess and to establish Julia in society, but instead, Rose proved entirely self-centered. She wasn't interested in filling the role of my wife but rather in using the position to pursue an agenda of her own. I came to regret my second marriage within months, and despite sharing a roof, Rose and I have been estranged for over a year." He paused, frowning faintly. "All that said, I had no idea she would stoop to or be silly enough to become involved in a scheme of this nature."

"I suspect," Louisa said, "that she fell victim to an arch manipulator in the mastermind, and he was clever enough to appeal to her vanity over her part in his plans."

Kirkpatrick grimaced self-deprecatingly. "I have to wonder if I might have done anything differently and averted this…disaster. She is my wife, after all. If I'd had any idea…"

"It's not your fault!" Leaning forward, Julia grasped her father's arm and squeezed. "You gave Rose every opportunity to lead a pleasant and carefree life, but she decided to go her own road. She made her own choices—her present position is entirely of her own making."

"I have to agree," Louisa said. "My assessment is that any sympathy directed toward Rose would be entirely misplaced." She met Kirkpatrick's gaze. "Even now, her only thought is to find her best way out of the mess and to gain as much as she can along the way."

Kirkpatrick's features hardened again. After a moment of staring at Louisa, he switched his gaze to Drake. "Given my position in the City— all I've stood for over the years—the notion that my wife has undertaken to distribute counterfeit notes is…a blow, both professionally and personally." He sat straighter, raising his head and squaring his stooped shoulders. "Regardless, I stand ready to make whatever atonement is possible for her role in this disturbing affair. I and my household will willingly render whatever assistance you need in apprehending this mastermind. Whatever you require, you have only to ask."

Drake inclined his head. "Thank you."

Julia patted her father's arm, her determined expression stating her firm support.

After lingering for a moment on Julia and Robert, Drake's dark gaze swept the company. "All those present here are trustworthy." He arched a mild brow at Kirkpatrick. "Your staff?"

"All are entirely loyal." Kirkpatrick paused, then added, "The only staff I can't vouch for are those Rose brought with her—her dresser, Archer, and her groom, Nettlefield. That said, both appear to have settled into the household under Mr. and Mrs. Secombe's rule."

Kirkpatrick glanced at Julia, who somewhat reluctantly conceded, "I haven't heard of any difficulties with either."

"Very well," Drake said. "In that case, I suggest you call in your butler and arrange for Nigel and Tilly Fontenay to be summoned to some room—a back parlor, perhaps—and kept there under guard for the moment. We will need to speak with them before leaving the house."

"If you wish…?" Robert, who had been sitting quietly beyond Julia and was closest to the bellpull, rose and, at Kirkpatrick's nod, tugged it.

The butler, Secombe, arrived, and Kirkpatrick gave him the suggested orders.

When the door closed behind Secombe, Kirkpatrick looked at Drake and arched his brows.

Drake replied, "We need to discuss how best to manage Rose."

Christopher listened as rapid consensus was reached that it would be preferable for Rose to remain at the manor and be brought to the Hall purely for the hours of the card parties.

"I cannot countenance her being free again within this house," Kirkpatrick declared. "I can ask the staff to guard Nigel and Tilly, but to ask them to guard their former mistress, who technically would still hold that position, might and very likely would place them in an invidious position." He paused, then added, "In truth, personally, I would rather not set eyes on Rose again."

They all found that entirely understandable. For her part, Julia nodded firmly.

It was agreed that Rose—they all now referred to her by that name rather than as Mrs. Kirkpatrick, avoiding further abrading Kirkpatrick's and Julia's sensibilities—would remain in custody, under guard at the manor.

"Perhaps, my dear"—Kirkpatrick looked at Julia—"you could ask Archer to pack a bag?"

"Yes, of course." Julia rose, bringing the men to their feet.

Louisa raised a hand, catching Julia's attention. "Merely tell Archer that her mistress has decided to stay elsewhere for the next week. No need to go into details."

Julia nodded, excused herself, and left.

The men resumed their seats.

"On the evening of each event," Drake said, "we'll escort Rose here in time for her to dress and be ready to receive her guests. She will, however, be closely supervised the entire time."

Kirkpatrick frowned. "Will she play along, do you think?"

"We believe so," Drake said. "Although she hasn't yet confirmed that in words, it's unlikely she won't, given that her only path to escaping the hangman is to behave as we direct."

After further discussion, Kirkpatrick called in his senior staff. Aided by Louisa, Ellen, and Julia, who had returned to report that Archer was preparing a small bag, he explained to the plainly curious staff that their erstwhile mistress was being held elsewhere in custody, having involved herself in an illegal plot that was extremely serious and that those present were now working to overturn.

"As part of that," Kirkpatrick concluded, "it's essential the upcoming card parties continue as planned."

Drake had been studying the staff. "We need to stress," he said, "that it is absolutely vital that no gossip of any sort regarding your mistress's change in circumstances leaks out. Not to anyone, not in any way."

Scanning the uncertain looks on the staff's faces, Ellen put in, "Also, you should know that, after acting as hostess for the three card parties— under close supervision—your former mistress will not be returning to this house."

Obvious relief washed over the four staff. Secombe half bowed to Ellen. "Very good, miss." He glanced at his wife and the two others lined up at the end of the rug. "That answers our most pressing question."

The staff's other questions—revolving about how they were to manage three major card parties likely to be bigger than any they'd hosted before—were answered chiefly by Louisa and Ellen.

"You needn't fear being overwhelmed," Ellen assured them. "We'll be bringing in extra staff from Bigfield House and the manor and even"— she glanced at Louisa—"London."

Louisa nodded. "Miss Julia, Miss Martingale, and I will liaise with you to make sure you have whatever assistance you require to ensure the evenings run smoothly."

"Today is Saturday," Ellen said, "and the first card party is to be on Tuesday evening. If you would think through your preparations and note any difficulties you foresee"—again, Ellen glanced at Louisa—"the marchioness and I will visit on Monday and go through everything with you and Miss Julia."

"I'm sure," Louisa said bracingly, "that working together, we'll manage everything satisfactorily."

The staff's—and Julia's—relief was palpable.

After confirming with Secombe that Tilly and Nigel had been confined in the back parlor and were, apparently, growing distinctly nervous, Kirkpatrick dismissed the staff and returned his attention to Drake. "What now, my lord?"

"Now," Drake said, catching Christopher's eye, "I believe it's time we met the Fontenays." Drake glanced around the company. "Any observations before we have them brought in?"

After a moment, Ellen asked, "What are the chances both of them know where Rose went last night and why?"

Louisa arched her brows. "High, I should think."

"So," Ellen went on, "by now, they must be quite exercised over what Rose's disappearance might mean for them—I got the impression they were every bit as self-centered as she."

Julia nodded decisively. "They are."

"I've had little to do with the pair myself," Kirkpatrick said. "They're not the sort of people I find entertaining."

Drake nodded at Robbie, who remained closest to the bellpull. "Let's have them in." To Kirkpatrick, Drake said, "It might be wise to have your senior staff back as well, so they hear what we say to the Fontenays and thus will be confident in acting accordingly."

Kirkpatrick agreed and, when Secombe reappeared, gave the relevant orders. Secombe departed, and shortly afterward, the other three members of the senior staff came in. At Drake's direction, they lined up along the wall; from there, they would be able to see the Fontenays and hear all that was said.

Seconds later, Secombe, flanked by two sturdy footmen, escorted a worried-looking Tilly and a scowling Nigel into the room.

Robbie and Christopher had placed two straight-backed chairs at the end of the rug, facing the assembled company. As Secombe joined the other senior staff and the door shut behind the footmen, Drake waved to the chairs. "Take a seat."

Tilly came quickly forward and sat, clasping her hands in her lap. Her gaze went from one face to the next, trying to divine what was going on. Nigel glowered as he dropped into the chair beside her. "What's going on?" he demanded. "Where's Rose?"

Although he scowled at everyone, the fear behind his attitude could not have been more evident.

"As to that," Drake said, "your cousin has been detained at Her Majesty's pleasure."

"*What?*" Nigel paled, then belligerently asked, "Who the devil are you?"

Drake smiled chillingly. "I'm Winchelsea, and my authority stems from those at the highest levels in Whitehall. Beyond that, you don't need to know more. What you do need to concentrate on"—his gaze switched to Tilly, then returned to Nigel—"both of you, is your own survival."

Tilly's eyes widened, and even Nigel drew back.

Drake tipped his head. "Indeed. The situation is this." Concisely, he told them what they needed to know—that the plan to pass on a large number of counterfeit banknotes had been rumbled, that Drake and those assembled were now directing the action, that Rose was in custody and would be assisting in putting on the card parties as originally planned minus the counterfeit notes, and finally, that Tilly's and Nigel's futures were in their own hands.

"At this point," Drake continued, "we are willing to view you as Rose's underlings—brought in by her to assist in carrying out her plan to distribute counterfeit banknotes via the card parties. She needed you both to give her the right contacts among the younger set and also to establish a certain credibility over providing appropriate entertainment."

Without pausing, he went on, "Should you agree to assist us in putting on a good show during the upcoming card parties by playing your customary roles in much the same vein as your cousin will be, then the authorities might be prevailed upon to turn a blind eye to your involvement in the wider illegal scheme. However"—Drake fixed both Fontenays with his gaze—"if you do not behave and do not adhere to the absolute letter of our plan, I can guarantee you will find yourself clapped in gaol with an alacrity that will leave your head spinning."

Christopher had to admit that Drake was an expert at instilling fear into his audience; the even, level tone of his voice—never rising or falling —somehow made the images his words painted all the more frightening.

Now, after a fraught pause, he said to Nigel and Tilly, "It's time to make your choice. In exculpation for your sins to date, are you willing to do exactly as I say henceforth, behave exactly as required by those in this room, or would you rather grow acquainted with the local cells?"

Fear was written all over Tilly's face, while Nigel was struggling to maintain a stoic demeanor but failing. Brother and sister shared a glance, then Tilly looked back at Drake. "I'll do what you want."

Nigel fought against the need to capitulate, but when Drake arched his brows at him, he swallowed and nodded. "I'll...play along, too."

Drake inclined his head. "A wise decision." He glanced at Louisa and Ellen, then looked back at the Fontenays. "For now, you are required to behave exactly as you normally would—as if nothing whatever has changed at Goffard Hall. We will speak with you again on Monday concerning your actions on Tuesday evening, but essentially, you will be doing exactly as you have been at your cousin's events. She will be in attendance as well and will be assisting us with our planning. I most strongly advise you not to attempt to alert anyone that, behind the façade of the card parties, anything at all has altered."

Christopher could almost see the wheels turning in Nigel's head. "You will be watched," he put in. "Constantly. Not only by the staff here but also by others of whom you won't be aware."

"Indeed." Drake studied the pair. "To be absolutely clear, should you make even one false move, you will be thrown into gaol and will hence-forth face the full consequences of being a willing accessory to your cousin's crimes."

He paused for a dramatic moment, glanced briefly at the attentive staff, then looked back at the Fontenays and reiterated, "You will be watched, all the time. If you have any sense at all, you will not put a foot wrong in any way whatsoever."

Tilly was eyeing the staff, who were staring woodenly back. "Will we be locked up?"

Drake looked at Secombe and arched a brow.

Secombe responded to the implied question with, "That might be best, my lord. It is a big house, and we've got our duties to attend to."

Drake returned his gaze to Tilly. "Yes, you will be locked in your rooms." He paused, then added, "You would do well to reflect that they're a great deal more comfortable than the local cells or, indeed, the room in which your cousin is presently sitting."

Tilly said nothing, and Nigel clearly thought better of his instinctive protest.

Drake sent an inquiring look around the others. When no one had anything to add, he glanced at Kirkpatrick and nodded.

Kirkpatrick dismissed the staff, consigning the Fontenays into their charge.

When the door closed behind the group, Drake looked around again and asked, "Is there anything more we need to arrange?"

Julia swiveled to look at her father. "Do you want me to manage the household?" When Kirkpatrick blinked at her, she appealed to Louisa and Ellen, seated on the sofa beside her. "Someone will have to take charge. For all her shortcomings, Rose did manage the household's reins."

Kirkpatrick cleared his throat. "If you feel up to the challenge, my dear…"

Julia's chin firmed. "I'm sure I can manage—I've lived here for years, and I know how things are done."

"And if you run into any difficulties," Ellen said, "you have only to send to Bigfield House, and I'll come over."

"I'll be happy to support you in any way necessary," Louisa added. "Especially over organizing these card parties."

Julia shifted to face the other ladies. "I must admit that running one card party would be challenge enough, but hosting three events, one after the other with only a day in between to catch our breaths…that will be quite a feat."

Despite the inviting glance Julia flashed around the company, Christopher kept his lips shut; he knew next to nothing about hosting events. However, Louisa and Ellen immediately responded; from the questions the pair put, they were attempting to get a clear idea of how the previous card parties had run.

Julia answered as best she could, imparting all she knew of the preparations, but she hadn't attended the parties herself. She twisted to look at Robbie, seated behind her, and appealed to him.

Happy to be able to help, Robbie applied himself to describing everything pertinent he could recall.

Christopher cut a glance at Drake; like Christopher, Drake was watching and listening, but making no move to offer any opinion.

Wise men know when to step back and leave matters to the ladies.

Christopher had heard his father, his uncle, and their cousins state that often enough to accept it as an inviolable truth. Neither he, Drake, nor Kirkpatrick made any effort to stick in their oar.

Finally, the three ladies were satisfied with what they had extracted from Robbie, and at Louisa's suggestion, Julia called Mrs. Secombe in.

The housekeeper was a no-nonsense motherly sort who ran her household like a well-regimented ship. When questioned about the previous and upcoming card parties, she threw herself into the discussion with evident zeal.

The planning covered a wide range of topics, from how many tables should be set up and where those should be positioned through to the amount of brandy—not of high quality—that might be expected to be consumed.

Eventually, the ladies looked at each other, then declared they had done all they could to that point.

Louisa patted Julia's hand. "We'll return on Monday"—she looked at the housekeeper and smiled—"and work through the finer details."

Mrs. Secombe curtsied. "The staff thank you for your help, my lady— and you for yours, Miss Martingale." Mrs. Secombe glanced at the men sitting opposite the sofa. "We've all been taken aback a bit by the news, but rest assured, all the staff are keen and eager to do our part to help catch this nasty mastermind person."

Louisa smiled, as did Ellen. "Thank you, Mrs. Secombe," Ellen said. "We knew we could count on you and the staff."

Blushing, Mrs. Secombe bobbed another curtsy to the men, then, at Julia's smiling nod, took herself off.

That was a signal for the others to rise.

"We've accomplished all we can to this point." Drake held out his hand to Kirkpatrick. "We'll return on Monday to help with the preparations for our first charade."

"Thank you." Kirkpatrick met Drake's eyes as he shook his hand, then shook hands with Christopher. "I can't say I'm happy about this situation, but I am grateful that you've stepped in. Learning the truth of what Rose was up to *after* the event—once she'd succeeded in distributing the fake notes—would have been…horrendous."

With goodwill all around, they parted. Robbie accompanied the four from the manor down the steps to where a groom was holding his horse a few yards behind the carriage.

In the forecourt, Ellen turned to Robbie. "How is everything at home?"

He grinned. "No disasters yet." He glanced at Christopher. "And the goats haven't eaten their way out of their pen."

Smiling, Christopher tipped his head Robbie's way. "That's always good to know."

Ellen clearly felt torn, yet... "With all that's going on, I suspect I had better dine at the manor again tonight." The look she directed at Christopher, Louisa, and Drake made the statement a question.

Drake nodded. "If you would, that will make our planning easier."

Ellen looked at Robbie. "Can you make my excuses to Aunt Emma and Uncle Humphrey, and tell Emma not to wait up for me? I can't say how late I'll be."

Robbie hesitated, and Christopher added, "I'll see your sister safely home."

Robbie's face cleared. He nodded to Ellen and grasped his reins. "I'll tell them."

He swung into the saddle, saluted them all, then set his horse trotting toward the bridle path that led to the rear boundary of the Hall.

After waiting for Drake to help Louisa up, Christopher handed Ellen into the carriage, then he and Drake followed.

The four settled, Christopher and Ellen on the rearward-facing seat, with Drake and Louisa opposite.

Drake leaned his head against the squabs. "The staff seemed very ready to render us any and all assistance."

"I think," Ellen said, "that like Mr. Kirkpatrick, they feel a need to prove themselves, to demonstrate that Rose's actions are as much an anathema to them as to us or any right-thinking person."

Louisa softly snorted. "They were also hugely relieved to hear that Rose would not return as their mistress. She's clearly made no friends among the staff, and it seems that Tilly and Nigel enjoy no better support."

Christopher, too, leaned back against the leather. "Regardless of their motives, I believe we're safe in trusting that the Hall staff, Julia, and Kirkpatrick himself will all do their utmost to further our joint aims."

~

They returned to the manor to discover that Toby had nothing whatever to report. "No action of any sort either at the inn or around Goffard Hall."

After filling Toby in on the arrangements thus far, they had Rose brought up from her room.

Once again, they spoke with her in the drawing room.

Drake informed her of Kirkpatrick's agreement to her continued incarceration at the manor, and that he and all at Goffard Hall, including her acolytes Tilly and Nigel, were committed to the plan to host the card parties as advertised and, after the last party, to use the fake banknotes—by then supposed to have been switched for the genuine article—to capture the villain behind the scheme.

"At this point, the only question remaining is whether you agree to join with everyone else in projecting the façade that the card parties are occurring as expected, in all ways exactly as anticipated, so that the mastermind who lured you into his scheme is, in turn, lured into contacting you to collect what he will believe are his ill-gotten but highly desirable gains." Drake held Rose's gaze and arched his brows. "Well? Do we have your oath you will perform as required, or should I summon men to escort you to the Tower?"

The hours spent alone had sobered Rose and drained a great deal of her haughty superiority. She'd listened to Drake with barely a flicker of emotion. Now, she studied him, then said, "As you're well aware, that's no real choice." Still holding his gaze, she dipped her head in acquiescence. "I will promise to do as you ask provided you give me your word that, at worst, I'll be transported—that I won't hang for my part in the scheme."

Drake let a moment elapse, then inclined his head. "You have my assurance that, should you do as we ask, your sentence in this matter will be transportation rather than hanging. Those here will bear witness."

Rose thought, then nodded. "Very well."

"Excellent." Louisa fixed Rose with her pale-green gaze. "You may commence demonstrating your bona fides by telling us about the young gentlemen you were hoping to entertain at the first card party. From how far afield will they come?"

Rose hesitated for only a heartbeat, then complied.

Both Ellen and Louisa peppered her with questions regarding the guests and their anticipated behavior, and she responded readily, especially once Louisa evinced a certain amazement at Rose's ability to lure young gentlemen to her events.

Rose couldn't resist preening and, thereafter, volunteered several details neither Ellen nor Louisa had, until then, thought of.

Eventually, Ellen and Louisa exhausted their immediate queries. Louisa looked at Drake. "I believe that's all we need for the moment." She returned her gaze to Rose and inclined her head regally. "We will, no doubt, have more questions on Monday."

Rose very nearly smirked, but then Christopher directed Pendleby and the two footmen to "see their guest to her quarters," and any inclination Rose had to self-congratulation fled.

She rose and, with a nod to Louisa and Ellen and a faint glare for Drake, went with the footmen.

Pendleby returned moments later to confirm their prisoner was back under lock and key and also to inform them that dinner was awaiting their pleasure.

Knowing better than to goad Mrs. Hambledon, they promptly rose and repaired to the dining room.

Over a mouthwatering four courses, they went over their plans, looking as far ahead as they were able, namely to the end of the third party.

"After that," Drake observed, "we'll need to take stock."

"Presumably," Christopher said, "we'll need to wait and see if and when the mastermind takes our bait."

Drake's eyes narrowed. "Somehow, I feel certain he will."

"Granted," Toby said. "But the critical point for us will be when."

After dinner, they agreed there was little point in further discussion. They returned to the drawing room and passed a comfortable hour exchanging news and information regarding their families.

Once the tea trolley had arrived and the tea was consumed, Christopher caught Ellen's eye. "As I promised your brother, I'll walk you home."

Ellen met his eyes, read the question and the hope therein, and fought to keep her answering smile from being too revealing. "Thank you."

She rose, made her farewells to the other three, linked her arm in Christopher's, and allowed him to steer her toward the front door.

Drake, Louisa, and Toby remained in the drawing room only long enough to allow Christopher and Ellen to be well on their way.

Toby yawned hugely. "I'm for bed. All this thinking, planning, and plotting is tiring." He looked at Drake. "I don't know how you do it."

Drake huffed, rose, and extended his hand to Louisa. "We'll retire, too. Tomorrow, being Sunday, might be a day of rest, but our past two days have been draining."

Louisa grasped his hand and allowed him to heave her to her feet. Upright, she tugged the bodice of her gown downward in a vain attempt to make the garment sit better over the bulge of her belly. Then she narrowed her eyes on her husband. "I might rest tomorrow, but be advised that I will not be left at home on Monday or any of the succeeding days." She linked her arm with Drake's and leaned on him as they made their way to the door.

Toby went ahead and held it open.

Louisa tipped her head at Toby in gracious yet haughty thanks. As she started up the stairs, she mused, "Sadly, I won't be able to appear at these card parties—"

"Thank God you realize that," Drake muttered.

Louisa shot him a glittering, narrow-eyed glance. "Of course I realize that. But I will need to be there, in the house with you—who also cannot appear for much the same reason—in case there are any last-minute glitches that Ellen, Julia, and the estimable Mrs. Secombe can't resolve." Louisa arched her brows. "Incidentally, I don't know if you entirely believed her, but I'm quite sure Rose's promise to behave—to perform as required, as you phrased it—will stretch only so far. If any alternative offers, she'll grab it."

Toby nodded. "That was my reading of her, too."

Drake humphed. "We're all so cynical, but yes, I agree. I wouldn't trust Rose any further than we absolutely must."

To accommodate Louisa, they'd been climbing slowly; as they neared the head of the stairs, Toby said, "One thing we haven't discussed—what about the counterfeit notes?"

Puzzled, Drake glanced at him. "They're here, in the safe."

"Yes, I know," Toby said. "But will that work, given that any communication from the mastermind will go to Goffard Hall?"

Drake frowned, stepped off the stairs, and halted in the gallery.

Toby halted, too, and went on, "Just think—sometime after the third card party, the mastermind is going to send Rose a message. If he's half as clever as you've painted him and immovably set on giving no one any chance to recognize him, then surely he's going to give Rose very little time before having to come out and meet him?"

"Hah!" Louisa had been listening intently. "No time to think too much, let alone inform anyone of her excursion."

"Exactly!" Toby looked at Drake. "In his shoes, isn't that what you would do?"

Drake grimaced. "Touché."

"And," Toby went on, "we want Rose to hand the mastermind the counterfeit notes so we can capture him with the most incriminating evidence in his hands."

Drake hesitated, then nodded decisively. "You're right. Remind me on Friday next, after the second party, to take the counterfeit notes to Goffard Hall. Kirkpatrick will assuredly have a safe in which we can leave them."

With that, the trio said their goodnights and made for their respective beds.

Strolling hand in hand, Christopher and Ellen reached the long pool in the Bigfield House shrubbery.

Christopher glanced at Ellen's face, wondering; he didn't want to make any incorrect assumptions.

As if feeling his gaze, she glanced sidelong up at him, then a sweet smile curved her lips, and with a confident tilt to her head, she tugged on his hand and drew him on.

Into the house, to her room and her bed.

Throughout the day, adjusting to their new relationship had come more easily than he'd anticipated, and judging by her bright smiles and laughing encouragement, she had found falling into the way of things as natural and as effortless as he. When she flung herself at him, he caught her; when he bent his head, she raised her face, and when their lips met and they kissed, that ineffable sense of promise flowered.

Eagerness, relief, delight, and a fizzing sense of joy—a wonder that this was truly real, truly theirs—infused the long minutes that followed. Acting as one, with one mind, one aim, they devoted themselves to exploring anew the landscape of passion and desire that opened up between them.

His hands traced, caressed, and sculpted, and his lips followed, tracing each line, each curve, with heated adoration.

Her fingers tangled and clenched in his hair, then released and, driven, splayed and swept over his shoulders, over his chest, exploring and learning, searching and possessing. When they closed about his length, his breath stuttered, then he found her slick softness and stroked, and she melted in his arms.

Desire-induced gasps and passion-laden sighs shivered through the night air as they battled to prolong the scintillating moments, yet no matter how they fought to dally, to savor the path and delay the inevitable, the compulsion to become one swelled, and soon they had joined and were racing, hearts thundering, as they strove to reach that elusive peak and the splendor that lay beyond.

Exquisite and overpowering, completion caught them, wracked them, shattered them, and ultimately, flung them free, buoyed on oblivion's pleasured sea.

Uncounted minutes later, Christopher's wits returned enough for him to gather his strength and lift from Ellen's arms enough to slump beside her. Already asleep, she murmured incoherently and turned to snuggle against him, pillowing her head in the hollow beneath his shoulder.

He looked down at her face, its perfection made only more glorious by the rosy flush of desire that had yet to fade. Something in him shifted; it felt as if some lock had clicked shut. For long minutes, he allowed his eyes to feast while a host of emotions, some new, others familiar, swirled contentedly inside him.

Nothing felt wrong or even out of place; everything felt right—as it was meant to be.

As *he* was meant to be.

Finally, he laid down his head and drew her deeper into his arms. He closed his eyes, certain beyond question that being there—beside her— was his fated place.

As sleep beckoned and he sank into the mists, one thought still shone in his mind: Being with her had filled the empty nooks and crannies of his soul.

The yawning emptiness within that he'd consciously carried over the past year was no more.

After all the years, with her, he'd finally learned the true meaning of contentment—of perfect peace.

CHAPTER 16

or Ellen, Sunday began with a hurried breakfast, followed by the drive to church.

Christopher was waiting in the porch to walk in with her, Emma, and Robbie; he sat beside her, and they shared a hymnal as they raised their voices in gratitude to their maker—and shared glances that lent that gratitude a new dimension.

After congratulating Reverend Thornley on his sermon, she and Christopher joined Emma and Robbie in making a beeline for Julia Kirkpatrick and her father, already on the lawn.

Ellen exchanged a smile and a nod with Mr. Kirkpatrick.

Christopher shook the older man's hand. "How are you and the household managing, sir?"

Mr. Kirkpatrick folded his hands over the head of his cane. "We are holding the fort, Mr. Cynster. The staff have been a great support."

Robbie had been consulting with Julia. Now, he looked at Mr. Kirkpatrick and asked, "Sir, Julia has mentioned that she would love to ride more. Would you consent to me escorting her on a jaunt around the lanes before luncheon?"

Mr. Kirkpatrick frowned slightly. "Just the pair of you?"

That had been Robbie's intention, but clearly that would be a step too far for Julia's father.

Christopher caught Ellen's eye. "If Miss Martingale would enjoy the outing, perhaps she and I might join you."

"Would you?" Robbie looked ridiculously grateful. He swung his gaze to Ellen. "Sis?"

"Yes, of course." She smiled brightly at Christopher. "It's a fine day, and an hour or so's ride would be lovely."

Thus it was that, half an hour later, Christopher and Ellen, mounted on their steeds, ambled in the wake of Julia, perched atop a nice-looking bay mare, and Robbie, on his roan. The leafy lanes were perfect for walking or trotting along, and Robbie, who rode every day, had learned where all the bridle paths were. Unerringly, he led them through a gate and onto a path that ran beside the stream, on the opposite bank to the gypsy encampment.

They rode along, letting the horses stretch their legs in a gentle gallop. The sharp-eyed gypsy children spotted them, then recognized them and ran to line the opposite bank, cheering and waving.

Ellen laughed and waved back.

Smiling and waving himself, Christopher glanced at her, and his smile deepened as he took in the sight of her ribbons bobbing about her ears. Strangely enough, these days, he barely saw them—or rather, they no longer signaled to him what they once had. Ribbons, rosettes, frills, and furbelows were no longer a sight that sent him running; now, they drew him in with the promise of passion, warmth, and a contented future.

Enjoyable, relaxing, and without incident, the ride was a great success. Mindful of instructions, Robbie turned them back in time to reach Bigfield House just as the luncheon gong rang out.

They dismounted in the stable yard and walked to the shrubbery—to where, beside the long pool, the staff had stationed two wicker armchairs. Emma sat in one, with Sir Humphrey in his bath chair alongside; both were chatting with Kirkpatrick, in the other armchair, while footmen and maids put the final touches to a repast laid out on several blankets spread on the grass.

In proposing the picnic, Emma had asked Christopher if his guests at the manor would care to join the company. Knowing all three were hoping for a true day of rest—a day of doing nothing at all—he'd demurred on their behalf.

It was a glorious summer's afternoon, with blue sky above and not a cloud to be seen. The drone of bees and the twittering of birds provided a muted background chorus as, with appreciative smiles and exclamations, the four riders disposed themselves on the blankets, and the wine and food was passed around.

Christopher had attended innumerable picnics, but none so simply pleasant and undemanding. Sir Humphrey was clearly having one of his better days; he'd recognized Christopher and was holding his own in a conversation with Kirkpatrick.

Christopher exchanged an encouraging look with Ellen.

She leaned closer and whispered, "Luckily, Mr. Kirkpatrick knows nothing about farming or local matters, so anything odd Uncle Humphrey says, Mr. Kirkpatrick simply assumes is correct."

Regardless, the two older men and Emma continued relaxed and content.

Likewise, Robert and Julia were getting on well—which left Christopher and Ellen to their own company, to sharing smiles, whispers, and soft laughs while they plied each other with morsels from the dishes arrayed on the blanket before them.

Eventually, the food was mostly gone, and two footmen arrived and carted the remnants away, leaving the company sipping wine and cider and lazing in semisomnolence in the afternoon's warmth.

Sir Humphrey's chair and the two occupied by Emma and Kirkpatrick had been set just in front of the hedge; soon, the three elders were nodding in the shade cast by the high green wall.

Before any of the rest of them fell asleep, Robert suggested a game of croquet.

Nothing loath, Christopher and Ellen got to their feet, settled their clothes, and followed Robert and an eager Julia out of the shrubbery and around to the square lawn set aside for the game.

Ellen halted under the spreading branches of an oak bordering the lawn. Christopher halted beside her. After a moment, he found her hand with his and, with his gaze on Robbie and Julia, who were collecting the hoops, balls, and mallets from a small cupboard to the side of the lawn, he raised Ellen's fingers to his lips and brushed a kiss over them.

She glanced his way, curious. He met her gaze and smiled, letting his feelings, his embracing of the simple pleasure of the moment, show, then he released her hand and set off across the lawn to help Robbie position the hoops.

They played as partners, Christopher and Ellen against Robbie and Julia, with much laughter, banter, and good-natured teasing, until a footman arrived bearing a summons from Emma to present themselves for afternoon tea.

They rejoined the trio beside the pool to find the older folk considerably restored.

After passing around the cups, sipping, and eating several delicious cakes, Christopher finally took his leave, sincerely thanking Emma and Sir Humphrey for a most enjoyable day.

Ellen walked with him to the stables. While they waited for Storm to be saddled, she heaved a happy sigh. Meeting his inquiring look, she explained, "Today has been simply lovely. I don't want to think of all we have to do tomorrow—I'm going to concentrate on enjoying the here and now."

Holding her gaze, he replied, "A wise and laudable sentiment."

Before the stableman returned and stole the moment, he dipped his head and kissed the luscious rose-tinted lips she tipped back her head and offered.

For a moment, the connection held—not flaring hotly but more in the nature of an anchoring sureness, a reassurance of unconstrained, unconditional togetherness—then the clop of a hoof reached them, and they broke the kiss, held each other's gazes for an instant more, then stepped apart.

Christopher mounted, saluted Ellen—she who he was now certain held his heart, for what else could this feeling of deep, unshakeable connection stem from?—then wheeled and rode back to the manor.

There, he found Toby and Drake relaxing in the library. Both were reading recent editions of *The Times*.

Christopher arched his brows. "Anything?"

Drake lowered the sheet enough to reply, "In the papers, nothing."

"As for any action here," Toby said from where he sat behind the desk, poring over the news sheet spread across it, "you've missed absolutely nothing." Looking up, he grinned. "It's been blessedly quiet all day."

"Rose?" Christopher dropped into the armchair opposite Drake.

"Not a peep," Drake replied.

Christopher studied Drake's for-once-openly mellow expression. "Louisa?"

Drake's lips curved slightly. "Believe it or not, she's resting."

"She said," Toby explained, "that tomorrow is going to be a hellishly busy day. She plans to head over to Goffard Hall immediately after breakfast."

"And," Drake said, his tone hardening, "to stay all day if necessary, which she believes will be the case. Incidentally, all three of us have been conscripted."

"We're to be her lieutenants, as it were." Toby shook his head. "We needed today to gird our loins for tomorrow."

Christopher sat back and imagined what tomorrow might bring while the other two returned to their reading.

Later, after dinner had been served and consumed and the four of them had dallied in the drawing room long enough to consume the tea Pendleby brought in, Christopher set out to walk through the gentle night to Bigfield House.

He hadn't said anything to Ellen about joining her that night, yet as he walked past the orchards and through the fields, the notion that she might not welcome his arrival didn't even enter his head.

An assumption, perhaps, but after that day of unalloyed togetherness, their slide into physical intimacy had been shown to be merely one strand in the connection linking them.

If she'd been looking out of her bedroom window, she would have seen him approaching the house.

Sure enough, when he strolled into the area of the shrubbery housing the long pool, there she was—waiting for him.

As he neared, the smile lifting her lips brightened, and she held out a hand.

He took it; when she would have turned and towed him on, he pulled back and stopped her. He stepped close, raised her hand to his lips, kissed her fingers, then with his other arm encircling her waist, drew her to him as he bent his head and pressed his lips to hers.

Eager joy and passion waited, like nectar on her tongue.

He'd never tasted anything so addictive. So enticing and alluring.

For long moments, he savored, and with her hands rising to frame his face, she supped and sipped and, in her own way, beckoned.

Eventually, they raised their heads and, hand in hand, with their gazes locked and both reluctant to break the link, they walked slowly on.

In her room, he closed the door and drew her to him. She came with anticipation lighting her face, with an effervescent joy that thrilled him.

Their lips melded, their tongues dueled, and passion and desire inexorably rose.

Heat welled and swelled, and they shed their clothes and gave themselves up to the pursuit of glory.

Tonight, he could feel a thrum in his blood that ran deeper, resonating more powerfully through him. It was, he supposed, their connection growing. Deepening and strengthening.

Ellen had never known that this—this joyous, glorious meeting of bodies and minds—was what intimacy was all about. He'd shown her. He'd opened her eyes to touch—to the scintillating pleasure of his fingers tracing her curves, of his palms sculpting her hollows. He'd lavished on her caresses—laden with passion, but also with a devotion to her pleasure—that elicited a response in her that was so intense and poignant, they drove her to the brink of insanity.

Into a madness of the senses for which only he held the cure.

Driven and needy, they joined, and sensation washed over and through her, battering her senses with unadulterated pleasure in so many different ways, she felt adrift from the world, as if only the two of them existed.

Her focus drew in, locked on the physical sensations of the moment.

She gasped, panted, and clung, and gloried in their headlong rush to fulfillment. Gloried over the way he closed his eyes and groaned, over the lack of restraint the moment—and she—drove him to display.

She knew—sensed—that, with her, he lowered his shields all but constantly, letting her see emotions he'd never shown anyone else.

Perhaps never felt with anyone else?

The fleeting thought made the tension building within her tighten to an unbearable degree.

She arched beneath him, gasping as he drove deep within her—and the coiled tension snapped, and her senses soared as the brilliant sun of ecstasy seared her, then exploded, and her awareness fractured into a million shards of bright, pulsing pleasure.

The wave of scintillating sensation rolled powerfully through her as he stiffened and found his own release.

While her senses floated somewhere in the void, the power in the moment—the strong, inviolable, and immutable bedrock of their connection—cradled her, cradled him, held them gently together as the physical impact faded and left, shining in her mind's sight, the rock formed of their joint emotions.

Even as she slid into slumber, she sensed them both reaching for and embracing the solidity of what had grown between them. The simple reality of love.

∾

After breakfast on Monday, Ellen looked in on Robbie. She found him in the study with Hopper, immersed in dealing with inquiries from various cider mills hoping to secure some of the Bigfield House crop. When Robbie looked at her absentmindedly, she merely smiled, waved, and left him to it.

She arrived at the manor to find Louisa ready and waiting to depart for Goffard Hall.

With the three men electing to ride, Louisa claimed the reins of the manor's gig and briskly tooled herself and Ellen down to the village and through it, to the lane that led north to Goffard Hall.

On arriving at the Hall, they were met by Julia and Mrs. Secombe; both were plainly ready to get as much accomplished as possible that day.

The first order of business was to throw open the drawing room and connected ballroom and rearrange or remove all the furniture.

Louisa and Ellen directed, Julia and Mrs. Secombe gave the orders, and the footmen heaved sofas, chairs, occasional tables, and sideboards hither and yon. Toby, Christopher, and Drake were roped in to help, each pairing with one of the footmen.

Next, the footmen—and their three male helpers—were sent first to the dining room and then all through the house to collect every straight-backed chair.

Drake, in his shirtsleeves, as were Toby and Christopher, halted beside Louisa and somewhat acidly remarked, "This isn't going to be a ball. Do we really need all these chairs?"

Louisa turned her head and met his eyes. "Yes. The chairs are for the card tables, of course."

Drake frowned. "Where are the card tables?"

"They," Louisa informed him, "are next."

It took time to refurnish the rooms as card-playing salons. It was lunchtime before Louisa, Ellen, Julia, and Mrs. Secombe declared that stage of the preparations complete. By then, the drawing room and ball-room between them played host to ten tables of varying sizes; the smallest would accommodate three players plus a dealer, while the largest, a circular table, would allow, at a pinch, seven players and a dealer.

After doing justice to the cold collation Mrs. Secombe had ordered set out in the dining room, Louisa and Julia took charge of reorganizing that room into a supper room, co-opting Toby and Drake as helpers.

Meanwhile, Ellen embarked on kitting out their card-playing salons appropriately. She consulted with Mrs. Secombe, then summoned Christopher from his current task of assisting a footman to ferry in the extra leaves to extend the dining table.

Christopher had been crossing the front hall; he caught Toby returning to the dining room and gave him his load.

Toby grunted at the weight and caught Christopher's eyes. "Who knew card parties involved so much work?"

Louisa, directing proceedings from just inside the door, had overheard; she swung around and brightly informed them, "And there's a great deal we haven't started on yet."

Toby rolled his eyes and carried the table leaves past her.

Christopher crossed the hall to join Ellen, who had produced a list from somewhere.

"We need cloths for the tables," she informed him. "Mrs. Secombe says they should be in the linen press at the top of the stairs."

He waved her to the stairs and fell in beside her.

As they climbed, frowning slightly, she added, "We might need to send to Bigfield House for more cloths and other items as well. According to the Secombes, they've run only six tables before, but Rose, Tilly, and even more Nigel seem confident that the number of guests liable to turn up for even the first of these special card parties is likely to be significantly greater than before." She looked at the paper in her hand. "It's annoying not having a definite number of guests. I'll need to make another list."

They reached the first floor, and she turned left. "Apparently, the linen press is somewhere along here. The door's one of those concealed-in-the-paneling sort."

It took them a few minutes to locate the door; Christopher finally spotted the seam and, by pressing on the right spot, released the catch. He pulled open the door. Light from the window above the stairs threw just enough illumination into the narrow room to make out the rows of shelves affixed to one long side and across the end wall, almost to the ceiling. On each shelf lay stacks of neatly folded linen. He blinked. "How on earth are you supposed to know which are tablecloths and which are sheets?"

Ellen nudged him aside and went in. "By the weight of the cloth, of course."

"Huh." He watched as she walked slowly along the shelves, touching the folded materials, pausing occasionally to take a piece of cloth between her fingers to gauge its weight before releasing it and moving on.

Three quarters of the way down the room, she halted. "Aha! Here they are."

She beckoned him forward, then started counting.

He ambled in and halted a foot from her.

"We need to take these downstairs." She pulled out two large, folded cloths, waited impatiently until he resignedly held out his arms, then laid the cloths across his forearms. "That's two."

He was surprised how heavy they were.

"We need ten, at least—in fact, we need more to allow for any spillages. Let's see." She continued to pull cloths from the shelf, steadily loading more onto his arms. Then she made a dismissive sound and loaded one last cloth on the pile. "They have only nine. We'll need to send to Bigfield for at least three more. No—wait!"

Confused, she met his eyes. "We'll need cloths—two large ones at least—for the dining table." She frowned at the shelves. "They must have had cloths on their supper table. How did they manage with only nine cloths before? Did they pray there would be no accident?"

He hid a grin and stepped forward.

She blinked at him and instinctively backed.

He continued to advance.

"What are you doing?" She continued to retreat until her shoulders hit the shelves at the end of the room.

She looked at him in confusion.

He allowed a wolfish smile to show. "I know the answer as to how they managed." He arched his brows at her. "What's my information worth?"

She stared at him. Then she faintly glared, shot a glance around him at the door, then flung her arms about his neck, stretched up and pulled his head forward, over the cloths stacked in his arms, and kissed him.

She would have cut her payment short, but he managed to balance the sheets on one arm and, raising his freed hand, cupped her nape and held her steady while he took charge and plundered unrestrained.

When he consented to raise his head, they were both short of breath.

She blinked up at him, patently struggled to assemble a stern expression, then gave up and asked, "So what's the secret?"

He grinned and, straightening and clutching the all-important cloths, backed toward the corridor. "The smaller tables downstairs are actual card tables—they're covered with green baize and don't need an additional cloth."

She'd followed him and now halted, clearly envisaging the tables in her mind, then uttered an enlightened, "Ah! Of course!"

Then she focused on him and, her lips twitching upward, waved him out of the narrow space. "So we have enough cloths, at least for the first party."

Together they returned downstairs, delivered the cloths into Mrs. Secombe's care, then Ellen turned to the next item on her list. "Cutlery." She looked around, then pointed to two heavy sideboards that now sat opposite the extended dining table, which had been moved toward one side wall of the dining room, closer to the door from which staff would ferry in the platters of delicacies for the hungry guests. "Let's look in those upper drawers."

"I'm not polishing forks," he warned her.

That earned him an exasperated look. "We're not going to polish them —we have to count them."

He tipped his head. "That, I can do."

About them, the others, including Robbie, who had arrived after lunch, were bustling about, doing this and that. The Hall's footmen and maids rushed here, then there, hunting out things and ferrying them around at the behest of Mrs. Secombe or Louisa.

As the afternoon wore on, Christopher, Drake, and Toby shared frequent glances, wordlessly conveying their amazement at the effort involved. Although all three had attended country house card parties many times in their earlier years, they'd never stopped to consider the logistics of what was involved, especially when entertaining on such a scale.

At one point, after the three ladies and Mrs. Secombe had paused to consult in what—from the safe distance of the wall against which all three gentlemen had chosen to lounge—had appeared to be exasperated vein, Louisa imperiously summoned Drake and dispatched him to wring as much insight as possible from Nigel and Tilly—for the day, confined in the back parlor—as to exactly how many guests might be expected.

"Because," Louisa declared, frustration ringing in her tone, "without having a more accurate notion of the number of guests, we're attempting to manage this charade blind!"

Drake went. He returned fifteen minutes later to report, "Their best guess is over eighty for the first event, but the numbers might be more like one hundred." He paused, then added, "For the succeeding events, the expectation is that the numbers will rise with each event, but exactly how high they might go is anyone's guess."

Hands on her hips, Louisa blew out a breath, then met Ellen's and Julia's eyes. "Don't panic. We'll manage."

Her *by the skin of our teeth* remained unsaid, but they all heard it.

They worked on the preparations until the shadows outside started to lengthen.

Finally, Louisa and Mrs. Secombe called a halt. By then, Ellen felt ready to drop; although glad to hear Julia ask Robbie to dine with her and her father, she was relieved when, also invited, Louisa graciously cried off, saying she needed to rest. As Ellen had arrived in the manor carriage, that gave her an excuse to leave as well.

They reached the manor as twilight deepened, and after confirming with Pendleby that they would dine as soon as Mrs. Hambledon was ready to accommodate them, the five of them slumped in armchairs and on the sofa in the library.

After a moment, Louisa stated, "I think we accomplished everything we absolutely had to get done today."

She placed a subtle emphasis on the last word, one Ellen comprehended without further explanation.

However, after a moment of silence, Drake, who had been staring unseeing at the ceiling, lowered his gaze to his wife's face and inquired, gently, "Do you mean to say there's still more to be done?"

Louisa stared at him. "Of course." When Toby and Christopher both groaned, she added, "You didn't think we'd finished, did you?"

Drake sighed. "What more is there to do?"

Louisa rattled off a string of tasks. "Ellen and I, and Julia, too, will be fully absorbed with finalizing the details of the supper and schooling the staff in how we need them to behave to ensure that all runs smoothly, and we need to put plans in place in case Rose, Nigel, or Tilly decides not to play to our script. Needless to say, that's critically important."

No one disagreed. "Am I right in supposing," Christopher asked, "that you're expecting our active assistance?"

Louisa nodded. "Naturally. The staff we've sent for from London—including those experienced in acting as dealers—should arrive here in the morning. You'll need to meet them, confirm they've brought sufficient packs of cards, then bring them over to the Hall, introduce them to Secombe and Mrs. Secombe, then show them the layout of the place."

She paused, then added, "We—Ellen and I—will take charge of merging the extra staff from Bigfield House and the manor with the staff at the Hall. You may leave that to us. However"—Louisa fixed her limpid eyes on her husband and second cousins—"given your combined experience of card games, you can further assist by ensuring all our dealers—including those from the Hall staff who have previously acted in that capacity—are fully conversant with the games Rose intended offering and also understand the need to occasionally lose."

Ellen added, "It might be helpful to include Nigel and Tilly in your lessons. They need to behave as they have previously if our charade is going to pass muster, and they can explain how the dealers have acted before."

"Indeed." Louisa nodded decisively. "There must be no suspicious changes for any guest to notice."

"Except for the lack of counterfeit notes," Drake wearily said, "but given none of the idiots noticed before, that shouldn't be a problem."

"Not the most observant bunch," Toby remarked.

"You can't rely on all the guests being unobservant," Louisa countered, "given that, from our first party onward, we're expecting guests who haven't attended before, and very likely, they will be rather more experienced and, potentially, more alert."

Christopher grimaced. "Sadly, that's true."

Drake sighed feelingly. When the others looked at him, he said, "I've just realized there's something else we'll need to do tomorrow, well before any guests arrive."

"What?" Louisa demanded.

Drake smiled and reached across to take her hand. "Nothing for you to do—this will fall to me." He met Christopher's and Toby's eyes. "We're going to have to decide where everyone who can't be seen is going to hide."

On the way to Goffard Hall that morning, they'd discussed who would be where, but only in general terms. Someone had to remain beside Rose Kirkpatrick throughout, to ensure she stuck to their script, and Ellen was the obvious and, indeed, sole candidate for that role. As a local lady, it was believable that she had made friends with Rose—who was, in fact, not that many years older and also a close neighbor; that Rose might have taken Ellen under her social wing was a story easy to swallow. Robbie and Julia had been delegated to keep Tilly in line; they would put it about that Tilly had finally prevailed on Julia to attend and, given Robbie's squiring of Julia, in such company, him sticking by her side and ignoring the tables was entirely understandable.

Meanwhile, one of the younger Cynster cousins by the name of Carter had been summoned to assist with Nigel. At twenty-two years old, Carter was the youngest Cynster cousin, yet he was only just young enough to join the expected company; they all hoped he'd received the message and would arrive with the additional staff tomorrow.

That left Drake, Christopher, Toby, Kirkpatrick himself, and Louisa to take up positions in and around the house where they wouldn't be seen by any guests, yet would still be close enough to respond in an emergency.

"The mastermind is not going to show his face, at least not at the first two parties," Toby pointed out.

Drake nodded. After a moment, he said, "For the first two parties, there's no reason we can't all take refuge in Kirkpatrick's study—I presume it's close to the reception rooms?"

Christopher shook his head. "No, actually. It's at the far end of one wing."

"It's a large house," Ellen pointed out. "There's sure to be another room much closer to the ballroom and dining room that you'll be able to sit in."

Christopher declared, "We can look and decide tomorrow."

At that point, Pendleby entered to announce that dinner was served.

Distinctly wearily, they rose and repaired to the dining room.

By unspoken consensus, they put aside all discussion of the card parties and, instead, focused on more normal subjects. Among other things, Ellen learned that Carter Cynster was a budding artist, currently in training under the great Gerrard Debbington, who, it transpired, was Christopher's uncle and therefore connected in some degree to the entire Cynster clan.

Eventually, they retired to the drawing room. Gauging their weariness, Pendleby brought in the tea tray earlier than was his wont.

No one complained. Louisa—slumped in the corner of the sofa—waved Ellen toward the tray, which Pendleby had placed between them. "Please…"

Ellen duly poured and handed around the cups.

She didn't see the look Louisa leveled at Christopher over the rim of her teacup.

For his part, on meeting that pointed gaze, Christopher chose to merely arch his brows. Louisa was too sharp for anyone else's good. He thought it likely she already knew that he wasn't spending his nights in his bedroom, but saw no reason to confirm or deny something she would learn about soon enough.

Finally, with the tea consumed, they were free to rise and retire. He and Ellen parted from the others in the front hall and set off on their now-regular stroll through the night.

As they walked, they traded idle comments about the day—minor observations each thought the other might find amusing.

Ellen found the sweet moments and the mutual understanding thus revealed both eye-opening and reassuring. She hadn't thought of what married life might be like, not over recent years while she'd dealt with her mother's death and her uncle's unanticipated decline. Consequently, she'd never formulated any firm expectations of how she wished *her* married life to be, yet this closeness of minds and hearts as well as bodies spoke to her, snared her, and drew her inexorably deeper into its spell.

They reached Bigfield House and made their way to her room. There, even though this was only the fourth night he had come to her bed, the ease with which he and she came together resonated with rightness—a clear indication that them, together, was how they were meant to be.

Cloaked in soft moonlight, she stood before him; the light was strong enough to illuminate his eyes as she raised both hands and framed his face. He looked at her steadily, his gaze open and unshielded. She searched his eyes and saw commitment and devotion waiting. Recalling the tenor of that stolen kiss of the afternoon, she drew him to her, but rather than kiss him, she offered her lips in invitation.

An invitation he smoothly accepted. He supped at her lips, then deepened the kiss and waltzed them both into the now-familiar dance.

She gave, and he took, and then he returned the favor.

Together, they explored, now confident and assured, certain in the other's reaction, in the other's pleasure and joy.

Hands linked, fingers clutching, they fed the wave and felt it surge, and when it crested and broke, with their limbs tangled and their hearts thundering as one, the power behind it swept them from this world.

Tuesday, morning to afternoon, went in not quite chaos—neither Louisa nor Ellen would have allowed that—but in a harried rush while everyone involved in what they now termed their grand charade raced hither and yon, striving to ensure that all aspects of the upcoming card party hit every last right note.

Christopher, Toby, Robbie, and Drake spent the day working with the staff who had arrived from London, together with the Goffard Hall footmen who had previously assisted in the card salons and would do so again. The four gentlemen put the dealers through their paces, ensuring they understood that the aim was not to win but to ensure no one lost by any great amount. The more-experienced staff shook their heads at such a fanciful undertaking; they then had to be instructed in how to cheat convincingly to ensure the inevitable losses were evened out.

Eventually, Drake summoned Tilly to explain how she'd judged the play and decided when to fold winning hands. Christopher asked, and Tilly explained that, in general, Nigel had been excused from dealing; his role had been to play the part of young gentleman-host to the hilt, moving about the room and encouraging his friends to play.

"Clearly," Drake said, "we don't need Nigel's assistance at this point."

"That's just as well," Toby murmured, "given none of us trust him."

With a speaking look, Drake took their crew of designated dealers, sixteen in all to allow for substitutions and rotation, into the ballroom and, with Tilly assisting, continued their lessons there.

That left Christopher, Robbie, and Toby to school the bevy of footmen in their somewhat expanded duties. Not only would they be passing through the crowd ferrying drinks, they would also be watching, alert to any unexpected happening, and standing ready to assist those shadowing Rose, Nigel, and Tilly.

To everyone's intense relief, Carter Cynster arrived midmorning, having ridden down from town and been redirected from the manor to the Hall. Tall and lean like all the Cynster men, black-haired, with bright greeny-hazel eyes that seemed to perennially dance with a cheeky and adventurous light, quite aside from being the only Cynster who might fit in with the expected guests, he was the perfect man for their job.

Toby greeted Carter with a slap on the back. "Good to see you, Dabbler."

As a budding painter from an early age, "Dabbler" had been the family's nickname for Carter, at least among the male members, although never, ever, in Carter's mother's hearing.

Christopher smiled and offered his hand. "We're grateful you could make it."

"London is boring at this time of year. I was happy to take a break."
After shaking Christopher's hand, eager and curious, Carter looked around. "So what's going on?"

Leaving Robbie to organize which footmen would pay particular attention to each of the key players—Rose, Nigel, and Tilly—Toby and Christopher led Carter aside and rapidly explained the situation.

Carter's eyes widened. "Good Lord! Counterfeit banknotes!"

"Exactly." Toby tipped his head toward the archway leading into the ballroom. "You'd better go and report to Drake. I suspect he'll be the best person to introduce you to Nigel Fontenay."

"Fontenay?" Carter's brow furrowed. "I can't say I recognize the name."

"You wouldn't," Toby said. "He won't have moved in your circles."

Carter continued to frown. "Will any of the guests recognize me?" He arched his brows at Christopher and Toby. "Should I use a name other than Cynster?"

It was a good question, but they decided that, as most guests would be unlikely to recognize him and the few who would wouldn't know what to make of his appearance there, that sticking with his own name and playing the part of dissolute artist who happened to be visiting at the manor was the best way forward.

"However," Christopher said, "you won't be able to pretend to be Nigel's best friend and stick to his side—there'll be too many of his real acquaintances present for that to pass—but if the crowd is anything like we expect, you'll be able to move with him, always close enough to hear anything he says."

Carter nodded. "I'll go and speak with Drake."

Christopher and Toby returned to Robbie and the footmen, who had progressed to discussing the points around the room at which the footmen would be stationed.

There were so many little details to be discussed and decided, Christopher's head spun.

Elsewhere in the house, Ellen felt much the same. She seemed to turn from one issue to the next as she and Louisa strove to ensure that every aspect of the card parties, from the food provided for supper to the lighting in the drawing room, ballroom, dining room, and elsewhere in the house would be as it needed to be to support their goal of pulling the wool over those unknown eyes that would be watching, assessing the success of the events in placing the counterfeit notes into the pockets of the unsuspecting guests.

Finally, in midafternoon, quite suddenly, the questions ceased.

Louisa surveyed the staff congregating in the servants' hall, then turned to Ellen. "I believe our work here is done—at least for now."

Ellen nodded, and they made their way to the front hall, where they found the others looking weary but satisfied. Drake was the last to arrive and brought a tall young gentleman with him.

"Carter! You came." Louisa hugged the young man, then introduced him to Ellen. "So"—Louisa glanced at Drake—"Carter will be keeping Nigel up to our mark."

Drake smiled, not humorously. "I've just introduced Nigel to Carter and explained that Nigel shouldn't think he won't be under constant supervision just because Carter won't be at his elbow every second of the evening."

Carter grinned, but his gaze was hard-edged. "I think he believed you."

Drake threw Carter a resigned look, then glanced at the others. "Any outstanding problems?"

For a wonder, there were none.

Over the past hour, Ellen had been conscious of a sort of brittle tension rising inside her and, she suspected, not just in her but in all those at the Hall. As she looped her arm with Christopher's, and with the others, they made for the stable and the horses and carriage waiting there, she realized the emotion squeezing her lungs was excited anticipation.

A waiting-to-see heightened expectation combined with a would-they-pull-off-their-charade excitement; she glanced around and was prepared to wager that feeling had infected them all.

CHAPTER 17

*T*he first card party commenced with every member of their company on very sharp tenterhooks.

Ellen arrived in the manor's carriage an hour before the first guests were expected, accompanied by Rose and escorted by Christopher and Carter. Louisa, Drake, and Toby followed in Louisa's carriage.

They drove around to the stable yard and entered via the side door, screened by trees and shrubs from anyone keeping watch on the front of the house. Julia, all but jigging with nerves, was waiting to greet them, along with Robbie, who had ridden across the fields from Bigfield House. Ellen sent Julia to check on Tilly, then accompanied Rose upstairs to her room and went inside with her while she changed.

Christopher stood guard in the corridor outside Rose's door, while Carter strode off to supervise Nigel's preparations.

For the occasion, Ellen had donned one of her London evening gowns; of fuchsia silk, the gown consisted of multiple rows of magenta-lace-trimmed frills, along with Emma's favorite ribbon rosettes, but was devoid of additional ribbons and bows. Regardless, their first sight of the gown caused Louisa to blink, and Rose to raise her brows in fatalistic resignation.

As Ellen was slated to play the part of Rose's newly acquired bosom-bow, fixed at Rose's elbow throughout the evening, Rose's reaction was, perhaps, understandable.

Now, after slanting a considering glance at Ellen's gown, Rose directed her waiting dresser to pull out from her wardrobe an expensive creation in satin of a blue that, at least, wouldn't clash with the fuchsia.

Despite that apparent accommodation, Ellen remained on high alert as, side by side and with Christopher trailing close behind, she and Rose walked toward the stairs to the front hall. The clocks in the house had just chimed for eight o'clock; they could expect guests to commence rolling up at any moment.

At the head of the stairs, Christopher touched his hand to the back of Ellen's waist, bent his head, and murmured, "Good luck."

She raised her head and watched him stride quickly down the corridor, making for the small alcove that lay behind the musicians' gallery above the far end of the ballroom. Mr. Kirkpatrick had suggested it as the perfect place for him, Louisa, Drake, Toby, and Christopher to wait out the evening. If they were careful, they could keep an eye on activity in more than half the ballroom and, to either side, in sections of the drawing room and dining room without anyone knowing they were there.

"Come on." Rose started down the stairs. "I need to be in position before anyone arrives."

They reached the open front door, guarded by Secombe at his most formal, just as the first carriage disgorged six laughing young men.

After that, guests arrived in a steady stream. Ellen lost count after sixty-three. Early on, she'd peeked into the drawing room and had confirmed that Tilly, with Julia and Robbie at her elbow, was acting her part, welcoming the young gentlemen with apparent pleasure and steering them toward the tables where the dealers stood waiting. Nigel—with Carter idling a yard away—had come forward to greet his friends; if Nigel's welcome lacked his usual sparkle, none of his friends, all openly delighted at the prospect of an evening's play, seemed to notice.

For her part, Ellen strove to maintain the appearance of a young lady anticipating an evening of unalloyed entertainment. She smiled on the silly young men to whom Rose introduced her, then was somewhat disconcerted when—presumably falling victim to her doll-like façade— several attempted to shamelessly flirt with her.

Being repressively severe in depressing their pretensions would not have fitted with the image she needed to project. And indeed, viewed against Christopher or even Toby, their behavior was more in the nature of errant puppies; rather than harshly putting them in their place, she brushed aside their protestations with a laugh and otherwise ignored them.

Once they quit the front hall, she moved with Rose as, incessantly smiling, the older woman wove through her guests, laughing a touch brittlely perhaps, yet constantly encouraging the young men to chance their hand and play.

Wine, which, in the interests of all concerned, would later in the evening be watered down, presently flowed freely, and minute by minute, the noise created by so many young men talking and exclaiming all at once escalated, building toward outright cacophony.

Ellen was tempted to look everywhere at once, to check that their preparations were holding up, but she had to keep her wits fully focused on Rose, monitoring each and every interaction.

This, after all, was merely the first trial of their charade—the first of the three challenges they faced. While everyone was on edge over maintaining their façade and keeping their acting skills up to the mark, thus far, all appeared to be advancing smoothly on all fronts.

The dealers, bolstered by the more experienced men from London, were interacting appropriately with the guests. The footmen tacked through the throng, offering various beverages. Perforce, there was not a maid in sight; that would have invited trouble. The only females in the room were Ellen, Rose, Tilly, and Julia, yet somewhat to Ellen's surprise —and she suspected the relief of those watching from above—the considerable crowd remained fully focused on the action at the tables, calling to each other, crowing over wins, and constantly egging each other on.

As she glided through the crowd by Rose's side, Ellen saw Julia and Robbie holding close to Tilly, overseeing her exchanges with the guests. In Ellen's estimation, if they were to have trouble with one of the Fontenays, it wouldn't be with Tilly; even more than Rose, Tilly seemed to have accepted on which side her bread was buttered and was being careful to play her part and not deviate by even a whisker from her assigned role.

Nigel, Ellen was nowhere near as sure of, yet every time she glimpsed him, he was playing his prescribed part of rowdy young gentleman-host to the hilt, with a glass in his hand and his eyes glittering rather feverishly in the gaslight. Carter was never more than a yard away, and Ellen suspected two other young men, neither of whom she recognized, were likewise unobtrusively dogging Nigel's steps.

Supper came and went; overseen by Secombe and his staff, the sudden rush of activity in the dining room passed off without incident, but the food proved merely a momentary diversion. Soon all the young men were back in the card salons, crowding about their favored tables.

The noise—and the tension of being so much on guard—started a faint headache throbbing behind Ellen's eyes. She ignored it and forged on.

Yet despite them all being so on edge, the evening rolled on without a hitch.

Finally, the crowd in the drawing room started to thin, with bosky young men staggering out to the tables set up at the rear of the front hall. On entering the house, they'd eagerly lined up at the same tables to buy gambling tokens and now sought to exchange the tokens they still held for cash.

Several footmen stood about the long, narrow tables, ensuring that the interactions proceeded without disruption or altercation. Unsurprisingly perhaps, the transactions were overseen by Rose in her capacity as hostess; Ellen stood beside her, behind the chairs on which two senior footmen sat, receiving the tokens and carefully counting out banknotes in exchange.

The departure of the guests continued in reasonably orderly fashion. Eventually, Secombe and some of the footmen helped the last stragglers to cash their tokens, then steered them out of the house and assisted them into their carriages.

When the last carriage rattled away, Ellen couldn't stop herself from regarding Rose with faint amazement; to the letter, the woman had stuck to the script Drake had dictated. In truth, Ellen hadn't expected such ready compliance.

Rose caught Ellen's look and interpreted it correctly. She raised a shoulder. "I'm not such a fool that I haven't realized Winchelsea is not a man to cross."

There was that, admittedly, yet as she trailed up the stairs in Rose's wake to watch over her while she changed back into her carriage dress, Ellen couldn't shake the feeling that, when it came to Rose, she needed to remain vigilant.

In the upstairs corridor, Christopher came striding up to join her. "Everything go all right?"

"Yes." She directed a look at Rose's back as she continued walking ahead of them. "Surprisingly, without any problem."

Rose paused outside her door, cast them a distinctly superior look, then opened the door and went in. Ellen exchanged a long-suffering look with Christopher and followed.

When, minutes later, the three of them rejoined the others in the front hall, the relief engulfing the company—excepting only Rose and presumably Nigel and Tilly, the latter two of whom had already been escorted back to their rooms—was profound.

Louisa raised her voice and thanked all the staff and the dealers, who were being put up at the Hall.

"We've met our first challenge," Drake added. "Now, we need to forge on."

Rose was duly loaded into a carriage and, along with two burly footmen from the manor, driven away to be returned to her "cell." After chatting with Mr. Kirkpatrick and Julia and consulting with Secombe as to whether any aspect might be improved for the second of the card parties, Drake, Louisa, Toby, and Carter climbed into Louisa's carriage and set off for their beds.

Robbie took his leave of Mr. Kirkpatrick and Julia, mounted his roan, and after Ellen assured him she would be perfectly safe walking through the orchards, pointing out that Christopher had remained to escort her home, Robbie met Christopher's gaze, then dipped his head and turned his horse for Bigfield House.

It was long after one o'clock, yet the moon still sailed the sky, providing sufficient illumination to light their way. After farewelling Mr. Kirkpatrick and Julia, Christopher and Ellen set out along the path that led to the rear of the Goffard Hall gardens, then wended through the Bigfield House orchards, all the way to the rear of the house.

Once they were out of sight of the Hall, Christopher caught Ellen's hand. The quiet of the countryside wrapped about them as they walked on.

Eventually, he said, "I really don't like the fact that it has to be you who sticks to Rose's side. I don't trust her."

"No more do I." Ellen glanced at his face and noted that his jaw was clenched. "But you were in the musicians' gallery—you must have been able to see us for much of the time."

"Believe me, that didn't make things any easier."

The tone in which the words were growled made her think back over all that had occurred...

She smiled, then chuckled and airily asked, "Did you see those silly young men falling over their feet, trying to fix my attention?"

From the corner of her eye, she noted the sharp glance he shot her; pretending she hadn't, she smiled widely. "One of them compared my ribbon rosettes"—she gestured to her bodice—"to roses and the lace to the tracery of butterflies' wings."

"Good God." He sounded appalled.

"Oh, that wasn't the most outrageous compliment—not by any means. I particularly liked the remark about my eyes being green topazes, which I'm not sure exist, and then there was the argument over whether the exact shade of my hair was guinea gold or ripening wheat."

He snorted, and she continued, relating some of the more fanciful flights of adoration her would-be admirers had indulged in; while he'd been able to see the young men fawning over her, he hadn't been able to hear what was said. By the time they reached the Bigfield House shrubbery, he'd relaxed and was smiling and chuckling, too.

They went inside and up the stairs to her room. Once the door was shut, she turned in to his arms, raised her face for his kiss, and proceeded to remind and reassure him in the most effective way she knew that she was his, and he was hers, not just for that night but forevermore.

On Thursday evening, the second card party commenced with a considerably greater degree of assurance on the part of all those tasked with ensuring that Drake's plan succeeded.

Once again, Ellen accompanied Rose to her room, where her dresser, Archer, assisted her erstwhile mistress to change into a suitable evening gown—this one in striking emerald-green silk—and to put up her hair and don her jewels so that she could fulfill her prescribed role of hostess.

Ellen sat in an armchair and watched the transformation.

The previous day—during which they were supposed to catch their breath—had, indeed, been spent in that vein. Christopher had ridden over from the manor in the late morning, just in time to give Robbie the benefit of his advice regarding how best to organize the workers to bring in the hops, which were ripening nicely on the vine.

He'd commended Robbie for making plans ahead of time, which had made her brother stand taller and left her even more grateful for Christopher's arrival. He'd stayed for much of the day, spending hours chatting with her uncle, even though it hadn't been a particularly good day in terms of her uncle's understanding.

Later, Christopher had ridden home to dine, and later still, he'd returned on foot via the shrubbery. She had been waiting by the long pool to walk with him to her room; what had followed had, at least to her mind but she hoped to his as well, set the seal on their relaxing day.

Midmorning today had seen them all back at the Hall to check over the preparations and ensure that all was well. As satisfied as they could be, they'd retreated to the manor to wait until it was time to dress and return to face the challenge of the second of the card parties.

Ellen kept a watchful eye on the interaction between Rose and Archer. She'd remembered Julia mentioning that Archer wasn't a local but had come with Rose to Goffard Hall; as with most dressers, Archer's loyalties very likely still lay with her mistress. But beyond the usual exchanges over which gown to wear and the style of Rose's hair—and a whispered discussion that Ellen hadn't quite caught, conducted over the contents of Rose's jewel box—the pair hadn't attempted any more-secretive or suspicious communication.

That said, from the narrow-eyed looks Archer threw her way, Ellen suspected that, if given the chance, Archer would do all she could to aid her mistress to escape her self-made snare.

She and Rose descended the stairs in good time to greet the first of the guests. The first party had seen a total of ninety-three attendees; that number was soon surpassed as more carriages drew up in the forecourt and disgorged more and more eager-eyed young gentlemen.

Rose and Nigel's boast that they had whipped up interest in the three successive card parties hadn't been an idle one.

Although rather more confident in her role the second time around, Ellen remained alert and watchful, by her very close presence reminding Rose that she wasn't in any way free to divulge her true situation to anyone.

Yet once again, Rose toed their line—more correctly Drake's line—without any backsliding. Although she kept her guard high, Ellen seized appropriate moments to gauge the reactions of the young gentlemen surrounding them; in none did she detect even the slightest sign that they sensed anything amiss.

And why would they? The façade of their grand charade was holding firm. No one and nothing had caused any cracks in the image they'd sought to project—that all was proceeding with the three card parties exactly as anyone might expect.

She'd just reached that comforting conclusion when she saw Carter, with his arm slung around Nigel's shoulders, leading Nigel from the room, flanked by the two young mystery gentlemen she'd spotted on Tuesday night; the sighting of the pair, once again in such close attendance on Nigel and Carter, strongly suggested—to Ellen at least—that they were Drake's men.

Thereafter, she divided her time between monitoring Rose's conversations and keeping an eye on the door to the front hall, through which Carter had steered Nigel.

A bare ten minutes later, Nigel returned to the party, with Carter following and the other two men slipping in behind. If any of the guests noticed that Nigel looked distinctly pasty, they would doubtless assume he'd overimbibed and suffered the usual fate, but Ellen suspected the effect was more likely to have been due to Drake.

Regardless, Nigel returned to his role with renewed vigor, laughing and whipping up his acquaintances, encouraging them to indulge in ever more outlandish wagers.

Ellen viewed Nigel's performance and the result with jaundiced eyes, yet for all those who had traveled to the Hall that night, the rising tenor of the evening appeared to be precisely what they'd hoped to find. One and all, they flung themselves into heated wagering on the turn of every card.

As a group, they truly were the gullible marks Toby had labeled them.

Tonight, the party showed no signs of running down of its own accord. It took Rose clapping her hands and announcing that, reluctantly, she would be calling an end in just ten minutes to remind the guests, flown with drink and the excitement of wagering, that their beds lay some distance away and they had yet to convert their tokens to cash.

Grudgingly, some ambled out into the front hall to do so, then the two mystery gentlemen who had been flanking Nigel left him to Carter and circled the tables, clearly passing on a message to the dealers, and subsequently, one by one, the dealers gathered up the cards and declared their tables closed for the night.

With some grumbling, the remaining guests headed for the front hall.

Stationed once more behind the tables at which the exchange of tokens was taking place and still very much playing her role to the hilt, Rose seized the opportunity to remind those leaving that the last card party on Saturday evening looked set to be a dazzling and very well-attended affair.

Several of those about to go staggering down the front steps perked up at that, and more than one swore he'd be there.

When, finally, the last of the guests had rattled down the drive, the company sagged. One and all, they appeared more wrung out than they had after the first party.

During a quick consultation with the staff, Secombe pointed out that there had been one hundred and twenty-seven guests present, and if more arrived for the final party, as now seemed certain, they would need more card tables if the guests were to be prevented from coming to blows.

Carter, Robbie, and the two neatly dressed men who had assisted Carter with Nigel agreed.

Carter regarded Rose, waiting to be escorted back to the manor. "From what I saw, the guests' desire to wager has been fanned to heights bordering on mania."

Drake's men caught his eye and nodded soberly.

For her part, Rose smirked. She might be a captive performing under duress, yet the evening and the young gentlemen's attitudes testified to her expertise in creating what would have been a devastatingly efficient means of distributing the counterfeit notes.

From the looks on many faces, few present were likely to forget that.

Finally, the gathering broke up, much as it had after the previous party.

Ellen and Christopher set off across the fields. Tonight, scudding clouds intermittently obscured the moon, yet they knew the way, and there was no denying that walking through the gardens and beneath the orchards' trees gave them time to slough off the tensions of the evening.

As they climbed the stile in the fence that marked the boundary between the Hall and Bigfield House, Christopher glimpsed the faintly troubled expression on Ellen's face.

Once they were walking hand in hand beneath the plum trees, he asked, "What's bothering you?"

When she looked up, surprised, he let his lips quirk upward and squeezed her hand. "Yes, I can tell. So what is it?"

She didn't immediately reply, but after they'd walked several more paces, she sighed, then said, "Despite Nigel's temporary lapse, which, due to our planning, was expeditiously dealt with, tonight, we succeeded in maintaining the fiction that Rose's card parties are proceeding as planned —and indeed, are building to a roaringly successful culmination."

His gaze on her face, Christopher nodded and mildly observed, "That was the plan."

"I know." After several seconds during which she plainly struggled over how to communicate what she felt, she went on, "I just feel...as if we're tempting Fate. Almost *baiting* Fate. We've got away with our grand charade for two nights, and now we're going to push for a third."

He raised his gaze and looked ahead. After a moment, he admitted, "Now you mention it...I can see, feel, what you mean."

"And that's just the last card party. How long afterward will it be before the mastermind contacts Rose? We'll have to keep the charade in place—make it appear all is normal at Goffard Hall and possibly even that Rose is still its mistress—until he makes his move."

Christopher grimaced. "True, but Drake believes he—the mastermind —won't wait too long. We discussed the point tonight, up in the musicians' gallery—as you might expect, that question is exercising Kirkpatrick as well. As Drake pointed out, the amazing success Rose has wrought—and the way the parties are escalating, increasing in size and fervor—makes it appear likely that, if the counterfeit notes were being substituted as before, even given the much larger amount, the exchange of fake notes for real would be quite easily accomplished by the end of the third party. Drake thinks the mastermind will contact Rose during the next day or, at the latest, the day following that."

He caught Ellen's gaze and smiled cynically. "Drake thinks the mastermind is unlikely to leave Rose contemplating all that money for longer than absolutely necessary."

Ellen humphed. "Given the mastermind's cautious nature, I can see that prediction makes eminent sense."

A few paces later, she glanced at him. "Anyway, what happened with Nigel? All I saw was Carter steering him out of the room, with those two other young men, who I assume are Drake's agents, helping."

"Yes, those two are Drake's men—he managed to pull them in at the last minute. They're skilled at what they do, which is something of a relief. Now Nigel knows they're there, he'll be more circumspect."

"But why did Carter pull Nigel out?"

"Nigel had started to grow maudlin and referred, albeit obliquely, to his changed circumstances."

"I see." Ellen's tone hardened. "What happened?"

"Drake happened. Which is enough to shock any young gentleman out of the deepest depths of drunken stupor straight into coherent sobriety." He shrugged. "That's more or less what happened to Nigel. I doubt he'll deviate from the plan again—he might even slow his drinking, at least for the final party."

"Rose made a point of chatting to those young men in front of whom Nigel had been indiscreet," Ellen said. "They were well away themselves and hadn't seemed to have read anything into Nigel's comments." She tipped her head. "In fact, it seemed doubtful they'd even remembered them."

They were almost at Bigfield House; as they turned out of the shrubbery and headed for the side door, Christopher said, "That is arguably the biggest factor in our favor—namely, that the guests are all young men of self-centered disposition. At that age, in such a setting, their minds focus on having a good time to the exclusion of all else."

Ellen laughed cynically. "I've seen enough to know that's all too true." She halted before the side door and met Christopher's eyes. "As those attending our last party will be of exactly the same type, I have to concede that there's a definite possibility that, baiting Fate or not, Drake's plan will continue to remain more or less on track."

Christopher tipped his head in gentle acknowledgment, opened the door and held it for her, then followed her inside.

The final card party commenced in much the same manner as the previous two. Ellen arrived at Goffard Hall decked out in a gown of pale-green satin sporting ribbons and bows in a darker shade of green, with a dark-green paisley silk shawl draped over her largely bare shoulders. The inevitable green ribbons cascaded from the knot securing her upswept hair. Joining her in the stable yard, Rose looked at the gown and shook her head. But she said nothing as she walked, escorted by two manor footmen, to the house. Ellen and Christopher, who had accompanied her from Bigfield House, followed.

Once again, Ellen trailed up the stairs to sit in the armchair in Rose's room while Archer assisted Rose to don her finery.

That evening, Rose chose a dramatic gown composed of swaths of black and white silks. With her dark hair and pale skin—and the long length of pearls waiting to be draped about her neck—Ellen had to admit the hostess of the evening would stand out among the horde they now expected to attend.

Three more card tables had been fetched from Bigfield House. Luckily, the London footmen had brought enough packs of cards to supply the extra tables as well as the original ten.

Archer was fussing with Rose's dark curls when a tap fell on the door. Ellen turned her head to see Julia peeking in. Julia's gaze went to her stepmother, then she beckoned Ellen.

Ellen rose. After a glance at her charge—who appeared fully absorbed in subtly applying cosmetics to her cheeks—she walked to where Julia hovered in the doorway. "What is it?"

With her gaze tracking Ellen in the mirror, her hands busy with a comb, Archer whispered, "I did as you said, ma'am. When I fetched your pearls from the master, I made sure I took a good look into the place he keeps them, and there is a package there, just like you thought."

Via the mirror, Rose met Archer's eyes and smiled. "Thank you, my dear. I knew I could rely on you."

The stiffly prim Archer softened. "Always, my lady."

Rose's gaze shifted to Ellen at the door. "Hush, now—and not a word to anyone."

"Of course not, my lady."

Across the room, her expression exasperated, Julia met Ellen's eyes. "Nigel just boasted to Carter that the number of guests attending tonight will likely be more than half again the number we had on Thursday evening. Apparently, there was a boxing match held this afternoon some-where south of Tenterden, and many of those from London who attended will have heard of the Goffard Hall card parties and are likely to head our way, following others who've been here before."

Ellen sighed. "Well, it appears this event will be a horrible crush—every hostess's dream." She cast a jaundiced glance at Rose, still seated at her dressing table with Archer fastening the pearl necklace, looped several times about Rose's throat, at her nape.

On turning back to Julia and noting the way the younger woman was gripping her fingers, Ellen said, "Never fear—we and the household will manage."

She looked past Julia to Christopher, lounging against the corridor wall, and smiled. "And look on the bright side. After such an event—one that will generate a good deal of talk among the young gentlemen of the ton—the mastermind will surely assume that Rose will have successfully exchanged the entire shipment of counterfeit notes and come calling sooner rather than later."

Christopher inclined his head. "Good point."

Julia didn't look convinced.

Remembering the younger woman's preference for quiet, Ellen closed her hand over Julia's twining fingers and gently squeezed. "If the crowd becomes too much to cope with, you can always retire."

Julia met Ellen's eyes. "I know." Then her chin firmed. "But with Robbie by my side, I've been managing." She raised her head. "We'll see."

"Good." Smiling reassuringly, Ellen patted Julia's hands.

Christopher glanced past Ellen. "Is Rose ready? It's time we went downstairs."

Ellen looked across the room and saw Rose rising from the dressing stool. "The answer appears to be yes."

Resplendent in her black and white, Rose walked toward them. As she neared, she arched a brow at Ellen. "Ready for the final act, Miss Martingale?"

Ellen stepped back and waved Rose ahead of her. "We're all more than ready, Rose."

As she followed her charge out of the room, Ellen caught Christopher's eye and rolled her own. She couldn't wait for the evening—now certain to be a horrendous crush—to be over.

An hour later, Ellen could confirm that Nigel's prediction had been accurate. She'd heard more than enough about the boxing match and its outcome, and there were far too many bodies for anyone's comfort now crammed into the rooms.

Not that jostling bodies and a lack of openings at the tables seemed to deter young gentlemen intent on gambling. Over the past three parties, she'd noted an increasing tendency for those gathered about the various tables to wager on the turn of a card or on the chances of a certain card appearing. Tonight, the only game being dealt was vingt-un, which gave plenty of scope for the onlookers to wager between themselves.

The footmen were having to fight their way through the throng, with eager hands reaching from all around to relieve them of the glasses of wine they were endeavoring to balance on their trays.

Behind her easy smile and pleasant expression, Ellen herself was distinctly hot and bothered. Courtesy of the crush, she had to exert significant physical effort to maintain her position by Rose's side.

And of course, because of that very crush, it was even more critical that she do so; she hadn't lost her suspicions of Rose, and regardless of the woman's unexceptionable behavior during the past two parties, Ellen didn't trust Rose not to speak to someone or pass on a message or do something that would scupper Drake's plan.

With her teeth gritted behind her increasingly strained smile, with dogged determination, she clung to Rose's company; at one point, she looped her arm in Rose's and literally clung.

This night cannot end soon enough.

Sadly, with the evening's festivities being a grand finale of sorts, they'd decided to let the tables run until at least two o'clock.

Through the crowd, Ellen caught occasional glimpses of the others—of Carter with Nigel, who was already well away to the point of almost staggering. Carter looked exasperated, as did Drake's men, but between the three of them, Ellen didn't doubt they would keep Nigel under control.

When she spied Robbie, he was very nearly grim faced as he sought to protect Julia from the worst of the crush while they stuck close to Tilly; indeed, even Tilly looked ready to claim Robbie's protection from the surging hordes.

Ellen regretted not being able to have Christopher beside her; he would have ensured she wasn't jostled and bumped. As it was, she had to rely on her fan and her elbows to redirect some of those less steady on their feet.

The evening wore on, and the atmosphere in the rooms thickened to that of a hothouse. Even Rose was affected; she drew to one side of the ballroom, where an open window let in some air, and while apparently scanning her guests, vigorously plied her fan.

Ellen halted beside her and did the same.

To Ellen's relief, no young men gathered about them; by now, all were intent on the action at and around the tables.

She seized the moment to ponder the "what comes next?" that Drake and their select company had, thus far, left largely unresolved. Once this party ended, they were going to have to wait for an unknown period of time for the mastermind to make his move. While they might hope he would contact Rose the next day, they couldn't count on it being that soon. They'd tossed around the prospect of Ellen, Drake, and Louisa joining the Hall household, and that Rose herself might need to be returned there, albeit kept locked away. They hadn't made any decisions and had left the matter to be dealt with tomorrow, once they'd weathered this event.

Rose snapped her fan shut, then with a resigned glance at Ellen, plastered on her hostess's smile and forged back into the shifting mass of bodies.

Ellen stepped out in Rose's wake.

They'd managed only three steps before a surging group of rowdy young men stumbled into them, knocking them almost off their feet.

The young men immediately leapt to save them; sobered somewhat by their own clumsiness, they steadied Rose and Ellen and even attempted to straighten their crushed skirts. Order of a sort restored, Rose and Ellen did their best to smilingly reassure the swaying men that all was well.

Finally, the group moved on, allowing Ellen and Rose to do the same.

Rose changed direction, heading toward the door to the front hall.

Following close behind, Ellen didn't see the crumpled paper Rose tucked into her bodice, and neither did those covertly watching from the musician's gallery above the far end of the ballroom.

One o'clock had come and gone, and to Ellen's eyes, the bulk of the guests were, finally, starting to flag.

She certainly was. She fetched up beside Rose, who had halted just inside the doorway.

Instead of turning to face her guests, Rose dipped her head closer to Ellen's and whispered, "I desperately need the withdrawing room."

Ellen blinked. She'd been aware that Rose had drunk rather more than she had. "Where is it?" She knew of the room to which the men were being directed, but presumed Rose was speaking of a room set aside for ladies. As the only ladies present were herself, Rose, Tilly, and Julia, three of whom lived in the house, Ellen was fairly sure they hadn't bothered to create a proper ladies' withdrawing room.

In obvious discomfort, Rose muttered, "I need to go up to my room."

Ellen sighed and nodded. "All right. Let's go." She wasn't about to allow Rose to wander the house alone. Ellen looked up at the musician's gallery, then followed Rose into the front hall.

The hall wasn't completely deserted. Two footmen stood by the front door, and at the rear, the senior footmen manning the tables for the exchange of tokens were quietly talking among themselves. But other than that, all the guests remained crammed into the drawing room, ballroom, and dining room; for what seemed the first time in untold hours, Ellen felt able to breathe.

She and Rose climbed the stairs. As they reached the top and stepped into the gallery, the sound of rapidly nearing footsteps had them both pausing.

Christopher appeared from the shadows of the corridor. His eyes went to Rose. "What's amiss?"

"Nothing." Ellen waved at Rose. "Rose just needs to answer nature's call."

"Ah." Christopher deflated. Halting, he studied Rose, then looked at Ellen. "I'll come and stand guard, regardless."

She smiled and tipped her head in acquiescence.

Rose made a growly sound, swung around, and head high, continued along the gallery and down the corridor to her room.

Christopher paced beside Ellen. His gaze on Rose, walking several feet ahead, he lowered his voice and said, "Drake's men on the floor—the two helping Carter—have reported there are several not-quite-so-young gentlemen they wouldn't have expected to see scattered through the crowd."

"Oh?" Ellen shot him an inquiring look. "What does Drake make of that?"

"He's not sure, but he's wondering if one or more of those not-so-young men are pawns of the mastermind, sent here to assess how well the card parties have gone."

"We did think that might happen," she reminded him. "That the mastermind would send spies. Given what any spies will report, surely that makes it more likely that the mastermind will conclude that all has gone swimmingly and will promptly contact Rose to get his money."

Christopher tipped his head. "We can hope."

They'd reached Rose's room, which lay at the end of one wing. She opened the door and swept in. With a glance at Christopher, Ellen followed and shut the door behind her.

Rose made a beeline for the large screen set up across one corner of the room.

Ellen strolled to the window and looked out at the gardens. From behind the screen came the rustling of fabric, then the tinkling sound of liquid striking porcelain.

Ellen focused on the view. Although there was no farmland attached to Goffard Hall, the gardens were extensive; she could see the waters of an ornamental lake glimmering between the canopies of the old trees that grew around the house. Her attention caught by a glimpse of white on the far side of the lake, she squinted and could just make out an archway amid the dark shapes of bushes and trees. *No doubt a folly of some sort.*

The susurration of silks followed by footsteps had Ellen turning to face the room.

Rose emerged from behind the screen. Her expression suggested severe distraction.

Given how self-confidently unruffled Rose had been to that point, Ellen found the change striking. "Are you all right?"

Rose had been staring, apparently unseeing, toward the door. She brought her gaze to Ellen's face. "What?" Then she frowned, shook her head as if to clear it, drew breath, and straightened. "Yes. Quite all right." She started for the door. "We'd better return downstairs."

Inwardly shrugging, Ellen followed.

Christopher pushed away from the wall and fell in beside her, and together, they paced behind Rose.

When they reached the head of the stairs, Christopher closed a hand about one of Ellen's and gently squeezed. "Another hour, and this will be over."

He released her and, with a quick nod, walked on, heading back to the musician's gallery, leaving Ellen to descend the stairs beside Rose.

The foot of the stairs fell approximately midway down the large front hall. The door to the drawing room lay ahead on Ellen's right, while the door to the ballroom, also on the right, lay closer to hand, with the dining room door beyond that and the tables for the exchange of tokens tucked away at the rear of the hall on that side.

Ellen stepped off the stairs onto the hall tiles.

"Oh!"

Sharp, pattering sounds had her whirling.

Rose had halted on the last step, her face a picture of horror as pearls slipped between her fingers to rain on the tiles. "My necklace broke!"

Desperately, Rose gathered the remnants of the long strands into her hands, then swooped to pick up fallen pearls. "Help me!"

Ellen already was. Crouching, she collected the small white beads rolling on the tiles.

"Ma'am?"

She turned her head and saw the footmen at the door, clearly wondering if they should leave their posts to assist. She waved at them to stay where they were. "It's all right—we'll deal with this."

It didn't take that long. Once they'd retrieved all the pearls they could find, Ellen added those she'd gathered to the pile in Rose's cupped hands, then met Rose's gaze. "Now what?"

Rose thought, then tipped her head down a corridor leading deeper into the house. "These are quite valuable—Kirkpatrick keeps the string in the safe in his study. We should leave them on his desk."

That seemed sensible. Ellen waved Rose on and followed her down the corridor. Kirkpatrick had been nothing but helpful and didn't deserve to lose what might be part of his family's jewels.

Rose led her to the far end of the corridor. Ellen recalled Christopher mentioning that Kirkpatrick's study was on the opposite side of the house to the reception rooms. When Rose stopped outside the door to the room at the corridor's end, Ellen obligingly opened the door, went inside, held the door for Rose, then closed it after Rose had entered.

As she'd intimated, Rose made straight for Kirkpatrick's heavy desk, which sat in front of a wall on which hung a full-length portrait of a lady —a lady who wasn't Rose. Ellen assumed the woman in the painting was Julia's mother, Kirkpatrick's beloved first wife.

Rose rounded the desk, and Ellen followed.

She watched as Rose carefully transferred the mound of pearls from her hands onto Kirkpatrick's blotter.

Several pearls rolled free and fell to the floor.

"Damn!" With her fingers spread to hold the bulk of the pearls in place, Rose looked down at those that had fallen.

Ellen stepped closer and bent to pick them up.

Rose shifted.

More pearls cascaded to the floor.

"What are you doing?" Before Ellen could straighten, a hard, heavy weight slammed down on her bent head.

She collapsed, and the world went black.

CHAPTER 18

$\mathcal{E}$llen had no idea how many minutes had elapsed before her wits returned and she managed to open her eyes.

She swallowed a groan, half rolled onto her side, and squinted upward —in time to see Rose lift the package of counterfeit notes from a now-open safe. Hugging the package to her chest, Rose shut the safe door and swung the picture of the lady back into position across it.

Ellen slumped and closed her eyes as Rose turned. She felt Rose's gaze as she studied her, then Rose muttered, "You shouldn't have got in my way."

With that, Rose walked out from behind the desk.

It took a moment for Ellen to register that Rose wasn't making for the door to the corridor but for the windows, beyond which lay the gardens.

She's getting away with the counterfeit notes.

Ellen heard Rose unlock the French door, open it, and step onto the terrace beyond.

Desperate, Ellen struggled to sit up. When she managed that, she tried to haul in a breath to scream, but her lungs felt as if a vise had locked about them; all she could manage was a hoarse call that lacked all power.

I can't let her escape.

Clenching her jaw against the pain in her head, she used the desk to haul herself upright. Clutching the desktop, she swayed and looked out of the window.

Rose was hurrying across the lawn toward the borders, thickly planted with established shrubs, which circled the bases of the huge old trees.

Ellen tried to think, but couldn't; just the attempt left her nauseated. She gritted her teeth, forced her feet to move, and staggered toward the still-open French door.

I have to follow. If somehow or other she's arranged to meet the mastermind, all I need is to see his face.

Rose vanished into the shadows beneath the trees.

Ellen lurched in pursuit. The cool and blessedly fresh night air bathed her face, and she discovered she could partially fill her lungs. By the time she was halfway across the lawn, the pain in her head was receding, and she was breathing more freely.

She was almost running when she reached the shadows beneath the trees. She paused. Searching the dimness ahead, she heard Rose's footsteps and glimpsed a flicker of white—Rose's gown. Rose was heading down a path Ellen thought would eventually take her to the lake.

Ellen considered screaming for help, but Drake's cordon of watchers was stationed around the perimeter of the property, too far away to hear. As far as she knew, no one was patrolling the gardens, and the reception rooms were on the other side of the house; no one there would hear her.

Besides, if I scream, I might scare away the mastermind, and we'll lose our only chance to identify him.

After all their hard work, that didn't bear thinking about.

She hauled in a deeper breath and set off along the path beneath the trees.

She was running through the heavy shadows cast by the towering beeches when a man crashed through the bushes on her right.

She almost shrieked, but he caught her by the arms, and recognition flooded her. "Christopher!" She almost swooned with relief. "Thank God!"

"What's happened?" His face a stony mask, his gaze raked over her.

"Rose knocked me unconscious and took the package of counterfeit notes." Ellen looked down the path. "She went that way."

Silently, another large shadow loomed out of the darkness and resolved into Drake. Apparently, he'd heard what she'd said. "How?"

"I'll tell you later, but right now, we have to catch up with her." Ellen pointed insistently down the path.

"Yes, we do." Drake set off along the path. "She's either escaping or going to meet the mastermind. I don't know how the bastard managed to contact her, but I'd wager he has."

Christopher released Ellen. "Wait here." He headed after Drake.

Ellen snorted. "Not likely." She picked up her skirts and hurried after him. Returning to the house to summon others wouldn't help. If they were going to interrupt a meeting between Rose and the mastermind, stealth had to be their watchword.

Three could be stealthy, especially when led by Drake.

The path ended in a circular area from which four other paths led onward. Drake halted; hands on his hips, he stared at the ground and listened. As Christopher came up, Drake muttered, "I can't hear anything. Which way has she gone?"

Christopher looked around, but it was Ellen, joining them, who pointed excitedly down one path. "There!"

When he and Drake peered into the darkness, then, puzzled, looked at her, she whispered, "Her gown—it's black and white. The white stands out in the moonlight."

Without further hesitation, Christopher and Drake took the path she'd indicated.

They continued to scan ahead and glimpsed flashes of white several times. They were, in truth, following Rose's trail.

The possibility of losing it kept them from running full tilt ahead, which allowed Ellen to keep them in sight; every time they slowed to get their bearings, she caught up.

At one such pause, she murmured, "It was in the crowd tonight. There was a moment when we were severely jostled—some of the young men patted down our skirts. After that, Rose made for the front hall and told me she had to use the facilities."

Christopher nodded. Drake set off again, and he followed. "Someone must have passed her a note then."

At their next pause, Drake muttered, "What I want to know is how the devil she knew the counterfeit notes were in Kirkpatrick's safe. I only put them in there this afternoon."

Ellen had worked that out as well. "Her dresser—Archer fetched Rose's pearls for her to wear tonight, and Rose told me they're kept in the safe."

Drake grunted and continued along the winding path.

At their next brief halt, he said, "She knows this place better than we do. We're falling behind."

Ellen caught up in time to hear him. Breathless, she gasped, "She's heading to the lake. There's a folly of some sort at the farthest point."

Drake cast Ellen a look as if wondering what else she knew, then ran on.

Rose reached the folly set among the trees at the far end of the lake. She didn't hesitate but went quickly up the steps. Two hours after midnight had been the time the note, passed to her by some young buck in the jostling crush, had stipulated; it had to be close to that now.

She stepped onto the marble floor and, panting slightly, walked to the center of the circular space, halted, and looked around.

The four open archways of the folly—one on each side—yawned, empty. But then the shadows wreathing one pillar moved, and a man stalked slowly toward her.

She blinked. He was tall and walked with a swaggering grace that was, somehow, familiar.

But this was it; she raised her chin and waited for him to reach her.

Only when he neared and the shadows between them thinned did she realize he was wearing a mask. A full-face mask that covered his cheeks and his chin, similar to what ladies wore to masquerades when they were intent on hiding their identity.

She frowned and fought an instinctive urge to step back.

He halted a yard away and tipped his head. His gaze had locked on the package she held in her hands.

"Is that all of it?" His voice was low and deep—and once again triggered a memory she couldn't quite pin down.

"Yes, and no." She'd thought of how to manage this meeting and of what she needed to achieve, but she hadn't counted on him being masked. "These"—she raised the package, but didn't yet offer it—"are the counterfeit notes."

"*What?*" Rapped out whiplike, the word stung.

Breaking the ensuing menacing silence, she gabbled an account of how Winchelsea had uncovered earlier steps in the scheme. "He used those people to lead him to me! He forced me to play out the charade of the card parties so it would appear that the fake notes had been successfully exchanged."

The man's attention refocused on the package. "But they haven't been."

"No, and I haven't been able to so much as touch the real notes traded for our wagering tokens." She hauled in a steadying breath. "But at least we—you—have these. Without me escaping and bringing them to you, you wouldn't even have that." She raised the package and stepped closer. "These have value—they're excellent forgeries and can still be exchanged in other places, passed off in other ways. I can help."

She couldn't resist a fleeting glance toward the house, then she refocused on the man's masked face. "But regardless of what you decide to do with them next, we need to leave now."

He drew back a fraction, scrutinizing her face. "They're searching for you."

His tone was harsh and accusing.

"No!" She had to convince him to take her with him. She stared at the slits behind which his eyes glimmered. "They'd set a silly woman to watch me—I knocked her out and fled with the notes. They can't possibly know where I've gone—they might not even know that I've slipped their leash and left the house!"

"Wait—you said Winchelsea?"

When, wary, she nodded, he said in a tone closer to horrified, "Winchelsea's in the house? He's the one you're running from?"

His tone had risen into a register that was increasingly familiar.

Ignoring the tug of memory, she stepped still closer and all but pressed the package of notes into his chest. "If we take the notes and run—"

"*No!*"

Rose jumped.

He'd stepped back and sliced one hand through the air. Now, with both hands, he clutched his hair and swung away. "Damn it all!" he snarled and abruptly swung to face her. "You couldn't even do a simple switch correctly. I need that money *now!*"

All the assumed glamour he'd used to disguise his voice had fallen away.

Barely able to believe her senses, Rose stared through the shadows. "Jonathon?"

Before he could react, she stepped forward, caught the mask, and hauled it free.

He straightened, his eyes narrowing to icy shards.

The mask dangling from her fingers, open-mouthed, Rose stared. "Good God—it *is* you!"

The oh-so-familiar classically handsome face, all hard angles and chiseled planes, contorted into a different mask—one of blazing fury.

He lunged and locked both hands about her throat.

Rose choked, and his fingers tightened. Eyes widening, then bulging, she dropped the package and desperately scrabbled at his fingers.

To no avail.

Her lungs burned.

Black spots flared behind her eyes.

Lips drawn back in a wordless snarl, her tormentor relentlessly tightened his grip, fraction by fraction, until Rose's eyes glazed and her fingers ceased scrabbling, then her hands slid from his and her arms fell limply to her sides.

Features locked, he growled low in his throat and squeezed still harder, then with a disgusted snarl, he flung her from him.

She crumpled and fell, a discarded doll sprawled on the marble floor.

He stared down at her. Slowly, his features eased back into their usual, arrogantly supercilious cast.

Footsteps padded on grassy ground, not yet close but nearing.

The man glanced in the direction from which the sound had come, then searched the floor.

He spotted the package; Rose hadn't been wrong about the fake notes still having value. He stooped, picked up the package, then slipped through one of the folly's arches and melted into the shadows.

He was going to have to use his head if he wanted to escape Goffard Hall.

Drake, Christopher, and Ellen had finally reached the lake. Across the dark water, at the farthest extreme from the house, a classically styled white-marble folly glimmered starkly against the dark backdrop of the trees.

Drake's expression tightened, and he nodded. "That will be their meeting place." He glanced at Christopher and Ellen. "We'll need to keep silent. Tread on the verges, not on the path."

They nodded and followed as fast as they could as, occasionally running, Drake hurried around the lake, keeping to the grass edging the gravel path.

Ellen waved at Christopher to go ahead; reluctantly, he did.

When Drake crouched beside a large bush a yard from the folly's steps, Christopher wasn't far behind. He hunkered beside Drake, and a minute later, Ellen joined them.

They listened, straining their ears, then Drake softly swore. "It's too quiet—we're too late."

He rose and went swiftly up the steps.

Christopher followed, with Ellen behind him. They stepped into the folly to see Drake circling a figure sprawled in the middle of the floor.

The froth of black and white skirts left no doubt as to who it was.

Ellen's breath hitched, and she halted.

Slowly, Christopher walked forward to join Drake.

Muttering an imprecation, Drake crouched beside the body and felt for a pulse at the heavily bruised neck. "Dead," he pronounced. He rose and added, "But only just."

He looked out through the folly's archways, as did Christopher, scanning for any movement in the dark.

They listened, but heard nothing—no footsteps, no twigs cracking, not even the shushing of leaves.

Quietly, Ellen came forward. She glanced at Rose's distorted face, but her gaze skittered away and snagged on something crushed beneath Rose's outflung hand.

Ellen bent, gently shifted Rose's limp arm, picked up what had been crushed beneath it, and rose. "A mask." She frowned. "This isn't Rose's —or at least, she didn't have it with her."

Drake came to Ellen's side and studied the mask. "The man—presumably the mastermind—must have worn it."

"His identity, after all, is his most precious secret," Christopher said.

"Yes, but why bother wearing it with Rose?" Ellen glanced at Christopher, then looked at Drake. "Rose had never met him—she didn't know who the mastermind was." She gestured about them. "The lighting in this place was never going to be good at this hour, so why go to the bother of wearing a mask—a full-face mask at that?"

"Because"—Drake's features sharpened—"Rose would have recognized him. She *didn't* know who was behind the counterfeit banknotes, but she *did* know our man. She would have recognized him had she seen him, even in such poor light. He knew that, so he wore a mask."

After a moment, Drake went on, "He could have taken the notes and fled, leaving her here to face the consequences. But despite his precautions, she recognized him, and so she had to die."

Christopher looked at Rose's body. "To keep his secret, he killed her."

Drake huffed in disgust. "Rose was born into a highly placed family —a minor if impecunious branch of a noble tree. Given her background, that she recognized the mastermind confirms that he almost certainly belongs to the upper echelons of the ton."

"Rose was very haughtily superior over who she consorted with," Ellen observed.

"Damn it!" Drake looked around in exasperation. "*Who* is he?"

"Whoever he is," Christopher remarked, "whether he knows it or not, he's within the cordon of our watchers. They were under orders not to stop anyone venturing onto the property, but they will stop anyone from leaving, other than via the main drive."

Drake nodded tersely. "But he might have spotted our men on the way in, and if he knows they're there, he might be skilled enough to avoid them on the way out."

With unimpaired calm, Christopher pointed out, "He still has to get away from the area. What are the odds he's driven himself here?"

Drake dipped his head. "I agree, and that means he's left a curricle, most likely, somewhere near." He looked at Christopher. "Where's the nearest, best, and fastest road to London?"

Before Christopher could answer, a sharp *crack* cut through the night. Both Christopher and Drake swung to face the sound, peering deeper into the gardens away from the house, toward the side boundary of the property.

The crunch of footsteps on gravel, followed by the click of heels on marble, had the three of them swinging to face the folly's main entrance.

Louisa marched up the steps. "There you all are! We've been hunting high and low for you. What's going on?" Then her gaze fell to Rose, and she halted. "Oh."

His lips thin, Drake waved her back. "We can't explain now. Christopher and I need to give chase. You ladies need to return to the house and alert Toby and the others. Send word to the men watching. The mastermind's been here, and he's trying to get away."

Drake collected Christopher with a glance, and they turned and ran out through the arch opposite the entrance; within seconds, they'd disappeared into the night.

"Well!" Louisa transferred her gaze to Ellen. "You can tell me what's happened on our way to the house."

Ellen looked down at Rose, then untangled the shawl she'd carried looped over her elbows, shook it out, and laid it over Rose's face. Straightening, she said, "Rose was no angel, but she didn't deserve that."

"No," Louisa agreed. After a moment, she shook herself. "Drake—as usual—is correct. We need to tell the others what's happened without delay."

Ellen nodded. Together, she and Louisa quit the folly and walked as fast as they could toward the house.

Telling Louisa all and answering her many questions left Ellen rather breathless by the time they reached the last stretch of path before the lawn, where the gravel walk wended between tall, dense shrubs under the old, thick-canopied trees.

Sporting their full summer growth, the bushes were rather overgrown and, together with the trees, cast dense shadow over the path.

Ellen and Louisa increased their pace, then both caught the sound of a soft footstep close behind.

As one, they halted and started to turn.

Before they could, some man roughly pushed them shoulder to shoulder and, before they could even gasp, locked his right arm about both their necks. He hugged them tight and forced them onto their toes.

Then his left hand appeared, brandishing a long, sharp-looking dagger far too close to their faces.

They froze.

"Excellent." The man's voice was a purr in their ears. "I'm glad to see you're both sensible enough to do as I wish."

Whoever he was, he was tall. As tall as Christopher, perhaps even taller.

But he wasn't as strong; Ellen was now quite a good judge of male physical prowess, and based on the muscles in the arm that lay across her throat, she was quite sure this man was significantly less strong than Christopher.

What use such knowledge might be, however...

When neither she nor Louisa so much as wriggled, the man went on, his tones cultured and cold, "And I'm sure you're both wise enough not to attempt to see my face. Indeed, I'll offer you a bargain—don't try to look at my face, and I'll leave you yours."

His words sent a chill slithering through Ellen, precisely as he'd intended.

"Ah." Louisa gave a tiny nod, barely moving her head. "The mask was yours. I take it you strangled Rose Kirkpatrick because she recognized you."

She'd touched a nerve; the man's breathing changed, becoming harsher. "And because she failed in the one task I'd entrusted to her. Rose," the chilling voice continued, "was inadequate in many ways."

He paused, then said in what almost passed for a conversational tone, "In case you're wondering, your menfolk are chasing hares that, with luck, will lead them far to the north." He chuckled, deep and low. "They were so intent on catching me, it was easy to draw them off."

Ellen swallowed. If he was to be believed, and she suspected in this case he was, then she and Louisa couldn't hope for rescue by Drake and Christopher, and Toby and the others in the house knew nothing of what was occurring among the shrubs.

To escape the fiend's hold and identify him, she and Louisa would have to act on their own.

Ellen didn't wait to think of everything that could go wrong. Angling her eyes sideways, she caught Louisa's gaze and mouthed, "Ready?"

Louisa read her lips, and her eyes flared wide.

The fiend was still gloating over his cleverness. Ellen seized the moment and slumped, boneless, as if she'd fainted.

The mastermind swore, but her sagging weight drew down his right elbow—dragging his right hand away from Louisa, forcing him to release her.

Ellen snapped open her eyes and fixed them on Louisa, who, freed, had staggered forward. "Run!"

Louisa didn't make the mistake of pausing to look back. Wrapping an arm protectively beneath her bulging belly, she raced onward along the path. In seconds, she'd vanished, and as she ran onto the lawn, even her footsteps ceased.

The mastermind uttered an obscenity, then viciously hauled Ellen upright. The arm about her throat pressed hard. He brought the knife up and laid it along her cheek. "I should cut you for that."

Her heart thundering, her mouth dry, Ellen managed to force out, "I don't like pain. If you cut me, I'll scream and faint, and then where will you be?"

He froze, and she realized what, in her words, had given him pause. "You can kill me," she said, "but then how will you get away?" He hissed through clenched teeth and shook her. "You," he grated in her ear, "are too clever by half. But you're right. In fact, one of you is preferable to two, and your friend didn't stick around long enough to hear where we're off to."

But Louisa would figure it out, just as Ellen had. Having come this close to the house, the mastermind had limited options for quitting the scene, and if he'd listened to their discussion in the folly—as she now suspected he had—he would have heard Christopher say that the only sure way to leave Goffard Hall without being stopped and questioned was via the main drive.

That was why he'd drawn Drake and Christopher off, then circled around and come after her and Louisa. It was also why he wouldn't kill her; he needed her as a hostage to secure a carriage or horse.

He started forward, propelling her ahead of him, almost on her toes. Within a few paces, she felt sure she'd guessed right; he was making for the stable.

He uttered a huff of dismissal. "Regardless, with any luck, with your friend in her present condition, by the time she reaches the house, she'll be too hysterical for anyone to make any sense of what she says."

Ellen almost smirked. She couldn't imagine Louisa hysterical.

She debated telling him who "her friend" was—to see if he recognized the name—then decided the course of wisdom lay in telling him as little as possible. That way, whatever relief came would be a surprise to him.

They covered the distance to the stable yard in far too little time.

He halted her in the shadows of the trees, far enough back so no one would see them, and there was no chance anyone could stop him from slitting her throat and vanishing into the darkness.

Having an excellent imagination has its drawbacks.

Although there were many carriages cluttering the stable yard and lined up along the drive, there was no sign of any horses, nor of any of the stablemen. Ellen assumed they were inside the stable, from which the glow of lanternlight spilled through the open doorway.

"Damn!" the fiend muttered. "I thought the party would be over and the idiots long gone." He paused; when he spoke again, his tone was hard and clipped. "No matter. Now, listen well." He spoke by her ear. "I don't know who you are, nor do I care. I need to leave and return to London, and given your foolishness in freeing your friend, I need to leave sooner rather than later. I require a good horse, saddled and bridled, so in a moment, we're going to walk to the stable door.

"What you need to do," he continued, "is walk calmly into the stable and order a horse to be saddled and bridled for me. I will remain close by your side throughout. If you perform as I require, when I step away to mount the horse, you will still be alive. If, however, you fail to secure what I want, I assure you I will have no compunction whatsoever in driving this knife"—once again, he brandished the blade before her face —"through your ribs."

He paused to let his words sink in; they effectively chilled Ellen to the bone. Then in an even tone, he asked, "Do you understand?"

She nodded, then added "Yes" for good measure.

"Excellent." He lowered the hand holding the knife, released the pressure on her throat, and stepped to her left, taking a position behind her left shoulder.

She felt the prick of the dagger through her gown, piercing between her stays just to the left of her spine as he stated, "I believe we understand each other."

She didn't try to glance at his face. If, as they suspected, he belonged to the nobility, seeing it would likely mean nothing to her.

Her forbearance amused him. "I approve," he crooned, once again bending close to breathe the words in her ear. "There really is no point in trying to identify me—much better for you if you don't."

She pressed her lips tight, stifling the urge to say something to banish the smug look his tone suggested was wreathing his face. She had no option but to dance to his tune and pray Louisa had alerted Toby, that they'd realized the fiend was making for the stable, and rescue was on its way.

"Now"—his voice turned brisk—"let's forge on. I need that horse."

He guided her forward, using the dagger's tip to enforce his edict.

Ellen raised her head and stepped out purposefully for the stable; she had to play her part and do exactly as he wanted until help arrived.

As the stable rose before them, she tipped her head toward him and said, "Just so we're clear, I have no wish to die."

Tonelessly, he replied, "We'll see."

She neared the stable doorway and felt, within her, the desire to live —to claim a life as Christopher's wife—rise like a tidal wave within her.

It gave her strength, mental and physical, and stiffened her spine; regardless of what happened with the mastermind, she would survive.

As if the fiend sensed some change in her, he glanced sharply at her and murmured, "Careful."

She tossed her head and walked confidently under the lintel and into the stable.

As she'd expected, a large knot of stablemen and visiting coachmen were gathered about several lamps set well inside the stable; they'd been sipping from mugs and rolling dice and, no doubt, exchanging stories of their masters.

On sighting her, they all leapt to their feet. Even though, from where they stood, they couldn't see the dagger pricking into her ribs, she suspected they sensed something was amiss.

A grizzled man she recognized as the Hall's head stableman stepped forward. "Miss Martingale." He ducked his head to her. "Can we help you and the gentleman?"

Ellen held up a hand, signaling to the stableman to wait. Tipping her head to the side, she spoke to the fiend beside and behind her. "A curricle would be faster—wouldn't you rather that?" A curricle would also take considerably longer to prepare.

He hesitated, then shifted restlessly. "No—a horse. I might need to cut across country."

"Very well." She looked at the stableman and gestured at the man beside her. "This gentleman requires a horse. He didn't ride here but must leave in a hurry. Do you have a suitable animal he can borrow?"

Several of the men in the group behind the head stableman narrowed their eyes, but the head stableman, thank heavens, was better at masking his suspicions.

"Aye." He nodded. "We've a hack that should do." Without looking away, he called, "Ben?"

"Aye?" came from a stable lad at the back of the crowd.

"Fig out the bay we keep for guests, boy—you know which saddle to use for the gentleman."

"Yessir." Ben turned and hurried off, down the long aisle of the stable.

The other stablemen remained where they were, staring at Ellen and her gentleman guest.

Under their concerted gaze, the fiend shifted, and the knife pricked more definitely. She sensed he was if not actually panicking, certainly growing nervous.

The knife was sharp; who knew what he might do if he panicked?

She hauled in a breath, held it, and willed herself to calm. She couldn't panic, either.

Where were the others? Louisa would have reached Toby minutes ago, and the stable wasn't that far from the house.

Briefly, Ellen closed her eyes and prayed for rescue—prayed she would live through the coming minutes.

Never in her life had she wanted anything so *fiercely*.

The clop of hooves nearing had her opening her eyes.

Ben was leading a heavy bay, saddled and bridled, up the aisle.

The mastermind straightened, becoming more alert and focused.

From the corner of her eye, Ellen caught movement in the stable doorway, then a single man materialized there, standing squarely in the entrance.

The mastermind had been studying the horse. Belatedly sensing the newcomer, he glanced that way, then snarled and, dragging Ellen around with him, causing her to stagger and nearly trip, whirled to face the new threat.

Then he cursed, wrapped his right arm about her waist, and hauled her against him—a human shield.

In moving, he'd taken the knifepoint from her back. Now, he brandished the blade in front of them. "Stay back!"

Ellen heard true panic in his voice. Wide-eyed, she focused on Drake in time to see him smile chillingly.

"Well, well—Jonathon Rattling." Drake cocked his head. "Who would have thought it would be you? But as I recall, you never did like getting your hands dirty, so I suppose that fits."

Where are the others? Ellen stared past Drake. She could see no one behind him. Yet if Drake was there, where was Christopher?

Rattling extended the blade before him, waving it left to right. "I warn you, Winchelsea. One step closer, and this lovely lady will die."

Abruptly, Rattling raised the dagger, angling the blade to lay it against Ellen's throat!

Horrified, she watched the silver blade sweep toward her neck—

An arm appeared, reaching around Rattling's left shoulder. A strong hand clamped about the wrist holding the knife and savagely wrenched hand and knife down and away—physically swinging Rattling around, forcing him to release Ellen in order to keep his feet.

Freed, she stumbled two steps forward, caught her balance, and swung around to see Rattling make a massive effort and wrench his arm free of Christopher's hold.

Rattling lashed out at Christopher, slashing the knife back and forth, forcing Christopher to weave and step back toward the line of closed stall doors.

Christopher's heel struck something in the straw, and he staggered backward, fetching up against a stall door.

Rattling snarled and raised the knife.

Ellen didn't stop to think. A metal pail sat before the next stall door. She raced in, grabbed up the pail, and as Rattling stepped forward, she thrust the pail, base first, sideways, ramming the metal edge into the side of Rattling's knee.

His leg gave way, and he stumbled.

Christopher pushed away from the stall door. With one hand, he grabbed Rattling's knife hand, holding the blade at bay, and with all the strength he could muster, slammed his fist into Rattling's face.

Bone meeting bone produced a satisfying crunch.

Rattling dropped the knife, reeled, then fell to his knees. He swayed, then his eyes glazed and he toppled sideways, landing in the straw.

Christopher hauled in a breath, told his heart to stop pounding—that all was now well—then he bent, swiped up the knife, and tossed it to Drake, who was ambling forward to secure his prisoner.

Despite his attention apparently being on Rattling, Drake plucked the knife from the air.

Losing all interest in Rattling and the knife, with his heart still thudding high in his throat, Christopher swung toward Ellen—in time to catch her as she flung herself at him.

Her hands clamped about his face, and she peppered it with kisses. "You came! You came!"

He trapped her fluttering hands under his. "Of course I came." Now was not the time to feel offended that she might have doubted him.

Instead, he seized a moment to bask in the glow lighting her eyes—a glow that succeeded, at least temporarily, in soothing the recently raging beast within—then he bent his head and kissed her soundly.

As she clung and kissed him back, he told himself—again—that all was well. That she was there, in his arms, and nothing else mattered.

But they did have an audience, so one kiss had to be the limit of their indulgence. When he raised his head, he smiled into her eyes. "Incidentally, thank you for your intervention. It was nicely timed."

She huffed and dropped back to her heels, but she didn't step away, opting instead to slide an arm around his waist and remain tucked against his side.

His inner beast settled a bit more.

Together, they turned to where Drake was standing over Rattling, who was slowly coming to his senses. A moment later, Rattling struggled up onto one elbow, groggily hanging his head.

After several more moments during which Rattling plainly battled to reassemble his wits, Drake looked at Christopher. "Did you have to hit him so hard?"

Christopher stared back, the beast rising again. "Yes."

Drake studied him, then sighed and returned his gaze to his barely conscious prisoner.

The stablemen and coachmen had moved into a semicircle, ready to support any action against the unwelcome intruder.

Drake acknowledged them with a nod, then the thunder of running footsteps in the stable yard heralded the arrival of Toby, Carter, Drake's men, and a bevy of others, including Louisa, Robbie, and Julia.

Drake smiled. "A trifle late, yet still welcome." As Louisa pushed through the cluster of large men now clogging the stable doorway, Drake waved at the figure slumped in the straw. "I give you our erstwhile mastermind."

Louisa halted beside Drake and stared at the downed man. "Jonathon Rattling!"

"Indeed," Drake confirmed.

Rattling chose that moment to finally raise his head and look blearily up at Drake.

Drake's chilling smile returned. "Jonathon Rattling, Viscount Melrose, by the power vested in me by the Prime Minister and Cabinet and Her Majesty, Queen Victoria, I'm arresting you on numerous charges of crimes against the realm."

Rattling slumped back on the straw. "Go to hell."

CHAPTER 19

*L*ater, they gathered in Mr. Kirkpatrick's study.

Carter, Robbie, Julia, Drake's men, and the staff who had rushed out to the stable had been the first to return to the house, where Secombe and the rest of the staff had held the fort and kept the by-then-flagging party going. Thereafter, Carter, Robbie, and Julia, now acting as hostess—with Nigel and Tilly coerced into assisting—had worked with the staff to bring the evening to an end. Eventually, Carter had announced that there'd been a serious accident elsewhere in the house, which had encouraged the last stragglers to leave.

Mr. Kirkpatrick had been informed of his wife's death by Christopher, while Toby had led a contingent of staff to retrieve Rose's body from the folly.

Meanwhile, the visiting coachmen who had witnessed the events in the stable were sworn to secrecy by Drake, then dispatched to ferry their young masters home.

Subsequently, Drake, assisted by Louisa, had spent half an hour interrogating Rattling before dispatching him with a significant escort to be incarcerated in the manor's cellar.

Drake had also given orders for the present occupant of the manor's cell to be released and sent home.

Now seated in an armchair opposite Mr. Kirkpatrick, Drake said, "Hardcastle was only a minor cog in Rattling's wheel—I doubt he had any clear idea of the wider implications of Rattling's scheme. It seems unfair that Hardcastle's life, and the lives of his family, should be ruined because Hardcastle fell victim to the manipulations of a self-centered, arrogant, and dangerous villain like Rattling."

After all the guests had departed, Nigel and Tilly, the only other living coconspirators, had been returned to their rooms, still under guard.

On being informed of that, Drake met Mr. Kirkpatrick's gaze. "Given they did their part in maintaining the fiction that all was well with your late wife's parties, and without that support, we would likely not have succeeded in capturing Rattling, I'm inclined to grant them clemency."

Mr. Kirkpatrick raised his shaggy eyebrows. "So they'll be released?"

"With a caution and a warning to never, ever, err in any way whatsoever again." Drake paused, then added, "I'll call tomorrow and speak with them. Until then, they can remain in their rooms."

"I'll come, too." From her position in the armchair next to Drake's, Louisa reached across, twined her fingers with his, and looked at Mr. Kirkpatrick. "I'll suggest that it's time for them to return to their home and, subsequently, make their own way."

Mr. Kirkpatrick inclined his head to her. "Thank you. They aren't welcome to remain here."

From her position in a corner of the chaise, with Christopher in an armchair beside her, holding her hand, Ellen studied the lines weariness and grief had etched in Mr. Kirkpatrick's face.

"If we're to speak of Rattling exploiting others," Louisa said, "I would have to say the most shocking example was his manipulation of Rose and, through her, drawing in Nigel and Tilly, too."

Louisa had already shared what she knew of Rose and Rattling's past with Drake, Ellen, and Christopher; now, she explained to the others, "Rose and Rattling are second cousins—he'd known her all her life. Years before she married, the pair engaged in a liaison that lasted for a year or more. Rattling knew Rose's character—what was important to her, how she might react to various scenarios. He knew which emotional strings to pull to lure her into doing as he wished. He knew she was drawn to money, that having it and spending it were important to her. More recently in London, he might well have heard direct from her of her wish for more funds."

Louisa paused, her head tipping pensively. "Indeed, even in hatching the scheme in the first place, he might well have had involving her in mind—not only would she jump at the chance to make money, but from their past association, he knew she possessed the required social skills to devise and pull off the critical distribution of the counterfeit notes."

Drake nodded. "He knew her well—well enough to seek to keep his identity from her. Whoever learned he was behind the scheme would have had a powerful hold over him for the rest of his life. So he approached Rose through an intermediary—the Frenchman, Millais—and when he came to meet her here, he chose a place drenched in shadow and wore a mask."

Louisa affirmed, "He wasn't about to trust her with his secret."

"You said he and Rose are family," Julia said. "Does that mean he's related to Tilly and Nigel as well?"

Louisa stilled; those acquainted with her knew she was consulting her capacious knowledge of the haut ton's family trees. Then she refocused on Julia and nodded. "Yes—they're on the same side of the family." She paused, then added, "Indeed, as a scion of the senior branch of the Rattling family tree, Jonathon's brought down opprobrium on the entire family, root and branch, in a fairly major way."

Christopher said, "Even if the public never learn of his crimes, the Rattlings themselves will know, and they'll also know that all those Drake has to tell of this—including Victoria and Albert—will know of the family's disgrace."

Louisa looked at Drake and cocked an inquiring eyebrow at him, plainly asking what he thought about that.

His expression unrevealing, he shook his head. "I can't predict how those to whom I report will choose to respond to Rattling's guilt. However"—he looked at Mr. Kirkpatrick—"while I will have to include Rose's name and the part she played in Rattling's scheme in my report to Whitehall and the palace, I doubt anything more will come of her involvement, especially given she was, ultimately, killed by the true villain of the piece."

Drake paused, then added, "Jonathon Rattling was always an exploiter—even at Eton. He rarely got his hands dirty, but instead grew adept at persuading—or intimidating or blackmailing—others to do his bidding."

After a moment of silence, Mr. Kirkpatrick harrumphed and looked at Julia, seated beside him. "I can't say I'm glad all this has happened, but, well, sometimes one makes mistakes, and Fate steps in and saves one from the consequences." Rather ruefully, he patted Julia's hand. "I'm simply glad this wretched business is over, and Julia and all of you and everyone else is safe."

"Actually," Drake said, "in this instance, I'm confident that the political sensitivity of the crime will work in your favor, ensuring that nothing will be said publicly about what's occurred or about any of those involved."

Toby arched his brows. "Not even Rattling?"

Drake tipped his head. "I wouldn't like to guess how things will go for him. While I'm perfectly certain he'll keep an appointment with the hangman in the not-too-distant future, what his route to that meeting will be and what his family will be told aren't my decisions to make."

Silence fell, but it wasn't restful—not yet. They were all still grappling with the implications and reverberations of what had occurred and who the mastermind had proved to be. According to Drake and Louisa, Rattling was extremely well-connected and had been making his way up the parliamentary tree. As Drake had feared, regardless of his scheme's success, Rattling would have represented a serious vulnerability for the government, given he would have been beholden to foreign crime lords in order to conceal his involvement.

Still openly concerned for Ellen, Robbie asked her to explain what had happened between her and Rose.

As most of the others also looked interested, Ellen recounted her story from the moment Rose had inveigled her to leave the party to finding Rose's body, then leaving the folly with Louisa to return to the house. Louisa asked what happened after she'd escaped, and Ellen found herself continuing her tale to her final action with the pail in the stable.

Mr. Kirkpatrick was shocked to learn that Rose had known the combination to his safe. Toby had spoken with Rose's dresser, Archer, and confirmed that, as Ellen had suspected, Archer had spotted the package of notes when, at Rose's direction given on the evening of the second card party, late that afternoon, Archer had asked Mr. Kirkpatrick to retrieve Rose's pearls from the safe. Subsequently, while dressing Rose that evening, Archer had passed on the information that the package was there.

Earlier, a search of Rose's gown had yielded a carefully printed note, bearing the half seal she'd described, appointing the folly as the meeting place to which to bring the exchanged notes and setting the time for the meeting as two hours past midnight.

"So she broke her pearls and tricked you into going with her into the study, then she knocked you out, opened the safe, took the package of notes, and ran to the folly." Julia sounded as if she couldn't believe her stepmother would do anything so desperate.

"I believe," Drake said, "that Rose intended to convince whoever came for the notes to take her with them. Essentially, she saw handing over the counterfeit notes as the way to buy her freedom."

"Hmm." Ellen wasn't proud of having been tricked, much less being clouted over the head with a heavy ledger, but... Frowning, she looked at Drake. "What happened to the notes? Rattling didn't have the package with him."

A small smile curved Drake's lips. "Rattling unwrapped the fake notes and stuffed them into his pockets. In terms of capturing him with incriminating evidence too definite to be argued around actually on his person, I couldn't have asked for better."

Louisa looked at Ellen. "I'm still feeling very unhappy that I had to run off and leave you in that devil's clutches."

"And I," Drake said, smiling sincerely at Ellen, "confess to nothing but admiration for how you managed from the time Rattling first got his hands on you to the moment in the stable when you hobbled him with that pail—first to last, that was laudable quick thinking."

With the remnants of the fear, anger, and determination that had seen her through those moments lingering in her blood, Ellen lightly shrugged. "I just did what seemed best at the time."

Finding herself the cynosure of all eyes, she sought to divert everyone's attention. "Actually," she said, frowning slightly, "one of the things I still don't understand was how Christopher"—she looked at him—"and Drake came to be out in the gardens when I followed Rose outside."

Christopher looked at Drake. "You'll have to reward those men of yours."

"The two helping me with Nigel?" Carter asked.

Christopher nodded. "They reported that, among the guests, they'd recognized several youthful scions of noble houses they wouldn't have expected to see in Kent in this season. More, those gentlemen hadn't attended the earlier card parties."

"The implication," Drake explained, "was that Rattling had already cast his net wider, possibly with the notion of creating situations he could later exploit for blackmail."

Ellen's eyes narrowed. "He truly was a rotter."

"Indeed. However, to answer your question," Drake continued, "I decided I needed to observe those unexpected young noblemen myself.

Christopher said it was possible to see into the drawing room and ball-room from outside while remaining hidden, and he accompanied me."

"We were rounding the house," Christopher said, "heading toward the front while keeping to the trees' shadows, when we heard footsteps running away"—he met Ellen's eyes—"then we heard your footsteps following."

"Obviously something had happened—something we hadn't anticipated," Drake said, "so we rushed to investigate."

"Well, that explains that," Louisa said, "but when Ellen sacrificed herself for me and our unborn child, as far as I, Ellen, and even Rattling knew, you two"—she eyed her husband and Christopher severely—"were racing northward, away from the house. Yet you reached the stable well before us." She waved at Toby, Carter, and Robbie. "You must have turned back soon after we parted."

The implied question hung in the air: *Why had they turned back?*

Drake looked at Christopher, and Christopher returned the look.

"Well?" Louisa demanded, rapidly attaining her most imperious tone.

"Let's just say," Drake carefully stated, "that as matters transpired, it's just as well both Cynster and Varisey males possess highly active protective instincts."

Louisa stared at her husband, then at Christopher.

Ellen mimicked the action in reverse.

Both ladies spoke simultaneously. "What does that mean?" From their tones, neither was sure it was anything good.

With his lips firmly sealed, Drake looked at Christopher.

Ellen and Louisa focused by-now-quite-pointed gazes on him.

Eventually, transparently reluctantly, he confessed, "We started off, as we'd said, assuming we were on the villain's trail and the pair of you, together, were returning to the house." His gaze fixed on Ellen. "But the farther we went, the...less certain we got." He paused, then acknowledged, "It might have been different had we been able to hear the master-mind ahead of us, but after that first crack before we rushed off, we heard nothing."

Ellen frowned slightly. "So because you couldn't hear him ahead of you, you turned back?"

Judging by his expression, Christopher was tempted to agree, but after a second of inner wrestling, he admitted, "Not just that. We"—he cut a sharp glance at Drake—"both of us, started to feel...that we'd done something unforgivably stupid in allowing the pair of you to walk off alone. With every step we took northward, the pressure to race back to you two and ensure you were safe ballooned and grew." He shrugged. "Finally, we gave in to it and came running back to find you."

"Given that both of us were feeling the same," Drake started.

"Given that instinct was prodding both of you with very sharp claws?" Louisa clarified.

Somewhat tersely, Drake tipped his head her way. "Given that, we realized it was possible that the mastermind had circled around and was also heading toward the house rather than away."

"Heading in your direction." Christopher's gaze hadn't left Ellen's face; his fingers tightened around hers. "When we caught up to you, he had the pair of you in his hold, trapped before him. But at that moment, you slumped, and Louisa broke free, and you snapped at her to run, which she did, and we realized what you'd done." His gaze turned severe. "That was a very risky maneuver. You couldn't know how he would react."

Feeling held, captured, by his gaze, by the vulnerability he allowed her to see, she squeezed his fingers back and replied, "I gambled that he needed at least one of us as a hostage. I couldn't think why else he'd bothered to seize us."

Drake nodded. "As I said before, that was quick thinking, and you were right. He had to have some leverage to get what he needed to escape, and you were all he then had. He couldn't risk harming or hurting you at that point."

"Once we'd seen all that..." Christopher paused, then went on, "We realized he was making for the stable and more or less guessed what he would do. While organizing the parties, I'd been into the stable and knew there was a second door opening to a paddock at the rear. That door wasn't visible from the main doorway or the area just inside the stable. So I left Drake to pick his moment and act as a distraction while I raced around the stable and came in via the paddock and the rear door. Once inside, the mob of stablemen and coachmen screened me from Rattling."

"Then," Drake said, smiling at Louisa, "it was up to me to draw Rattling's attention and keep him focused on me as the sole threat."

Ellen smiled at Drake, then returned her gaze to Christopher. "I have to admit I was never so grateful to see anyone in my life."

Drake's smile widened. "I feel compelled to point out that it was me you saw."

"But," Ellen countered, her hand tightening on Christopher's, "as soon as I saw you, I knew Christopher was there. That was enough to bolster my courage."

Everyone smiled at her, and Drake inclined his head in a half bow. "Your courage, my lady, was never in doubt."

She shook her head at Drake and the rest of them, but her eyes, her gaze, her focus were all for Christopher.

He looked into her eyes and felt the tension of the last days—especially of the last hours—seep away.

What had Kirkpatrick said? *Everyone was safe.*

The mission had ended, the villain had been caught, and everyone Christopher cared about was hale and whole.

That reality sank in, yet couldn't eradicate or even really mute his newly acquired understanding of...the vulnerabilities of love. Of the powerful swell of hopes, desires, passions, needs, and fears—most of all the fears—that seemed intricately and ineradicably entwined with loving and being loved.

If anything, the impact of those was worse than even he had imagined.

Yet Ellen sat beside him, unharmed and apparently content, and for now, he told himself that was enough and that he could stare his fill at her and bask in the warmth of her eyes and her smile.

Among those gathered, it seemed that all the immediate questions had been answered. By general consensus, they rose, made their farewells to Mr. Kirkpatrick and each other, and headed for the front hall.

As, hand in hand with Christopher, Ellen was about to quit the study, she glanced back to see Robbie standing beside Julia and speaking with Mr. Kirkpatrick.

Ellen smiled, glanced at Christopher, and still smiling, walked on.

Drake, Louisa, Toby, and Carter left in the carriage for the manor. Robbie had ridden over and, at this hour, would go directly to the stable for his horse before riding home to Bigfield House. Ellen looked up at the clear, midnight-black sky, settled her hand in Christopher's, and with no need for any words to signal their intention, they descended the Hall's front steps and set out to stroll through the summer night.

The moon had set, leaving the stars to be their guide. She raised her face to the silvery light and breathed deeply, savoring the scents that came to her on the light breeze—night-flowering stock, the lingering scent of cut grass, the zest of ripening hops, and the fainter aromas she now associated with tilled earth and bearing fruit trees.

Until she'd moved to Kent, London had been home for all of her life, yet, she realized, she didn't miss the bustle of the streets, the constant noise and city sounds that filled one's ears even in the dead of night.

Against her initial expectations, she felt more at home here—crossing grassy fields, strolling beneath the branches of an orchard, pausing to climb a stile.

There was a peace in the country she hadn't known she was missing until she'd come to live there, but now she'd experienced it, grown to savor it, she couldn't imagine leaving that peace behind.

They were walking through the Bigfield House apple orchard when Christopher, his gaze on the ground, murmured, "Your brother seems to have...I think the correct phrase is 'grown into his own' over the past weeks."

She pondered that, then replied, "He stepped up when I started to spend more of my time helping you with the investigation." She paused, then, knowing it was right, stated, "I had to get out of his way and give him room to grow. I hadn't realized that." She glanced at Christopher's face. "That by filling the role that was rightfully his, I was holding him back."

He met her eyes, searched them, then gently smiled. "I think it was more a case of the right happening at the right time. The investigation drew you away, giving him the chance to show you, himself, and all others what he was capable of, and"—with his head, he indicated Goffard Hall behind them—"the events of the last weeks have placed him in positions that have forced him to mature still further." His smile grew deeper. "In truth, I've been impressed by his willingness to learn and how rapidly he's done so. And he's found his way in dealing with Kirkpatrick, too."

Ellen pressed her shoulder to Christopher's arm. "Thank you on his behalf." After a second, she slipped her hand free and wound her arm with his. "Although Robbie will always be my little brother, I know it's time to let go."

She felt Christopher's gaze touch her face.

"So you won't be returning to your previous role of running virtually everything at Bigfield House?"

She pulled a rueful face. "That wouldn't be fair, now we know Robbie can manage." She slanted a glance upward and met Christopher's eyes. "I'll have to look for some other endeavor to occupy my time."

They'd reached the shrubbery and were walking beside the long pool. Ahead, the archway framed a section of the side of Bigfield House.

Christopher slowed and halted, and as Ellen obliged and halted, too, he drew her to face him. Their gazes locked and held; his was hopeful, hers curious. "We worked as partners throughout the investigation. Perhaps, together, we can put our minds to finding a new endeavor to fill your time."

Her smile was beatific as she reached up and drew his lips to hers. "I'm sure that, together, we'll think of something."

They kissed—once, twice, three times—then, hungry for more, repaired to her room.

There, in the summer-scented starlit darkness, the passions stirred by the dangers of the evening—by the undeniable vulnerability of loving—swelled and rose in an ungovernable tide and swept them away.

Into a landscape that was familiar yet not, to a place where each witnessing the other's close brush with death had honed a fine edge to their passions. That night, they came together in a world where desire was sharper, brighter, where need pounded an irresistible tattoo through their veins, and pleasure lanced, excruciatingly titillating, boundlessly exciting and exhilarating, and utterly, overwhelmingly devastating, through them both.

Gasps rose and fell, sighing through the night. Hands gripped; fingers clenched.

Palms stroked, while hands sculpted and possessed.

Joy welled, silver and gold, and threaded through the mounting urgency, adding another layer, another dimension, to their joining.

To their loving.

The end, when they seized it and it seized them and ecstasy roared over them, was shattering in the extreme.

It left them wrung out, sated as neither had ever been before, awash on a sea of pleasured completion, wrapped—safe, secure, and forever-more—in each other's arms.

∽

Later, Christopher rose and, drawn by he knew not what, walked through the darkness to Ellen's window.

He stood before the open panes; hands rising to his hips, he looked out and realized that, in the distance, standing above the canopies of the trees between, he could see the roofs of the manor. The lane lay in a dip, and the manor, like Bigfield House, was built on a slight rise. The play of the starlight on the different angles of the roofs was strangely fascinating; he'd never seen his home from this angle before.

He heard a soft patter and felt the warmth of her nearing. He turned and, lowering his arms, smiled and drew her into his embrace. He brushed a kiss to her forehead. "I didn't mean to wake you."

"Hmm. You didn't." She'd grabbed a shawl and wrapped it about her shoulders, but the night air was soft, not even truly cool. Her hands resting on his chest, she turned her head and peered out of the window. "What were you looking at? You seemed transfixed."

He pressed a kiss amid the unruly curls above her temple. "I was thinking of our future."

She looked up at him. "Oh?" She blinked. "What about our future?"

He could have smiled and, with some light comment, led her into the less threatening aspects of that subject, but...now and forever, he owed her the truth. All his truth.

He turned her and nudged her forward, then he sat on the window seat and drew her down to sit before him, between his widespread thighs, with her back to his chest. He urged her to relax against him, which she readily did.

Resting his chin on her curls, he snugged his arms about her waist and, before she could ask, confessed, "I thought *everything* would be easy, because it *was* so very easy to fall in love with you."

He was grateful when she didn't immediately react, didn't prompt or hurry him. He gathered his thoughts and went on, "But tonight, seeing you trapped in that bastard's hold with a knife at your back, and later"— involuntarily, he closed his eyes and shuddered—"seeing him raise that knife toward your throat— *that* wasn't easy at all." He opened his eyes and went on, "In that moment, I felt, truly felt, the threat of having my heart ripped from my chest—the feeling hovered so real and so close I could taste my fear."

He paused, then, voice lowering to an almost guttural register, admitted, "I'm not a fanciful person, but it was as if having my soul ripped to shreds was just about to happen before my very eyes."

He hauled in a huge breath, then slowly exhaled. "I was so frightened, yet over and above all else, my principal fear was for you. Even being swamped by those riotously wretched feelings and gripped by that presentiment of devastation, I didn't fear for myself so much as I feared for you."

After a moment during which he breathed in and out, he murmured,

"I've never felt like that about anyone or anything before. I thought I knew about love—about how powerful it was—but I wasn't prepared for what happened tonight. I didn't realize how deep love could reach, that it could alter my perceptions of life—of my life and what was important to me—to such a fundamental extent. But it did. It has."

Several seconds of silence passed, then he sensed her filling her lungs, and he tightened his hold about her waist and, bending so he was speaking close by her ear, quickly said, "I'm telling you this by way of explaining that I'm still grappling with loving you—with what that truly means for me. Consequently"—he lightly grimaced even though she couldn't see—"I'm likely to have ideas and reactions and suggestions that you might view as a trifle extreme."

He felt her lungs quake, just a little, but she didn't laugh. Instead, she wriggled around, and even in the weak light, as she looked into his face, he could see and sense and quite literally feel the love that shone in her eyes.

She raised her hands to frame his face, something she often did and he now welcomed, seeing it as a sign of her claiming him.

She searched his eyes, then replied, "No, love isn't easy. Love—real, true, active love—is too powerful to ever be easy, facile, much less controllable. It's the opposite of superficial—its roots reach deep into one's soul, into one's very being."

Her eyes, gloriously certain, held his effortlessly, and her lips gently curved with rueful understanding. "Love is too powerful, wonderful, and precious to be without cost." Her gaze was direct, open, and true. "And I've come to know and understand that, too."

The question rose to his lips without the slightest thought. "Are you willing to pay love's price?"

Her answering smile was radiant. "You know the answer to that. I couldn't give you up if my life depended on it. In fact, my future life, certainly the quality of it, depends entirely on keeping you in it."

He exhaled. "Good." Then he returned her smile. "Very good."

She arched a brow. "So are we in agreement, sir?"

"I believe we are, lady mine."

She wriggled around again, so she was, once more, leaning against him and looking toward the manor. "So what about our future do we need to discuss and decide?"

He rested his chin amid her curls and gazed at his home. "Given we've already agreed to share our futures, the only detail I really want to decide is when we should marry. However, I should warn you that I strongly suspect the instant we tie the knot, my parents will declare the positions of master and mistress of the manor vacant."

She turned her head and cast him a faintly frowning glance. "Why?"

He grinned. "Because they've had enough of running the show, here in Kent, and have been talking of moving to live with their closest friends, my father's cousin and his wife, the Duke and Duchess of St. Ives. Their residence in London is St. Ives House, and the ducal seat in Cambridgeshire is Somersham House, and both are huge, so there's plenty of room." He paused to cuddle her close, then added, "I think my parents are using this holiday of theirs as a trial to see how I cope with the estate entirely on my own."

"You know everything there is to know about running the manor estate. Everyone local knows that—you even coped with marauding goats."

"That's true enough, but I think my parents—my mother, at least— was thinking more along the lines of forcing me to cope without a lady to assist me, in order to open my eyes to how much I needed a wife."

"Hmm. Your mother sounds a bit like Louisa."

He considered that, then replied, "No—Louisa is far and away the more manipulative."

She chuckled, then he sensed she sobered. A moment later, in a smaller voice, she asked, "Do you think your parents will accept me as your wife?"

It was his turn to laugh. "I *know* my entire family will welcome you with open arms."

She turned her head and arched a brow at him. "Have you really been so difficult to please?"

He held her gaze for a moment, then replied with the truth. "Yes. I've been waiting all these years for you."

Her smile made his heart soar.

She raised her head and touched her lips to his.

As she drew back, he murmured, "So if you're up for becoming mistress of the manor…?"

"I believe I'll be equal to the task, especially with you and the staff by my side."

"Then when can we marry?" He tightened his hold on her. "Please make it soon. As much as I appreciate being here with you, I'd rather I didn't have to slip in and out under cover of darkness."

"I'll be delighted to marry you as soon as may be." She widened her eyes at him. "How soon do you think we can arrange it? Your parents are in America and will need to be summoned home, and that might take time."

"Not that long—hell and high water won't delay them. An express letter will have them on the next steamship home."

They discussed the prospects, including whether Sir Humphrey might be able to accompany her down the aisle, and eventually settled on a date four weeks away.

With that decided, they repaired to her bed and gave their full attention to a related endeavor, namely, to reaffirming their commitment to their joint future in the most fundamental and emphatic way.

Later, with the first hints of a rosy dawn streaking the lightening sky, Christopher lay beside his sleeping wife-to-be and listened to the contented thud of his heart.

The restlessness that had dogged him over the past year had vanished, replaced by this contented certainty. He knew which path his feet were on, knew it was the right one for him, and was looking forward, eager and expectant, to learning where that path would lead, to what dips, heights, and joys.

He'd found the right companion for his journey—his fated helpmate, his other half, the lady who would be his wife. With her by his side, he would accept and weather even the troughs in their road, sure in the knowledge that the heights would dominate and outweigh any sadness.

That was life—the good and the bad—and the challenge was to go forward and embrace it.

He glanced at her face, then smiled, turned on his side, slid an arm around her, and settled to sleep.

For the first time in a very long while, he was happy—simply and sincerely happy—to the very depths of his soul.

EPILOGUE

$\mathcal{E}$llen stood in the foyer of St. George's Church in Benenden while Emma and Julia, Ellen's bridesmaid, fussed with her train. Louisa, of course, was there, twitching the layers of Ellen's wedding gown straight; at eight months along and waddling, Louisa couldn't bend to touch the train but was determined to do her part.

Naturally, Drake was hovering in the shadows nearby, supposedly manning the side door; he didn't need to pretend he wasn't seeing the bride before her groom because, in truth, his dark gaze remained locked on his wife.

It was the first week of October, and the harvests were in throughout that part of Kent. The church had been decorated with the bounty of the season as well as with sprays of crimson and gold autumn leaves. Although the doors to the nave were presently shut, the decorators had paid considerable attention to the foyer; they'd constructed a straw-based arch of seasonal color that covered the stone frame of the double doors and was duplicated over the main entry, currently at Ellen's back.

She waited with outward serenity while a curious mix of excitement and joy bubbled and fizzed inside her. Now the moment was nearly upon her, she was able to smile on her attendants with patience as she watched them tweak her gown into perfect array.

Indeed, this gown would be the last her aunt had a hand in bedecking, yet even Louisa appeared rather impressed with how the design had turned out. It had seemed unfair to disappoint the Rollinses, who had, courtesy of Hardcastle, come up with the required twenty yards of exquisite lace at a bargain price. With a wedding gown required after all, Ellen had bought the lace and allowed Emma to work with the local seamstress and an enraptured Mrs. Rollins to fashion a suitable bridal gown. The result was a fairy-tale affair, created from layer upon layer of gathered lace. Seed pearls had been stitched randomly over the whole, to the point where, in the gown in strong light, Ellen glimmered and gleamed.

She'd been pleased that, even though, as Drake had prophesized, Rattling had been thrown into the Tower, apparently to face a trial in camera, Hardcastle as well as Tilly and Nigel had been freed with stern cautions. Tilly and Nigel had left the area—Ellen didn't know to where and didn't care—but Hardcastle had returned to his post behind the inn's bar counter, and the village had settled into its customary unremarkable round of minor village events.

Peace had settled on the district once more.

While waiting by the double doors to lead Ellen down the aisle, rather than watching his sister, Robbie was staring at Julia with a silly and rather proud smile on his face. As the new de facto master of Bigfield House, he continued to learn and impress, and Ellen expected to hear any day that he'd finally screwed his courage to the sticking point and asked Mr. Kirkpatrick for Julia's hand.

As for Julia, under Robbie's admiring and encouraging attention, she'd blossomed and bloomed; indeed, she was one step away from vying with Ellen in radiance, and her retiring, overly reserved side seemed to have sunk beneath her emerging confidence.

Given Robbie's and Julia's ages, their engagement was likely to be a long one, yet Ellen felt certain the news would be welcomed by all the local matrons.

In coming to Kent, she and her brother had found their right places and settled in.

Then the organ swelled, and Louisa whispered, "It's time!"

Emma clapped her hands before her face and looked at Ellen with tears in her eyes. "My dear..." Words failed her.

Ellen smiled, stooped, and kissed her aunt's cheek. "Thank you for everything."

Brisk despite her ungainly state, Louisa took charge and steered Emma toward Drake. He opened the side door and let Emma and Louisa hurry through, then looked at Ellen, and as she laid her hand on Robbie's arm, Drake smiled and saluted her. "Welcome to the club." Then he whisked through the door, and it closed.

What club, Ellen wondered, but then Robbie caught her eye.

"Ready?"

She smiled. "I've been ready for the past four weeks."

Her brother laughed and hauled open one door while an usher waiting inside—one of the Cynster cousins—smiled and pushed the second half of the door wide.

The long church was packed; there were even gentlemen and a few ladies lining the side walls. The entire congregation craned their heads to catch a glimpse of Ellen, but she had eyes only for the man waiting for her at the end of the aisle.

The music changed, and she stepped out, walking steadily toward him—toward her destiny.

Robbie paced beside her; their Uncle Humphrey had been delighted at the news that Ellen was to marry Christopher, but he hadn't felt strong enough to escort her down the aisle, even in his chair. He'd patted Ellen's hand, told her the day should be all hers, and given her and Christopher his blessing.

Ellen was dimly aware that the Cynster side of the church was filled to overflowing, but the far-flung Martingales were well represented as well. As she neared the end of the aisle, she was momentarily distracted by Christopher's parents, who, as he'd foretold, had hotfooted it home the instant they'd received his letter. The couple were now beaming, utterly delighted and with open expectation of joy to come. Also as Christopher had predicted, his father and mother had announced their intention of taking up residence with the ducal couple in London and Cambridgeshire, leaving the manor for Christopher and Ellen to make their own.

Ellen swallowed and hoped she—and Christopher, too—could live up to everyone's expectations, not just those of his family but also those of the manor staff, who had embraced her wholeheartedly. From the tales Pendleby and Mrs. Marsh and even the redoubtable Mrs. Hambledon had shared with her, it was plain that Christopher was their golden boy, even if he didn't seem to realize that.

Before allowing her gaze to refix on her husband-to-be, Ellen spared a quick glance for the gentleman beside him—Christopher's brother, Gregory. He caught her eye and smiled encouragingly. Yet from what Ellen had witnessed over the past days, Gregory, along with all the other unmarried Cynster males, regarded her in ambivalent fashion—on the one hand, charmingly welcoming her as Christopher's chosen bride, while on the other, they seemed to view her as some harbinger of an unspecified doom. She'd mentioned her analysis to Christopher and asked what possible doom she represented, but he'd only laughed and advised her to leave them to it.

To what? she'd asked, but had yet to receive any coherent reply.

Then, finally, her long progress was at an end, and she looked at the man who was holding out his hand to her.

Joy—pure and intense—flowed through her. Lost in Christopher's moss-and-agate eyes, she drew in a huge breath, felt Robbie transfer her fingers from his sleeve to Christopher's hand, and smiled in utter delight.

Christopher closed his fingers about Ellen's and felt his heart swell until it seemed it might burst. Not for the first time, he wished that one of those who had gone before had warned him of his likely reactions; instead, they'd smiled smugly and left him to his fate.

Left him to weather this day and all its revelations.

Yet with Ellen smiling in radiant delight, he discovered that nothing else truly mattered—not even his unruly, overintense reactions. Hand in hand, they faced Reverend Thornley and, in something of a daze, followed his prompts through the service.

Then, at last, the good reverend declared them man and wife, and as Christopher turned to Ellen and met her eyes, he felt something shift inside him—a change so profound it could never be undone.

This was a turning point in his life; of that he had not the slightest doubt.

This moment joined them as a couple, with the promise of a family to come.

From this moment in time would flow all he now craved in life—the future he and she, together, would create.

His eyes locked with hers, he drew her to him and bent his head.

She stretched up, and their lips met in a simple, chaste, yet meaning-laden kiss—one that, to them both, signified so much more.

They drew back, gazed at each other for a glorious second, then hand in hand, with uninhibited smiles, they turned to face the congregation.

Happiness and good wishes hit them in a wave, one of almost palpable joy.

His father was one of the first to clap him on the back and wring his hand, while his mother exuberantly hugged Ellen and looked over her shoulder at him with tears shining in her eyes.

Others crowded close to press their congratulations. Courtesy of the quips and observations, it dawned on him just how anxious the rest of the clan had become over whether he would ever marry.

They'd actually doubted the Cynster curse?

Well, the curse finally turned its sights on me, and here I am, having, in the end, surrendered gladly.

His entrenched cynicism hadn't stood a chance.

Life isn't meant to be lived alone.

Christopher glanced around for Gregory, but his brother had already slipped into the crowd.

The rest of the day passed in a whirl, with a sequence of organized events sweeping them effortlessly through moments filled with neighbors and friends, with family and laughter, with good food, good wine, and good cheer. The wedding breakfast, held at Bigfield House, was a riotous success, during which Christopher seized the opportunity to introduce Ellen to his various cousins as well as their parents.

Soon after the speeches—which, with Louisa watching narrow-eyed, went surprisingly smoothly—the musicians struck up for the wedding waltz, and the guests cleared the floor.

Christopher drew Ellen into his arms and set them whirling. A genuinely delighted smile on her lips, her gaze remained trained lovingly on his face.

In response, he smiled even more proudly and drew her closer. "Do you remember our first waltz at Benenden Grange?"

Her eyes said she did, quite clearly. "We were circling each other then, as you pointed out, on several planes."

"True," he returned. "But we found our way, our path, and now we're together in every sense of the word."

Her face lit with agreement, and he laughed and whirled her around, driven by the moment, by overflowing happiness.

Sometime later, they took refuge in a knot composed of the married Cynsters of his generation, together with their spouses.

Pru leaned forward and tapped Christopher on the arm. "You need to stir your stumps, old man, if you want to have any hope of catching up with the rest of us in the matter of filling our nurseries." Pru grinned widely, unrepentantly leaving Ellen blushing, although not for the reason Pru and the others assumed.

Christopher squeezed Ellen's fingers and wearily arched his brows at

Pru and her husband, Deaglan, who, unsurprisingly, was hovering close; Ellen was, in fact, already expecting.

Louisa, of course, leapt to the correct conclusion. "When?" she demanded.

"What?" Pru said.

"Did I miss an announcement?" Antonia asked.

"No," Christopher replied sternly. "Not yet." Ellen wanted to wait, and so they would—and he was quite prepared to make that plain to his peers.

The ladies retreated, but they were smiling warmly—not just at him but even more at Ellen.

Inclusion. As of today, with her, I've joined—or more correctly rejoined—their world.

That his cousins were patently pleased at that outcome left him feeling a different kind of happiness.

Meanwhile, Ellen was thanking her stars that she'd first become acquainted with Drake and Louisa during a fraught investigation. That had eased her into their world. Now, having dealt successfully with Drake —a tall, powerful, lethally focused nobleman intent on forging his own path in life—and Louisa, who was Drake's female counterpart in every way except height, Ellen could weather interacting with an entire group of similar people, male and female both, without feeling overwhelmed— indeed, with passable aplomb.

She was especially interested in learning the ladies' names, along with where they lived and when they were expecting or had had their first child. Lucilla, who lived in Scotland and had married first, had two-year- old twin daughters and a son of just three months. Lucilla's sister-in-law, Niniver, had married next, and her son was now eight months old. There had, Ellen learned, been two other recent additions—a son and heir, ulti- mately to the dukedom, born to Antonia and her husband, Sebastian, a few weeks before Lucilla's son had made his appearance. Most recently, a girl had arrived for Cleo and Michael; their little one was barely three weeks old and was currently being passed around among the older generation.

Louisa's baby was expected within the month, while Prudence and her handsome Anglo-Irish husband were anticipating the birth of their first- born early next year.

It was hardly surprising that the ladies put their heads together, largely ignoring their spouses, who looked on with proud expressions on their faces as their wives discussed all the usual issues pertaining to incorporating infants into one's life.

Ellen was included in the group by right, and she couldn't have been happier or felt more welcomed. These women were now her family circle, and they embraced her warmly in every way.

At one point, she managed to mentally draw back and catch her breath. Struck by how easily she'd meshed with the ladies and glancing at their husbands, talking in a circle nearby, she realized that this—family writ large—was what made clans like the Cynsters so powerful, not just socially but from bedrock up.

They might tease and laughingly taunt, but if anyone or anything threatened one of theirs, they would close ranks and defend as one.

She'd witnessed that in Toby's and Carter's readiness to support Drake, Louisa, and Christopher throughout the investigation.

She saw it now in the way the ladies interacted, with offers of advice, assistance, and more freely exchanged.

This was what she was now a part of—that family writ large.

The Martingales were a large family, but only loosely connected; they didn't stand together against the world. The Cynsters' level of support, of solid and invincible connection, was new to her, even if she recognized the forms and structures, the links.

A mix of confidence and eagerness buoyed her. She'd found her place, and she was determined to meet its challenges.

She refocused on the ladies' conversation and discovered they'd moved on from discussing children to evaluating the prospects for the next Cynster wedding.

"Surely," Pru opined, "it'll be one of that recalcitrant group hugging the wall to our left."

The others scrutinized the bevy of five males, and for Ellen's benefit, Louisa recited, "Starting with Gregory, who you know, to his left is Justin, who is Rupert and Alathea's eldest son. Then comes Aidan, who is Justin's first cousin, being Alasdair and Phyllida's eldest child—those three are all thirty, now. Then there's Aidan's brother, Evan, who is a year younger. And the last, the only one with fair hair, is Nicholas, Pru's brother, who's the same age as Evan."

"Meaning twenty-nine," Pru added, "and a man more stubbornly wedded to his career would be hard to find."

"By all the signs," Antonia observed, "it appears they're circling and putting up defenses."

Lucilla smiled with serene confidence. "That won't save them."

"No, indeed," Louisa agreed. "It never ceases to amaze me that they so consistently fail to see their fate coming."

"More," Pru added, "despite all the evidence to the contrary, they cling to the mistaken belief that they actually have some say as to when Fate will strike."

Louisa smiled at Ellen. "As we've just seen with Christopher, when it comes to Cynsters, Fate gives no quarter. No matter what they think, those five won't escape."

Louisa's smile deepened, and she turned to bestow it on the five males. Judging by their expressions, that only made them even more wary.

By the wall, Gregory, Justin, Aidan, Evan, and Nicholas shifted restlessly under the beam of Louisa's smile. They all breathed easier when she of the unnerving pale-green gaze, the one of their number slated to follow in their Great-aunt Helena's footsteps, looked away.

Gregory frowned. "I wish she wouldn't do that. It's unsettling."

"Indeed," Justin replied. "And no matter what Louisa thinks, I, for one, have far too much to do to go hunting for a wife. At this point in my life, my sole goal is to establish myself in Papa's shoes as an expert investor."

"And I," Nicholas declared, "have far too much on my plate managing the racing stables. Even with Toby helping with the breeders, there's a never-ending litany of decisions to be made. Wife-hunting isn't even on my list of possible distractions."

Evan snorted. "I don't think I'd label wife hunting a distraction, not in this company."

Aidan looked around the circle and shook his head. "I'm in the same boat, but it's fairly clear that now Christopher has fallen and most of our sisters of marriageable age—with a few exceptions, admittedly—have already dragged some poor blighter to the altar, then the combined attention of our grandmothers and great-aunts will, inevitably, focus on us."

Nicholas shrugged. "They can focus all they like, but it's not them living our lives. That's our responsibility, our paths to choose. At least for the next five or so years, wife hunting will have to take second...no, make that seventh place."

The others made sounds of agreement, and they stayed where they were, on the edge of the crowd, and sought to ensure that their grandmothers and great-aunts, especially their Great-aunt Helena and her terrifying companion, the now-ancient Lady Osbaldestone, who were clustered in armchairs farther down the room, couldn't draw a bead on them and beckon, demanding their attendance.

Louisa was bad enough; the older generation were infinitely worse.

As it happened, the topic of discussion in the older ladies' circle did not center on any of the as-yet unmarried males, nor even on the few Cynster girls of marriageable age yet to meet their match. Instead, the grandes dames of the older generation were covertly observing an already married couple on the other side of the room.

"I still feel a thrill on observing how much like me my namesake has become," Lady Osbaldestone announced.

"Indeed." Helena, Dowager Duchess of St. Ives, nodded sagely. "One has to wonder if, being acquainted with you as she grew, she consciously or even subconsciously took her lead from you. The likeness of character is striking."

"Regardless of how it came to be," Therese Osbaldestone returned, "I will be forever indebted to Patience for naming her daughter after me."

"And somehow guessing the gel's future character so correctly," Celia Cynster put in. She eyed the couple in question, who, apparently, were merely exchanging idle observations, yet there was something in the pair's stances vis-à-vis each other that screamed of a closeness that went well beyond that generally seen in a couple of the haut ton. "Do you think he knows?"

Horatia Cynster, the "gel" in question's grandmother, twisted in her chair to observe the pair. "With Devlin, who can tell? But to my mind, the more interesting question is whether *Therese* has realized."

"Hmm," Lady Osbaldestone said. "I take your point. From my own past, I can testify that, while seeing the connections between others might come easily, sometimes, what is under one's own nose can pass largely unremarked."

"That is very true." Helena nodded regally. "However, in this instance, I believe the veneer is wearing thin and, very soon, we shall see fully revealed just what lies underneath."

All four ladies spent another minute studying the intriguing pair, then studiously transferred their gazes elsewhere.

Across the ballroom, Lord Devlin Cader, Earl of Alverton, breathed a trifle easier. These days, in Cynster family settings such as this—impossible as they were to avoid—he constantly felt as if he was walking on eggshells. There were far too many perspicacious females among the company for his peace of mind.

Beside him, his wife, Therese, continued her observations—pointed and, for Devlin's money, entirely on the mark—regarding her eldest brother's inevitable tumble into matrimony's snare.

Devlin knew perfectly well that remaining beside Therese for too long was inviting exposure, yet still he lingered. *If I keep weakening like this, I'll be doomed.*

Therese glanced up at him, her fine silver-blue eyes filled with the pleasure of a lady thoroughly vindicated in her predictions. "I am so utterly in charity with dear Christopher. I'd virtually given up all hope that he would ever be sensible enough to choose a lady like Ellen as his bride—that he would recognize the possibilities, the prospects, even were she to appear before him, pressed upon his notice, as, indeed, I gather occurred."

She returned her gaze to her eldest brother and sighed happily.

Later, he was to wonder if it was a touch of irrational jealousy provoked by the quality of that sigh that had him suggesting, "Perhaps your dear Christopher finally opened his eyes and took his cue from me."

He heard the words fall from his lips and very nearly closed his eyes and groaned.

Of course, it was too much to hope that Therese hadn't heard him clearly, much less that she would lightly dismiss his words.

His wife rarely glossed over anything to do with him.

Now, after a fractional hesitation during which, no doubt, she replayed his words, analyzed his inflection, and tried to make sense of her conclusions, she turned a faintly frowning gaze on him. "What on earth do you mean?" The frown grew more definite. "If you recall, you didn't choose me. Quite the opposite! I chose you, as all the ton and his dog are well aware!" She warmed to her thesis, and a hint of misusage crept into her tone. "If you will cast your mind back five years, my lord, you will remember that I had to badger and hound you into marrying me!"

He told himself the course of wisdom was clear; he should meekly agree and airily claim a faulty memory regarding the steps that had led to their union.

Only his memory of those days and nights was crystal clear, etched in his mind like a picture carved in stone. Then he met her eyes, saw the faint hurt she tried to hide behind the nearly reflective pale blue, and impulse took over; he grinned devilishly at her—allowing his true self to show—and as her eyes widened, softly said, "Oops."

Her eyes flared, her jaw dropped, and he couldn't help himself.

He laughed, low and irredeemably seductively, then swooped, lightly bussed her lips, and smoothly moved off into the shifting crowd, leaving Therese, stunned more comprehensively than he'd ever seen her, staring after him.

~

Dear Reader,

From his earlier appearances in his cousins' romances, it was clear that whenever love finally caught up with Christopher Cynster, it wasn't going to be in any ton ballroom or drawing room, but in some unanticipated, unlooked-for way. And indeed, in Ellen, Fate found the perfect foil with which to challenge all Christopher's preconceived notions of the lady he would want as his bride.

I hope you enjoyed reading of Christopher's surrender to love, inevitable as it was. I particularly enjoyed imagining Ellen's confronting gowns and exploring her character as it unfurled through the book. And having Drake and a distinctly pregnant Louisa turn up, along with Toby, was an added bonus. If you feel inclined to leave a review here, I would greatly appreciate it.

As usual, the last pages in this book switch our focus to the subject of the next novel in the series, but in this case, it wasn't who I thought would be next – Gregory, Christopher's brother, or perhaps Nicholas, Pru's brother. Instead, the next Cynster Next Generation novel will address the romance of Christopher and Gregory's sister, Therese, and her already wedded husband, Devlin, Earl of Alverton. That novel is scheduled for release in early 2021.

Meanwhile, the rest of 2020 will see the release of the last in The Cavanaughs series, *The Obsessions of Lord Godfrey Cavanaugh*, scheduled for release on July 16, 2020, followed by the fourth volume of Lady Osbaldestone's Christmas Chronicles, *Lady Osbaldestone's Christmas Intrigue*, for you to enjoy in the lead-up to the festive season.

With my best wishes for unbounded happy reading!

Stephanie.

For alerts as new books are released, plus information on upcoming books, exclusive sweepstakes and sneak peeks into upcoming novels, sign up for Stephanie's Private Email Newsletter http://www.stephanielaurens. com/newsletter-signup/

Or if you don't have time to chat and want a quick email alert, sign up and follow me at BookBub https://www.bookbub.com/authors/stephanie-laurens

The ultimate source for detailed information on all Stephanie's published books, including covers, descriptions, and excerpts, is Stephanie's Website www.stephanielaurens.com

You can also follow Stephanie via her Amazon Author Page at http:// tinyurl.com/zc3e9mp

Goodreads members can follow Stephanie via her author page https:// www.goodreads.com/author/show/9241.Stephanie_Laurens

You can email Stephanie at stephanie@stephanielaurens.com

Or find her on Facebook
https://www.facebook.com/AuthorStephanieLaurens/

COMING NEXT:

The fourth volume in THE CAVANAUGHS
THE OBSESSIONS OF LORD GODFREY CAVANAUGH
To be released on July 16, 2020.

Lord Godfrey Cavanaugh, now an expert in authenticating works of art, pursues a commission for the National Gallery that lands him in a snowstorm in North Yorkshire. Godfrey battles through the blizzard to reach his destination, and at Hinckley Hall, he finds the lady he hadn't known he was searching for, along with a family who embraces him and fills a long-standing emptiness within him—yet all at Hinckley Hall is not as it seems, and danger lurks, threatening the futures of all within its walls.

Available for e-book pre-order in mid-April, 2020.

PREVIOUS CYNSTER NEXT GENERATION RELEASES:

A CONQUEST IMPOSSIBLE TO RESIST
Cynster Next Generation Novel #7

#1 New York Times *bestselling author Stephanie Laurens returns to the Cynsters' next generation to bring you a thrilling tale of love, intrigue, and fabulous horses.*

A notorious rakehell with a stable of rare Thoroughbreds and a lady on a quest to locate such horses must negotiate personal minefields to forge a greatly desired alliance—one someone is prepared to murder to prevent.

Prudence Cynster has turned her back on husband hunting in favor of horse hunting. As the head of the breeding program underpinning the success of the Cynster racing stables, she's on a quest to acquire the necessary horses to refresh the stable's breeding stock.

On his estranged father's death, Deaglan Fitzgerald, now Earl of Glengarah, left London and the hedonistic life of a wealthy, wellborn rake and returned to Glengarah Castle determined to rectify the harm caused by his father's neglect. Driven by guilt that he hadn't been there to protect his people during the Great Famine, Deaglan holds firm against the lure of his father's extensive collection of horses and, leaving the stable to the care of his brother, Felix, devotes himself to returning the estate to prosperity.

Deaglan had fallen out with his father and been exiled from Glengarah over his drive to have the horses pay their way. Knowing Deaglan's wishes and that restoration of the estate is almost complete, Felix writes to the premier Thoroughbred breeding program in the British Isles to test their interest in the Glengarah horses.

On receiving a letter describing exactly the type of horses she's seeking, Pru overrides her family's reluctance and sets out for Ireland's west coast to visit the now-reclusive wicked Earl of Glengarah. Yet her only interest is in his horses, which she cannot wait to see.

When Felix tells Deaglan that a P. H. Cynster is about to arrive to assess the horses with a view to a breeding arrangement, Deaglan can only be grateful. But then P. H. Cynster turns out to be a lady, one utterly unlike any other he's ever met.

Yet they are who they are, and both understand their world. They battle their instincts and attempt to keep their interactions businesslike, but the sparks are incandescent and inevitably ignite a sexual blaze that consumes them both—and opens their eyes.

But before they can find their way to their now-desired goal, first one accident, then another distracts them. Someone, it seems, doesn't want them to strike a deal. Who? Why?

They need to find out before whoever it is resorts to the ultimate sanction.

A historical romance with neo-Gothic overtones, set in the west of Ireland. A Cynster Next Generation novel—a full-length historical romance of 125,000 words.

The first volume of the Devil's Brood Trilogy
THE LADY BY HIS SIDE
Cynster Next Generation Novel #4

A marquess in need of the right bride. An earl's daughter in search of a purpose. A betrayal that ends in murder and balloons into a threat to the realm.

Sebastian Cynster knows time is running out. If he doesn't choose a wife soon, his female relatives will line up to assist him. Yet the current debutantes do not appeal. Where is he to find the right lady to be his marchioness? Then Drake Varisey, eldest son of the Duke of Wolverstone, asks for Sebastian's aid.

Having assumed his father's mantle in protecting queen and country, Drake must go to Ireland in pursuit of a dangerous plot. But he's received an urgent missive from Lord Ennis, an Irish peer—Ennis has heard something Drake needs to know. Ennis insists Drake attends an upcoming house party at Ennis's Kent estate so Ennis can reveal his information face-to-face.

Sebastian has assisted Drake before and, long ago, had a liaison with Lady Ennis. Drake insists Sebastian is just the man to be Drake's surrogate at the house party—the guests will imagine all manner of possibilities and be blind to Sebastian's true purpose.

Unsurprisingly, Sebastian is reluctant, but Drake's need is real. With only more debutantes on his horizon, Sebastian allows himself to be persuaded.

His first task is to inveigle Antonia Rawlings, a lady he has known all her life, to include him as her escort to the house party. Although he's seen little of Antonia in recent years, Sebastian is confident of gaining her support.

Eldest daughter of the Earl of Chillingworth, Antonia has abandoned the search for a husband and plans to use the week of the house party to decide what to do with her life. There has to be some purpose, some role, she can claim for her own.

Consequently, on hearing Sebastian's request and an explanation of what lies behind it, she seizes on the call to action. Suppressing her senses' idiotic reaction to Sebastian's nearness, she agrees to be his partner-in-intrigue.

But while joining the house party proves easy, the gathering is thrown into chaos when Lord Ennis is murdered—just before he was to speak with Sebastian. Worse, Ennis's last words, gasped to Sebastian, are: *Gunpowder. Here.*

Gunpowder? And here, where?

With a killer continuing to stalk the halls, side by side, Sebastian and Antonia search for answers and, all the while, the childhood connection that had always existed between them strengthens and blooms...into something so much more.

First volume in a trilogy. A Cynster Next Generation Novel – a classic historical romance with gothic overtones layered over a continuing intrigue. A full-length novel of 99,000 words.

The second volume of the Devil's Brood Trilogy
AN IRRESISTIBLE ALLIANCE
Cynster Next Generation Novel #5

A duke's second son with no responsibilities and a lady starved of the excitement her soul craves join forces to unravel a deadly, potentially catastrophic threat to the realm - that only continues to grow.

With his older brother's betrothal announced, Lord Michael Cynster is freed from the pressure of familial expectations. However, the allure of his previous hedonistic pursuits has paled. Then he learns of the mission his brother, Sebastian, and Lady Antonia Rawlings have been assisting with and volunteers to assist by hunting down the hoard of gunpowder now secreted somewhere in London.

Michael sets out to trace the carters who transported the gunpowder from Kent to London. His quest leads him to the Hendon Shipping Company, where he discovers his sole source of information is the only daughter of Jack and Kit Hendon, Miss Cleome Hendon, who although a fetchingly attractive lady, firmly holds the reins of the office in her small hands.

Cleo has fought to achieve her position in the company. Initially, managing the office was a challenge, but she now conquers all in just a few hours a week. With her three brothers all adventuring in America, she's been driven to the realization that she craves adventure, too.

When Michael Cynster walks in and asks about carters, Cleo's instincts leap. She wrings from him the full tale of his mission—and offers him a bargain. She will lead him to the carters he seeks if he agrees to include her as an equal partner in the mission.

Horrified, Michael attempts to resist, but ultimately finds himself agreeing—a sequence of events he quickly learns is common around Cleo. Then she delivers on her part of the bargain, and he finds there are benefits to allowing her to continue to investigate beside him—not least being that if she's there, then he knows she's safe.

But the further they go in tracing the gunpowder, the more deaths they uncover. And when they finally locate the barrels, they find themselves tangled in a fight to the death—one that forces them to face what has grown between them, to seize and defend what they both see as their path to the greatest adventure of all. A shared life. A shared future. A shared love.

Second volume in a trilogy. A Cynster Next Generation Novel – a classic historical romance with gothic overtones layered over a continuing intrigue. A full-length novel of 101,000 words.

The third and final volume in the Devil's Brood Trilogy
THE GREATEST CHALLENGE OF THEM ALL
Cynster Next Generation Novel #6

A nobleman devoted to defending queen and country and a noblewoman
wild enough to match his every step race to disrupt the plans of a
malignant intelligence intent on shaking England to its very foundations.

Lord Drake Varisey, Marquess of Winchelsea, eldest son and heir of the Duke of Wolverstone, must foil a plot that threatens to shake the foundations of the realm, but the very last lady—nay, noblewoman—he needs assisting him is Lady Louisa Cynster, known throughout the ton as Lady Wild.

For the past nine years, Louisa has suspected that Drake might well be the ideal husband for her, even though he's assiduous in avoiding her. But she's now twenty-seven and enough is enough. She believes propinquity will elucidate exactly what it is that lies between them, and what better opportunity to work closely with Drake than his latest mission, with which he patently needs her help?

Unable to deny Louisa's abilities or the value of her assistance and powerless to curb her willfulness, Drake is forced to grit his teeth and acquiesce to her sticking by his side, if only to ensure her safety. But all too soon, his true feelings for her show enough for her, perspicacious as she is, to see through his denials, which she then interprets as a challenge.

Even while they gather information, tease out clues, increasingly desperately search for the missing gunpowder, and doggedly pursue the killer responsible for an ever-escalating tally of dead men, thrown together through the hours, he and she learn to trust and appreciate each other. And fed by constant exposure—and blatantly encouraged by her—their desires and hungers swell and grow...

As the barriers between them crumble, the attraction he has for so long restrained burgeons and balloons, until goaded by her near-death, it erupts, and he seizes her—only to be seized in return.

Linked irrevocably and with their wills melded and merged by passion's fire, with time running out and the evil mastermind's deadline looming, together, they focus their considerable talents and make one last push to learn the critical truths—to find the gunpowder and unmask the villain behind this far-reaching plot.

Only to discover that they have significantly less time than they'd thought, that the villain's target is even more crucially fundamental to the realm than they'd imagined, and it's going to take all that Drake is—as well as all that Louisa as Lady Wild can bring to bear—to defuse the threat, capture the villain, and make all safe and right again.

As they race to the ultimate confrontation, the future of all England rests on their shoulders.

Third volume in a trilogy. A Cynster Next Generation Novel – a classic historical romance with gothic overtones layered over an intrigue. A full-length novel of 129,000 words.

If you haven't yet caught up with the first books in the Cynster Next Generation Novels, then BY WINTER'S LIGHT is a Christmas story that highlights the Cynster children as they stand poised on the cusp of adulthood – essentially an introductory novel to the upcoming generation. That novel is followed by the first pair of Cynster Next Generation romances, those of Lucilla and Marcus Cynster, twins and the eldest children of Lord Richard aka Scandal Cynster and Catriona, Lady of the Vale. Both the twins' stories are set in Scotland. See below for further details.

BY WINTER'S LIGHT
Cynster Next Generation Novel #1

#1 New York Times bestselling author Stephanie Laurens returns to romantic Scotland to usher in a new generation of Cynsters in an enchanting tale of mistletoe, magic, and love.

It's December 1837 and the young adults of the Cynster clan have succeeded in having the family Christmas celebration held at snow-bound Casphairn Manor, Richard and Catriona Cynster's home. Led by Sebastian, Marquess of Earith, and by Lucilla, future Lady of the Vale, and her twin brother, Marcus, the upcoming generation has their own plans for the holiday season.

Yet where Cynsters gather, love is never far behind—the festive occasion brings together Daniel Crosbie, tutor to Lucifer Cynster's sons, and Claire Meadows, widow and governess to Gabriel Cynster's daughter. Daniel and Claire have met before and the embers of an unexpected passion smolder between them, but once bitten, twice shy, Claire believes a second marriage is not in her stars. Daniel, however, is determined to press his suit. He's seen the love the Cynsters share, and Claire is the lady with whom he dreams of sharing *his* life. Assisted by a bevy of Cynsters

—innate matchmakers every one—Daniel strives to persuade Claire that trusting him with her hand and her heart is her right path to happiness.

Meanwhile, out riding on Christmas Eve, the young adults of the Cynster clan respond to a plea for help. Summoned to a humble dwelling in ruggedly forested mountains, Lucilla is called on to help with the difficult birth of a child, while the others rise to the challenge of helping her. With a violent storm closing in and severely limited options, the next generation of Cynsters face their first collective test—can they save this mother and child? And themselves, too?

Back at the manor, Claire is increasingly drawn to Daniel and despite her misgivings, against the backdrop of the ongoing festivities their relationship deepens. Yet she remains torn—until catastrophe strikes, and by winter's light, she learns that love—true love—is worth any risk, any price.

A tale brimming with all the magical delights of a Scottish festive season. A Cynster Next Generation novel – a classic historical romance of 71,000 words.

THE TEMPTING OF THOMAS CARRICK
Cynster Next Generation Novel #2

Do you believe in fate? Do you believe in passion? What happens when fate and passion collide?
Do you believe in love? What happens when fate, passion, and love combine?
This. This...

#1 New York Times *bestselling author Stephanie Laurens returns to Scotland with a tale of two lovers irrevocably linked by destiny and passion.*

Thomas Carrick is a gentleman driven to control all aspects of his life. As the wealthy owner of Carrick Enterprises, located in bustling Glasgow, he is one of that city's most eligible bachelors and fully intends to select an appropriate wife from the many young ladies paraded before him. He wants to take that necessary next step along his self-determined path, yet no young lady captures his eye, much less his attention...not in the way Lucilla Cynster had, and still did, even though she lives miles away.

For over two years, Thomas has avoided his clan's estate because it borders Lucilla's home, but disturbing reports from his clansmen force him to return to the countryside—only to discover that his uncle, the laird, is ailing, a clan family is desperately ill, and the clan-healer is unconscious and dying. Duty to the clan leaves Thomas no choice but to seek help from the last woman he wants to face.

Strong-willed and passionate, Lucilla has been waiting—increasingly impatiently—for Thomas to return and claim his rightful place by her side. She knows he is hers—her fated lover, husband, protector, and mate. He is the only man for her, just as she is his one true love. And, at last, he's back. Even though his returning wasn't on her account, Lucilla is willing to seize whatever chance Fate hands her.

Thomas can never forget Lucilla, much less the connection that seethes between them, but to marry her would mean embracing a life he's adamant he does not want.

Lucilla sees that Thomas has yet to accept the inevitability of their union and, despite all, he can refuse her and walk away. But how *can* he ignore a bond such as theirs—one so much stronger than reason? Despite several unnerving attacks mounted against them, despite the uncertainty racking his clan, Lucilla remains as determined as only a Cynster can be to fight for the future she knows can be theirs—and while she cannot command him, she has powerful enticements she's willing to wield in the cause of tempting Thomas Carrick.

A neo-Gothic tale of passionate romance laced with mystery, set in the uplands of southwestern Scotland. A Cynster Next Generation Novel – a classic historical romance of 122,000 words.

A MATCH FOR MARCUS CYNSTER
Cynster Next Generation Novel #3

Duty compels her to turn her back on marriage. Fate drives him to protect her come what may. Then love takes a hand in this battle of yearning hearts, stubborn wills, and a match too powerful to deny.

#1 New York Times *bestselling author Stephanie Laurens returns to*

rugged Scotland with a dramatic tale of passionate desire and unwavering devotion.

Restless and impatient, Marcus Cynster waits for Fate to come calling. He knows his destiny lies in the lands surrounding his family home, but what will his future be? Equally importantly, with whom will he share it?

Of one fact he feels certain: his fated bride will not be Niniver Carrick. His elusive neighbor attracts him mightily, yet he feels compelled to protect her—even from himself. Fickle Fate, he's sure, would never be so kind as to decree that Niniver should be his. The best he can do for them both is to avoid her.

Niniver has vowed to return her clan to prosperity. The epitome of fragile femininity, her delicate and ethereal exterior cloaks a stubborn will and an unflinching devotion to the people in her care. She accepts that in order to achieve her goal, she cannot risk marrying and losing her grip on the clan's reins to an inevitably controlling husband. Unfortunately, many local men see her as their opportunity.

Soon, she's forced to seek help to get rid of her unwelcome suitors. Powerful and dangerous, Marcus Cynster is perfect for the task. Suppressing her wariness over tangling with a gentleman who so excites her passions, she appeals to him for assistance with her peculiar problem.

Although at first he resists, Marcus discovers that, contrary to his expectations, his fated role *is* to stand by Niniver's side and, ultimately, to claim her hand. Yet in order to convince her to be his bride, they must plunge headlong into a journey full of challenges, unforeseen dangers, passion, and yearning, until Niniver grasps the essential truth—that she is indeed a match for Marcus Cynster.

A neo-Gothic tale of passionate romance set in the uplands of southwestern Scotland. A Cynster Next Generation Novel – a classic historical romance of 114,000 words.

And if you want to discover where the Cynsters began, return to the iconic

DEVIL'S BRIDE

the book that introduced millions of historical romance readers around the globe to the powerful men of the unforgettable Cynster family –

aristocrats to the bone, conquerors at heart – and the willful feisty ladies strong enough to be their brides.

ALSO AVAILABLE:

The first volume in Lady Osbaldestone's Christmas Chronicles
LADY OSBALDESTONE'S CHRISTMAS GOOSE

#1 New York Times *bestselling author Stephanie Laurens brings you a lighthearted tale of Christmas long ago with a grandmother and three of her grandchildren, one lost soul, a lady driven to distraction, a recalcitrant donkey, and a flock of determined geese.*

Three years after being widowed, Therese, Lady Osbaldestone finally settles into her dower property of Hartington Manor in the village of Little Moseley in Hampshire. She is in two minds as to whether life in the small village will generate sufficient interest to keep her amused over the months when she is not in London or visiting friends around the country. But she will see.

It's December, 1810, and Therese is looking forward to her usual Christmas with her family at Winslow Abbey, her youngest daughter, Celia's home. But then a carriage rolls up and disgorges Celia's three oldest children. Their father has contracted mumps, and their mother has sent the three—Jamie, George, and Lottie—to spend this Christmas with their grandmama in Little Moseley.

Therese has never had to manage small children, not even her own. She assumes the children will keep themselves amused, but quickly learns that what amuses three inquisitive, curious, and confident youngsters isn't compatible with village peace. Just when it seems she will have to set her mind to inventing something, she and the children learn that with only twelve days to go before Christmas, the village flock of geese has vanished.

Every household in the village is now missing the centerpiece of their Christmas feast. But how could an entire flock go missing without the slightest trace? The children are as mystified and as curious as Therese— and she seizes on the mystery as the perfect distraction for the three children as well as herself.

But while searching for the geese, she and her three helpers stumble on two locals who, it is clear, are in dire need of assistance in sorting out their lives. Never one to shy from a little matchmaking, Therese undertakes to guide Miss Eugenia Fitzgibbon into the arms of the determinedly reclusive Lord Longfellow. To her considerable surprise, she discovers that her grandchildren have inherited skills and talents from both her late husband as well as herself. And with all the customary village events held in the lead up to Christmas, she and her three helpers have opportunities galore in which to subtly nudge and steer.

Yet while their matchmaking appears to be succeeding, neither they nor anyone else have found so much as a feather from the village's geese. Larceny is ruled out; a flock of that size could not have been taken from the area without someone noticing. So where could the birds be? And with the days passing and Christmas inexorably approaching, will they find the blasted birds in time?

First in series. A novel of 60,000 words. A Christmas tale of romance and geese.

The second volume in Lady Osbaldestone's Christmas Chronicles
LADY OSBALDESTONE AND THE MISSING CHRISTMAS CAROLS

#1 New York Times bestselling author Stephanie Laurens brings you a heartwarming tale of a long-ago country-village Christmas, a grandmother, three eager grandchildren, one moody teenage granddaughter, an earnest young lady, a gentleman in hiding, and an elusive book of Christmas carols.

Therese, Lady Osbaldestone, and her household are quietly delighted when her younger daughter's three children, Jamie, George, and Lottie, insist on returning to Therese's house, Hartington Manor in the village Little Moseley, to spend the three weeks leading up to Christmas participating in the village's traditional events.

Then out of the blue, one of Therese's older granddaughters, Melissa, arrives on the doorstep. Her mother, Therese's older daughter, begs

Therese to take Melissa in until the family gathering at Christmas—otherwise, Melissa has nowhere else to go.

Despite having no experience dealing with moody, reticent teenagers like Melissa, Therese welcomes Melissa warmly. The younger children are happy to include their cousin in their plans—and despite her initial aloofness, Melissa discovers she's not too old to enjoy the simple delights of a village Christmas.

The previous year, Therese learned the trick to keeping her unexpected guests out of mischief. She casts around and discovers that the new organist, who plays superbly, has a strange failing. He requires the written music in front of him before he can play a piece, and the church's book of Christmas carols has gone missing.

Therese immediately volunteers the services of her grandchildren, who are only too happy to fling themselves into the search to find the missing book of carols. Its disappearance threatens one of the village's most-valued Christmas traditions—the Carol Service—yet as the book has always been freely loaned within the village, no one imagines that it won't be found with a little application.

But as Therese's intrepid four follow the trail of the book from house to house, the mystery of where the book has vanished to only deepens. Then the organist hears the children singing and invites them to form a special guest choir. The children love singing, and provided they find the book in time, they'll be able to put on an extra-special service for the village.

While the urgency and their desire to finding the missing book escalates, the children—being Therese's grandchildren—get distracted by the potential for romance that buds, burgeons, and blooms before them.

Yet as Christmas nears, the questions remain: Will the four unravel the twisted trail of the missing book in time to save the village's Carol Service? And will they succeed in nudging the organist and the harpist they've found to play alongside him into seizing the happy-ever-after that hovers before the pair's noses?

Second in series. A novel of 62,000 words. A Christmas tale full of music and romance.

AND RECENTLY RELEASED:

The third volume in Lady Osbaldestone's Christmas Chronicles

LADY OSBALDESTONE'S PLUM PUDDINGS

#1 New York Times bestselling author Stephanie Laurens brings you the delights of a long-ago country-village Christmas, featuring a grandmother, her grandchildren, an artifact hunter, the lady who catches his eye, and three ancient coins that draw them all together in a Christmas treasure hunt.

Therese, Lady Osbaldestone, and her household again welcome her younger daughter's children, Jamie, George, and Lottie, plus their cousins Melissa and Mandy, all of whom have insisted on spending the three weeks prior to Christmas at Therese's house, Hartington Manor, in the village of Little Moseley.

The children are looking forward to the village's traditional events, and this year, Therese has arranged a new distraction—the plum puddings she and her staff are making for the entire village. But while cleaning the coins donated as the puddings' good-luck tokens, the children discover that three aren't coins of the realm. When consulted, Reverend Colebatch summons a friend, an archeological scholar from Oxford, who confirms the coins are Roman, raising the possibility of a Roman treasure buried somewhere near. Unfortunately, Professor Webster is facing a deadline and cannot assist in the search, but along with his niece Honor, he will stay in the village, writing, remaining available for consultation should the children and their helpers uncover more treasure.

It soon becomes clear that discovering the source of the coins—or even which villager donated them—isn't a straightforward matter. Then the children come across a personable gentleman who knows a great deal about Roman antiquities. He introduces himself as Callum Harris, and they agree to allow him to help, and he gets their search back on track.

But while the manor five, assisted by the gentlemen from Fulsom Hall, scour the village for who had the coins and search the countryside for signs of excavation and Harris combs through the village's country-house libraries, amassing evidence of a Roman compound somewhere near, the site from which the coins actually came remains a frustrating mystery.

Then Therese recognizes Harris, who is more than he's pretending to be. She also notes the romance burgeoning between Harris and Honor Webster, and given the girl doesn't know Harris's full name, let alone his fraught relationship with her uncle, Therese steps in. But while she can engineer a successful resolution to one romance-of-the-season, as well as a reconciliation long overdue, another romance that strikes much closer to home is beyond her ability to manipulate.

Meanwhile, the search for the source of the coins goes on, but time is running out. Will Therese's grandchildren and their Fulsom Hall helpers locate the Roman merchant's villa Harris is sure lies near before they all must leave the village for Christmas with their families?

Third in series. A novel of 70,000 words. A Christmas tale of antiquities, reconciliation, romance, and requited love.

ABOUT THE AUTHOR

#1 *New York Times* bestselling author Stephanie Laurens began writing romances as an escape from the dry world of professional science. Her hobby quickly became a career when her first novel was accepted for publication, and with entirely becoming alacrity, she gave up writing about facts in favor of writing fiction.

All Laurens's works to date are historical romances, ranging from medieval times to the mid-1800s, and her settings range from Scotland to India. The majority of her works are set in the period of the British Regency. Laurens has published over 75 works of historical romance, including 40 *New York Times* bestsellers. Laurens has sold more than 20 million print, audio, and e-books globally. All her works are continuously available in print and e-book formats in English worldwide, and have been translated into many other languages. An international bestseller, among other accolades, Laurens has received the Romance Writers of America® prestigious RITA® Award for Best Romance Novella 2008 for *The Fall of Rogue Gerrard*.

Laurens's continuing novels featuring the Cynster family are widely regarded as classics of the historical romance genre. Other series include the *Bastion Club Novels*, the *Black Cobra Quartet*, the *Adventurers Quartet,* and the *Casebook of Barnaby Adair Novels*.

For information on all published novels and on upcoming releases and updates on novels yet to come, visit Stephanie's website: www. stephanielaurens.com

To sign up for Stephanie's Email Newsletter (a private list) for heads-up alerts as new books are released, exclusive sneak peeks into upcoming books, and exclusive sweepstakes contests, follow the prompts at http:// www.stephanielaurens.com/newsletter-signup/

To follow Stephanie on BookBub, head to her BookBub Author Page: https://www.bookbub.com/authors/stephanie-laurens

Stephanie lives with her husband and a goofy black labradoodle in the hills outside Melbourne, Australia. When she isn't writing, she's reading, and if she isn't reading, she'll be tending her garden.

www.stephanielaurens.com
stephanie@stephanielaurens.com